SORCERER'S SPIN

MAYFLOWER MAGES #3

ANISE RAE

1

THIRTEEN SORCERESSES STOOD in a circle in the crumbling parking lot behind Blue Light Mills. Weeds poked up here and there in a determined bid for survival, dandelions with puffy heads, ragged blades of grass, and a scattering of vibe violets. Though charm and beauty lacked a place in the setting, none of the women paid attention as they cast their ritual spell. Instead, they darted glances at their boss.

Mara Rand's glowing eyes—a terrible quirk of her wayward mage power—were a definite distraction.

She resisted the temptation to lower her eyes and hide. Her forewoman must have sensed her unease from across the circle. Esther shook her head at her as if to say she couldn't back out now.

And Mara wouldn't. Without her, they'd be short on power for the ritual.

Much too short.

Blue Light Mills was a haven for weak and damaged sorceresses. Mara made it her policy to hire them, though she herself had enough mage vibes to power the entire mill.

Wayward vibes, that was.

Like every wayward mage, she'd been taught to keep her shameful, imperfect energy tucked out of sight. A trickle of nervous sweat dripped beneath her ceremonial gown. She resisted fidgeting at its unwelcome touch.

Though no one but an aurist mage could sense the extra frequency that ran through a wayward's vibes, everyone could see their glowing eyes. Other wayward mages hid their bronze glow with *concealing* spells or lenses that fit over their corneas. But Mara's waywardness was so extreme nothing could keep the light hidden when she gave her power free rein. Her glow shined through everything. There was no denying her true nature.

Unblessed.

A freak.

Cursed with the evil eye.

But this was her mill, these were her employees, and the fine thread they were spinning in the early morning ceremony would be woven into a blessing dress for her assistant's new baby.

She checked her supply of fiber on her distaff, the tall rod she held beside her, its top bunched with flax for spinning. Each of the thirteen women stood with her own distaff.

The ends of the long, old-fashioned devices rested on the ground. To some, they might have looked like upside-down brooms since the flax at the top resembled the straw on a broom's end. Like a mage's broom, each sorceress might have mounted her distaff and flown away. In theory at least. Only the truly powerful sorceress who had bonded with her distaff for a lifetime could manage that. It didn't happen often anymore. For much the same reason, few mages could fly on their brooms nowadays either.

Fluffs of fiber drifted out from each sorceress's distaff with gentle pushes of her fingers, connecting to the new thread forming from the twist of her drop spindle. Held on the opposite side as the distaff, the spindle, a short wooden rod with a small saucer of wood skewered at one end for weight, pulled and twisted the fiber into thread.

It wasn't the only way to spin. Her factory was filled with spinning wheels of all kinds, but drop spindles were portable and more ritual-friendly than the wheels.

Mage energy whirled among the sorceresses until the center of their circle was littered with skeins of the fine thread.

Spinning was a sorceress's domain.

Mara could have filled the circle with yarn in a mere moment, but she held back, letting her employees contribute their share at their own pace.

Stella, the young mage beside her, looked up from her drop spindle and gave her a closed-mouth smile, happiness pulling her cheeks into cherries. Her spinning was the slowest by far. The girl was so damaged after being conscripted by the electric company to spin copper wire that she had almost no vibes at all. Nor hair nor teeth. A scarf covered her head. Despite all that, Stella had bravery in spades. Though she was new to the mill, she didn't shy away from Mara's glowing eyes.

Truth be told, none of them did. Their glances might have held curiosity and wonder, but they also held acceptance.

As the thread piled high in the center of their circle, the first sliver of sunshine joined the morning star and the crescent moon in the still-dark sky. As dawn pulled the world into a new day, Mara directed her power at the fine thread and guided her sorceresses to cast the weaving spell. Vibes sparkled as threads wove on a loom of air until soft fabric floated before them. Only the luckiest baby was gifted with a blessing dress that was born at the same time she was.

Their ritual complete, their vibes faded away. Mara gathered the fabric into her arms before it fluttered to the ground. To her mage sense, it shimmered with beauty.

Now for the tricky part.

She looked over at Esther, tempted to give the task of the

blessing to her. For all that her forewoman had suffered—forced to work for Power United like Stella—Esther had a belief in the Goddess that had only strengthened from the forced labor she'd endured.

Mara didn't believe in the Goddess. The only prayer she ever muttered was to the lost girls and that wasn't going to work here.

"It's all you, lady boss." Esther's voice was rough. Spinning hay into copper for so long had damaged her vocal cords. When she'd first arrived at Blue Light Mills years ago, she too had been missing her hair and a few teeth. But Mara's mill had a hair mage on staff and a contract with a bone mage. Now, Esther looked as normal as she was willing to appear.

Mara looked up at the sky as if the words for a blessing might slide along the curve of the crescent moon and shower down on her. Or perhaps they might burst out of the tiny light of the morning star like a celestial *fireworks* charm.

But no such luck.

She forged on, as always, and concocted a blessing on the spot. "Bless the babe born under starlight and moonbeams, the morning sun's ray and night's dark cloak. May the light and shadows twined through this gift bring love and happiness to your path upon this world."

"Blessings," a chorus of voices sang out with joy. Their job complete, the circle of sorceresses scattered apart.

"Someone else needs to have a baby so we can do this again," Esther said, heading toward the picnic tables where the workers lunched on sunny days and where the Tea Time food truck pulled up every Wednesday for four o'clock tea. She sat down. "How 'bout you, lady boss?"

Mara's lips went tight. She yanked her power back and shut it away. Her vision, perfect with her vibes free and open, went blurry and dim. It was a cruel trick of fate that she couldn't see well without her power flowing...and without her eyes glowing.

She pulled her spectacles from the pocket of her robes and slipped them on.

No mage ever willingly wore spectacles. Such a physical imperfection was an embarrassment.

"Not me." She tapped the nosepiece of her red-rimmed specs. "No mage would make a pass at a sorceress with these."

"Then find a fairy." Esther's bold suggestion was met with horrified gasps.

"I can't believe you just said that!" Stella cried.

To most mages, whose power was either of the pure light or dark, fairies were the murky in-between...the gray. They were the children of the Goddess's disgraced consort.

But to Mara, they simply held another type of the universe's power. And she never called them the gray or fairies. Both words were considered a slur. The people with the in-between power had their own name for themselves—glister—but few mages knew it. Mara was one of those few.

Esther continued, "Why not a fairy? They won't mind the spectacles. They're bound to like you, lady boss, especially considering you spin with the webs of the fairy's spiders."

The webs.

Mara straightened. It wasn't a topic she talked about freely. She was skating a dangerous edge by using the fairy spiders' silk. Considering most mages didn't like fairies, using the silk could end up being a public relations nightmare for the mill. If she weren't careful, she'd be swirling in a cauldron of scandal—or worse—because of it.

She'd sold clothing made of the spider fabric only to a few clients, but it had enormous potential. The fabric helped heal mages with sense sickness or those burdened with too many vibes. It could also help people like Stella, whose power had been crushed.

"I'm positive some handsome fairy man would do you." Sometimes her forewoman didn't know when to stop.

Mara started to respond, but Stella beat her to it.

"She can't have a baby with a fairy!" the girl cried. "They're all in the West and, anyway, can you imagine what she'd get? A freak!"

The women went still.

A freak.

It was a common term for waywards.

"I mean...." The young woman lowered her gaze. "That's not what I meant."

"I know." Mara knew what she was. She'd accepted it long ago. She was content—delighted even—with the power that spun through her. The labels couldn't take that delight away. Still.... "I wouldn't pass on my wayward blood. No child deserves that." Not the way things were now. And there was no hope for change. Mages worshipped perfection. Wayward power fell far outside the boundaries of perfect.

She handed the fabric to Lara, one of the mill's best seamstresses. "Ladies, it was a privilege to be a part of your circle this morning," Mara said.

"We made a fabric worthy of a princess thanks to you," Lara said. A chorus of agreement followed from the others. Everyone was desperate to change subjects, something other than fairies and freaks.

Mara smiled at the gentle attempt to soothe her. This was a time for celebration, and the boss needed to exit.

"Esther has coffee and doughnuts for you all. Enjoy yourselves. I'll see you inside." She walked toward the south door of her mill, their goodbyes echoing behind her. Turning at the corner of the long wing of the blue building, she moved out of their sight.

"She'd be so pretty," one of the women whispered. "Except for those eyes."

Mara almost stopped. She almost turned back to explain. She had no use for *pretty*. *Pretty* attracted goods she could not afford to covet much less buy. *Pretty* was on the surface. It was a covering that hid what lurked below, things even she didn't want to look at.

But they wouldn't understand. Their eyes didn't glow. None of them was wayward.

She straightened her spectacles and quickened her pace to the door, reviewing the day's schedule in her mind. First up was changing out of this ceremonial gown and into the crisp white blouse and black suit that waited in her office.

She opened the factory's door and a paper fell to the ground with a smack.

No, not a piece of paper. An envelope.

Another one.

The shush of her blood filled her ears. Her face grew hot. She gave a quick look left and right.

She was alone.

She picked it up. Her hands were steady, but her soul trembled.

The stationary was always the same—thick and expensive. It was the message that varied, odd prophecies, poems, nursery rhymes, or sayings that had nothing to do with her and everything to do with the glister...or the fairies, as her sorceresses would say.

Which one would it be this time? Would it be the prophecy warning about evil clutching one of the glisters' mythical relics and killing the entire Republic? Or maybe it would be the one about wielding a relic, a deadly choice if one wasn't a glister prince or princess. Perhaps it contained the childish ditty about the white spinning wheel, the largest relic.

A proper mage would know nothing about the relics since they belonged to the glister. But the author of these neatly written messages knew that Mara was not a proper mage. He...or she...likely believed that wayward was a synonym for evil, as so many mages of the Republic did.

She opened the flap.

No matter where she was, the notes always found her as if they were written by an all-knowing pen pal. In her mail slot at home, in her desk drawer at her office, on the driver's seat of her car. They'd been arriving for fifteen years.

No citizen but the High Councilor should know about the prophecies. Mara would be in a dungeon so deep she'd never get out if the old crone found out about these letters.

Mara freed the paper inside.

As she stared at the simple words, the envelope fell from her hand.

She knows.

2

GREGOR WHITMAN STOOD guard at the front entrance of Blue Light Mills while his team—he used that word loosely—confiscated the last of the spinning wheels. They needed ten more minutes.

They weren't going to get it.

Judging by the vibes flowing in the ritual behind the building, they had three minutes. Maybe four. He and his team were going to get caught. Then he'd have to face the woman he knew of only through her file. Based on what he'd read, Mara Rand didn't deserve this.

It had been a damn long time since he'd had to carry out a mission that he disagreed with as much as this. But these orders had come from on high. Very high. Refusing would have been detrimental to his continued existence. Then again, the same could be said if this undercover mission was exposed.

A sense of unease hissed through his mind and not for the first time. The old crone had to know that their intel about Blue Light Mills was as cracked as an ass because it made little sense that the place would be empty at this hour. His so-called team should have been deployed in the dark of night instead of less than an hour before the mill's first shift started.

They would have been caught the moment they'd arrived if it hadn't been for his fast spell. The sorceresses in the back lot would have heard their vans pull in. It had taken an enormous amount of lightning-fast vibes to seal the dome of silence throughout the interior of Blue Light Mills and around its front parking lot and driveway, but Gregor had cast it with ease.

And then he'd sighed with relief.

His vibes had functioned. Though it had been three months since the incident, he still didn't trust his power. He wasn't sure he ever would again.

He eyed the front lot and the street as he focused his mage sense on the women at the back of the building. Based on the different energy signatures, there were twelve of them, most of them so faint he could barely sense them. But one had power that would have sung a symphony to his ears if he'd still been able to hear the melodies of mage vibes. The incident—as the army called it—had stolen that ability.

Don't go there. Don't.

Too late. Grief waved over him. Its battering was familiar, but the pain was still raw and fresh. He tightened every muscle to hold it back like it was a physical force. As if in answer to the wave of grief and despair, the women's power flowed higher, reaching its zenith. The one crystal clear note among them vibed with purity and strength.

It had to be the Rand woman. Her vibes showered around the land, a silent, gentle mist to his mage sense.

Was it cowardly that he didn't want to be unmasked as the leader of this mission by her...the one wayward who dared to live openly? How had he not heard of her before her file was slapped into his palm? She helped those no one else would—the weak, the damaged, the ill, the wayward—the people that mage society preferred to ignore. She risked censure...or worse...for her actions. He had to wonder if the High Councilor was taking revenge on the sorceress by stealing her spinning wheels because it was clear the wheel they were looking for was not here.

Behind the building, the ritual vibes eased and then faded away. The ceremony was complete.

"Hurry." Gregor pushed the word with his mage vibes straight to the men inside the building. Sound was a cadence mage's specialty.

No one responded. He hadn't expected them to. With one exception, none of the men in the building was strong enough to respond using a spell. But no one appeared in the doorway either, so maybe they were ignoring him.

A distinct possibility with this team.

"They're as slow as fucking turtles," Captain Dane Smith responded with a *comm* spell. His frustrated sigh came through. "Perhaps a *prod* spell up their asses? Please? I'll be gentle."

Lie.

Most mages could sense them. To Gregor, they prickled against his ear.

"Just get the hell out of there," Gregor said with another push of energy.

Two minutes passed. He almost headed inside when he sensed vibes approaching. Five of his men filed past him, exiting the building with spinning wheels. He bit back a dozen admonitions. They'd do no good. He'd never encountered such an ill-disciplined lot. They wouldn't last sixty seconds in the army.

The men headed toward the third van—the first two were already full—and crammed the wheels in. Instead of rushing back to the mill, they lingered, poking their fingers into his silence spell that stretched over the entire place. It seemed to be a game to them, stabbing at the spell like it was a giant upside-down bowl full of jelly, as if they could pop it and watch as its power flooded out. None was strong enough to damage it, but their constant pokes were annoying.

Gregor cast his vibes, readying them to capture his next words. "Break it and it'll burst your eardrums." With an easy spell, he pushed his warning to whisper in their ears, isolating the noise. "You don't want that."

"Screw you," one of them muttered in a quiet voice.

The others laughed. They thought he couldn't hear them.

Dane, his best friend, strode out the mill's door. He wasn't really a part of the team, more like a specialist tacked on at the last minute. He was one of the army's best tracker mages and he was dressed in uniform.

Shortly after the incident that had damaged his power, Gregor had stuffed his uniform in his fireplace. It was still waiting for a *flame* spell.

Dane shook his head at the men. "These are the biggest bunch of assholes I've seen since we deported those trolls. There are ten more wheels on the upper floor. Then we're outta here." His job was to track the vibes that emanated from the sorceresses' spinning wheels and ensure the team located them all. But tracking wasn't his only ability. He, too, could pull the men's sound waves to him and eavesdrop, though not as easily as Gregor.

Mages were like that.

Most were born with specialties, but even average-powered ones could cast a wide gamut of spells across many areas.

Neither Gregor nor Dane were average...which had made Gregor's deceit upstairs much more difficult.

Gregor had known that if he'd refused to participate in this mission, the government would still confiscate these wheels. His refusal wouldn't have stopped the mission. So he'd done what he could to right it and to ease his conscience.

If his deception was discovered, he'd be branded a traitor to the Republic. But he'd be long gone by then.

Besides, the Republic had betrayed him first.

Three months ago, the High Councilor had requested that he

undergo an inoculation to make him immune to a fairy's hypnotic power, a trait that would keep him safer should he encounter the creatures in the line of duty. He'd agreed, of course...Goddess and country above all.

A thick gray cloud of pain shrouded his memory of the event, but he remembered his certainty that something was wrong the moment a fairy had walked in.

No matter what the medical officer had claimed afterwards, Gregor didn't believe that the fairy—or any of the fucked-up creatures—was an ally to the Republic. He couldn't remember what that fairy had looked like, but the memory of the needle glowed with clarity. It had vibed with an ancient wickedness that still turned his stomach, as did the memory of the searing pain when the fairy, with the Republic's blessing, had pricked him.

When Gregor woke three days later, his mage power was permanently damaged. His life was ruined. And no one had any idea if the procedure had actually done what it was supposed to.

The men sauntered back to the building. The burliest of the men pointed at it. "Did you guys see those sorceresses out back?" He pulled out a dollar and waved it at his friends.

Oh hell. Gregor knew exactly where this was going to go.

It was a well-known fact that sorceress power thrived on any type of spin—spinning on their toes like ballerinas, spinning bicycle wheels, spinning a tale, even spinning around a pole. The best strippers were sorceresses. Though it had been a long while since he'd seen one, he'd witnessed a few unforgettable performances.

"You think if I shove this down one of their dresses they'll give up spinning yarn on a wheel and spin around a pole for us and strip?" the burly man asked.

What the hell was wrong with these assholes?

Beside him, Dane sucked in a breath. "I think it's going to take more than one dollar," he muttered, just loud enough for Gregor to hear him.

"Save your dollar, Johnny," another man muttered. "One of 'em is wayward. If she danced, her vibes would shrivel our dicks."

Wayward. At the sound of that cursed word, the dark ocean that had threatened to pull him under for the past three months surged forward. Its towering wave was utterly silent though it ought to have roared and howled considering its mass. Its silence made it even more powerful and foreign to his senses...and frightening. Goddess, he hated this rage, and that only fueled it more.

"What's wrong?" Dane squinted—confused, concerned. And oblivious. After all, his power worked perfectly.

"She can't help how her vibes resonate," Gregor said with clenched teeth.

"Gor, come on, you're not like her." But Dane was wrong. He was exactly like her now.

Coming to a halt at the steps that led to the front door, Johnny cupped his crotch protectively. "You shittin' me? Wayward vibes can shrink dicks?"

Enough.

Gregor summoned his vibes into his throat and hummed a chant in the language of the cadence mages. The *mute* spell formed with enough energy that it should have sounded like an engine revving in his head, but it was as silent as his dark ocean of rage. He couldn't hear the sound of his own power anymore.

He thrust the spell out, a vicious punch. The five went pale, stumbling. He'd hit them hard...harder than he'd meant to, but he'd lost confidence in his power. He still wasn't sure that it functioned properly.

The men flapped their mouths and flung their arms in alarm, temporarily as stuck in silence as Gregor was in permanent, partial deafness. Then they scrambled inside the mill like their asses were on fire, nearly running over the other men in the team who were exiting with more wheels.

"Nice." Dane gave him an approving nod. "See. Your power

works fine. Now, buck up. Rescind your resignation and get back to our unit. The general is pissed all the time without you there to shut me up."

Gregor shook his head. "It doesn't feel the same."

"That doesn't matter. Power's power, man. It's like fucking a different girl from your usual. It doesn't feel exactly the same, but it's still a fuck." He wiggled one eyebrow. "Probably a damn good one, too."

Thankfully there were no women around to hear. Gregor would have had a hard time defending his friend from their justified attack. "Someday you'll find a girl you want to keep, and she's not going to have anything to do with you."

"Why not?" Dane frowned.

"Because you're you."

Dane crossed his arms over his chest. "Still a little grumpy, I see. Going on three months now. Is this a permanent change? Guess I'll have to get used to it."

"Guess so." He rubbed the scars on his throat, the remains of the fairy needle's touch. How the hell was he supposed to live like this? It had stolen the sounds of his vibes, made him deaf to his chants, deaf to the beauty of all music, sheer torture for a cadence mage to whom sound equaled power and pleasure.

Fortunately, after more than two decades of chanting spells, he didn't need to hear them to use them. Still, the partial silence made him want to punch a hole in the stars.

Dane raised one eyebrow and lowered the other, giving him a devilish look. "You can't want to quit the army and work for Power United with these idiots. How'd you get stuck with them? You sure as hell picked the short straw."

"Luck," Gregor drawled.

"Seriously, man. Vin didn't mention you would be here, and if the general doesn't know, then no one else in the army does either."

He shrugged that off. He and Vin weren't on good terms.

Gregor couldn't remember exactly what had happened right before or after the incident. All he had were snatches of memories that flicked through his mind like a deck of shuffled cards. The general was among them.

"So who put you on this job?" Dane wasn't one to let things go.

"I woke up early this morning with the High Councilor leaning over my bed and whispering in my ear," Gregor explained. He tried to shove back the anger and resentment he felt toward her. He refused to call it hatred even to himself. She could read minds, and he wanted to get out of the Republic with his head intact. Besides, the fucking fairies were the true culprit. "She ordered me here."

"Are you fucking kidding me?" Dane shouted.

He'd wanted to shout too, especially when she'd rifled through his underwear drawer and pulled out a black silk thong he'd never seen before. He could only guess she'd planted them as a joke. She'd found it hilarious. Her cackles still echoed in his ears.

At Dane's shout, the men loading the vans looked over. Flickers of excitement lit their vibes. This group loved violence.

Just then, the silenced men returned and scrambled past, carrying the last of the spinning wheels. Gregor and Dane marched out on their heels.

Finally.

As Gregor climbed into the first van, a car turned into the mill's front lot. Sporty, sleek, and bright red.

Shit.

It stopped behind the vans, blocking them in. Cecilia Garnet, director of Power United's mage resources, waved at him from behind the wheel. He wasn't sure where she fell on the chain of command on this mission. She probably thought she was his boss. She might have been right. He was only a temporary consultant leading a team of her workers. She got out and strode over, her long legs strutting with all they had. They damn well had a lot.

Dane, beside him, whistled in quiet appreciation. "And who do we have here?" he whispered.

"What we have is a fucking roadblock to getting out of here undiscovered." Gregor was careful to keep his face blank as they got out of the van. In the short time he'd known her, it was obvious that, unlike most executives, Cecilia enjoyed getting her hands dirty. There was plenty of dirt to stir up here.

Her long dark hair draped over her shoulders, one curl circling around the outline of her nipple poking through her shirt. He couldn't help but notice. But he didn't return her smile.

"Cecilia, we're all done," Gregor called out as she strutted forth. "You pull out and we'll be right behind you."

But she just kept coming.

Goddess above. It was like Fate was pulling on his chain and dangling him over a cliff. There was a part of him that wouldn't mind if she just let go.

His jaw cracked as he clenched down. Cadence mages were supposed to be the epitome of calm, but it had been a shit day and the sun had yet to clear the horizon.

"Captain Whitman," she purred. "I'm impressed. The vans are all loaded up. You crack the whip well."

He wasn't a captain anymore, but he didn't bother to correct her. "Yeah, thanks. Lead us back to Power United and we'll unload. We'll debrief there."

She pursed her gleaming red lips. "I can't stand to think I've missed all the fun." She winked at Dane. "Well, hello there. Did Captain Whitman tell you I love men in uniform?" She looked him up and down, taking in his black army uniform. "I'd like to thank you for your service."

Dane gave her a quick smile. "It's my pleasure, ma'am." But he refocused as footsteps sounded from inside the building, unmuffled and at a furious pace. "Incoming."

In a blink, Gregor resigned himself to his mission being exposed. Antipathy flowed through him with surprising ease. It was like swallowing down a cool glass of *who the hell cares*. It quenched a deep thirst, the kind that somehow made water taste sweet. This wasn't how he thought he'd feel. He took a deep breath and went with it. After all, this sure as hell wasn't the worst thing to happen to him.

Mara Rand, CEO of Blue Light Mills, burst through the building's doors, her green gown flowing out behind her. Her red spectacles dominated the portrait she made simply because he could count the number of mages he'd seen wearing specs on one hand, minus a few fingers. They framed her brown eyes, which sparked with fury. Her chin-length curls blew back from the force of her approach.

She was taller than he'd expected, and she stood straight, upright in a way that made him think she'd been tested and had come out of the battle stronger. He recognized that look. The best warriors in the army had it—the experienced ones—though it always came with a mess of scars, visible or not, and a stubbornness that bordered on impossible to defeat. Still, she was no warrior mage. Her vibes were tucked away, her muscles too slender to fight and win.

She radiated a sophistication that equaled Cecilia's, only Mara's was crisp and poised and cool instead of dripping with heat. He hadn't expected that either. But now that he thought about it, that cool poise had been apparent in her *image* spell in her file. He just hadn't been looking for it.

She stood on the stoop of her factory like a queen ready to defend her castle from marauders.

"Oh goody. I didn't miss it. I've been waiting years for this." A cruel glee vibrated in Cecilia's voice.

"Cecilia. I should have known you'd be behind this." Mara Rand's voice snapped with disdain as they approached.

Nowhere in the intel on this mission had the words *mortal*

enemies with Cecilia Garnet been listed. Yet another instance of fucked-up-ness for the morning.

Behind him, he could hear men shuffling out of the vans to get a closer view of the show. He looked back. The men he'd casted the *mute* spell on had stayed in the van.

A mark of intelligence. Finally.

Cecilia linked her arm through Dane's. "Let's go ruin this freak's day...and her life." She pulled him forward and paraded closer to the sorceress.

"I'm handling it," Gregor spoke softly and overtook the pair in three strides. Cecilia might have outranked him, but she couldn't fire him since his orders came from the High Councilor.

"You can't stand to let your cast-offs succeed, can you?" Rage flashed in Mara's brown eyes. Wayward mages were supposed to be downtrodden and submissive, not ready to cast someone's head through the nearest window.

Somewhere inside him, a faint spark glimmered, and it took him a moment to recognize it. Satisfaction and a hint of pride in his own kind...the wayward kind. He might have tried to mirror it back to her, but he could not take pride in what he was about to tell her. He stopped at the bottom of the three steps that led to the front door and looked up at her. "Miss Rand, by order of the government of the Republic of Mage Territories and the High Councilor, you are hereby ordered to surrender your spinning wheels into the custody of the Republic."

She was the first wayward he'd met face-to-face, or rather she was the first mage he'd met who admitted to waywardness. She met him head-on. She did not flinch. She did not blink. She did not bend. "Ordered to surrender them? There's nothing for me to surrender. You've helped yourself." She gestured toward the vans as her crisp tone cracked through the air.

Courage under fire. Gregor admired that. There was part of him that wanted her to march over to the vans and take back what was hers. If he could take back his perfect power, not even an army could stop him.

"Ma'am, I want to caution you. Acting against anyone here will be considered an act against the government," Dane said from beside him.

Gregor glared at him. Dane was showing off his power for the sexy executive next to him. Sometimes his best friend was an ass.

"Cecilia Garnet doesn't work for the government." Mara pointed at the men dressed in the work overalls of Power United. "These thugs don't work for the government." Her finger encompassed him in the category of thug, a judgment that might have snapped the chain that Fate held in her fingers. It left him sinking into the abyss.

"That's Captain Gregor Whitman. You should speak to him with respect," Cecilia snapped.

Mara's eyes burned fiercely as she stared at Cecilia. And then she turned her gaze on him and he was pierced to the core. He could see the words in her eyes. She might as well have said them aloud.

You are not worth my respect.

The same words whispered at him whenever he looked at his reflection. He'd spent hours trying to convince himself he was wrong. But the incident...it had left him a fraud. He'd hoped no one would notice, that he could walk around with his empty shell intact, masquerading as what he once was. Dane sure as hell didn't seem to see anything amiss.

With one glance, Mara Rand had seen through his façade.

MARA KNEW why they were here. They were searching for the white wheel.

She knows.

Based on the prophecies delivered by her unknown pen pal, that could be the only reason for this raid.

Now Power United was carting away everything she'd worked for...everything she needed to keep her people in paychecks.

"These men are ensuring the future of our country," Cecilia drawled. "A freak-free future. You and your weak-ass sorceresses have only one way to contribute something positive to society: spinning copper wire for Power United. Otherwise, all you are is shit under the shoe of the Republic."

The blond man stepped up beside Mara. "Cecilia, please. That's uncalled for."

"This is all uncalled for." Mara turned to face him. She'd get nowhere with Cecilia. Not that she expected this man to do anything other than steal from her. She did not harbor the foolish hope that pleading her case would change anything. Still, she studied her opponent as if she might find his weakness and exploit it.

Unlike the uniformed man standing next to Cecilia, Captain Gregor Whitman wore street clothes.

Dark brown cargo pants and a black shirt. Tailored. It had to be to fit his sizable shoulders.

It was quality cloth. She could tell at a glance.

He was tall enough to carry his broad shoulders with ease though he was slightly slumped. His blond hair, almost a burnished gold, went every which way as if it bore the brunt of his dissatisfaction with life and it was trying to flee in any direction it could manage. His blue eyes were serious, their bright hue striking as he stole her livelihood in the name of the government.

"I apologize, Miss Rand, for the intrusion, but this is for the safety of the Republic." Judging by his tone, she wasn't sure he believed what he said. She certainly didn't.

"The safety of the Republic. You expect me to believe that?" Mara eyed the vans. "Those spinning wheels are as dangerous as a bag of cotton balls. By taking them, you're stealing the food off my employees' tables. How does that keep the Republic safe?"

"Oh please," Cecilia spat.

Mara ignored her. Nothing agitated Cecilia worse than being ignored. Besides, the ugly gleam in the other woman's eyes was nothing new. She'd seen it before. In fact, she could almost guess what Cecilia's next words would be.

"The government doesn't need to keep people like you safe." The highbrow Power United executive narrowed her eyes to slits. "Your mere existence is a traitorous smear on our land."

Mara gave a mental nod. Yes, she'd guessed it almost perfectly. She took a moment to imagine what it would be like to spin the other woman in a tight, sticky spell, roll her out of here, and leave her in the middle of the street. But Mara could never commit violence with her power. The truth was, she wasn't that skilled.

"I will not stand for this," Mara said softly to the blue-eyed man. "I will fight this with everything I have."

He nodded as if he'd expected as much. He opened his mouth, but Cecilia beat him to it.

"Well, you don't have much, freak." Cecilia folded her arms across her chest, lifting her cleavage high. "You're finally getting your due. Blue Light Mills won't recover from this. No wheels, no thread, no cloth, no money." She tsked. "Just remember, Power United can offer you employment spinning copper wire. We believe in charity for the weak and disgraced."

That last bit was more than Mara could ignore. "Your charity murders its target audience." The whispers of the dead stirred against her skin. They had for a long time. She'd do almost anything to lay the whispers to rest, but that, too, was beyond her skill.

"If that were true, you wouldn't be here. You'd be in a grave." Cecilia glared at her for a moment and then she smiled at the two men in charge. "Since you gentlemen have this under control, I'll leave you to it." She winked at the uniformed man. "Maybe Captain Whitman will lend you my calling card. He has one. I'd like to hear from you." With that, she sashayed away, her red high heels silent on the pavement as she muffled her footsteps like every polite mage.

A familiar tap of gentle vibes pressed against Mara's shoulder. Lady Henrietta Alden—Harry, for short—alerted Mara to her presence as she silently stepped out of the mill. "Was that the notorious Cecilia Garnet in action? I missed it." A regretful frown crossed her face and then disappeared. "Maybe next time. For now, I've called my contact at *The Dispatch*. She's saving room in the afternoon edition for the story about the theft of our spinning wheels which was apparently aided by the army." Her cool gaze landed on the man in uniform. The man wiped his hand over his face and shook his head as if Harry had just made his life harder.

Good.

"Thank you, Harry," Mara replied. The story wouldn't make the front page, nor would it make any difference, but it was something.

"Just doing my job, lady boss." As Blue Light Mills' PR woman, Harry had done everything possible and then some to right the mill's reputation.

"Lady Alden, I wish you'd waited to do that." Captain Whitman was well-informed if he recognized one of the aristocratic daughters of Alden Territory. It was far away from here, tucked in the southwest corner of the Republic. Harry was a long way from home...and employed by a wayward mage. Mara still couldn't believe the woman worked for her, but she was grateful.

"Waited?" Mara asked. "Why? So you could smother the story before it got out?"

A rush of footsteps pattered down the hall before she could pursue the topic further. She turned to see her sorceresses spill out the door, still dressed for the ritual. Mara braced for the showdown.

"You can't take our wheels!" Esther shouted, shoving toward the front, thrusting out her barrel chest, hands on hips. "Who the hell do you think you are?" She glared at the uniformed army man and Captain Whitman.

Stella dashed forward, her head covered in a cloth, her lips curling inward where her teeth should have been. She halted next to Mara and pointed her drop spindle toward the men at the vans. "I'm not afraid of you anymore. You're not taking me back! And you can't have my wheel!" Her hand shook.

Mara's heart jumped in fear. Before she could step in front of the bold girl, the uniformed army officer yanked the spindle from her as if he thought she could actually cast a spell. The jerk on Stella's arm cascaded through her body and her kerchief fell back, exposing her bald head. Stella's shoulder's crumpled, and her face went white.

The men of Power United laughed.

"You're not going back. Ever," Mara whispered, wrapping one arm around her and pulling her kerchief up with the other. "And I'll get your wheel back. I'll get them all back."

The laughter disappeared, cut off in mid-chuckle as if someone had turned their volume off. Their mouths were moving, but no sound came out.

"Sorry about that, ma'am." Captain Whitman gave her a nod. His gaze was tight at the edges, and his broad body spoke of coiled power as if he were waiting for an attack. "I don't think these men learned proper manners as children. But it's never too late to learn." He took the confiscated drop spindle from the army man. The other man gave it up with a dark look. Powered waved between the two of them—even Mara could sense it—as if some unspoken communication flitted between them. Captain Whitman handed the spindle to Stella. The girl took it with shaky fingers.

Mara nearly pressed her hand to her heart in gratitude.

Sorceresses couldn't cast energy without some type of spin to conduct it through. Her employees used the spin of their spindles or their wheels to cast power, the most elementary of sources due to their ease of control. Mara, however, was different. She was the only sorceress she knew who didn't need an outside source of spin to use her vibes—another quirk of her odd power. It was one of her most tightly held secrets, and she had a lot of secrets.

"You put that away," the uniformed army man snapped as if Stella was someone to fear.

"One last thing." Captain Whitman handed Mara an envelope, taller and wider than the one she'd just received. "An invitation. The High Councilor requests that you appear tomorrow afternoon at a quarter past high sun at the Council House. You can find it by—"

"I know where it is." As the personal tailor to the old crone, she'd been there dozens of times.

She turned her back on him, ushered her sorceresses inside her mill, and tied the handles of her doors shut with a thread she spun right there with her vibes.

She knotted it tight...as if it would actually keep them safe.

Though no mage had ever broken through such a thread of hers, the High Councilor could get to her anywhere...just like the person who been sending her those notes for so many years.

3

NIGHT SHROUDED THE THIN, rocky path that led toward the moat surrounding the Rarified Library. Mara navigated it carefully, struggling to see in the dim light. Tonight, she planned a last-ditch effort to arm herself with as much information as possible about the white spinning wheel and the other two mythical glister relics.

The library, fashioned of stone, looked like a towering eight-legged beast with a tall, pointy body on top. Every inch of the thousand-foot structure was covered in detail, decorated with hundreds of carved faces, statues, gargoyles, arches, and buttresses. It resembled a castle gone mad and skinny from a hunger strike.

It sat on the outskirts of the city's main cemetery as if the scrolls had been laid to rest, never to be disturbed again. Though it was one of the oldest buildings in the Republic, few knew it existed. Some complex spell far beyond her ability or under-standing hid it from view of the general public. Mere knowledge of the building's existence broke the *concealment* spell for an indi-vidual, but that knowledge was reserved for the mighty and elite. She was neither. A client had told her about the library as payment for a Blue Light Mills' blouse. Mara wasn't opposed to occasionally bartering with clients who couldn't afford to pay her cash. Tonight's visit, like all her trips to the library, was also a bartered arrangement.

A young woman, pale gold hair streaked with a single, thin line of blue, met her at the edge of the bridge that crossed the moat. Jane Witt, assistant to the librarian of the East Legs, had a long way to go before she resembled the blue-haired mages who ran the Rarified Library. Mara had caught glimpses of a few of them on one of her visits. Something about the job turned hair blue. Mara had asked Jane about it, but she claimed it was a trade secret.

Mara crossed the bridge. Beneath it, the great-vibed sharks jumped and snapped with iron teeth. "Stop it, boys," Jane ordered. The sharks obeyed and swam away. "They're always testing me. One of these days, I'm going to smack one with a *scroll* spell and roll the life out of it."

Mara lifted her eyebrows at the petite woman.

"Viciousness is all they understand. Some creatures are like that."

Some mages were like that too. They were all the worse when they could hide their viciousness, swimming through society with their cruelty concealed beneath pristine layers of handsome smiles and faux kindness, unnoticed until the sting of their bite tore the life out of their victims. It was why she'd concluded that of all the people involved in stealing her spinning wheels today, the most dangerous person there had been the blond captain who'd returned Stella's drop spindle. She'd wondered at that all day, a dozen questions about his motivation spinning through her mind.

Jane led Mara to the first of the two East Legs. The door was heavy and warped as if the flow of molten metal had cooled before it could lay flat. Mara suspected the waves were caused by the power bulging inside the building. Despite the door's uneven front, it blended perfectly with the structure, enough that the eye passed over it. A mage could circle the building for hours in search of the entrance, assuming he could get past the sharks. Despite her previous visits, Mara couldn't have found the entrance on her own.

Inside, Mara held out her package, wrapped in paper.

Payment for this visit was a scarf, its threads spun with a *concealment* spell, though nothing as powerful as the one that hid this building.

Unlike Mara, the other woman was a normal wayward and could conceal her glow...when she remembered. Jane was a moderately powerful finder mage—a brilliant thinker but absent-minded. While occupied on fact-finding missions, she tended to drop her concealment spells for her glowing, wayward eyes. The scarf would hold that spell for her.

Jane took the package. In return, she held out a piece of paper. "Directions. And good news...the scrolls you want are on a lower shelf. You can reach them just fine."

Mara sighed with relief at that.

"It's a popular spot lately." Jane disappeared into the enormous stacks of scrolls before Mara could ask for clarification.

She looked around. There were ancient spells at work here. Based on the outside dimensions of the library, only a couple of scroll cases should have fit in the first of the two east legs. Instead, shelves stood in rows as far as she could see and stretched thirty feet high. They were packed so tightly together there was no room for a ladder to access the scrolls at the top. A mage would have to cast a *levitation* spell to get them. A good thing the scrolls she needed were on the lower shelves...of the upper tower, that was. She could handle climbing the two-hundred plus stairs, but she would have been hard pressed to cast a *levitation*.

She followed the directions on the paper to the stairs. The first three staircases took her to the main body of the Rarified

Library. The remaining steps were housed in a tiny tower that clung to the main structure.

She began the hike in the tight, coiling space. It was dark, and the skinny windows admitted mere slivers of moonlight. The power of the knowledge contained in the library vibed around her, emanating from the walls as if the building were alive. She sensed it even with her own power tightly wrapped away. As she climbed, the scent of old stone and paper and the dusty robes of a thousand scholars brushed against her nose.

With every step, she listened for a pair of feet coming down. It had happened once when she'd been researching syphon mages, one of whom was now a client. She'd come face-to-face with a giant of a man. She still wasn't sure how he'd fit in this small area. He'd had to bend down, so he didn't bump his head on the low ceiling as the staircase twisted around and around. Plus, his width should never have fit. She could only guess he'd cast a *greased pig* spell. She'd had to return to the main floor to give him room to pass and restart her climb after he'd exited.

Glancing at her directions, she let a hint of her power unwind from its tight spin inside her and cast a mage light in the darkness of the circular staircase.

Tenth floor. Stack three. Shelf four. Scrolls 118.34A through 118.34AB.

She was out of breath by the time she made it to the top.

The door to the tenth floor was four inches shorter than she was and at an odd angle. She ducked and tilted to the left to enter.

She cast another mage light, doubling the brightness, preparing to read the call numbers on the scrolls' handles. She paced through the shelves. She'd assumed stack three would be close to the front. Instead, the shelves went backward starting at ninety-seven. It felt like it took her five minutes to make it to row three.

She entered the row and jumped back. Captain Gregor

Whitman stood in the aisle, his blue gaze focused on the entrance of the row. Evidently, he'd heard her coming.

She certainly hadn't sensed him. "You!" Fright pulsed in her temple and demanded immediate retreat.

"Miss Rand, this is a nice surprise." A small smile crossed his lips.

"Nice?" she snapped. "Why in the starry vibes would this be nice? What are you doing here? Are you spying on me?"

He rolled up the scroll he was reading and stuck it under his arm. "Definitely nice. You were like the grand champion of the weak and beleaguered today, and lately I'd given up hope anyone like that might exist."

She rolled her eyes. "And yet, you stole my wheels." Her voice echoed around the stacks like an eerie warning to flee. To do anything else was beyond foolish. He was at least six inches taller than she, his shoulders were broad with powerful muscles, and he probably knew all kinds of spells that could do horrible things to her.

"Yeah." He dropped his chin with the rough word, but he didn't look away from her. "I agreed to carry out the mission. As ordered. And I do my duty...did my duty. But I'm done. Today was my last day. I'm unemployed as of this afternoon." He squared his body to her though his shoulders still had that faint stoop.

"Why? Did you get fired?" It was a nosy question, but maybe the answer would hold a clue about her stolen wheels.

A small chuckle lifted his shoulders. "No. I didn't get fired." He looked around them as if there was something to see other than shelves and scrolls. "The reason is too long of a tale for such an uncomfortable space. We should sit down for that story."

His answer made her warier yet. "So, you don't work for Power United?"

"A side gig. Temporary at that, and it's over."

"But Power United has my wheels."

"Yes."

"How do I get them back?" She tried not to sound desperate. She was certain she failed. Blue Light Mills' factory floor was empty and silent. Her sorceresses were a sad, scared lot after this morning's awfulness.

"I don't know." His voice was calm, but a bleak note ran through it. "I wish I did."

He sounded sincere, but she couldn't believe him.

Silence built between them for a moment. "Any other questions I can answer for you?" he asked.

She backed up one step. "No. I don't want to know anything else about you. In fact, I wish I hadn't met you." Cruel words. But true.

He pulled in a long, slow breath. "I can understand that. You'd probably like to confine me to the still-hells with the fallen god."

She gave a single, decisive nod. "I thought that very thing this morning." She hadn't. But she should have.

"In which case, before I'm cast down, I have a confession."

She braced for bad news when she caught sight of the number written on the side of the scroll tucked under his arm.

118.34A. The relics.

"Why do you have that scroll?" Her words burst out, accusing, and interrupting his confession-to-be.

He didn't even glance at the scroll. "The spinning wheel in your office. I left it there."

For a minute she didn't follow. What did that have to do with the scroll? "That's your confession?" He nodded, and she shook her head right back. Her curls scattered against her cheeks at the brisk move. "No, you didn't." She'd been in her office for most of the day meeting with her forewoman, brainstorming ideas on how to keep her mill running without spinning wheels.

She knew darn well there was no spinning wheel in her office.

"It's hidden with a *don't look* spell exactly where you left it. In the corner. To find it, all you have to do is reach out and touch it.

It will reveal itself to its owner, but no one else. Just don't let anyone around it or they might trip."

"But that means you disobeyed the High Councilor." Disbelief crept over her.

Treason.

The word sounded in her mind with perfect clarity as if his admission had triggered some *surveillance* spell that hovered over every citizen of the Republic. "No one disobeys her orders," she whispered.

He continued, "And by telling you this—"

"Stop." She backed away. For a moment, she couldn't catch her breath around this revelation. He'd risked his freedom—his life—to save one of her wheels. Her favorite wheel, in fact. It hadn't been taken into the clutches of Power United. "Why would you risk that?"

"Because your mage power soars. I've never felt anything like it." His voice was low and something about it enticed her as if he cast a spell with his words.

She could have leaned into them. But she didn't, of course. "I beg your pardon. My vibes are nowhere near you."

His smile reappeared, the one he given her when she first showed up. "Right again. But this morning, whatever you were doing behind your mill, they were like a note of beauty among a dozen ugly chords."

"Ah." She gritted her teeth. "You were spying. And of course, you were surrounded by ugly vibes. You're with Power United. That's who they are."

He lowered his eyebrows. They made a dramatic line across his forehead. "That's not who I am."

"No? You're not one of the privileged and powerful who can take whatever they please from the weak and poor and then reap the accolades and benefits. So today was an exception?"

He opened his mouth, but his words didn't fall until after a long pause. "Yes," he said finally.

She'd expected a handful of excuses. "At least you're honest about the flexibility of your moral code."

"But I'm not spying on you." He held up a finger, halting her protest. "Not anymore. Though I did recognize your vibes coming toward me."

"I wasn't broadcasting my power."

"Your mage lights were. And your vibes really are the prettiest energy I've ever sensed...as pretty as you are."

"Oh, just stop right there." She held up her hand, something no normal mage would do, but she wasn't normal. "Do not bother trying to charm me."

Pretty. That word again. And from him!

She'd been called pretty once before by another tall and handsome man. She'd fallen for it with all her soul. Then he'd abandoned her to drown in a hell so deep and murky only the sharks could survive.

Her cheeks burned so badly they might have started steaming, but it wasn't embarrassment. It was fury. It rippled through her.

"Why are you slumped over?" she asked. It was rude and offensive. It was her version of a slap to the face. Which she would never do.... So why had she said it?

She dropped her gaze. Now it was shame burning her cheeks. She worked with damaged and sick mages all the time, and she never would have demanded such a question of them. It was not wise to hang around this man. She couldn't find her balance with him.

"I'm slumped?" He straightened, slow and still crooked, as if he'd been off-kilter for so long he'd forgotten how to stand straight. She might have reached out to fix him, but too much of a divide stood between them for her to brave that.

She pulled the scroll from under his arm, put it on his right shoulder and pressed down gently until it came into line with the left. "That's better."

"I wonder how long I've been standing like that."

She let him ponder that while she unrolled the scroll. It was thick and heavy. She glanced around for a scroll stand, but the shelves were the only furniture around. "You never answered my question about why you have this scroll." A safer topic compared to *pretty* and slumps.

"It contains information about the spinning wheel the High Councilor is looking for."

Not a safer topic.

"The wheel is quite ancient. It was made by the fallen consort," he continued.

"The wheel is a myth. It doesn't exist. It never has." She struggled to turn both ends of the old scroll.

"May I?" He held out his hand for it and she passed it over. He wound the scroll with efficient expertise and much greater strength than she had. He paused at a set of drawings. "This is what it looks like."

"I know. I've seen pictures before. That doesn't mean it exists."

He pointed to another drawing. "This is the sewing needle. It's also one of the relics." He looked at her, his eyes dark and lost. "It exists. I've seen it. Felt it. I thought it was going to kill me. Instead it left me...." He swallowed so hard she could hear it. "Slumped. It damaged my power and there's no undoing it."

Few mages shared their weaknesses, certainly not with strangers. It had to be hard to admit such an injury. Especially for a man like him.

She didn't believe for a moment that a relic had caused such damage to him, but whatever had happened, sympathy welled up in her, even though he was a thief. Damaged power...that was something she was much too familiar with. "I'm sorry you were hurt." In the face of his pain, she wouldn't argue further about gods and their supposed crafting tools.

He moved the scroll to one hand and lifted his other hand to the scars that lined the left side of his neck. Any hint of his smile was tossed away like broken threads. "Stay away from the white wheel," he whispered.

"I don't think that's going to be a problem for me."

Silence fell for another moment. Eventually, he gestured with the scroll. "The story of the relics' creation is in here. It reads like a fairy-tale, a sad one. A few of the sorceresses don't fare well, I'm afraid."

She knew that story well. The sorceresses in it were known as the lost girls, consigned to the still-hells of the fallen consort forever. "You've been standing here a long time to have read it all."

"Yes. My feet are tired."

She looked down at his feet shod in heavy black boots. He was so big and powerful. The idea of his feet hurting was incongruous to his physique.

"Just so you know, my feet are tougher than they sound. I read six scrolls standing here."

"Six?"

"Okay, five. I skimmed the sixth."

"You must have learned a lot."

He swiped the broad swath of his hand over both of his cheeks. "There's surprisingly little of substance in any of them. Except for this." He rolled the scroll for a long minute, finally stopping at a small poem.

Her chest tightened when she saw its form.

He read it aloud.

> *"In the hand of royal's heir,*
> *Three relics claim the regal chair.*
> *It sits in east and rules in west,*
> *Destiny shall manifest."*

"It's a prophecy," she said. One she'd never heard. She stepped away. She wanted nothing to do with this. "You should put that back. Prophecies are dangerous. They're trouble."

He frowned. "This can't be a prophecy. Only the High Councilor has those. I don't know much about the Rarified Library, but I know prophecies are not kept here."

"Then this one escaped."

He straightened, his lips tightening, his eyes alert. "Someone's coming." He rewound the scroll and slipped it back. "Come on. We need to hide. Whoever this is, he's not friendly. He's nervous." He cocked his head. "Coming fast and silent."

"It's probably just a librarian. They're very quiet people."

His nostrils flared as if he were scenting the air. "This guy is no librarian." He put his hand on her elbow and tugged her out of the aisle and into the last row. He stepped in front of her, shielding her body with his, and then wrapped his hand around her wrist. "Stay close." His vibes circled around them both, sealing them together.

"What are you doing?" she whispered, her words tight and fast.

But his gaze stayed focused straight ahead.

Every breath she took was full of him—his warmth, his spice. Her nose was an inch away from his shoulder.

A thousand tiny jitters raced through her veins and it had nothing to do with their incoming visitor. It was him. For all that he might have been ready to fight, his touch was gentle, and his warmth was welcome against the coolness of the library. Though he was alert and focused and had an air of aggressive readiness, his vibes were composed and tranquil. How did he manage that? Whenever she was angry or scared, her vibes were tight and harsh and tucked away.

His power was like silk. It was oddly reassuring. She leaned closer. Her cheek almost brushed his shoulder. By the starry vibes, what was she doing? She pulled back and he tightened his grip on her wrist, a warning squeeze.

She hadn't let a man touch her in two years. It had been on the final night of a textile conference. After that evening, she was content that she wasn't missing much. But the captain, even if he was slumped, had that confident swagger. He probably knew how to show a girl a good time. Not her, of course.

For her, he had *wrong guy* written on every line of his *Potential Lover* application, from the *current employer* line to the *work skills* line because theft wasn't a talent she was interested in. Plus, he had a misplaced belief in mythical relics.

"You didn't hide when I came up here, Captain," she whispered.

"That's because I recognized your vibes." His voice was barely audible. "And call me Gregor."

Ahead, the door opened. Its creaking noise carried to them. It was a long moment before the man came into view through the cracks in the shelves. He was tall and meaty, his hair dark and curly, his skin well-tanned. He wore black from head to toe. Fingerless leather gloves covered his hands. A pair of dark spectacles sat high on his head.

He paced down the aisle, his shoulders strutting with the move.

Power emanated from him, warning her to stay back. He flashed *danger* like a gun, and it stole her breath. The newcomer stopped in the same spot they'd vacated. He pulled out a scroll. It could have been the one the captain had just returned, but she was too far away to see.

She tried to get a closer look through the cracks in the shelves, leaning into her would-be protector, and she became very aware of his solid wall of muscle that smelled of clean male, the woods, and sunshine.

The visitor put one scroll and then four more inside a bag that rested on the floor. He sealed it up and made his way out. After a moment, the door creaked open and then shut.

Mara stepped back.

"Not yet." Gregor tugged her closer by her arm. "He might sense me break the spell," he whispered.

"Who was he?" She cleared her throat, hoping her breathy words passed for a whisper.

"No idea." He turned and looked back at her, holding her gaze, and an unexpected awareness snapped between them.

Foolish.

She twisted free and stepped away from him, deeper into the row of scrolls. His spell shattered in a soft wave. Cool air rushed between them and a shiver ran across her shoulders, missing his close warmth. "He stole those scrolls. We need to tell a librarian," she said. "Did you get a good look at him? He had dark spectacles on his head like they were for the sun." Strange, because mages typically used a spell to cast sun shields in front of their eyes, not specs.

Gregor shook his head. "Only the center of the specs was dark. The edges of the lenses were clear."

She hadn't been able to see that high. "What's the point of that?"

"I don't know. They wouldn't be for the sun...or for seeing much of anything."

She gestured toward the aisle's exit. She couldn't get past him unless he moved. "We have to tell someone."

"I admire your honesty, but I don't think that will be necessary. He can't get the scrolls out. This place has *alarm* spells packed in everywhere." His vibes pressed out again. Though they weren't intended for her, they brushed against her and tickled at her skin. He frowned and stepped out of the aisle, holding her off with a raised hand.

"What's wrong? Is he coming back?" She was as good as blind to other mages with her sense tucked away.

"He's gone. Completely. No vibes. Unless he fell down the stairs and died, something's wrong." He strode off toward the door, giving her a long look at his broad shoulders. "Stay here."

Not happening.

She followed him from the room and into the stairway, crooking her head and shoulders to fit through the tiny door. She raced behind him as fast as she dared down the steep, tight, windy stairs. He stopped at a broken window, staring out at a flying....

"Is that a horse? A Pegasus? Do those exist?" She blinked trying to clear the image before her eyes. "That's as impossible as the white wheel popping into existence...as impossible as a wayward ruling the world."

He turned to her, a breath away in the tight space.

She stood on a step higher than he did, their height matching and bringing her close to his blue eyes. Out the broken window, a half-moon glimmered in the dark sky. It shined through and graced his face, glinting against his blue eyes. If the Goddess existed, she'd just focused her spotlight on him.

"I've seen and felt things that I thought were impossible." His tone was light, but sadness echoed behind it. "Now I know better. Nothing is impossible."

4

MARA KEPT up with Gregor's fast pace, racing down to the Rari-fied Library's ground level, but the spiral of the stairs called out to the twist of her mage energy. She had to focus to keep her power wrapped tight inside her. It threatened to spin out and bring the shine to her eyes. If they'd descended any faster, she'd be glowing like dual stars.

"Jane?" she hollered, uncertain where to look for the woman or if she should. She was only here on an exchange of favors, not because she had any right to be. But they needed to tell someone about the theft.

"I'll alert the Librarian tomorrow," he offered. "It's late. I'm sure everyone's gone home for the night."

"I'll wait for Jane. You can leave." She needed him to go away, along with his silky vibes and his blue eyes. Even Stella had commented on the latter after he'd left this morning.

"No, ma'am. I'm seeing you to your car. It's dark and there are flying horses carrying thieves in the vicinity. Shall we?" He held out his hand toward the slender door.

She didn't move. "That's not necessary. I rode my bicycle."

He nodded, his lips mashing together in a thoughtful frown. "Perfect. I missed my second workout today. I'll run alongside you. That way I know you'll get home without getting plucked out of your seat and tossed to the sky."

"Don't you have a car"—she paused—"somewhere around here?" There was no lot nearby. For that matter, no road ran through here. Just the rocky path. The librarians either walked to work or simply lived among their scrolls. Then again, for all she knew, maybe they unwound a scroll and flew on it like an enchanted carpet.

"I took a taxi to the edge of the cemetery and walked the rest of the way."

"Then you should summon another taxi. You can't run next to me. Your feet are tired, remember? And those boots look heavy."

"I see I need to prove the strength and manliness of my feet to you." He spoke absently as he opened the door, stepped outside, and scanned the area, star-studded sky included. Apparently satisfied, he gestured for her to exit.

She hadn't meant to challenge him. "I fully believe your feet are capable." She pressed a hand to her chest. "I'm capable too. I'll get home on my own."

He nodded at her like he cared but was going to do as he pleased. She sighed in capitulation. He cast a string of mage lights to guide their way. They crossed the bridge over the moat to her bicycle.

He frowned at it. "No *lock* spell?"

"Who would steal my bike here? No one knows about this place. And besides, there are great-vibed sharks around."

"Speaking of the sharks, where are they? Did you sense them when we crossed?"

She squinted at the water, cautious even though they were a good distance away. She didn't want to disturb the creatures with the weight of her gaze. But nothing stirred in the moat. "Eaten by a Pegasus?" She mounted her bicycle, kicked the stand up, and put one foot to the pedal. "Running beside me is going to be very awkward. You'll struggle to keep up and you'll huff and puff everywhere."

"I promise not to blow your house down."

A smile stretched her lips against her better judgment.

He patted her handlebars. "Let's go." He took off at a fast jog, his stride easy.

She pushed off. "Do you often escort girls home while they ride bicycles?"

"Do I look like a professional? I am in the market for a new job. I wonder if that's a viable business. How am I doing? You're my first." He looked back, and his vibes spilled out.

"Quit with the vibes," she ordered.

Two mage lights circled around her, one stopping at the front, the other floating behind her.

"Why? It's dark. You have no visibility."

His power was like a lasso that tugged her with a gentle pull, enticing her. Tempting her.

He stopped running and she passed him.

"I know what your issue is," he hollered.

"You're tired already? No wonder you need to work out twice a day."

"You like my vibes." He caught up with her in seconds.

She scoffed and then lied as only a sorceress could. "I do not. Why would you think that?" Her bicycle wobbled, channeling the unsteadiness he inspired in her.

He smiled.

Oh, don't do that.

Men like him should come with warnings. Maybe there was some kind of spell that would hover a banner over his head. If such a thing didn't exist, someone should invent it because his smile was like sunshine and rumpled bed sheets, warm and seductive, something to snuggle up to. She had to look away.

"You leaned into me when we were hiding," he said. Neither huffing nor puffing. "You were intrigued."

"Maybe I simply lost my balance." She pedaled faster.

He kept pace. "I believe I mentioned that I like your vibes, too."

She sucked in a light breath. How long had she imagined meeting someone who could see past her specs and the labels society chained around her? Inside her chest, something small blossomed. She braked and put a foot on the road. "Fine. I admit that you have nice vibes. They're tranquil." She tightened her lips. "It's too bad you're a thief. And worse, it's too bad you work for Power United." She pushed off again, leaving him behind, and ruthlessly squashed the wistful flutter in her heart.

He caught up before she was ten feet down the road. "I don't work for them."

"You did. And now you're tainted."

"I disagree. Despite what you've seen of me, I'm a nice guy."

"Nice guys say *no* to committing theft."

It wasn't exactly fair of her. The High Councilor had issued Gregor an order, and no one said *no* to her. Except he had in a way…he'd hidden her spinning wheel in her office, keeping it safe for her.

He might have groaned as she pedaled faster, but he didn't fall behind. Maybe he was using some type of *jogging* spell to keep up with her. Did those exist?

"So I have room for improvement. But in my defense, may I point out that I returned your employee's drop spindle?" This time there was a slight panting in his voice. "No mage should have the conduit of their power taken away. I vow I will never do that to a fellow mage." The energy of the vow vibrated through the air.

She scrunched up her nose. She hated vows. "Here's a lesson in dealing with wayward mages: never vow to the Goddess around them. She's not a fan of our imperfections."

"That's not true." His voice was sharp with the denial as if he'd taken her lack of godly favor personally. Silence fell between them for a moment, broken only by heavy breathing. "What else is there to this lesson?" he prompted. "I'm listening."

But she wasn't interested in convincing him of the truth. "That's all there is. It's pretty simple." Focusing on pedaling, she called out the directions to get to her home.

They turned down Redbud Alley that led to the old carriage house she used as a garage. Half a block in, she squeezed the brakes, stopping at its doors. The alley was secluded and dark, and the tree limbs stretched over them, hiding them from the sky...hiding them from scroll thieves riding on an impossible Pegasus.

"You didn't learn what you came for tonight. What were you seeking?" He took one deep inhale and his breathing evened out as he stood beneath the soft glow of his mage lights. A bead of sweat dripped down his cheek to hide among the golden whiskers that shadowed his face. He lifted the hem of his T-shirt to wipe it away. Her glance to his belly was automatic, the lines of his muscles glistening in the light. She didn't even try not to look. The best she could claim was that she kept it quick.

Warnings clanged in her mind, reminding her that she'd been lured in by a handsome face before. She'd almost forfeited her life for it.

"I was looking for proof that the relics don't exist." She lifted her gaze to him, expecting to find a flirtatious smile because if he'd noticed she liked his vibes, then he hadn't missed her glance at his abs.

But his gaze was focused and sharp, his lips in a serious line. "Instead you found me, and I've seen a relic for myself. They exist. Do you believe me?"

"No." She climbed off her bike.

He sighed hard and then his attention caught high, toward

the upper floor of her house. "You left a light on and the curtains open. Might want to rethink that."

Her most powerful wheel sat highlighted in the dark of night.

She couldn't catch her breath at the thought of losing anything else today. She'd shuttered away the grief at the loss of her wheels for the sake of her sorceresses, but it burst to the surface now. "Are you going to turn me in?" The words quivered.

"I swear by the Goddess not to tell anyone or anything." Vibes waved around him at the power in the words.

She flinched. "Captain, you didn't heed my short lesson."

He held up his hands, palms in, surrender, mage style. "Habit. I apologize. And it's Gregor."

She pushed the button on the garage remote that sat in her bicycle's basket. Catching his glance, she knew he was surprised she hadn't spelled the door open, but she never used her power in public. "Thanks for the protection against the Pegasus." She walked her bike into the garage. His mage lights accompanied her. She would wait to extinguish them until after he left. Even the small amount of energy needed for that would cause her eyes to glow, and she refused to expose that to him.

He stood there, a silhouette of grays and blacks. "Mara, I'm leaving soon."

She waited. He didn't move. "Okay. I'm closing the door now."

"No, I meant I'm leaving to...go far away."

She didn't ask where. *Far away* didn't invite questions, and the less she connected with him the better.

His shadow didn't move. "Can I take you to dinner tomorrow?"

She might have laughed. "No. Whatever you are...a government agent, a soldier, a Power United employee, I know your type. Lure them in and lead them to their doom."

"A flair for drama wasn't in your file."

"You admit you read my file." It was evidence against him,

though she wasn't surprised there was a file on her or that he'd read it. She could imagine what it contained.

"It was thin. I'd say it's missing a few details. I'll bring you my file. You can read it over dinner. Then we'll be on even ground."

"You and I will never be on even ground." She closed the garage door with another push against the remote.

He bent down as it lowered, keeping her in sight. "Please?"

"No."

5

GREGOR WALKED into the High Councilor's vast throne room and surveyed it. The throne stood at the center of the back wall and was elevated on a dais. Enormous tapestries hung throughout the room. The exits were peppered among them. He made a note of them. Habit.

There was a door ahead, close to the throne, another behind him and one each on the right and left walls. It was always good to know how to escape when the High Councilor was in the vicinity.

Beside him, General Vincent Rallis cleared his throat. Something nervous and uncertain rang through the sound to Gregor's mage sense. He braced himself for questions that would be uncomfortable for them both, and then decided to be proactive. "No."

"No, what?" Vin asked.

"I'm not returning." He wasn't changing his *no* to a *yes*. Though he spent most of last night wondering how to get Mara to do the very same to his dinner invitation. "I'm not rescinding my resignation."

Vin asked him each time they'd been together since Gregor

had quit. The question was usually followed by a spiel claiming that he didn't know anything about the plans with the fairy needle and he wanted him back in his unit and that Gregor needed to move on.

"I would like you to reconsider." Vin's tone turned formal. He was a member of a founding family, practically a prince of the Republic. His occasional stuffiness was a side effect of his birth.

It had never bothered him before.

Gregor eyed the other man in the room, Lincoln Sinclair, chief of the High Councilor's guards. He didn't know him well, and he didn't want to have this conversation in front of him. But considering Sinclair's position, he probably already knew about the incident.

"The army doesn't welcome waywards. You know that as well as I do. The only reason you're asking me is because you're my friend." Or rather they used to be friends. Gregor couldn't trust him anymore. "No one would willingly follow me or partner with me."

"Dane." Vin held out his hands.

"Again, because he's my friend."

"And many others."

Wrong. Vin was just too stubborn to admit it. Gregor couldn't go back, but he had no idea how to go forward. "You say I need to move on." He met Vin's gaze. "So do you."

The right door opened, and Cecilia Garnet entered, along with her Power United colleague, Nils Lusman.

Their arrival killed the conversation. Thank the Goddess.

Both wore business suits, Cecilia's tight with a short skirt. Nils's suit was much less remarkable, as was everything else about him. He was tall and slender with brown hair, sharp eyes, and the manners of a polished businessman. But today he looked pale. He puffed out his cheeks. "Holy vibing shite. I can't believe I'm in the throne room." His voice wavered. "Captain Whitman, I am glad you're here. You have a capable presence." He pulled at his tie. "Pretty much what I need right now. Goddess, I'm nervous. By the way, you did quite a job coordinating the men at the mill. I know they weren't the easiest men to handle. We're always a little short-handed on the night shift."

Gregor stifled a frown at the excuse. Those men had orders and they should have followed them to the letter.

"I hope you'll consider joining us permanently." Nils glanced at Vincent. "Sorry, General. We offer better pay, better benefits. It's less dangerous by far. I know we're a step down in prestige but considering...."

Gregor raised an eyebrow. "Considering that I've had a step down in prestige as well?"

"No, no, not at all. I just want you to know we do not discriminate. We are an equal opportunity employer. As you know, we hire even the weakest of sorceresses."

When Gregor had overseen the delivery of Blue Light Mills' wheels yesterday morning, he'd witnessed the women spinning green hay to copper. He'd made it a point to check it out. Their working conditions were nothing like what Mara had claimed—her protests were recorded in her file, but she had no proof of wrongdoing by the electric company.

"We've been looking for the right man to head up security for a while," Nils continued, smiling.

"We've got great toys to do the job." Cecilia handed him a flat rectangle, about the size of his palm.

"Pocket-sized tracker," she explained.

He knew what it was.

"No spells. Just Non-mage tech, so no mage can sense it on him...or her." Her smile brimmed. He could guess what was coming. "We've been tracking Mara Rand at the High Councilor's request. A smart move. She can't be trusted. I hear you're taking over the job."

"What?" He raised an eyebrow. That was news to him.

Sinclair snapped straight and opened the door ahead of him

with a push of his vibes. No one but the High Councilor's guards could cast spells in her presence. Not even the senators.

The old crone entered, her white robes flowing around her. Her long white hair, parted in the middle, streamed down her back. Wrinkles lined her round face. At first glance, she looked like a kindly grandmother walking around blind, her eyes closed, with long black eyelashes gracing her sightless eyes. But on a closer look, those eyelashes focused into black stitches. Her eyes were sewn shut, the better to see the future, or so the story went. But only the foolish assumed she couldn't see exactly what was in front of her and more.

Power radiated from her and it took Gregor a moment to remember how to breathe again. She always had this effect on him.

Everyone bowed low until she was seated on her throne.

She turned her blind gaze to Cecilia and Nils. "How many wheels have you confiscated?"

"From Blue Light Mills, there were one hundred seventeen," Cecilia replied. "From Rallis Territory overall, we've collected about a thousand. And Power United's branches in the other territories are right on track with us. In total, we've confiscated over ten thousand."

Gregor absorbed that new piece of information as calmly as possible. No one had told him this was a nation-wide seizure.

Nils cleared his throat. "None resonate with the power of the gray according to our tests."

"Your tests?" Gregor's words busted out, driven by horrified instinct. "You don't need to use it to know it's a relic. Trust me. You'll be able to sense its evilness simply being in the same room with it." He flung his arm out with the words, the small tracker box still in his grip. What the hell was he supposed to do with it? He stuck it in his pocket.

"Some of the sorceresses who spin for Power United have

taken on the duty," Nils responded as if it were no big deal. "We need to be certain in our identification process."

Goddess above, they didn't know what they were asking.

"As soon as the relic is identified, it will be taken into custody and delivered to the Council House. No one will be worse for wear." Nils smiled.

Three months ago, Gregor had been meant to walk away from his encounter with a relic too. Stronger than ever. No worse for wear.

Nils was clueless about the power of the relics just as the army officials had been. The med mage had even assured Gregor that the inoculation with the needle would strengthen his power. Not ruin it.

Gregor eyed the man. "If you find the wheel and test it on one of those women, you'll destroy her."

Nils shook his head. "I don't—"

"Lusman and Garnet. Out. Now." The High Councilor waved at both Cecilia and Nils.

They didn't wait. Both almost ran out of the room. The door clicked shut behind them.

Vin stepped forward, his mouth in a tight line. The general was highly displeased. "With all due respect, Lady, this is something the army should lead. Not Power United."

"They are spinning wheel experts, Vinny. Can anyone in the army claim that? I think not. Besides, I have my little monk mage on the case." She pointed at Gregor.

Monk mage—it was another term for cadence mage because of the chants they often used in their spells.

"My little monkey."

Experience kept him from grimacing. She'd called him that more than once. His bigger concern was that he'd thought his part in this was done. He wasn't on the case. He was here to report his findings and then he was getting back to his prepara-

tions for his trip. He was leaving for the West on a search to find...
something. Answers. Hope. Himself.

The High Councilor shook her head at him as if she
disagreed with his thoughts.

Goddess, he was tired of this. His slump intensified. He was
aware of it this time.

"The handsome Captain Whitman is right. He knows exactly
how a fairy relic feels," she said.

He wasn't a captain anymore.

Beside him, Vin stiffened. "He knows how one feels because
you've destroyed his life with it."

"He's still standing, isn't he?" she snapped. "I did not destroy
his life." She held up a long, pointy finger. "But I can destroy
yours, General. Best remember that." She nodded at Sinclair.
"Hide these two away before my army boy gets angry and
commits treason. When it comes to children it's best to limit their
opportunities to misbehave. Besides, I promised him he could
watch his wife." Her voice dropped a few notes lower. "It's a little
kinky, General...your inclination to spy on her. Does she know?"

Vin wisely remained silent.

Gregor followed the general and Sinclair behind the hanging
tapestries. Whatever the hell was going on now, he knew better
than to ask.

Three feet of space stood between the wall and the tapestries'
thick fabric, one of which was coated in a *transparency* spell,
making a one-way window into the receiving room. The moment
they were hidden, ladies-in-waiting entered and bowed to the
High Councilor. Gregor had witnessed similar scenes dozens of
times over his years of guard duty.

The old crone waved them away and then watched from her
throne, seemingly bored, as the women mingled.

Mara Rand walked in a moment later. Gregor straightened as
he drank her in.

Her eyes were clear behind her red-framed specs. Her chin

was high. Her black pantsuit outlined her long legs. The trim jacket followed the curves of her body with equal perfection. She might have looked like she belonged, except for the spectacles and the solitude that hovered around her. She bowed, unacknowledged, and took a seat against the wall and waited alone, a meal fit for any one of the privileged women circling like the library's sharks.

A fist punched against the inside of his ribs as if prodding him to go to her, to stand beside her, but all he could do was watch.

FROM HER SECLUDED corner of the receiving room, Mara eyed the High Councilor. She no longer shivered at the sight of the stitches that held the High Councilor's eyes shut. Instead, she wondered which sorceress had spun the black thread. Though it was done long before she was born, some ambitious, prideful part of her wished she'd been the one to spin it.

A waste of a wish for a wayward.

The thread had probably been spun by a sorceress who was related to one of the ladies milling about the chamber. They were all born of privilege and power. The group was composed of the female members of the Council, one senator, and some of the heiresses of the Mayflower families—their ancestors were the founders of the Republic.

The three-dozen women gossiped and cast curious glances Mara's way. The *muffle* spells that hovered over the room clogged their words like they were stuck in a drain. But Mara didn't need to hear them to comprehend their disdain.

She wondered if any of them knew that some of her spells circulated here. The original tapestries of the room that graced the wall to her left were woven with threads she'd spun and imbued with the power to absorb mage vibes. Thanks to her

spells, the room wasn't overwhelmed with the energy of the high-
powered mages who frequented it. The ladies-in-waiting didn't
seem to notice the spells, but they weren't they meant to.

However, Mara was certain she was meant to notice the new
set of tapestries that hung over the throne. She'd taken stock of
them the moment she'd arrived. They were a message to her.
Although considering the messenger, who happened to be sitting
beneath them, it was more accurate to call them a threat.

The largest tapestry, a depiction of the mythical white spinning wheel, hung in the middle, in line with the throne. Within
the fabric, the large wheel and its twelve spokes gleamed under a
night sky sparkling with stars. Its spindle was very long and
sharp, and an even longer strand of yarn trailed out from it,
everything the ancient stanza claimed it was.

A white fairy oak wheel
And a silver spindle's prick
Twelve moonbeams spokes whirl
And endless threads twirl.

The nursery rhyme was a frequent message from her mysterious pen pal.

The two remaining relics were depicted in the other new
tapestries. To the left of the throne hung an image of the Goddess
sewing with the singing needle. In the other, to the right, the
Goddess used the dancing scissors to snip threads in her
embroidery.

Legend claimed that the Goddess's fallen consort had made
the relics to win back her love after he'd cheated on her with
some of their daughters...daughters who were sorceresses.

A horrific tale and bad juju for sorceresses to this day.

Mara didn't believe a word about the gods or their unfortunate incestuous habits.

The three other tapestries, hanging on the wall to her left, had been here every time Mara visited. These tapestries portrayed the herds of unicorns that pulled the Goddess's carriage, the mermaids that graced her fountains, and the wolfmen who guarded her castle.

All a bunch of mythical vibe shite.

Except for the wolfmen, but they only dwelled in the Wild West, along with the glister.

Surely the High Councilor knew that five out of six of her tapestries showed myths. The woman was no fool.

"Why are you late?" the High Councilor croaked suddenly.

Mara jumped, trying to think of her answer to that question even though she hadn't been late. But just then Lady Bronte Casteel entered, her violin and bow clutched in her right hand. She was the latecomer to this unfortunate party.

Lady Casteel's lacy dress, made by Blue Light Mills, high-lighted her to perfection as she curtseyed to the crone. "My apologies, Lady High Councilor."

"Were you unable to shake your mate off your tail or something? Did he stick to your dress like a spider's prey?"

Mara's heart stopped.

Lady Casteel's dress was woven from threads that Mara had spun with gray repose spider silk. The dress allowed the syphon mage to function safely in society. The beautiful woman, mate to the commander of the Republic's army, no longer had to worry about syphoning too much energy from the mages around her when she wore it.

Mara hadn't been sure Lady Casteel would have the courage to wear the spider silk fabric. Especially in public. As a rule, mages hated spiders. They were all creatures of the glister...the fairies...who were equal parts despised, feared, and obsessed over by mages.

But their gray repose spider made silk that could reset unbal-anced systems.

Mara's thread was revolutionary. But was the Republic of Mage Territories ready for such a revolution?

"No, ma'am, he did not stick to my dress," Lady Casteel replied simply. "Shall I play?"

The High Councilor waved her hand. The gracious woman took her spot next to the throne and lifted her instrument. Her beautiful tune drifted out.

The other women turned back to their conversations as if the musician was hired help instead of the most talented violinist in the Republic.

Typical.

The high-powered were interested only in their own world. They were involved only in themselves. This was why injustices happened all over the Republic, such as those against weak-powered sorceresses conscripted into Power United's army of copper spinners. Mages like Stella and Esther. The powerful of this world simply didn't care.

Mara leaned her head against the wall. She needed to return to her mill. If she didn't get back there soon, her sorceresses would start plotting some ill-advised action to recover their spinning wheels.

She tried to focus on the music as a distraction.

Lady Casteel played with her eyes closed as if she'd been caught in the spell of her melody, and it had transported her soul elsewhere. Mara recognized the feeling. She felt the same when she was spinning, or better yet, dancing, though she never let herself do that anymore.

She snuck a glance at the High Councilor sitting on her throne. Her robes had hiked up and a pair of Blue Light Mills' jeans stuck out beneath. Unlike Lady Casteel's dress, Blue Light Mills' denim was spider silk-free. It was also free of all mage vibes until its owner put them on.

The High Councilor was her best customer when it came to her jeans. She preferred all white.

Blue Light Mills' denim was woven with specially spun threads that had a hollow core designed to hold the wearer's vibes. Therefore, the wearer had nothing but her own energy pressing against her. It was like walking through a universe that was custom-made for an individual—peaceful and powerful. And very expensive.

The manufacturing process was arduous. Only Mara had the skill to spin the thread, but even she couldn't weave the threads into denim fabric. The weaving had to be done with someone with zero mage power. If a mage wove the threads into fabric, then the hollow tube of the threads would fill with the weaver's energy, rendering the fabric's special powers useless.

The only mill that could weave her special thread into the denim and not contaminate it was in the Wild West. That mill was run solely by Non-mages.

Mara had originally made the jeans to thumb her nose at the establishment, a favorite hobby of hers. Jeans were illegal in the Republic because the style originated in the Wild West. Nothing from that anarchic land was welcome inside the tightly controlled Republic.

She'd been shocked when the jeans had earned a following among some of the younger members of the founding families... and then the High Councilor had ordered a pair.

It was hard to enforce a law when the High Councilor herself flaunted it.

Blue Light Mills wasn't the only company that made jeans in the Republic. There were a few other companies that did too. But none were as special as Mara's. No one else could spin the unique hollow-core threads. Likewise, no other jeans company had to go to the Wild West to have their denim woven. But Mara made up for the cost with the exorbitant price tag attached to BLM jeans.

As Lady Casteel's melody ended, the High Councilor clapped. Her slow applause picked up volume as the other women around joined in. The musician tilted her head in acknowledgment.

"Lovely, Bronte," the High Councilor said. "Incomparable music from our Republic's only syphon. We all breathe easier with you around to syphon away our excess power. And how do you breathe around us? Is the dress living up to expectations, or do I need to summon your man to whisk you away from our torture? I promised the general I would ask."

General Vincent Rallis was the scariest man Mara had ever met, powerful enough to blow away the force of one of the Old World's mushroom bombs.

Ten years ago, he'd been her first official customer for her exclusive jeans. So exclusive she hadn't even cut a pair from the then-newly developed and unadvertised fabric, but the Rallises, the rulers of Mara's home territory, had spies everywhere. Including her tiny mill.

"Considering the amount of mage power around here, it ought to be in tatters by now. But it looks as pristine as ever," Lady Casteel replied.

The crone gave an exaggerated frown and turned her blind eyes to Mara. "Impressive, wayward sorceress."

The women in the room turned to her. Their narrowed eyes carried suspicion, dismay, and more than a few held disgust. Mara ignored them as she stood. She was stiff, as if her body didn't want to move, and she was reminded of Gregor's tired feet. At least she'd had a chair.

She strode forward with as much confidence as she could muster. "Blue Light Mills produces quality clothing, Lady. We train our sorceresses to spin outstanding threads and yarn even though they all register as three or lower on the Frederick-Johnson power scale." She never missed a chance to spread her message.

Gasps ricocheted around the room. It was a serious faux pas to reveal information about power levels, especially about such low, shameful numbers. But they needed to know.

She continued, taking advantage of the shocked silence. "This is proof that the weakest sorceresses among us are capable of contributing to society in ways that are gentle to their health and well-being." Unlike what Power United did to them. "Regardless of their strength, they deserve fair treatment. It is Blue Light Mills' mission to further the well-being of sorceresses and their families by providing on-the-job training and equitable pay."

From the start, Mara had become an expert at developing methods of spinning that used minimal power, not because she was weak, but because her power was so odd she'd been forbidden to use it in public.

"Bully for you," the High Councilor said. "You've got a factory full of weaks and freaks."

The insult emboldened Mara. She stared at the woman's blind eyes. "No, ma'am. I'm the only freak."

Another round of gasps played harmony to the High Councilor's loud, sharp laugh. She held out her hand and addressed her ladies. "Do you see why I keep her around? Tell me, sorceress, does one have to be a freak to spin the spider silk?"

"It has nothing to do with being wayward, just skilled." Highly skilled. She was the only sorceress who could create fabric from the gray repose spider silk. Most likely, she was the only one who'd tried.

A woman stepped out of the crowd. It took Mara a moment to place her. Lady Prower...that was her name, wife to Senator Prower. The newspapers often featured her for her so-called impeccable style and her occasional charitable works.

"The spider silk fabric should be illegal," Lady Prower stated. "Anyone who stoops to using such energy ought to have her hands removed!"

And so it begins, she thought. She swallowed down the seeds of panic. The woman's declaration wasn't an original idea. It was the standard punishment for any low-powered sorceress who refused to do her duty if she was conscripted to spin copper for the electric company.

"How could you wear something from those dirty gray, Bronte?" one of the younger women in the crowd asked. She gave a dramatic shiver. "Fairies are nasty."

"My dear Calendra, we must always be kind to the weak and less fortunate among us, those such as Lady Casteel." Lady Prower bestowed a gentle smile on Calendra, but cunning lurked beneath it to anyone paying attention. "I do wish you would accept my invitation to travel to the Wild West. Our missionary work brings such comfort to those in need. Afterwards you would appreciate how much you truly have."

Mara made sure to keep her face blank, but she couldn't stop from clenching her teeth.

Lady Casteel's sister, a pale blonde woman, stepped to the violinist's side. "Oh please, Prower." Senator Selene Glender-Casteel was known to be vicious and cold, but Mara admired the woman. "We all know why you go over there. You're hooked on the gray's hypnotic power. And your little manifest destiny fetish isn't as secret as you think."

Manifesters believed the Republic should stretch from the Atlantic to the Pacific. It wasn't a view the Council or the Senate condoned.

"Lady Prower, I could never go to the Wild West. It's dangerous over there!" Calendra cried.

That was true. Few mages dared to cross the Mississippi for good reason.

Lady Prower shook her head. "The glister are truly gentle."

Mara laughed. Every eye turned to her. "I've encountered a few glister in my time. I assure you they are fierce and proud. Gentle is not a term I would use for them."

"Glister?" Calendra asked in her prissy voice. Mara estimated the young woman was about Stella's age. They'd certainly led different lives.

One of the ladies scowled. "Another word for fairy scum."

"Best watch yourself over there, Prower," the crone said. "If the fairy scum don't turn on you, the Black Skulls might. I don't know what I'd do without you and your conniving husband in my Senate."

"Regarding the dress," Senator Glender-Casteel's tone was laden with impatience. "I don't see what all the fuss is about. It's useful and safe if the general allows his wife to wear it."

"Allows?" Lady Casteel squinted at her sister.

Senator Glender-Casteel continued, "I hereby propose Bill 45.73 stating that the gray repose spider is a valued resource and is granted full protection accorded by the law of this land."

Was it that simple?

"Denied," the High Councilor declared.

Of course it wasn't.

"A mistake," the senator countered.

As she sat on her throne, the old woman's robes fluttered in a gust of power. Her staff appeared in her hand from thin air. "Mara Kathryn Rand, you are hereby ordered to cease spinning the webs." The High Councilor's voice vibrated with power. The tapestries swayed with the force.

She gasped, a strident protest on the edge of her tongue. She bit it back but not quite in time. "No—" It was a whisper, but it still gripped the room in utter stillness as if she'd shouted. The High Councilor lifted an eyebrow and waited, but Mara had her mouth under control. Her mind raced. She needed more webs to help heal Stella.

The High Councilor looked at Bronte. "Did all that power bother you?"

"No, so why—"

"Look at that. It really works." The High Councilor laughed and then her face morphed into solemn lines. "All remaining silk will be confiscated immediately."

Mara held out her hands. "I don't have enough left to make it worth your while to confiscate, Lady High Councilor." She'd used the last of the spider silk to make Lady Casteel's dress, and then

Stella had arrived at the mill so damaged, so in need of the silk's healing powers. She'd been working to acquire more ever since.

"Also, the silk is hereby banned from importation." The old crone slammed the end of her staff against the floor with the proclamation.

It was like a cement block tied to fragile wings of hope. She swallowed hard and flapped those wings with every joule of courage she could muster. "This fabric has the potential to change lives, from sense sick mages to those whose power is too heavy a burden, to the poorest of Nons who are unable to afford shelter or to heat their houses in winter."

"Yes! And that is why it has shrunk the Senate's tiny little senses to microscopic proportions! Power for Nons? You're a dim-wit to even suggest it. The webs are being confiscated as we speak."

The unfairness of it all was a slap in the face. A cold flame struck to life inside her. Its flicker fueled her forward. "Just like you took our spinning wheels? What next, Lady? Our roving? Our looms? We've done nothing wrong. I've done nothing wrong...merely tried to help the sick and ailing and poor."

The High Councilor stood and strode forward, her staff tapping against the floor like a third foot.

A gust of power pushed at Mara. She fought to catch a breath, but the air skipped past her mouth as if it had somewhere else to be...some place safer.

The High Councilor's robes blew up to her knees. Inky black strands drifted out from her, like long hair that detached and floated through the air in macabre streamers.

"Oh no!" Calendra whispered. "A prophecy. My clothes!"

The door and windows rattled as the High Councilor's words boomed out.

"When evil's clutch shares the relic's touch,
All joy the Wheel will steal.

> *Then West devours the mages' powers.*
> *The Lady's cry, her land to die."*

Someone screamed. Blackness descended, pressing against everything. The walls cracked under the force.

Mara's lungs sank from the weight. She stumbled, hands out, reaching for the floor. Her palms and knees smacked the ground. And then, just like that, the air cleared.

It was a long moment before she could lift her head.

Sticky black coated the tapestries, the furniture, and the walls. Slowly the stains faded—expensive *stain-resistor* spells—until the room was clean, but everyone's clothes were streaked with black.

"Eww!" That came from Calendra, cowering on the floor like everyone else. "Is it in my hair?"

The High Councilor burped loud and long. "Oh, excuse me. I hate it when prophecies revisit me like that. They're like bad fish. They just keep coming up. I had that one last night. It's a bouncer." She peered at Lady Casteel. "You still with us, syphon?" She squinted at the dress. "Is it naturally stain resistant?" She lifted the hem of her robes. "Too bad my jeans aren't."

6

GREGOR STARED through the *transparency* on the tapestry. The black, sticky clouds of the prophecy hadn't touched him, but its power had flowed through the thick fabric, shoving the three of them against the wall. Machismo had forced them into a race to recover, and they all stood straight, trying not to gasp for air.

Much closer to the source, the prophecy's energy had knocked the high-powered ladies off their feet. Anyone who didn't have *stain resistor* spells on her clothes was regretting it now. Many of the highest-ranking women in the Republic were covered in the sticky strands, including the High Councilor. Her white jeans were ruined.

Mara was sprawled on the ground. If she'd been his to guard, he would have thrown himself over her, taking the hit for her. She was alone out there. As alone as he was behind this damn rug. Goddess, how did she stand it? How did she keep her head up, exposing her weakness to everyone?

She needed a protector. His power readied, surging into his throat at the thought. He had to swallow it back. That was the first time it had done that since the needle.

On the other side of the tapestry, Mara tripped over her feet as she fought to stand up. She'd be safer if she just stayed down. It hurt to watch. He was afraid of what would come next. The prophecy had spoken of evil. The word was synonymous with wayward, and its mention would not go unnoticed. He knew damn well that it was the relics that were evil, along with the god who made them. Not Mara.

The High Councilor raised a leg to showcase her stains. She kept her balance with her staff. Her jeans looked like she'd waded through ink. "You should work on this, sorceress."

"If you want jeans that only hold your vibes against your skin," Mara began, "then I can't weave them with *stain resistor* spells. If I did that, the jeans would hold my vibes."

"Then we have a problem! I need a new pair with plenty of backups. I want a dozen! No, two dozen! And make them tighter." The High Councilor slapped her own bottom.

"Goddess help us," Vin whispered, backing up a step.

"Tight like a second skin," the crone continued. "I want them by Saturday next. I have a hot date."

The room went quiet.

Senator Glender-Casteel gave a long-suffering sigh. "Is this date scheduled for before or after the West devours the Lady's land?"

"Are you questioning my judgment, you speck of a girl?"

"Here they go again," muttered Sinclair.

"Always, Glender," Senator Glender-Casteel replied. The crone had been a mother, of sorts, to the now-senator, a fact Gregor had learned in his time as bodyguard to Lady Bronte.

The pair faced off.

Power flashed, burning up in a blink and taking the warmth in the room with it. The air turned so cold it hurt to breathe, even behind the tapestry, as the two powerful women battled in silence with their energy.

"Oh Goddess, we're going to die." Calendra backed up to the edge of the crowd until she was hiding behind Mara. "My mother sent me to court, and she as good as turned me into a corpse." For once, the flighty, young woman wasn't overreacting.

Vincent poked at the tapestry. "I want Bronte out of there."

If Gregor's mate were in there, he'd feel the same. As it was, he wanted Mara out of there too.

Mara stepped forward. "If I may interrupt?"

He closed his eyes. Hell, this kept getting worse. No, you may not interrupt, he thought. Have a care, woman.

"Shit," Sinclair muttered. "She is too damn brave for her own good. I warned her to stay quiet."

Unexpected jealousy raised its head. Someone else had noticed that brave goodness...and probably those legs, too. Those were impossible to miss. "You know her?" Gregor asked.

Sinclair smirked. "Interested? You'll never get her. You're not her type."

"And you are?"

He laughed softly. "Anyone who's connected to her"—he pointed at the High Councilor—"or any other part of the government doesn't stand a chance with Mara Rand."

The crone dashed forward and in less than a blink, stood nose to nose with the sorceress. "You want to interrupt, evil eyes?"

Power rocked the tapestry. Gregor clenched his teeth.

The High Councilor tossed her staff in the air and it disappeared. She grabbed Mara's hands and peered at her palms as if she could see a fortune there. "Is your clutch as evil as those glow balls rolling around in your skull behind those spectacles?"

Mara lifted her chin high though fear tightened her brow. "You do know that the idea that waywards are evil is outdated and incorrect. When was the last evil wayward you can remember?"

All around her the ladies-in-waiting backed away, bracing for the retaliation they were certain—he was certain—would come from standing up to the most powerful mage in the Republic.

"Eh." With the casual sound, the crone shrugged. "There's always a first."

"Well, I'm not it. And, also, I can't get you a new pair of jeans by Saturday, much less two dozen." She held up her hands, palms toward her chest in a pleading mage's non-threatening pose. "The spinning alone will take me over a week and the closest mill that has the proper conditions to weave it is in the city of Kansas. The threads must be woven into fabric by Non-mages or they get contaminated, and the Republic certainly doesn't have a mill that meets that requirement."

The Wild West. Gregor cocked his head.

"I have to book two months in advance to get time on their looms," Mara explained.

"Figure it out, sorceress," the High Councilor snapped. "I'll give you three days to spin the thread, starting tomorrow. Wednesday, Thursday, Friday." She ticked off three fingers. "Saturday for travel." Another finger. "I give you Sunday to rest." Her voice went light with that little gift.

"Generous, Lady." Sarcasm drawled through the words. "Most Nons don't work on Sunday anyway. But your plan has a problem."

Oh, Goddess, so damn dangerous.

"What the hell is she thinking?" Vincent muttered. "Does she not understand to whom she is speaking? She's going to be a flake of freak dust if she doesn't stop."

Gregor narrowed his eyes at the condescension in his former boss's tone. This was why he could never go back to the army. Prejudice ran deep, and now he was cast out among the rest of the imperfect to fight against its swift current.

"How do you expect me to spin thread when you confiscated my spinning wheels?" Mara demanded.

Gregor caught Mara's hint of nerves as she shifted her eyes right and left. The High Councilor couldn't know about the wheel he'd left behind, could she?

"I've taken care of that." With another breath, the crone was back to her plan and on to the next hand, ticking off those fingers. "Monday to get it woven. Tuesday to travel home."

"There are no trains on Tuesday." Mara's anger came through the words. "The train that goes between the city of Kansas and the border only runs on Saturday and Monday."

"The West is so weird. Fine, then. Monday to get it woven and travel home. You'll be a busy girl that day, but do whatever you want on Tuesday. You've got Wednesday, Thursday, and Friday to cut and sew." She lifted both hands. "Delivery on Saturday next at noon. Simple! Even I could do it."

Mara gave her a hard, defiant look.

A silent pause stretched and then the crone poked a bony finger against the middle of Mara's forehead. "Watch yourself, sorceress."

"She's reading her mind," Lincoln whispered. "Mara knows better."

"What's the wayward doing?" Calendra gasped, apparently oblivious to the High Councilor's mind-reading ability. "Is she going to give us the evil eye?"

"I went to school with Mara." Sinclair spelled the words to his ear, shutting Vincent out of their conversation.

"You went to SWWM?" Gregor cast back. He knew his surprise showed on his face.

If Lincoln Sinclair attended the School for Weak and Wayward Mages—its initials were pronounced *swim* for short—then that meant the chief of the High Councilor's security was wayward.

Sinclair stared at him. Yes, he definitely knew about Gregor's incident and its results.

"Wayward vibes are contagious!" Calendra cried, standing in the middle of the ladies-in-waiting.

Sinclair laughed out loud.

The High Councilor gasped too, mocking the woman. "You

don't say! We should vacate the room so we don't catch it! Run!" The word roared through the room, shoving the women toward the door on an ocean wave of power. But just before Mara got there, the doors slammed shut. The bolts slid home.

Mara was locked in with the High Councilor.

7

HER HANDS WERE SHAKING, but she stood her ground, holding the crone's gaze. She adjusted her specs with quivering fingers. "I have a business to run, Lady. I need to—"

"Where is the white glister oak spinning wheel?" The High Councilor's voice turned so sharp and vicious that Mara's cheeks and hands stung from its force.

She looked down. Red welts streaked her palms. Her breath came in short, silent jumps. The air was disappearing again, sucked away like a *vacuum* spell had descended over the entire room.

"I don't know," she gasped.

Black spots dotted her vision. Mara fell to her knees as thick, smoky streams surrounded the High Councilor once again. This felt different from the last time. Power streaked over her skin like a thousand tiny lightning strikes. Gravity multiplied by a hundred.

She fell flat to the ground.

"*Glow Eyes spins webs as Luck commands!*" The crone's voice expanded, punching against every inch of the room, the building, the world, as if she channeled the Goddess's voice. "*Abandoned!*"

The word scraped through the little air left with a harsh roar. She screamed, pain filling the sound.

Glow Eyes. Lost girls, help her. This was about her.

She knows.

She tried to cover her head, but she couldn't lift her arms. She was pinned to the ground by the strength of the prophecy.

"*The relics...await!*" The words were disjointed. The High Councilor choked on them, like they were too big and powerful for her mouth to hold. "*Their fate!*"

And then everything returned to normal. The air reappeared in a silent snap. Gravity relaxed its tight pull.

Mara took a loud breath of air and managed to lift her head to survey the room.

The High Councilor swayed on her feet and then sat down on the floor beside her, legs out straight, her robes caught up high, exposing her stained jeans. For a moment the woman sat there slumped, her face slack with exhaustion. Mara wanted to inch away, but she couldn't move yet.

The crone leaned back on her hands. The color slowly returned to her cheeks. "Was it good for you?" She wiggled her feet back and forth.

It was all Mara could do to get to her hands and knees, which felt less dignified than lying flat. She twisted to let gravity take her hips to the floor so she could sit facing the leader of the Republic.

"I could feel that coming. They're like burps that won't bubble up. Such indigestion." The High Councilor patted her stomach and then pointed her thumb over her shoulder. "That's why I sent those sissy women out. They couldn't have handled that. Don't tell them I said that though. They'd be insulted. Now, you, tough stuff, I knew you would survive. Nothing knocks you down, does it?"

"I'm knocked down every day, Lady, case in point." How could the High Councilor possibly assume otherwise? How could anyone? "And to set the record straight about that prophecy, Luck does not command me to do anything." A tired anger popped up that fate would dare to stir its finger through the threads of her life.

"You think not?" the crone asked. "That prophecy is new. They're a bitch to birth, but I always feel like I'm doing my job when they come up. That one is not fully formed.

"*Glow Eyes spins webs as Luck commands. Abandoned.... The relics await their fate,*" she recited. "No shit that the relics await their fate. But what is their fate? That's the question. I had another new prophecy last night." She recited it, too.

> "*Glister mistress, twined delight,*
> *Wields the relics a royal right.*
> *Wield without line of blooded descent,*
> *A deadly choice, spin and lament.*"

The High Councilor paused for a moment. "A glister of blooded descent, straight from the king's line. There aren't any of those. The glister king has been missing for a long time."

"Everyone in the Wild West knows that."

"Pfft. Been there so many times, have you?"

"As a matter of fact, yes." The Wild West had given her a temporary home years ago. She'd been desperately poor with nowhere else to go. She'd stayed west of the Mississippi long enough to earn the funds to start her mill by selling shirts and pants woven with *bulletproof* spells, her own creation, one that few needed in the Republic since citizen mages shot vibes at one another, not guns. Although the Republic's army or enforcers might have been interested, she would never approach either party.

Thanks to her denim, Mara was still a regular visitor to the Wild West. "Don't you have that in my file?" she drawled.

The High Councilor shrugged. "Don't ask me. I've never read

your file. I have no need. Besides, your name comes up in every other prophecy I speak."

"What?" she gasped.

"Well, just this one. But trust me when I say, one is enough. Prophecies are nothing but trouble. Last night's prophecy came up easily. That means I'm not the first oracle to speak it." She sighed. "Some other oracle already knows it."

Mara already knew it too. It had arrived numerous times from her mysterious pen pal.

She knows.

But did she? Surely if the High Councilor knew about Mara's collection of prophecies, she wouldn't be so relaxed at the moment. She'd be squeezing Mara for every drop of information possible.

The crone lifted an eyebrow. "What was that thought?" She cupped her ear as if she was trying to hear better.

Shit. Mind reader.

"No, seriously. I missed it. Think it again, would you?"

Mara tightened her nose as if she could squeeze the thoughts to stay in her mind.

"Oh, come on. You're no fun." The High Councilor nudged Mara with her foot. "*Wield without line of blooded descent. A deadly choice.* Soooo," she sang the word long and loud. "Apparently"— she hung on to that word too—"according to that prophecy, it's a bad idea to touch the damn relics. Unless you're royal."

The crone gave a humph. "Wish I'd known that earlier. But that's a hazard of the job. Acting without knowing everything. I vomit up words, phrases, and fragments that come from some-place else...someplace other than my mind...until the entire story is formed, and then I must make sense of it." She scooted across the floor until she was side-by-side with Mara. She leaned in, their foreheads nearly touching. "Day and night, they whisper at my mind."

A chill ran over Mara's skin.

"They don't always come up as rhymes and riddles. Sometimes they're images or messages for specific people. Regardless, they are my reason for breathing, for casting every vibe of power. And you, my foolish sorceress, have spun yourself into the heart of it all. Stupid Glow Eyes." She stroked the back of her wrinkled, veined hand along Mara's cheek. "Evil child."

Mara stiffened.

"There are other prophecies about the relics. Here, listen to this."

Black smoky trails encircled the crone again as her words overflowed with vibes, carving a path into Mara's mind like a canyon gouged out by countless floods. It hurt.

> *"Whoever claims the relics three*
> *When midsummer moon shines bright,*
> *Sets mageland's fate upon its course,*
> *Their hearts' desire as its force.*
>
> *If under that moon's pure white light,*
> *Cruelty bears what Luck bestowed,*
> *The borders of mageland will erode.*
>
> *But if under summer's full Rose Moon,*
> *High Blood finds Luck's Lady's three,*
> *Then safe the western borders be."*

The High Councilor tipped her head back as the aftermath of the prophecy landed on her face. She blew a perfect ring of smoke. "The Rose Moon," she whispered and held up her fingers as if she were counting on them. "Seventeen days and the clock is ticking. The Goddess's wheel in cruel, evil hands. What do you think of this, sorceress?"

"I think there is no Goddess. There is no wheel. There is only a fairy-tale."

The High Councilor cackled a hard laugh. "Stubborn, aren't you? But you will learn. And how you will wish for oblivion. Glow Eyes, Luck speaks about you...and the relics...and their fate. He, too, exists, else I would not speak prophecies of him. The wheel will destroy everything we live for. The Lady cries." She waved her hands, impatient. "The land dies. Blah blah blah!"

"If evil has a spinning wheel, we both know who wields it," Mara said

The crone frowned. "Power United? We've searched high and low through their stores of wheels, through the ranks of their sorceresses. There is nothing there. I wish it were so simple." She clapped her hands. "Bang! Poof! Tada! Evil identified. Problem solved. But they don't have it. Evidently, you don't either." She shrugged. "I can only guess that the West has it. And so I'm sending you."

"Me? I don't know how to find it." This time, a dangerous mix of desperation and rebellion welled up in Mara's voice.

"Monkey!" the old crone called over her shoulder.

Mara glanced around the room trying to figure out where the High Councilor was leading this conversation now, but there was no monkey present.

Gregor stepped out from behind a tapestry.

"You," she whispered. Betrayal squeezed around her. Had she seriously believed he'd seen past her specs yesterday? What had she been thinking? This man was the government's agent...and Power United's. She could not afford to forget that.

She took a slow inhale as if she might pull back the whims their previous encounter had momentarily loosened.

His gaze darted over her form, inspecting her. She didn't hesitate to do the same to him. His slump was back. His forehead was lined with what she guessed was worry, but his stride was loose and long. It devoured the distance between them. He wore the same clothes as yesterday like they were a uniform for him.

He stopped beside her and only then turned to face the old

woman as if he were declaring his allegiance with Mara. "Lady High Councilor." He bowed and knelt down, putting them all on the same level.

Mara glared at him. He'd been spying on her again. He was like a gnat that would not buzz off.

"A gnat?" the High Councilor said. "I bet it would be quite satisfying to give him a good swat. You'll have plenty of opportunity, sorceress. I am sending my monkey with you to the West. It's a dangerous place, and I care very much about my jeans. Gregor Whitman, I hereby release you from my service and render you to Mara Rand."

"What?" Mara said. "You can't give people away. And even if you could, I don't want him."

Gregor flinched, but she didn't apologize. His throat bobbed as if he swallowed down her rejection. "If you're sending her after the wheel, she needs a team of bodyguards to keep her safe."

"You're not man enough?" the High Councilor demanded. "You have a gun, don't you? Spells galore?"

"My power is not what it once was. She deserves more than me."

"What's wrong with his power, girl?"

Mara tightened her brow, confused, appalled...trapped. "I have no idea."

"Well, he's wayward! You should know what's wrong with him. You're the only expert I've got on the waywards." She thrust a hand at Gregor. "Open up, monkey. Now, sorceress, look at him. Tell me what you see."

GREGOR FOUGHT AN INSTINCTIVE FLINCH. The High Councilor might as well have ordered them to strip naked. Power, like a heart's deepest hopes and wishes, was private. But he didn't have a choice. If he refused, the old crone would open him up herself.

Mara pulled off her spectacles, her cheeks pink, her head low. She secured the earpiece of her specs in a button of her shirt. She tried to hold his gaze but looked away, her embarrassment at the enforced intimacy obvious.

This wasn't right. He fought not to cover up, to cast a *blanket* spell over them both. "Lady," he began. "Miss Rand is—"

"Shush, monk mage." The High Councilor tilted her head as if to get a better look through her blind eyes. "Thoughts, sorceress. Spill 'em. Now."

Mara's vibes fluffed around her, expanding like a towering cloud that warned of powerful storms brewing in the sky. For a moment, he was distracted.

Goddess, the noise that would make would be heavenly, but he would never have the privilege of hearing it. It stole his breath, that loss.

"I've never done this before." Mara's words jerked and stuttered. "His power looks...imposing. Huge." Her chest lifted and fell as if she struggled to stay calm.

He wished he could tell her everything would be all right, to give her some kind of encouragement, but he was fresh out of those sentiments.

"That's all you've got?" The High Councilor snorted like a dragon losing patience, ready to breathe fire. "Come on! Reach in there. Comb it out. I know how you work. He's a bag of fleece ready to be spun."

"No. He isn't. He's a person who deserves his privacy." Despite her protest, she reached for his power with hers. Goddess, it was like she'd touched the very core of him. He had to fight to stay still and if he lost that battle he wasn't sure if he'd yank away from her vibes or rush into their power.

"It's strong. It flows like it's already been combed," she offered weakly.

Her vibes were a tangled fluff, inviting and soft. The longer he looked at her power, the more he was certain that if he stepped into them, he might never want to come out. She was cozy and he wanted to roll in it.

"Like a pig in mud?" the High Councilor asked him.

"Not quite." His words were strained from the task of remaining still under Mara's touch.

"Keep going, sorceress."

Mara shook her head, frowning. "It's steady. It has a rhythm like it's dancing or something. Or rather, it makes you want to dance. And I can't see the end of it."

"Me either," the High Councilor said, frowning harder than Mara. "But what's wrong with him?"

"Nothing. He's perfect."

He might have puffed his chest with pride, but the tone of her voice held no admiration. Besides, wayward vibes weren't perfect.

The High Councilor gave a dissatisfied shake of her head. "I don't understand wayward power. And that's a problem. I ought to know all. But he's your guard now. You're welcome, by the way. I always give the best gifts. People don't believe me, but it's true. Now find me that wheel."

"No."

"No?" The High Councilor chuckled with malicious glee. "I don't encounter outright refusal of my commands very often. Ever, actually. I have so many *punishment* spells I could deploy right now." She tapped a finger against her lip. "Hmm. Which to use?"

Mara shoved on her spectacles with a sharp, quick move and wrapped her energy down tight. Her eyes were hard, her lips flat. She dared what few would, saying no to the crone. If he could, he'd hold her back, shield her from her own bravery, but even when his power was pure and true, he couldn't have managed that.

"I don't want your gift," Mara said. "And I don't know how to find the wheel."

"Of course you don't! If I don't know how to find it, how can I expect you to?" she spat. "You are bait seasoned with a tasty sprinkle of evil. I'm fishing for enemies."

"But you said I would be alone and abandoned. How can I live up to your prophecy if you send him along?"

"I'm not abandoning her," Gregor said.

"See!" Mara cried.

"Eh." The High Councilor shrugged. "Fate has a way of working these things out. All I need is for you to be as sticky as a spider web and the wheel will cling to you."

"I thought you didn't want me to touch it!"

"I thought I didn't have to worry about that since you claim you're not evil. Are you telling me differently now?" the crone cried.

"I'm not evil! But if I touch it, I'll die. Right? A deadly choice?" She argued as if she were the old woman's equal, and if he didn't know a thing or two about her, he would have questioned her intelligence. Her courage outmatched any soldier he'd ever met. It worried him.

The old crone shrugged. "I'm willing to risk it. But if you do die, please die *after* you make my jeans. You wouldn't believe how hard it is to find jeans that fit perfectly. I should never have worn them today, but they're just so comfy. And damn sexy."

Mara bit her lip as if to keep from speaking.

The crone shook her finger at her. "I can hear that thought tumbling through your mind and you're right. Begging for mercy would do no good. I have no mercy. The West is coming, sorceress. Either it comes on our terms, caught on my hook and squirming in terror at my power, and our way of life is preserved for generations, or it comes on their terms, and we all become violent victims to our basest instincts. What do you say about that?"

"All I want is to get my spinning wheels back."

Guilt ate at him. That was his doing.

The High Councilor turned toward him. "Monk, it is not your

destiny to become a hermit, to don robes, and grow a long beard on a mountain peak in the wilderness."

How had she plucked that from his mind? He hadn't even been thinking about it.

"I found the map in your underwear drawer with the big red circle in the middle of the western range of the Wilds. Boxer briefs. Best of both worlds." She shook her finger at him. "Let me tell you, monkey. Hermit robes are a bitch to keep clean even if they're spelled to the nines. They drag everywhere and the friction against the ground wears away at the *keep clean* spells. And you're much more kissable with smooth cheeks than a scraggily assed beard.

"Oh boy!" The crone held up her hands. "Hold the landline! Here comes another!" Smoke poured from her mouth as if she'd lit a potion stick.

"The needle sings for the stitcher's dance,
But claims the songs of warrior chants.
Guard the quest of the one who spins.
Seek the truth and healing begins."

She smiled as the smoky clouds settled. She'd spoken this prophecy with ease. "Huh. There ya go." Thrusting her hand out, she pointed. "West! Giddy up. Tallyho. Don't forget your lasso."

Healing begins.

The words echoed in his mind with a song of possibility.

Guard her quest. Seek the truth.

He could do that. He'd do anything to get his power back. Hope thundered through his energy. He wanted to grab Mara's hand and run west.

"When the relics are safe, and I have proof that you are not the prophesied evil, then you will have your wheels back. So find the white wheel!" The High Councilor stood and made her way to the door, leaving Gregor and Mara to scramble to their feet as well. Side by side, they watched her go.

"Guards!" The crone hollered as she walked. "Take them away."

His hope sputtered. What the hell was this now? He spun around as six men poured through the door at the back of the room. Lincoln came from behind the tapestry. Gregor's power snapped to the ready, but he didn't have a chance at getting them out of there.

He could not stop whatever this was.

"Oh, relax, monkey." The High Councilor stopped just short of the exit. "You've survived far worse. As for you, sorceress, you will spin the thread for my jeans in my dungeon. The monkey will be your plus one."

The dungeon. He gritted his teeth. What the hell kind of hope would he find there?

"Maybe he'll sing you a song." The old crone clapped her hands as if the idea filled her with joy.

"No." The denial busted out of his throat. That he would not do. He had no songs. The needle had claimed them. His gut turned hollow at her suggestion, a familiar feeling these last months, as if the needle had aspirated his insides. It left plenty of room for rage, and it poured in on cue, leaving him a repository for a thunderous fury that would peal out for eternity if he let it loose.

"Suit yourself."

The guards rushed them.

8

Surrounded by the dark gray stone of the dungeon's cell and with the slam of the door five stories above echoing through the chamber, Gregor paced their confines. Mara huddled against the wall. The room was cool, too cool for long-term comfort, but he barely noticed. A sharp burn of anger roasted him from the inside out.

Healing begins.

The crone had dangled the promise before him only to yank it away and toss him in the damn dungeon.

"I can't sing you a song." His voice was sharp.

Mara looked at him from the corner of her eye. "That's all right." She sounded as if she were speaking to a wild beast who'd promised not to eat her but was still salivating in the shadows.

"No, it's not. That's what's wrong with my power. That's what's damaged inside me. She wanted you to see it." He paced on.

The circular room was about ten feet in diameter. Skinny stairs wound around the wall to the entrance above. With no railing, if a prisoner fell, he'd have to cast a spell fast or he'd be dead.

The sole break in the stone was a wooden door to his left. He broke away from his path to open it—a sink and toilet. This dungeon offered sanitary conditions. He swallowed down a wild, bitter laugh.

"I don't know what a lack of songs looks like in a mage's power." Mara crossed her arms over her chest like she was cold already.

"No reason why you would. Not many people have seen a man drained of his chants and songs. Not many people have had a fairy prick them with a fu—" He bit back the curse. "With a needle so old it belonged to a god."

He wanted to strangle the High Councilor until she blurted out what the hell she was playing at. Dangerous thoughts. Goddess, his mind was falling through the cracks if he was thinking that kind of vibe shite. Who knew how close the crone had to be to read his mind? But she had sucked away his songs, his chants, his life. When she offered him the hope of healing, she promptly threw him in a dungeon.

He rubbed his hand down his face.

Why the hell had she done this? Mara could have spun the yarn in a guarded room with comfortable furniture and easy access to food and water.

"Why would someone do this to you?" she asked.

"Promise me hope and then throw me in a dungeon?"

"No. The...other."

He clenched his jaw. It popped again. He really needed to stop doing that. "The needle's prick was supposed to make me immune to a fairy's hypnotic power. Instead, it made me wayward."

She flinched.

"My power is broken—I'm broken." All of his bitterness poured out with the words. He'd held onto it for three months, and of all the places to unload it, this was not the one he would have chosen.

She was the last person he wanted to know his insurmountable flaws, but the crone's hint of healing had rocked him off his axis. He wondered if this might be the moment he shattered to pieces, right here in the dungeon in front of a pretty girl who walked the world with her skin on inside out, exposing her secrets instead of hiding them.

She pressed her fingers to her lips, concern rippling across her face. "Does the High Councilor know?"

"She ordered it."

"By the lost girls," she breathed. Her eyes were sad and he suddenly felt guilty for burdening her with this. She stepped toward him. "How could she do that to you? How can you not hate her?"

Of course, I hate her.

He bit down on his tongue as if that might stop the words from floating through his mind. He couldn't hate her...not if he wanted to live.

"I agreed to it. I'd encountered a fairy once before. He was not a nice man." In fact, he was evil, the most fucked-up creature he'd ever encountered. But he'd keep that part to himself at least. "I was sixteen. I swear he held my mind for three days. I'd do anything to keep that from happening again." He reached into his pocket and pulled out his lucky charm. He'd been doing that a lot in the last three months. He was trying to stop. It was a bad habit. Besides, the damn thing hadn't exactly worked lately.

"Is that a tuning circle?" she asked gently. She took two steps closer to see. He caught the flowery scent of her hair as she looked down.

The silver piece, the size of a large coin, was shaped in a swirl, designed to pull more energy into a mage. "You seem awfully powerful to need one," she said.

He surprised himself and smiled. She'd complimented him. "I found it at the same time the fairy found me. I don't think I would have survived without it."

"I'm sorry."

"Do you believe me now? About the relics?" he asked.

She parted her lips but didn't respond right away. That was answer enough. "Denial is not an effective defense, Mara." He wanted to wrap the truth around her and seal it tight, a shield against whatever the future held.

Truth.

Seek the truth. About what? The white wheel? The needle? Mara?

He put the coin back in his pocket. "The crone is planning to wave you out there like a red flag to a bull in hopes that the white wheel will run you down." The plan screamed *danger* with a banshee's cry. He stepped closer to her, forming a *silence* spell around them. "You should be the one running...as far away as you can." He'd go with her. He had nothing to hold him here. Except for his parents. But they'd understand.

She held up her hands. They might have brushed against his chest or he might have wished for her touch so much he imagined it.

"I can't run. I have my mill, my sorceresses."

"None of that will matter if the wheel finds you."

"Wheels don't find people." She moved back and his *silence* spell broke. She wandered toward the spinning wheel that stood in the center of the cell.

Goddess, she was stubborn. He lifted his head and looked up at the ceiling, shadowed by darkness and hidden from view. "At least you're not alone." His whisper slithered around the cavernous space. A song would have soared in here.

"I work best alone. I don't need a hero if that's what you're thinking, not one who pops out of the woodwork everywhere I go." Her soft words struck him like tiny fists.

He looked away for a moment. "I suppose I was talking about myself. I'm glad I'm not alone."

"Oh." She opened her mouth again but didn't say more. She reached down to the bulging bags piled by the wheel. She opened one. Cotton fluff spilled out. "You can't cast a spell," she said. "You can't cast anything."

A protest punched up inside him and he fought not to jut out his chin and puff his chest. His magehood was insulted. Hell, so was his manhood. "I *can* cast. Everything works. I just can't hear vibes—"

"I know you can." Impatience lined her tone. "Just don't do it. Don't even cast a light." Her voice was tight. Her lips were tighter. "You'll contaminate the spinning process. It's a special thread. I only spin it when I'm alone." She adjusted the stool in front of the wheel.

"You're getting down to work right now?" He'd expected rage, crying, complaining. Hell, he was doing two out of the three. Which made him wonder.... "How many times have you been in her dungeon?"

"First time. But I've been in a room like this before." She didn't look at him as she pulled out a wad of cotton and dragged it apart until it fell in short stretches of fluff as if she was testing it. "And I ended up in that dark, cold room because of a man who reminds me a little of you." A dark thread sang through her soft voice, carrying the promise of a tale.

He narrowed his eyes. "A man like me."

"The story is rather cliché, I'm afraid." She sat on the stool before the wheel, preparing to work, and with the simple move, an intimacy flickered to life around them. He would see her work. It distracted him from the sharp edge of his anger.

He crouched down beside her. "Tell me."

She sighed, the cotton fluff in her hands blowing in her breeze. "Just as I graduated from SWWM, a man came along and charmed me off my feet." Her voice fell into an easy rhythm. A sorceress was a natural storyteller. "He had the nicest smile, blond hair." She studied him. "Darker than yours. More bronze and light browns. He kept it brushed across his forehead in a perfect wave, and he had this light in his eyes. Though he wasn't wayward. It wasn't that kind of light." She yanked at the cotton with a hard pull. "I thought it was kindness. I was wrong. Little did I know that his light was a beacon into a world of evil."

She did have a flair for drama.

"He claimed I was the girl for him, that he would protect my poor wayward self from the big, bad world."

His vibes hummed through him, reacting to the danger, ready to defend, but there was no defending anyone from the past. There was only moving on.

She tugged and adjusted a piece of string that attached to the wheel. "It was a common tactic for some Power United bounty hunters at the time. Since then, sorceresses have wised up. Most know of the ploy." Her voice turned wry. "There has never been such a foolish girl as I. I had no idea what was going on when he dropped me off at Power United. Their holding cell is lined with stone. It's underground too. It's not round though."

He inhaled, slow and controlled. "Power United has a dungeon?"

She gave a small, tight smile. "I'm used to people not believing me."

He opened his mouth to reassure her, but he stayed silent. He wasn't sure he did believe her. Perhaps she'd been too scared to see the truth, and for good reason. "What was his name?" When they got out of here, he'd look up the bastard. He'd bet no one had done that for her. Hell, he'd do it for all the waywards who'd ever been helpless before a bully. Maybe that would help him move on.

She shook her head at his question. "And now here you are with your charming smile that lights up your handsome face, and here I am in a dungeon."

He filed away the handsome comment. "Here *we* are in a dungeon. And I'm not a bounty hunter. I'm your guard, bound by a prophecy."

"A prophecy that harmed your mage power. I'd think you'd want nothing to do with it."

"You can't outrun fate. Or your own foolishness." He held up his hands at her gasp. "Talking about myself again." He rubbed the scars on his neck. "Case in point. I was foolish to trust anything related to fairies. I knew better. I hate fairies."

"Ah. I know one. He's a friend." She spoke with a crisp beat, her words building a wall between them as if she were siding with the fairies over him.

"Fairies are no mage's friend."

"And many would say the same of waywards." She turned her back to him as she looped the fluff of cotton around the string she'd adjusted. "It's going to take me every second I have to spin the threads for this." Her tone made it clear that she was done talking.

He studied her fingers, gracefully moving over the spinning wheel. He'd been no friend to waywards. Not until he'd become one.

He wondered again, before the incident, would he have looked past her spectacles and her waywardness? He couldn't imagine not being intrigued. She had the bravery of a warrior mage...and the legs of every man's fantasy.

"I'll help you get back to your sorceresses. I vow it."

She slashed the air with her hand and gave him a sharp frown. "Oh, stop with your pointless vows. No wayward with any sense believes in the Goddess and if they do, then they certainly don't look to her for blessings or hope. We're her cast-offs, her imperfections."

"Well, I wasn't always wayward, so you'll have to tell me what I'm doing wrong." He fingered the side of his throat where the scars sat.

Maybe it would have been better if he'd been born this way. He wouldn't know what he was missing. His strength drained with the thought. From his skull to his feet, it slithered through him as if his body was suddenly too weak, too imperfect, too broken to hold him. "I hate being wayward."

HOW MANY YEARS had it been since she'd had the same sentiment? She'd never talked about it with anyone, not even as a student at SWWM. She'd been isolated from the others because of the extremity of her waywardness.

Her heart hurt at his confession. The pain was so unexpected that she skipped a breath. "You're certain you're wayward?"

He lifted an eyebrow in her direction. "I'd take off the *concealment* spell on my eye—only one glows, by the way—but I've never even looked at it in the mirror."

She pulled off her glasses and let her eyes shine with her power. She'd let her sorceresses see them when she didn't have a choice. But she'd never done this before.

He sucked in a loud breath. "Goddess, Mara, your eyes are beautiful."

No one had ever told her that. Nor did she believe him. His words hit a shield that had been growing for a lifetime, honed by too many taunts to remember. Besides, compliments weren't why she'd showed him.

"Being wayward doesn't mean you're broken. It shouldn't mean anything to anyone. Except for the glow, there's no real difference. The average wayward does fall lower on the FJ power scale than the general population, but I've seen your power." It had been like dipping a cold toe into a warm pool. She'd wanted to jump in and immerse herself. She cleared her throat. "You're enormously strong. It was almost hard to look at...hard to sense without...." Without reveling in it. There was no other word for it. Remembering, her breath caught in her chest.

She didn't try to explain further, to convince him that his

power was sound. Maybe he too had a mental shield that blocked compliments from soaking in.

For a long moment neither spoke.

"Do you know how dark the forest can be at night?" he asked, his voice soft.

"What?" His change of subject yanked her away from her memories of the feel of his power, a reminder that she shouldn't have been lingering there in the first place. He was a danger not an ally.

"The trees are darker than the sky. Even if there's no moon, the trees are the blackest shadows. Their darkness towers over you. But if you're lucky, fireflies will come along and offer a little light. That's what you remind me of. You're my firefly in the darkness."

She laughed, a sudden case of nerves. "I don't know what to say to that." She put a hand against the back of her neck as if she might cool off the embarrassed burn firing over her skin. "Just don't get any ideas. We're not having pet names for each other. I'd have to call you *thief* or something and I don't think you'd like that."

GREGOR LOST count of the hours as he watched her spin. As the fine yarn piled up, he paced to the wall and back; he leaned against the wall; he sat against the wall. Helplessness sucked. Fretting and worry were worse. The first time she'd shut her eyes and then jerked awake, he'd almost pulled her off her stool and carried her to a corner to rest, but she'd shooed him away.

"If I sleep, I won't finish in time," she'd protested.

Her fingers cracked and bled. Her shoulders seemed to shrink even as her power clouded through the room, strong and steady. On the eighth time that her eyes closed—he'd counted—she slumped over.

He jumped up in time to catch her, wrapping his arm around her and pulling her into his body. Her head came to rest on his shoulder as he crouched next to her. Her breathing was steady.

"Mara," he whispered. "You have to take a break."

She opened her eyes to half-mast. "I'll just lie on the floor right here." She turned into him, aiming for the floor, but he didn't let her fall, keeping her soft curves braced against him.

He looked at the door high above. She was an easy target here in the middle of the floor, and he didn't trust anyone up there. Not considering how they kept throwing down food, the occasional canteen, and a bunch of straw. Except for the straw, so far, they hadn't hit Mara. Every time they opened the door, he moved to stand over her, protecting her from their falling objects. "How about under the stairs?"

She didn't answer.

He picked her up, braced for rejection. But she didn't open her eyes until he laid her next to the wall.

"Just for an hour. No more," she said.

He didn't have a way of keeping time, but he'd try. She curled up around herself. He brushed a lock of hair from her cheek. "Goddess, Mara, you're freezing." The temperature in the cell was too cool for comfort, but he'd stayed warm. Moving around helped, but the *temp regulating* spells in his clothes did most of the work. "Don't you have spells in your clothes to keep you warm?"

"Not in the summer," she muttered. "Only to keep cool."

Instinct said to cast a spell and warm her, but she'd told him not to cast. Since there was no blanket, he had one viable option. He lay beside her, molding his body to hers. Goddess, if it was wrong to take pleasure in this, then he didn't care.

"What are you doing?" She opened her eyes. He could tell because the room brightened the faintest amount.

"If I can't cast *warming* spells, then you get me because I'm not letting you die of hypothermia. The people I guard stay alive."

"Don't get any ideas," she muttered and then the light dimmed slightly as she closed her eyes.

He had ideas nonstop. He'd spent the last day and a half immersed in her power. It flowed around the room in a never-ending current, tugging at him, whispering against his skin, twining through him. He'd had to fight not to let his power answer hers and brush it gently across the slope of her shoulders, through the curls of her hair, around the curve of her waist.

As he held her, her scent surrounded him. She smelled like nighttime in the forest with a wisp of moonglow blossoms. The flowers had grown in the forest around his school. Their pure white petals pulled the light of the moon, their scent like lemons and sugar.

As he'd watched her spin, he kept thinking about his apprenticeship under the monk mages. He'd thought back to the monastery, the huge stone building on the hill, and the songs and chants that flowed out of it day and night, the pure energy that, after generations of powerful inhabitants, soaked through the walls and the land.

Mara's power reminded him of that. He'd never known one person to fill a space so completely with her power. It danced everywhere as if each vibe heard its own tune and spread out to fulfill the potential of that space. In the rest of society—in the army, especially—every mage kept his energy to himself. But the monks had been different. They'd let their power sing out and be heard and savored by all. He'd forgotten how that felt.

He shifted closer to her, burying his nose in the soft curls of her hair.

But just like he couldn't return to the army, going back to the monastery was not an option either. Even the monks wouldn't welcome him now. Not without the perfection of the Goddess's power.

He was lost. Where the hell was he going to go now? He'd thought he'd have a lifetime career in the army, that someday he'd hear the vibe song of his mate, they'd get married, she'd be content with the unpredictability of life as a warrior mage's mate and have his babies and build their home. It was a happy picture. And now it was gone. He had nothing to hold on to anymore. Only things to hide away, an incurable disease that society didn't want to see.

Mara made them see.

His gut twisted that he wasn't as brave as the woman in his arms. The damn fairy had aspirated his songs and chants and his courage. Fear and anger curdled through his blood. And hate for the fairies.

None of those was anything he wanted to offer her.

After an hour, or thereabouts, he woke her and she returned to her wheel.

Gregor got to hold her once more after another day had passed, and she slept for another hour. His arms craved more.

She finished the yarn just shy of her deadline and stuffed it in one of the bags the cotton fluff had sat in. She turned to the straw piled haphazardly on the floor and gulped audibly. Her power dried up, leaving the room empty, and his soul emptier yet.

9

STRAW WAS the raw material for spinning gold, and sometime during the last three days, a guard had thrown down a bucket full. It had flown everywhere. Caught in a haze of spinning, Mara eventually noticed that Gregor had gathered it up. She'd sensed his anger burning in his vibes.

She gathered a handful of the brittle material. Straw was next to impossible for a sorceress to spin. Mara suffered much less than most, but this time it hurt like a thousand flames beneath her skin. She was far too tired for this, but finally, the gold wire clanked to the ground. She leaned forward on her stool, reaching for it, moving as if a hundred years had worn into her bones.

Gregor scooped it up for her. He placed it in her hand, curling her stiff fingers around it. "I don't know what you just did, but until you spun this hay—"

"Straw." The word hurt. Her throat was dry.

He left her side for a moment and returned with the canteen of water.

She took a drink. "Straw makes gold. Hay makes copper, and white clover spins into silver."

"Fine. Straw." The words had bite. "Your vibes were as light and full as a white cloud on a sunny day. They vaporized the moment you spun the straw. I saw it."

"You were watching? With your mage sense open?" She eyed the gold wire and summoned her vibes. One by one they coalesced, each a sharp sting as her power pulled the wire into a tight weave. Round and round the gold spun until a coin solidified in her palm.

She panted, trying to give her body enough oxygen to stay upright.

"My mage sense has been open for almost three days now."

She hadn't noticed, focused only on the rush of power flowing through her as she'd spun dozens of skeins of yarn. She was so exhausted it hurt to breathe. A drop of blood fell to the floor from her cracked fingertips. Thank the lost girls that hadn't gotten on the white yarn.

"Why in the name of the Goddess are you spinning straw?" he demanded.

"Gold coins are the only accepted fare to cross the Mississippi River and enter the Wild West. It takes two for a round-trip, and though the High Councilor is sending me on this mission, she isn't paying for it."

"Then I'll figure out where to get the gold from. But you aren't doing that again."

Lying in his arms had been a warm luxury. His touch had soothed some part of her soul she hadn't known was rumpled. But it was a delight that would lead to a painful end. She'd had a firm talking to herself while she'd spun the last bags of yarn.

The sooner this ended, the better. And she certainly wouldn't rely on him to pay for her crossing.

The sound of fabric ripping crackled through the chamber. He took her hand, his shirt missing its hem, and wrapped the worst of her injured fingers, tying off the strip. He reached for another.

"No. I need the others free." Otherwise, she wouldn't be able to spin as easily. She tried to summon enough energy to create another coin. She pulled the scraps and bits of straw scattered on the dungeon floor to her with her vibes. They swirled through the air, following the circular pattern of sorceress energy, landing in her hand.

And if she weren't utterly exhausted, she wouldn't have forgotten to spin something as she cast those vibes...the wheel, perhaps, to continue to hide her odd ability at being able to cast without an outside source of spin. All sorceresses needed to spin something in order to cast a spell...a drop spindle, a wheel, a bicycle, a pirouette on her toes.

But not Mara.

She sucked in a tight breath and glanced at him with wide eyes. He stared at her. She was caught.

"This isn't the first time you've done that," he said.

Her empty stomach lurched. When else had she slipped up? If the government learned how powerful her wayward energy was, they'd never let her out of here. "I don't suppose you could pretend you didn't see it?"

Silence fell for a moment. Her hand shook. The straw sitting in her palm slithered around.

"See what?" he asked.

She exhaled, closing her eyes. She couldn't trust him, but she had no leverage to pry out promises of confidences to be kept. That would have to do for now.

She eyed the straw. Though darkness lay heavy against the room, with her mage power open and her energy spreading around her, she could see every detail in her cell, including the minuscule amount of straw in her hand.

It wasn't nearly enough.

Above, the door creaked open. She jumped, nearly toppling backward on her stool as her vibes spun back inside her in a rush. It was instinct, beaten into her from her first day of school to the last.

"Easy." Gregor steadied her with one hand on her shoulder and kept it there. She leaned back into him without thinking.

"Time to go, sorceress," the guard yelled. "Move it, freak." The ugly command shattered against the stone and stung her ears.

Her clear vision had vanished, which meant the bronze glow of her eyes was extinguished as well. She pulled her spectacles from the top button of her blouse and slipped them on.

She lifted her gaze to the door high above. Judging by the number of steps that lifted and twirled against the circular room's walls, the dungeon had to be six or seven stories underground. Starry vibes, she was never going to make it.

"Listen to me," he whispered. He wrapped an arm around her waist and pulled her to standing, keeping her pressed against his chest. Her muscles ached and burned.

"This is how it's going to work. I'm going to carry your yarn bag and lead the way up. You're going to hold my hand the entire way. I need to know if it's safe to cast spells yet. Will your yarn be damaged? If the asshole up there throws anything down on us, a spell or otherwise, can I cast back?"

Something warmed beneath her skin that he'd asked. "It's safe. And I can carry—"

"You can barely stand. I'll carry the bag." He guided her toward the stairs.

If she'd had the chance, she would have given the spinning wheel one last caress. It didn't deserve to be banished to the dungeon.

She thought of her wheel in her office, waiting for her, hidden away. It was her source of comfort, of peace. It didn't judge her glowing eyes or turn away from her abnormal power. It had stood strong and true, a reliable partner against a world that despised her kind.

He'd saved it for her.

A lump of tears rose in her throat. By the lost girls, she was tired. She sniffed and tried to swallow past that lump.

She clung to his hand though she hadn't planned to. Every step was a struggle. By the time they reached the top, she moved at a crawl. Gregor adjusted his pace to hers.

The guard studied Gregor with caution, but when he looked at her, he sneered. "You have hay all over you."

She looked down at her suit to find a few pieces stuck here and there. It hardly qualified as all over, but what did he expect? Sunshine fresh and pretty?

"It's straw," she said. "When you threw down the bale, it went everywhere."

"What's the matter, can't catch, Rancid?" He smirked and the expression grew more hateful as she stiffened under the insult. "Marred and Rancid." His laugh echoed in the empty hallway.

She hadn't heard that nickname since she'd left SWWM. Within those walls, *Mara Rand* had quickly become Marred and Rancid.

Gregor let go of her hand, eyed her as if inspecting her state, and then in a single move he punched the guard with a ferocious fist. That sound, too, echoed in the hallway and the guard collapsed, his spit flying.

Mara raised her eyebrows high, shock splashing over her. A laugh bubbled out, more nerves than delight. Maybe. She leaned around Gregor's shoulder to look down at the man, a wave of energy bursting through her. "I see someone read my file to you."

He growled at the insult, backing away and coming to his feet in the same movement. The foolish man stepped toward her again.

"Hands off, Dawson!" The hard command came from Lincoln Sinclair, rounding the corner. Her hiking backpack was over his right shoulder. Another pack was on his left.

"You will treat the honored lady's tailor with respect." Lincoln was a Blue Light Mills client, a secret one, as were most of her clients. He was wayward but kept his bronze eyes concealed behind his own spells with ease. He had ample power, but it sometimes tightened up and got stuck, like air in an asthmatic's lungs, a common problem for mages with great power. His power seizures were rare, but the High Councilor's guard would never have accepted him with such a deficiency. Years ago, she had designed a cloth that constantly pulled a thin stream of power through it for just such a problem, keeping the energy pathways open. They were BLM's top-selling undershirts.

"Whitman." Lincoln nodded and set both packs on the floor. Mara took the knapsack of cotton thread from Gregor and shoved it inside hers.

"Everything you both listed is in your packs. I did it myself."

Sometime during their three days in lockup—she'd lost track of time—Lincoln had walked down the spiral stairs and asked what they needed. Her first need had been a landline to make a call to Thompson Mill in the Wild West. They would weave the yarn into denim for the jeans. Gregor was the one who suggested she list the items she'd need to pack from home for the trip.

She was grateful, though it meant Lincoln had been through her underwear drawer.

The man knocked on the side of the pack. It made a dull thunk. Something hard was tucked inside. He gave a slight nod.

She always took her longest, sharpest spindle when she traveled to the Wild West. This particular spindle was designed to go on a spinning wheel, but she didn't have one that fit it. The spindle was so long that most mistook it for a sword when she had it strapped to her side. No one roamed the West without a weapon and the spindle suited her perfectly. Its tip was coated in *sleeping* potion. A single poke and any would-be attacker was fated for a snooze.

Lincoln pulled out her car keys from a side pocket of the pack. Most mages used a spell to start the engine, but Mara couldn't afford to have her eyes glowing every time she drove.

"It's fully vibed and waiting on the other side of the portal." He handed them over to Gregor, but she intercepted them, pocketing them with her gold coin. Gregor tipped his head at her, but he didn't protest.

Dawson sneered. "You into freaks, Sinclair? I always knew there was something wrong with you."

Lincoln's fast spell pinned the guard to the wall. He left him there, turning his back to escort them down the hall at a clip.

She looked back at Dawson. "Are you just going to leave him there?"

"The spell will wear off eventually. Quicker if he stops struggling. He should know that."

She tripped over her feet, too tired to walk straight, and Gregor tucked her arm into his. Her head bumped against his shoulder and she was tempted to let it rest there. It was definitely broad enough to cradle her head.

Outside, night gripped the land.

"What time is it?" she asked. What day was it, for that matter?

"The wee hours of Saturday. A half-turn past the maging hour," Lincoln replied.

Saturday for travel, the crone had said. Right on time. Sprung free at midnight. She'd have to drive all night to make the ferry and then the train.

Linc walked them to the portal and looked at Gregor. "That Power United man has left two messages for you. The job offer. He wants an answer."

Mara tripped again. Gregor's hand on her arm burned against her sudden cold. She jerked away.

"I don't work for them." He held up his hands in surrender. "I'm not accepting their offer, Mara."

She just shook her head.

"I vo—" He sighed. "I promise. My answer is no."

It didn't matter what his answer was. He was connected to them and that alone was too much. She'd needed the reminder.

"Can I talk to you for a minute?" Lincoln asked Gregor.

"I'll wait for you on the other side." Her voice wobbled as she jumped on the excuse to give them privacy. "I need away from here."

"Give me the keys. You're going to leave without me." Gregor held out his hand.

"I won't leave without you." She spun a swirl of energy into the words. It wasn't easy. The vibes were rough and too few, but her tale—her lie—was spun. She wasn't sure he was completely fooled. He was still frowning, so she gave him the keys.

The moment he turned to Lincoln, she crossed the portal. Its energy hummed against her skin. She stepped out in her hometown, hundreds of miles away from the Council House. Her car waited at the curb where she'd left it three days ago. Retrieving the spare key spelled to the underside of the back bumper, she unlocked the trunk. She threw her pack in, jumped behind the wheel, and peeled away.

He'd be pissed. But her life always seemed to circle back to Power United. The only thing she feared more than that massive company was herself and what she'd done to escape their hell. She'd spun that experience so tightly around her that she might never be able to unwind it.

She needed to keep Gregor far beyond arm's reach. Keeping people at a distance usually wasn't a problem for her. One look at her specs and every mage knew she was flawed and to avoid her at all costs...unless they needed her expertise. Then the specs acted as her trademark. But she'd taken them off for him. What had she been thinking? It's not like she'd forgotten about his Power United connection. She sped out of town, heading west, leaving him behind.

She'd felt sorry for him...horrified. Plus there were his broad shoulders. His smile. Those blue eyes.

She bit her lip, holding in the tears building in her throat. She did not cry. That was not her. She was just tired. That's all this was. It wasn't guilt. Or loneliness.

She drove as fast as she dared and she didn't look back, stopping only three times. She powered her drive with one catnap and a trio of *stay awake* potions purchased from behind the counter at a vibe-fuel station. Along the way, she changed out of her dungeon clothes and into her travel outfit—packed by Lincoln. The journey stretched six hundred miles from the heart of the Republic to the western border. Though the roads were small, the car was mage-engine fast. She made it in six hours, crossing the borders of four territories and their checkpoints, guarded by bounder mages who held those borders on behalf of their ruling families.

By the time she arrived at her destination, she was shaking with exhaustion. She'd passed the entrance to the small clearing in the woods three times before she'd finally spotted it. Such a waste of time. He'd catch up with her if she weren't smarter than this.

She parked her car and then dropped her head to the steering wheel. Had she ever been so tired?

Grabbing her last *stay awake* potion from her purse, she fumbled with the packet, too tired to get a grip. Her purse dropped to the floorboard as she finally yanked it open. Powder flew. Her nose got a swift dose. It stung. Her eyes watered, but energy zoomed through her. Snorting the stuff was more effective than swallowing it. She needed to move while it lasted because the downside of this would be like swimming in trash vibes. She jumped out of the car, brushed off her pants, and extracted her pack from the trunk.

An envelope fell to the ground.

Not again.

She closed her eyes. What was the point of these things? There was nothing she could do about any of the prophecies. She'd tried to stop the notes from coming, casting *security* spells as best she could around every spot they'd been left. But either her spells were poor or the delivery person was powerful. She'd even tried writing back to the unknown culprit, scribbling a message that asked what the hell she was supposed to do about these things, leaving her reply where the message had arrived. Naturally, no one had picked it up.

She pondered leaving this one on the ground and walking away. But she'd tried that too...leaving them unopened. That hadn't changed a darn thing.

She picked it up and pulled out the paper. The envelope was never sealed shut, merely open and waiting for her.

She spun her fluffy power into a usable thread and cast a light.

Glow Eyes spins webs as Luck commands...

Abandoned....

She crumpled the note and shoved it in her vest pocket. Flinging her backpack over her shoulders, she fastened her long spindle around her waist like a sheathed sword and hiked through the deep forest toward the bank of the Mississippi where she'd dutifully take on the role of bait.

Little did the fallen god know that the High Councilor had soundly trumped his command to spin webs by confiscating them and banning their import, proving that no one was more powerful than the crone. Not even a god.

GREGOR LEANED against the dilapidated ferry tied up along the Mississippi's east bank. The fairy who owned the boat had nodded at him from the edge of the forest and then disappeared. Even getting that close to him had sent an icy slush through his veins.

Damn fairies.

He gripped the good luck charm stashed in his pocket. It had protected him once a long time ago from a fairy and, Goddess willing, its luck would continue for him today.

He couldn't believe he had to get on this fucker's boat. But Mara would be here soon and he'd do it for her. To keep her safe.

He'd tracked her across the Republic, staying close enough to keep an eye on her. She'd never suspected. The woman had no defensive instinct. She hadn't even sensed the *cushion* spell he'd cast around her car when she was in the bathroom at her first stop, in case of a wreck. She was too damn tired to be driving, but if he'd tried to stop her, she would have fought like a wet cat.

Lincoln had shit bad timing with his little *can I talk to you?* But Gregor hadn't wanted to refuse a fellow wayward man.

Footsteps crunched through the leaves and twigs of the forest still claimed by night. Mara was almost here.

She would accuse him of spying on her...again. And she'd be right. He crossed his arms over his chest. This would be the only time she managed to leave him behind. He would not let that happen again.

He kept his mage sense open and waited.

10

Mara gazed at the Mississippi. The muddy water licked at the bank with whispered kisses, languid and calm beneath the sliver of pale moon that hung in the sky. Smoke lingered in the air, likely from an old campfire of Daegan's, the ferry pilot, who was also a fairy. Few made any joke about that twice. Indeed, no one with any intelligence used the word fairy or gray in front of him. He was a proud glister.

His rickety boat waited in the shadows, docked with the power of a glister spell. It was barely visible under her dual orbs of mage light, but she could see the craft was minus its pilot. He wasn't expecting her. Advanced tickets were not an option. This boat was first come, first served, and sometimes not served at all if Daegan was in a bad mood.

The pilot and his supposedly unwholesome gray power and shabby boat were the stuff of wicked legends. Other legends, more wicked still, abounded about the Mississippi's monsters, the river maidens. They devoured mages—head to toe, skin to bone —with their vicious teeth if a mage dared to cross without permission. They were much more dangerous than the mere glister, who could hypnotize a mage with a single glance, force them to their will, and uncover their darkest secrets.

Fortunately for proper Republican mages, the glister dwelled only in the West, along with native tribes, renegade mages, and tens of thousands of powerless Non-mages who'd either escaped the cruel hand of the Republic or had immigrated from other countries seeking a better life. Beneath much of society's disdain and fear of glister was a curiosity, a forbidden fascination that fueled dozens of romance novels starring the unholy fairies. Gregor, however, had made his feelings clear to her. He harbored no love for the glister.

Guilt strummed through her again at leaving him. He'd been attentive and kind while she'd spun out every joule of her energy into making that yarn. She hadn't had many people treat her like that. Certainly not a man. But thoughts of him at Power United chilled the warmth of those memories.

Reaching into the bottom left pocket of her travel vest, she palmed the single gold coin. She'd have to barter for more straw from the Third Street Stables when she arrived in the city of Kansas. The barn manager would drool when he saw her coming again, knowing she'd pay him with a small piece of gold. It was a vibing good deal for him but draining for her.

She tossed the coin through the pre-dawn's shadows and into the black water. Without a sound, the river swallowed it up.

Hadn't it? Surely, she didn't miss. Granted, she was beyond exhausted, but her target was enormous.

Nothing moved.

Daegan didn't appear.

The train was scheduled to depart at half past seven, Non-mage time. It was the equivalent of fifth past bottom morning in standard mage time. By either measure, she couldn't wait much longer.

"Daegan! Where are you?" she called toward the forest. "It's Mara. I need to cross."

Silence.

She'd never known him to be far from his post. She studied the water. She had no plan B. There wasn't another train until Monday. If she missed this one, she'd miss her scheduled slot on Thompson Mill's guaranteed vibe-free loom—the only one east of Denver. If she missed that, she couldn't deliver the jeans on time. It was a domino chain of doom.

She strode into the forest to find him, doing her best to dodge the sticks and weeds as she went, but her hand brushed against a prickly twig. A sticky tightness adhered to her skin. She looked down.

Through the shadows, she could see a long line of crisp, blackened branches and twigs marring the forest floor. This was the source of the smoky smell. On top of the burned foliage, white spider silk draped in thick webs.

She frowned. The gray repose spiders were not supposed to live in the Republic. They inhabited burned-out forests in the Wild West. They were healers to the trees and plants.

But here, unexpectedly, was her plan B.

"I'm sorry," she whispered to the hiding spiders. "I'm hoping you all have lots of silk left in you because I'm going to need this batch."

She slipped off her spectacles. There was no reason to hide the true depths of her power here, though she always kept a tiny drop spindle in the pocket of her travel vest for the very rare instances when she was in public and needed to cast spells, keeping up appearances for a proper, normal sorceress. But she was alone, a good thing, since she needed a great deal of energy for this endeavor.

She let the chaotic bundle of her mage power coalesce around her. In a blink, she spun it into focus.

The world crystallized.

Perfect vision. Abundant power.

She didn't need a mirror to know her eyes were glowing.

She turned her gaze to the broken, tangled webs that draped over the burned forest brush. It was an odd place for a fire. If it had been deeper into the Republic, she might have worried about being set up, as if the High Councilor were spying on her to ensure she obeyed her commands. But Mara had never seen another mage wandering this forest so close to the Wild West.

Despite the fire, the land was already recovering. Tiny green buds dotted the twigs as the silk webs restored the plants to equilibrium and rightness. Holding out her hands, she let her power flow, using it to spin the webs and ply them into a thin yarn. As the yarn drifted out, she cast a *knit* spell. Lace stitched to life before her. She let it pile into her hands, a fine shawl with the potential to right an unhealthy energy system.

Somewhere in the forest, an owl sang out as if acknowledging her work.

She walked back toward the river, heaving her pack over her shoulder as she passed it. She took a breath, stopping in front of the water. Did she want to risk this? Did she have any choice?

"Last chance, Daegan!" she hollered to the forest.

"Mara."

She jumped, twisting toward the voice. A rush of nerves leaped through her.

That wasn't Daegan. It was Gregor.

She stepped back. Her foot brushed the water.

"Careful!" He grabbed her by the shoulders and yanked her into him.

Surprise stole her breath. On its heels, a whisper of relief tumbled like a lone thread drifting on the wind. "How did you get here?"

He set her directly in front of him and leaned down to her eye level. "You lied to me. That was the one lie you get. You don't get any more."

She couldn't promise that. She'd spin whatever tales were

necessary to get this job done so she could get back to her sorceresses. Her anger at being forced to abandon them fueled her next words. "Have you been here the entire time?"

He pointed at the edge of Daegan's ferry. "I've been sitting right there with my mage power wide open." He pulled his lips in a tight, thoughtful frown. "To be honest, I thought you'd seen me. You looked right at me. And then when you stomped into the woods, I realized you hadn't."

He studied her, his gaze intense as if he saw something he'd never noticed before. She wanted to step back under his scrutiny, to hunch her shoulders as if she might protect her secrets.

"I didn't mean to scare you," he said, finally. The simple words rang with honesty.

"You're lurking in the dark in complete silence. How could you not expect to scare me? My heart is still pounding." But the answer to her question blew through her mind like a fluff of cotton fleeing its field.

He was broadcasting his mage power through the air. It waved in a calm flow. He wasn't hiding a thing. She just hadn't been paying attention.

"Right," she whispered. She shoved on her spectacles and twirled her energy back inside her.

"You didn't sense me at all." The tight wrinkles in his forehead conveyed concern and a worry she didn't want. "Which makes me wonder...do you know any defensive spells?" He was much too perceptive.

She lifted her chin. "They didn't teach those at SWWM. But I have a weapon." She patted her spindle.

He eyed her hip. "I see. What kind of sword is that?"

"A sharp one. With a poisoned tip."

"A poisoned tip. Smart." He nodded. Tiny vibes of his power drifted out, rustling against her. He focused on her sword. "It's not a *kill* potion. Its vibes are too soft, and it doesn't vibe with hate. A *sleeping* potion." His tone dripped lower with those last words as if he disapproved. "It feels very old, that sword. For your sake, I hope whoever made it knew what they were doing."

"You can tell that just from touching it with your vibes?" She squinted at him, unable to see him clearly against the shadows.

As if he'd read her mind, he cast a dozen mage lights with a gentle hum. They spread out, softly lighting up the area.

He moved to a large log laying on the bank. He sat down and patted the space beside him, offering her a seat. She looked into the trees, hoping for a glimpse of Daegan, but all was quiet and still. She sat next to him with an exhausted sigh and let her pack drop off her back. She draped the newly made scarf over the top of it and stretched her legs out next to his. Her yawn caught her by surprise.

"You could have slept for five hours while I drove us here," he said. "Hell, we could have both slept and had the army fly us in."

"Or Power United?"

His nose flared. "I don't work for them. I don't want to work for them. I'm turning down their job. That's the truth. Can you sense a lie, firefly?"

"Don't call me that." But her voice was too soft to hold much of a challenge. She had to fight not to drop her head. The truth was she couldn't do much with her mage sense except for her specialties and the basic spells of life.

He sighed hard as if he knew the answer to his question.

"Am I disappointing you?" she asked.

He put his hands on her shoulders, turning her with the slightest pressure. He leaned forward. Their gazes locked. The space between them felt like it crumpled, narrowing existence until it might have been just them. "Nothing about you is disappointing. Nothing."

"Oh." His closeness stole any other response.

He let her go. She swayed with the freedom, not expecting it, and having forgotten, even, that she should want it.

He pulled out his wallet and removed a card. "Here's my calling card. On the off chance—the very off chance—that we get separated again."

Wait. Her wallet. Her purse.

"Oh no." Disaster trickled over her. She'd left it on the floorboard of her car. Snorting that *stay awake* packet had thrown her off. Now she had no money and no permit papers, the documents permitting a citizen mage to return from the Wild West, necessary if the bounder mages caught her.

"What's wrong?" he asked.

A hundred curse words tumbled through her mind and morphed into the crooked prayer of the hopeless and cast-off. "Lost girls, spin me a rope," she whispered. She had no time to return to her car and get it. There was only one option. She'd have to spin even more gold coins to pay for everything.

"The lost girls, eh? Does that prayer ever work?"

She glanced up, expecting a smirk. Few stooped so low as to plead to the banished lost girls instead of the beloved Goddess.

But there was no smirk, just curiosity.

"No." Her voice was rough. "Better to spin your own rope and pull yourself up as best you can. That's my philosophy."

"That's a lie, little witch." Daegan's whisper popped in her ear. "But let it be your truth."

She jumped up to face him, her heart struggling to keep up with the disasters and frights. "What is it with everyone today?"

Gregor yanked her behind him. His shoulder brushed against her, and she felt the fearful shiver run through him. He was as afraid of fairies as she was of Power United.

"It's all right, Gregor." She slipped his calling card into her pocket and put her hand against his back. She stepped between him and Daegan. "He's not going to hurt me." She frowned at the other man. "And Daegan's not going to hurt you either."

But the glister's eyes swirled with the dreaded silver of his power. In all the years she'd known him though, his power never made good on the promise.

"Are we really going to start out this way?" she asked.

"I told you to stop spinning the webs!" His shout hurt her ears, and she covered one with her hand.

"Back off, fairy," Gregor ordered.

The swirl in the fairy's eyes deepened as he turned to him.

This was getting out of hand. "Daegan, quit." She held her hands out between them, palms down. "I have stopped spinning the webs. The High Councilor ordered me to, so it's a moot point." She spoke calmly. "My supply has been confiscated."

Daegan snorted. "You should never have had any webs in the first place. And I know damn well you haven't stopped spinning them." He looked pointedly at the delicate white cloth resting on her pack. "Spin and lament," he whispered, almost as if he were talking to himself. "Foolish girl."

Her breath caught in her throat. "Spin and lament? Are you the one who's sending me the prophecies?" She yanked the crumpled note from her pocket and held it out. Her hand shook, anger, not fear.

He took it and smoothed it out. The hypnotic silver faded from his gaze. He read silently and then he flung the note into the river. "It wasn't me." His voice snapped. "But you've brought this on yourself. It didn't have to be this way. If you'd left the spiders alone—"

"I couldn't. A lot of people need that spider cloth. It can give them a fuller life."

"And ruin yours." His face turned red. "I didn't want this for you!"

"Sweet of you." She waited until his breathing evened out before she spoke again. "I don't understand any of it...prophecies about mythical relics—a spinning wheel, that I haven't seen, by the way, scissors—"

"And a needle," Gregor stated, his powerful voice close to her ear. "And it exists. It's not mythical."

Daegan narrowed his eyes. "Oh, they exist. Monk boy is right about that. Luck made them. He charmed the wheel to spin tales to entertain his Lady while she spun her precious threads. The scissors endow anything they snip with the power to dance. And the needle sings, as your monk friend knows.

"Walk away from this, *mi minliha,*" Daegan whispered. "Walk away. The West may or may not be destined to devour the mages' land, but you will be its first victim if you keep on this path. Go home. Forget the webs. Ignore the Luck damned notes." His eyes deepened with silver again. His hypnotic swirl pulled at her mind, but she flicked it away like a fly. "You do not want to cross the river, Mara," he said.

Gregor yanked her back and thrust her behind him, his shoulders blocking her view. "Get your fucking trance off her!"

She put a hand on his arm and squeezed gently. His cold soaked through her, a startling difference from the heat of the already hot summer day. "I've known Daegan for years. I've argued with him for just as long. He pretends to try to catch me with his eyes, but he never gives it his all."

"Your guard protects you, Mara." Daegan's tone turned light. "Gregor Whitman. Born in Standish Territory. Raised by the singing peace men of the Green Mountains. Now a man, who's never had his own door, one who's so scared of his reflection that he thinks to flee from his homeland and take up residence on a lonely western mountain." He sneered. "Perhaps I misspoke when I called you a man. More like a sniveling boy. And not a very smart one at that."

"Cut it out," she said.

Across the water, the train whistle blew a warning. She grabbed her pack and slung it on her back, taking the lacy shawl in her hand. "All I need to know is if you'll take us across."

Daegan looked at her. "You're not very smart either, Mara, obeying that bitch without a thought. Dumb fool."

She flinched at the scorn in his voice. "What's gotten into you?" She shook her head, knowing it was past time for plan B. She turned her back on him and looked up at Gregor, tugging on his hand. "I have to get across. I have almost a hundred employees depending on my return, and I will come through for them no matter what. You can come with me."

He frowned. "How? There are no other options. You can't swim across." Then he refocused on Daegan. "How the hell did you know all that about me?"

Temporarily dismissed, she took it as a sign...because there was another option. And she was going to take it. As she came to her decision, she imagined stepping up to Gregor, rising up on her tiptoes and kissing his cheek. Just a simple brush to say goodbye and perhaps to say thanks for caring for her in the dungeon. But that was a slippery slope and her heart didn't wear thick tread to catch itself.

She turned on her heel and headed toward the river, leaving the men behind her.

"I know everyone who crosses my river," Daegan replied to Gregor.

The water lapped at the shore as if its gentle touch would console her. Its foaming edge reached out. She folded up the newly knitted shawl and tossed it into the air. "I need a ride, please," she whispered to the water. "Safe passage in return for my gift." That shawl could have been Stella's salvation, but Mara would get more webs on her return trip.

The lace drifted for a moment, caught on a breeze, as the men behind her argued.

"If you cross the river today," Daegan said, "all you're doing is moving the pawns further onto the playing board." His tone was cutting.

The lace touched the water and disappeared beneath in a flash.

"I'm afraid you have me at an advantage, fairy, because I don't understand the rules of this game," Gregor replied. "Clue me in and I'll play, but you leave Mara alone."

"Only if you plan to stick around to finish the game, witch boy. You're no fun if you go off pouting with the tip of a mountain up your ass."

Mara sucked in a breath at the insults, but she didn't turn around to referee.

"You may not know this, but we don't call ourselves witches." Gregor's voice was matter-of-fact.

"Then again, you're probably not smart enough to play. You let your power be drained away by a glister relic," Daegan continued. "Idiot."

A river maiden stuck her head above the water. The white lacy shawl was draped over her head. It stood out in relief against her dark, wet hair. As Mara watched, the maiden's pale face grew fuller. Her cheeks brightened.

That was fast. The webs were a marvel, though she shouldn't be surprised at how quickly they helped a river maiden. After all, both the spiders and the maidens were of the glister. Their power was in sync.

The last time Mara had seen this creature her cheeks were hollow, her eyes bloodshot, and her hair stringy. The creature had stared at her from beneath the water as Daegan had ferried her across. The desperation in her eyes had pleaded for help.

At the time, Daegan had shrugged away Mara's concern. "The king's creatures suffer in his long absence." He'd refused to say more.

Mara knew about suffering. Each of her clients suffered in some form or another due to mage energy. She'd gambled that the creature's ills were similar and might share a cure.

The river maiden swam closer. A glint of light played just above her ear. She'd claimed Daegan's gold coin, too.

A raft formed from the mist. It slid onto the bank, stopping an inch from her feet. "Gregor," Mara called.

"What the hell are you doing? That's a river maiden!"

"She'll take us across."

"No! It's too dangerous!" His face drained of color. He held out his hand. "Come on. Move away from there." He calmed his voice, like he'd decided he was talking to a crazy person and needed to negotiate her off the ledge before she jumped. He stepped toward her cautiously.

The train whistle blew again.

"I have to catch this train. Come with me." With her pack on her back, she stepped aboard the worn planks. The boat surged away in an instant, so quick she should have stumbled, but its movement was smooth and easy as if the water was ice. "Wait," she cried toward the head of the boat, but not even the shadow of the river maiden's sleek body was visible beneath the water.

Twenty feet already separated her from the shore. Even she wasn't bold enough to jump in this water and swim back to him. Gregor ran for her, but it was too late. "Tell it to turn around!" His voice bounced over the river, fading already.

Mara swallowed hard. This wasn't quite what she'd intended.

She turned back to him one more time. He was looking at her, or so she guessed. She took off her specs and let her energy surge forth. He came into focus with her mage power. His face was tight, his eyes wide. Fury. Anguish. But mostly fear.

"I'm sorry," she whispered though there was no way he could hear her. "It will be all right. I am not afraid. Not of this." The truth of her words spun strength into her bones, and she stood a little taller. "Please don't be afraid for me."

A tendril of his energy brushed against her and then disappeared. From the shore, he held out his hands as if he could grab her. She put her specs back on, wrapping her power down. Turning away, she looked ahead.

"Danger awaits in the West, Mara Rand!" Daegan's voice shimmered over the water.

"It always does," she whispered again. She didn't have a choice but to face it. If the boat hadn't been sturdy, she might have sunk beneath the weight of her responsibilities.

"Too many threats to defend against alone. *Saliiy Sueytie a tuu*," he said softly. "May Luck shine upon you. You're going to need it."

11

GREGOR SPUN to the fairy as Mara drifted away. "I paid your fee. Get your boat underway. I'm not letting her get away from me." Within him, raging helplessness stormed, a thousand times worse than watching her spin cotton until her fingers bled. If it hadn't been for a near-lifetime of training, he wouldn't have known which way to turn under its force.

The next time he caught up with her—and he was damn well catching her— he was attaching them with a spell.

Daegan lunged for him. Gregor jumped back, a furious shout bursting from him. His mage power shot forth. But the fairy had been playing him. The fucker jerked to a stop short of touching him.

Gregor's heart raced so fast he couldn't hear a break in the beats.

Daegan bent over laughing. "You're afraid of me." His chuckles rasped against Gregor's nerves.

He experienced a new level of hate—dark and fathomless. Its chill froze his blood. He got ahold of it before it overtook him completely. But it was a near thing. He stared at the fairy's chest, avoiding his eyes. "I'm going after her. Are you driving the boat or am I?" He walked backwards, unwilling to turn his back on the man.

"Tell me why you're afraid and maybe I'll take you." Daegan stood relaxed and easy as if Mara wasn't out there alone facing death. "I hope it's a good story because the price of your passage is quite costly."

"I already paid you."

"Price just went up."

"You people are all evil," he snapped. That's why he was afraid, and he had no problem admitting that. Evil was something to fear. He jumped on the boat. The craft didn't even bob in the water from his quick move. Some type of fairy's spell held it.

"Evil. Really. Met many of us?"

"Yes. The one who did this." He pointed at his neck. "And another when I was sixteen and he peeled my mind open and held it for three days."

"Three days! That's a lie. An impossible lie," Daegan shouted as if he were personally offended.

"I wish it were." He jerked his chin toward the disappearing boat on the river. "Now hand over the keys to this piece of shit." He eyed the ferry for a set of controls, not that he expected to find any. This thing would be powered by spells.

"No glister here today has the power to hold open a mage's mind for three damn days. Also, it would be a very sick fuck who would even want to look at a mage's mind for that long. You all are a tangle of insanity inside."

"It wasn't *here today*. It was about twenty years ago."

Daegan shifted on his feet, something uneasy in the movement.

Gregor eyed the power surrounding the boat, his mage sense wide open. The fairy's spells morphed into view. He blinked, surprised. That had never happened before. But maybe that was because he'd never really tried to see a fairy spell.

He eyed the silvery energy encasing the boat. That amount of power...it was a bit of overkill. A waste of energy and effort. He glanced at the man as if he might actually ask him why he'd used so much.

Daegan stared blindly up the river, thoughtful and worried, as if Gregor's story had rattled him. Or perhaps he was finally concerned for Mara.

Good.

Mara was a silhouette, frail and alone, heading west as the sun dawned and the eastern sky turned to fire. Gregor paced to the helm of the boat, getting as close to her as possible.

He was an excellent swimmer, and if it had been any body of water except the Mississippi, he would have jumped in, but he had no defenses against the river monsters. They'd eat him alive. What the hell had she been thinking getting on that boat?

"You're like a rabid dog whose bone is floating away. Why do you care about her?" Daegan asked. "She's a pretty form, I suppose." The fairy shrugged. "A steady paycheck. I've heard you mage men are turning into slouches, relying on your women to provide for you."

Not him. And not anyone he knew. Although now, with his power scarred and damaged, he had no official paycheck coming in for the first time since he'd left the monks. But he'd sure as hell figure it out.

He reached into his invisible pocket—a spell that Lincoln had cast for him in private upon his departure, a gift from one wayward to another. He pulled out his gun and holstered it with a spell at his side. It would be faster to draw it from there.

"What's that supposed to do? Show me you're tough?" Daegan shook his head. "You can't shoot me. If you try to cross the river without me, the maidens will devour your bones. Their queen leads your witch across now." He nodded toward the river. "They're hungry."

Long, sleek shadows darted through the water, from the edge of Daegan's boat all the way to Mara's.

The fairy nodded at the gun. "You can't stop a glister's power with that. But I can tell you how you can stop it."

Right. He didn't believe for a second that the fairy would tell him.

He studied the boat's spells. He swallowed hard, his throat dry with fear. Sound spells worked oddly over water, and the Mississippi was probably a thousand times worse. But what choice did he have?

He formed the chant in his mouth and let it into the world, silent to his own ears. Every cell in his body vibrated with its energy. His vibes morphed into a sharp blade and sliced the gray spells that anchored the boat to the land. The boat started to drift. He heaved a sigh, relieved.

Daegan gave a cruel laugh. "Impressive, monk." With a single bound, he leaped aboard. "No mage has ever broken my spell before. More than a few have tried. You don't need the gun. You've convinced me. Even though I hate mages."

Gregor adjusted his position so that both Mara and the fairy were in his sight. "And I hate fairies." As he watched, she looked back, biting her lip as if she felt bad about leaving him.

He hoped she did.

How had she managed to survive her dozen trips to the West if she made decisions like this?

The ferry cut through the water. As the wind danced past him, the distance between the two boats lengthened. "The creature is speeding up," Gregor said over the sound of the wind. Daegan's boat would never catch her.

"I don't think the river maiden queen likes you."

"The feeling's mutual." Nerves danced across Gregor's shoulders at being so close to a damn fairy. "Why didn't you take Mara across when she asked you?"

"Because I didn't want her to go." Daegan looked over. "Relax. It's unlikely the river queen will eat her."

His gut turned to lead. He felt for his gun. His hand against it, he soundlessly chanted a *waterproof* spell over it. If the queen moved against Mara, he'd go into the damn river after her. Surely if he cast an *impenetrable* spell over his body it would last a few minutes in the water. "Can this piece of shit go faster?"

The fairy ignored his question. "Guard the quest of the one who spins. Seek her truth and healing begins," Daegan quoted.

Gregor clenched his teeth so hard they rattled. "How did you know that?"

"Do you actually believe it is your destiny to go West because an old woman croaked out a black cloud of sticky shit?"

"You have a spy in the High Councilor's court." Who was the snitch? As the river smacked against the sides of the boat, he wondered...did he even care? He pulled in a slow breath. He cared if it impacted Mara.

"You should know that prophecies can change," the fairy said. His gray power spread around the bottom of the boat, fluctuating in silvery shimmers of energy visible to Gregor's mage sense.

"Don't get hung up on this one," Daegan continued. "You can be replaced."

Gregor put his hands on the boat's railing and squeezed. "No one is replacing me. Mara is mine to guard."

Daegan shook his head. "And the game plays on."

She was now sixty yards distant. Between her boat and this one, a river maiden raised her head and called out, the sound like static to his damaged hearing. The power in her song lifted the hair on his neck with a painful tingle.

If one of them made a move, he'd throw every vibe he had at her and pray it would be enough.

He caught Daegan eyeing the water. Was that desperation on his sweaty brow?

"Are you worried about her?" He wondered if the arguing and the insults were just a big show. "She told me she had a friend who was a fairy...a glister. For her sake, I hope she wasn't talking about you. You're a shit friend."

Daegan gave an icy laugh. "Fairies do not like anyone, witch."

He wasn't buying it, not considering the fairy's clenched fists and tight brow as he stood at the helm. "You've escorted her across the river multiple times. Why put up a fuss today? What do you know?" He would have shaken it out of him if the man had been a mage. As it was, he was afraid to look him in the eye. He fingered the gun at his side.

"Done some research on her, have you?" Daegan asked.

"As you have researched me, apparently. Where I was born, my schooling, that I have no door?" He squinted. "What the hell does that mean?" And what else did he know?

"You want to know how I learned your fascinating facts?" The gray man took a breath. "*Sueytei wiesi.*"

The words blew against Gregor with a power that chilled deep inside his skull. Like the blessing the fairy had whispered, he knew their meaning. Somehow, his mind understood.

Luck whispers.

He wanted to chalk it up to his years-long apprenticeship under the monks—learning languages, speaking in tongues, chanting, singing the Goddess's songs.

But no mage had anything to do with the god, Luck. The former consort to the mages' Goddess was loathed for the harm he'd caused their beloved Lady.

Daegan looked over his shoulder at him. "You are Luck's man more than you are the Republic's. You are consort-marked."

He pulled his gun, keeping it at his side. "The fuck I am!" Rage renewed its boil. "No mage would ever be Luck's man."

"Two pricks in the neck with Luck's needle. You could not be more clearly marked. Deal with it. If you are to guard the quest of the one who spins, then you must let go of your anger and your fear." His soft voice was a taunt. "Poor simple monk boy. You've been kicked off your pinnacle of superiority, and now you're floundering in some dark sea that you think is your doom. You should relax. Go for a swim. You might like that dark sea."

He hated that dark sea. It was filled with rage and fear and pain. Swim in it? He did everything he could to avoid it.

Daegan nodded toward the sorceress, so far ahead of them now. "You are not worthy of her. None of you witches are."

"Mages, not witches." His tone was absent, his mind focused on the blackness.

Ahead, the river maiden's boat bumped against the shore. Mara tossed her pack to the small dock and hopped off. The creature bobbed up, her head and shoulders above the water and she bowed, long and slow. Mara bowed back.

"Thank the Goddess," he breathed.

She gave him a wave and his heart lurched. She lingered for a moment, but the train whistled and she dashed up the hill and into the wild, unclaimed land that thrived on chaos and tumult.

He wasn't surprised. She had a mission to complete in order to return to her sorceresses. But he'd caught her hesitation and he clung to it. He patted the small tracker still in his pocket, the one Cecilia had given him. He hadn't planned to use it, but neither had he tossed it away.

Daegan shot in front of him, a streak of silver lightning. That was all it took. Gregor was caught. The silver swirl sucked him in. He couldn't move. His mind screamed. A soul deep fright shook him to the marrow of his bones. The cackle of the fairy's laugh brought an instant sweat over his skin.

"Warrior, you want to flee from my grip? You can. I'll tell you how, secrets only my people know." He poked at Gregor's scarred neck. "Luck has changed your magic." He touched Gregor's temple. "I can change your mind."

A low growl burst from his throat, helpless rage. His power was harnessed like a slave to the fairy. His gun hung useless at his side.

"You are not unique. Did you know that?" Daegan's smooth, low tone circled around him. "They tried the needle on another soldier...three decades back. He is marked by Luck, too."

Gregor's body and power might not have been under his control, but his mind still was. A wave of hope washed through him.

"Don't get excited. He did not fare well. He can't help you, monkey." Daegan tipped his head as if he could see into his mind. "It remains to be seen if the god's gift can overcome the prejudices of your mage mind. I wonder, will you harness it, monkey?"

Gregor tried again to shake off his grip, but he couldn't move.

"If you quit fighting, it won't be so hard."

Quit fighting? No way in hell. He reached for his power, but all that happened was the gun fell to the floor. "Is this how Luck overcomes prejudices?" Gregor found his voice, but his tongue flopped like rubber and his words slurred. His heart pounded, slow and hard, as if it needed to race faster but the fairy held it hypnotized too. His chest ached from it.

"It is not Luck with whom you should be angry. Nor are the glister to blame. She betrayed you, monk. The old bitch. She knew it didn't work. Her first victim was Major Stanford Madding. Know of him?"

"The leader of the Black Skulls?" His surprise powered the words out of him.

"The Mad Prophet himself. And yet she tried it again on you." He tilted his head. "Is that evil's clutch at work or just stupidity?"

Gregor's chest rose and fell as if he'd sprinted miles around the raft. "The gray. You're the evil ones."

"We do not subscribe to evil. Did she tell you our king is missing? That without his magic to anchor them all, my people grow restless and dangerous? Did she tell you about the outlaws brimming forth? That the Mad Prophet leads his men east and plays for control of the Wild West?" He leaned into Gregor's face, his power pulling him deeper. "And yet she sends Mara into their clutches. The crone will blame her for everything that goes wrong." He leaned closer. "And so many things will go wrong."

The boat bumped against the shore hard enough to knock Gregor over, but Daegan's hold kept him on his feet.

"Let me go," he seethed. He shook so hard trying to free himself that his vision was blurred.

"First, I must tell you how to defeat a fairy's power. Don't you want to know?"

Fairies were damn hard to kill—even with a gun. They were impervious to mage spells, had quick healing powers, and were impossible to detect. They were as blank as Nons until they turned on their energy. The species had few weaknesses.

As quickly as he'd caught Gregor, he let him go.

Gregor grabbed the gun from the floor and pulled the trigger. Once. Twice. Three times.

Just as fast, a wall of water formed high between them— muddy and solid and obliterating everything. It collapsed in a huge wave. Three bullets lay on the wooden deck.

The fairy stared. "I'm your only ally."

"I will never be a fairy's ally. And don't you ever fucking hypnotize me again, asshole." He grabbed his pack and hopped over to the dock.

"You may not know this, but we don't call ourselves that." Daegan mocked him. "We are not fairies or the gray. We are the glister." He said the words as if it were a grand pronouncement.

"Glister. Right. 'All that glisters is not gold.'" He quoted the old play as he took the first steps of the hill. No, the fairies weren't gold. They were silver.

"He was one of ours, you know. Shakespeare."

Gregor stopped to face the man. "Shakespeare was a mage. He was not a Goddess damned fairy." Offense boiled through him as if he'd known the bard personally. He sure as hell knew his writings. It was one of the two books in his pack at the moment.

"More fool you, but that is a topic for another day," Daegan said. "The Republic is creeping ever closer to bleeding power through its borders, its energy streaming forth like a mortal wound flooding the wild lands. Even I am not sure why that is happening. You can be sure that the glister do not want the Republic to fall. We do not want their kind here."

He didn't believe him. Fairies, like sorceresses, were synonymous with lies and secrets and cunning.

A train whistle shot through the air again and Gregor ran up another two steps before Daegan spoke again.

"Wait. Don't you want the secret to stopping glister power? You already have the first part, the mark that changed you. The second part? It's the simplest and most deadly of weapons. It's the unsung song of hearts."

12

DAEGAN'S WISH for Luck shining down on her wasn't working. Mara wandered through her third train car seeking a vacant seat. So far, she'd found only one. No matter her exhaustion, she was not sitting beside the man with three chickens shoved into a cage built for one.

She continued down the skinny aisle, fighting to keep her heavy pack balanced on her shoulders and fighting equally hard not to think about Gregor. She didn't have the energy to feel guilty about leaving him. Again. She fingered his calling card in her pants pocket, wanting to connect the spell, to check in, but too many Nons surrounded her. Mage power was painful to them. They'd turn on her in an instant.

She paced through the car. An opened newspaper, held high by its seated owner, caught her eye and then stole her breath. Her face smiled back at her from the image spell printed on the front page. *Sorceress's fabric cures mage ills with fairy power.* The subheading read *Federal government confiscates spinning wheels.*

That last part was Harry's work, but someone else had spilled the vibes about her gray repose spider fabric, most likely one of the ladies in the High Councilor's receiving room.

Lovely.

She'd be lucky if she wasn't lynched when she crossed back over the border.

A hard punch of what-have-I-done? slammed into her gut.

She should have kept her head down and her spectacles concealed instead of testing the waters with such a high-profile client like Lady Casteel. Too late now.

The train lurched forward with a dull boom, starting its two-hundred-mile journey to the Wild West City of Kansas without Gregor.

She bit her lip, her mind rattling in her skull as if it wanted to reach out to him. She'd connect the *calling card* spell the minute she was alone in her room in the city.

Reaching for the seatbacks to steady herself, she headed for the next car. There had to be a seat somewhere onboard.

A sharp smack to her pack tossed her forward. She fell. Her hands shot out in time to save her nose from breaking against the floor. The hard length of her long spindle jammed into her thigh, the dawn of a new bruise. Twisting slowly through the remnants of the jolt, she looked up to see someone jump over her.

A dark-haired woman, petite and ragged, looked back, tears in her eyes, dirt smudging her cheeks. Utter fear lined her face. Without a word, she turned away and raced out the door at the back of the train, slamming it shut.

The man with the newspaper leaned out, frowned, and then returned to his paper.

Welcome to the Wild West where every man is an island.

She straightened her specs, lumbered to her feet, and brushed herself off. Her palms were scraped and blood dotted both of them. She didn't expect anyone to inquire if she was all right. Everyone here was assumed guilty of something...Non-mages fleeing their sponsors; mages accused of crimes and running from their sentences or debts; fairies too dangerous to glance at. A smart woman on her own knew that if anyone talked to her, they probably wanted something she didn't want to give.

The door at the front of the car clicked opened and the roar of the train engine rushed in. Mara looked back, hoping it was someone vacating his or her seat. Instead, a brawny man entered the train car. He was so large he took up the entire aisle—side to side, top to bottom.

A lightning bolt badge was pinned to his chest.

Bounty hunter.

Mara's throat went dry. The train spun around her as ghosts of the past twirled through her mind.

Please. Not me. Not again.

Gregor would never know what happened to her. No one would.

The bounty hunter held up a picture that looked like a mug shot. "Ladies and gentlemen, has anyone seen this woman?" he hollered. His audience obeyed his call and turned toward him. In the picture, the woman was pale, her eyes half-closed, her lips bracketed with heavy lines. It was the woman who just ran through the train car. "She's a dangerous sorceress."

Perhaps. But only because a cornered creature, no matter how powerless, could be dangerous if fighting for her life.

Suspicion flooded through the car as the passengers looked around at each other, ready to accuse their seat-mates of wrongdoing.

Mara clutched the strap of her pack until her fingernails dug into it. "Power United." Her soft words carried in the silence. "So mighty and strong yet you enslave defenseless women." No matter how scared she was, she could not step aside for this man. Silence was not an option.

He lowered his hand and the picture crumpled against his thigh. "Ma'am, we're just doing our jobs and trying to keep the West free of dangerous mages."

She put her hand on her spindle. "No. That's not what you do.

You take weak sorceresses, strap them to a wheel, and gut their vibes from their souls."

"You misunderstand." He looked her over. "Or perhaps you don't." He strode forward, his hulking shoulders shifting right and left with each step as if they were connected by strings to his feet. "Sorceress. Your fingers give you away. I know my targets."

"But not the sorceress we're looking for." Another man, this one in a suit and tie leaned out from behind him, his frame much leaner. He patted the bigger guy on the shoulder. "And it's more her charming face that clues one in than her poor battered fingers. Miss Rand is well-known to Power United, Frank." Nils Lusman nodded to the bounty hunter.

She almost sighed with relief.

Nils played his role to perfection. An executive in the upper echelon of Power United, he was the only ally Trail of Strings—the organization that helped conscripted sorceresses escape—had inside the company. Mara was a volunteer, one among many whose names were buried within the group.

Whoever the escaped sorceress was, Nils had most likely facilitated her escape only to be roped into retrieving her by the higher-ups at P.U. That sometimes happened.

Mara donned her role almost as easily as Nils, stuffing back her fear as best she could. "Lose another one, Mr. Lusman? Considering her lack of power and that you practically starve them, it doesn't say much for your competency."

Frank shrugged. "Oh, we'll get her back." He gave a chin up nod to Nils. "My partner is coming the other way, sir. She's trapped. Guaranteed. And then it's a fat payday for me."

By the stars, what they did to those poor women. Anger rolled through her like a yarn ball on the loose, tangling her in its threads.

Nils pinched the bridge of his nose. "Guaranteed, you say? This girl has dragged us from the far end of the Republic and into another country for vibes' sake."

"Sir, this ain't no country. You're asking for trouble if you think this place comes with laws and civilized folk." He whipped out a pair of mage cuffs, square pieces of metal that prevented a mage's power from working. He nodded at Mara. "I'll getcha this one too, and then it's an extra five hundred for me. You can make use of her somehow, even considering she's got something wrong with her." He tapped his temple, mirroring where Mara's spectacles rested on her face.

She lifted her chin. "Yes, something's wrong with me. You should pass on this one."

Nils nodded. "We certainly will, Miss Rand. Your name is not on our list of conscripted sorceresses."

Vibe-poor sorceresses had few career options, and spinning copper wire for the power company's hungry grid was the bottom of the job pool. It was a slow death sentence, one that came without a choice. The government conscripted low-powered sorceresses every year through a lottery and handed them over to Power United. It was a four-year sentence. Most never reappeared in society.

Even when Nils was able to find a candidate to free, most of the sorceresses chose to flee to the Wild West instead of staying in the Republic. Mara didn't blame them. She might have had enough of the Republic if she'd been stuck in Power United for a long time, too.

"Although we will happily offer you employment, Miss Rand, if you are interested. Our sorceresses work for the betterment of the Republic. Where would our great country be without the electricity that keeps it running?" Nils smiled with pride.

"Great, my ass!" a passenger hollered. "Elitist power-hungry pricks who keep the normals as third-class citizens."

An approving chorus of yeas filled the car, proving that it was populated with Nons...normals in Wild West lingo.

Mara wasn't about to argue with them. Even Frank looked wary. Everyone in the West was armed, hips strapped with guns, knives, and more guns. If they weren't careful, they'd all be lynched before the train was out of sight of the station.

A rush of noise flowed in behind her as the car's front door opened again. She turned to see Gregor pacing toward her.

A gnawing ache in her chest loosened, but a sudden pressure around her wrist grabbed her attention.

The bounty hunter had lunged forth and locked the cuff around her. Shock rode in hard, a sense of panic on its tail. Stone walls closed around her mind.

Gregor pulled a gun from nowhere and pointed it at the man. "Remove them. Now." He squeezed her arm, keeping her close as she struggled to shake the metal off. "Easy, firefly. He's not taking you." His voice was calm.

She turned into his shoulder, hiding her face, her arm stretched toward the awful bounty hunter.

"Put the gun away, sir," the hunter said. "I'm acting on the authority of the Republic of Mage Territories."

"I have to call vibe shite on that, hunter," Gregor replied, low and easy. He wrapped his arm around her. "The Republic has zero authority here. You take that off her. Now. If I have to do it, it will be while standing next to your corpse."

"That would be a mistake, sir. Power United carries the same authority as the enforcers and even the Republic's army."

"Remove the cuffs," Nils snapped. "Or I'll have your name taken off our roster of consultants."

"With all due respect, you ain't my boss. This woman's five hundred bucks to me. And if you erase my name, Miss Cecilia's gonna have something to say about that. She'll approve of this. She'll probably give me another bonus."

"Frank. Seriously, you're in deep trouble here." Nils held up his hand. "Captain Whitman, I'm certain my consultant is going to see reason considering you're a warrior mage."

"You know each other?" Mara gasped. She lifted her head away from Gregor as conspiracies circled through her mind.

"I assisted Power United with *one* mission, Mara." Gregor said, crisp and precise. "That's over. But that's how I met Nils. And Frank here is going to eat a bullet if he doesn't let you free."

The bounty hunter shrugged. "Whatever. You ain't worth my life." The handcuff fell off with a twist of his key. Gregor yanked her out of the man's hold and lowered his gun.

Another roar of the open door and the fleeing sorceress dashed back in. Her eyes wide, she puffed for air. A cut along the top of her hand bled as she gripped the seatbacks. A man rushed in behind her.

"Ah, there we are." Nils smiled and straightened his tie. "I'll see that you get paid double for this one, Frank, in light of our troubles here."

"I am not going back. Ever!" The sorceress caught Mara's eye. "Please help me! I'm not one of their conscripted girls."

"That's what they all say. Ignore her," Nils muttered, an authentic tone of disgust in the words.

The door opened again. Another bounty hunter and Cecilia, of all people, strutted in behind the fleeing sorceress.

She smiled when she saw Mara and then tilted her head in surprise when her gaze landed on Gregor. "Well, hello, Captain," Cecilia purred. She eyed his arm around Mara. "Playing in the dirty end of the vibes, I see. That can be fun...for a while. Is your friend with you?" She winked and continued without waiting for an answer. "I hope you're not concerned about what you see here. AWOLs don't happen often. The SLSS means we get a few random crazies now and then."

The Sorceress Lottery Selection System was the root of all evil as far as Mara was concerned.

"Your system ruins lives," Mara said.

Cecilia rolled her eyes. "Sometimes our lottery picks are a bit wild. Dangerous even." She yanked a yellow paper from the sorceress's hand. "How did you get this train ticket?"

Mara knew. She provided an easy distraction. "This is the

usual treatment for sorceresses under the control of Power United. Now you can see it for yourself, Captain."

"I'm not a captain anymore," he said softly.

"I am outside the laws of the Republic!" the sorceress cried. "You have no right to take me back." She looked at Nils. "How can you do this? You bastard!"

"Case in point," Cecilia offered. "She wouldn't be saying such things if she wasn't really conscripted."

"You want this one, Miss Cecilia?" Frank thrust his thumb at Mara. "'Cause I'll get 'er for you." He held up his cuffs by his finger.

"Frank, you're a slow learner," Gregor said.

Cecilia smiled. "I'll pass on that one. For now. Let's focus on little Miss Runaway, here."

The desperate sorceress would never get out again if they captured her, and she wouldn't survive at her wheel for long. Even Nils wouldn't be able to help her. If freedom was in this girl's future, Mara had to do something. She knew what it was like to be chained to a wheel. She'd experienced the results for herself, so had many of the women in her mill. This girl would not be taken back to hell on her watch. Reaching into her vest pocket, she tossed the sorceress the tiny drop spindle tucked inside.

The sorceress spun it immediately. Mage power swirled through the car with the force of a miniature tornado. Mara's pack pushed her off balance and she fell to the floor, nearly taking Gregor with her.

Shouts of rage burst from the crowd of Nons at the mage power. They stood en masse. Trouble was coming. The sorceress dashed out of the car at one end. Cecilia and the second bounty hunter pushed past Mara's prone form to escape out the opposite end. Nils and Frank were fast on their heels.

Gregor yanked her to her feet, but not fast enough.

The passenger to her right, a balding man with a pot belly,

pulled a gun, so close to her she could smell it, sour and sharp. He started a chain reaction among the rest of the passengers. Before two seconds passed, at least thirty black metal barrels of varying shapes and sizes pointed at them. They promised death. The fearful, angry people beyond were mere extensions of their guns.

The man closest to Mara pressed his gun to her temple. The cold, hard pressure throbbed against her. She was going to die on this train because of Power United.

"We don't want any trouble." Gregor's voice was calm and soft.

How did he always manage that?

"Watch, I'm putting away my gun." He moved slowly. "We just want to leave. We're going to back out of here and everyone's gonna be okay."

Farther down, a group of men marched forward. Anger burned in their narrowed eyes.

"Mages don't rule here!" The tallest of them pointed a meaty finger. "You think this is the Republic where you can cast your spells willy-nilly?" Mage vibes provoked a primitive fight-or-flight reaction in Nons. Apparently, the former was leading the way today. "Let me tell you, witches, this is the West. You can't go shooting energy whenever you want."

"Get 'em off the train!" a woman behind them called out.

Echoes of agreement surrounded them. "Oh, they're leaving all right," the man beside her said. "Move." He bumped the gun's barrel against her temple. Pain blossomed.

Gregor pulled her back, one slow step at a time. "We apologize for the disruption. We meant no harm."

The balding gunman followed them out the door and onto the platform between the cars. Beneath the open pattern of the metal floor, the ground rushed past. The hot wind of the train's movement blew her hair across her face, the pressure popping her ears.

The Non-mage cocked the gun.

She might have breathed out a prayer if she believed any deity was listening and if she could have managed to form any words. They were going to die right here and her sorceresses would lose their only protector.

Gregor yanked her into his chest and wrapped his arms around her, a tight fit with her full pack. He gave a hard yank and then he jumped, taking her with him. They went flying.

GREGOR ENCIRCLED his spell around them just in time. A sphere of vibes surrounded them like a giant, cushioned bubble. The first bounce against the land squeezed the breath from his lungs, but his spell held. They rolled over the land as the train stretched out, a snake in his peripheral vision, leaving them behind.

Good riddance.

He had Mara. That was all that mattered.

He held her tight, one arm around her lower back beneath her pack and the other against the nape of her neck.

Mara was stiff, her body clenched. He wanted to tell her to relax, to go with the fall, but the words pressed out of him every time they flipped.

The *bubble* spell kept them from touching the ground. No rocks scraped their sides. No dirt marked their skin. No dust settled over them, though a dirty cloud stretched out behind them, a lengthening trail. He caught a glimpse of it every time they spun around. He fought the temptation to close his eyes, but someone needed to drive this thing. Better yet, someone needed to stomp on the brakes.

Their packs jostled hard. Mara grunted with a steady rhythm each time he flipped on top of her, pushing her weight into the uneven surface of her huge pack, her legs flopping beneath. Her long sword bumped against them, caught between their hips.

"Hang. On." His words jerked with the swirl of their ride.

Her energy puffed against him as they went round and round. The power grew, tickling and cushioning the jolting ride.

Finally, they slowed enough that he risked popping their vehicle with a snap of his energy. Hot air burst around them as they rolled to a stop against the rocky ground. He lifted his weight off her.

Mara lay on her pack, panting for air as she stared at the sky. Her feet tilted out to the sides; her arms drooped to the ground. Power fluffed around her. It encompassed him in its soft touch, its strength skating toward the sun. Her eyes glowed softly bronze.

He sat up, his mage sense open and seeking. "Are you all right? Does anything hurt?" He could have formed a *scan* spell and checked her for broken bones, but it wasn't his finest ability.

"I'm good." Her voice was high and light. "That was an impressive spell." She moved toward him like she might rest on her side, but her pack's straps stopped her.

He pulled it off her, helping her to sit. Her curls dashed every which way and he brushed a lock from her face.

"That spun my power right out of me," she gasped. "That's never happened in my life."

He knew that if she were able to put it back inside her, she would have. She was the equivalent of a mage parading naked.

Her cheeks were bright red and she couldn't hold his gaze.

"It probably would happen to every sorceress who got thrown off a train and spun circles over the ground," he offered politely, though it was untrue and they both knew it.

She arched one eyebrow, revealing her disbelief, as she waved her hand through her power. The vibes moved as if they were a physical substance in the air. Though he knew mages who were extraordinarily powerful—he was no slouch himself—he'd never heard of anyone who could let their power free like this. "You said I get to lie to you once. Is that *your* one lie?" she asked.

He narrowed his eyes. "That reminds me. I'm adding to the rules. You get one lie—already used up. Also used up are all of your chances at abandonment. That's twice now. Goddess, Mara! I watched you float away with a river maiden. Have you seen their teeth?" He wanted to shout. No cadence mage ever shouted. They were too controlled, too appreciative of sound to abuse it like that.

"I haven't." She scanned the ground and found her spectacles. She tucked them into her white blouse. "And I don't believe you have either."

He practically sputtered. No cadence mage sputtered either. "I've seen *image* spells."

"Images designed by mages who likely doctored them to appear scary and dangerous. You can't trust things like that."

"I'd like to be able to trust you."

She pressed her hand against her chest. "My trustworthiness is not in question, Mr. Thief. I asked you to cross the river with me. I have to get to the city of Kansas on time and get back to my mill." She spoke with matter-of-factness. "I'll do whatever it takes to make that happen."

"Funnily enough, that's my goal too. Imagine if we'd gotten on the train together. There's a damn good chance we'd still be on it and heading to our destination in a timely manner."

She looked away, her chin high. Her power retreated as if her stubbornness helped her regain control of it. She donned her specs. "Daegan wasn't going to take me across."

"He might have had a good reason to refuse."

Her brown eyes went wide with surprise. "You agree with a glister? You hate them."

"Yes, and Daegan did everything he could to reinforce that sentiment. However, look what's happened to you so far and you've only been here for a fifth of morning."

She drooped. Guilt punched him in the chest. "Yeah, well, I still have a job to accomplish," she said.

Screw the job. That's what he wanted to say. It would have been a waste of words. She'd made her goal clear.

For now, they were alive and unhurt. He just had to keep them that way. "I'm here to help. If you'll let me." He tucked a curl behind her ear. His hand brushed the line of her jaw. She met his gaze and went still except for the pulse at the base of her neck. It fluttered. She was close enough to kiss. He'd been thinking about kissing her since he'd dropped her off at her house on her bicycle. He felt the energy between them heighten, but a rush of caution followed it.

Don't mess this up.

She cleared her throat, leaning away an inch or two. "Thank you for whatever that spell was. That's some power you have." She put her hand on his wrist. "You saved my life."

He turned his hand so their palms met. Her slight inhale registered to his ears, every noise amplified with his mage sense fully open. Threading his fingers gently into hers, they held hands on the dusty ground, a light touch, a soft connection that he made sure she could pull free of easily...and she did.

"Your waywardness hasn't broken you." She stood and swiped at the dirt on her pants. "I hope you believe that someday soon."

Until then, don't bother holding my hand.

She didn't say the words, but he heard them nonetheless. It was a logical sentiment...something he'd expect of her. Because if he didn't accept his wayward power, then he couldn't accept hers either.

The realization was like the sharp pop of a firecracker in his mind, followed by the stunned silence that always came after the noise. If he wanted a chance to hold her tighter, he knew what he had to do: accept his waywardness. He just didn't know how.

She reached for her bag and he forced himself to move, standing and taking both of their packs.

"No." She held out her hand for it, her chin high, her lips tight. "I carry my own bag."

He recognized a threatened mage when he saw one. "We have a long walk. You'll have more energy to go farther if I carry it."

"It has my yarn in it," she said as if that was reason enough for her refusal.

He held up his hands, palms in. "I won't steal it. I vow—" He cut himself off, running into a chasm he didn't know how to cross...he couldn't fathom accepting his waywardness if it meant believing the Goddess had turned her back on him. "Explain. Please." He snapped the words. He didn't mean to, but the anger and the confusion busted out.

She didn't flinch. "It's written in the Book of Spells. I'm sure you know it. *For the power lines birthed when she was betrayed, her heart's love was quelled, her blessing withheld.*"

She was right. He did know the story. But those lines used to be only vaguely familiar until he'd looked it up three months ago. Now he, too, knew it by heart. "That's from the appendix, written by a questionable authority. And most likely written only two centuries ago. It's not taught." He'd reeled with the idea that waywards were unblessed. Ever since, he'd spent hours trying to prove that it couldn't possibly be true.

Cadence mages had a special place in the Goddess's holy court. They sang her songs, chanted her words, and vibrated in resonance with her voice. He'd never imagined something could take that away.

"How would I know about it if it wasn't taught? I've not even read the book, and I know that much. Rest assured, it was read to me. The important parts." Her voice drawled with sarcasm. She froze, a tight squint on her face.

"What's the matter?"

She put a finger against her lips and nose as if she needed to silence herself so she could think. "I don't remember hay fields being here the last time I was on the train. Wasn't this all forest?"

"Why would you remember?" The vast clearing radiated with sunshine, leaving everything in varying colors of orange. Huge bales dotted the landscape. The nearest one sat twenty feet away. It would have made a good brake for their air bubble.

"Any sorceress would remember hay fields. I'm certain this used to be forest. Look." She pointed straight ahead at the long, tall stack of cut tree trunks so far away he was surprised she could see it without her mage sight activated.

"Someone must have a helluva herd of livestock around here," he said.

"Or someone's planning to spin enough copper wire to string the entire length of the Mississippi." She looked up at him. "That's what hay is to a sorceress...and to Power United. This is like miles and miles of hell as far as the eye can see. Maybe Power United owns it."

"No. Republic companies are forbidden from owning anything in the Wild West." He went still, listening with his mage power. Somewhere from the west, vibes shimmered through the air. "Mage motors. Headed this way."

Hope boiled in his chest with a dangerous burn...if this was who he thought. But Mara's safety was at stake. "Go sit by the tracks. I'll cast a *don't look* on you. Stay put. If they take me, I vow —I promise I'll come back for you."

"If they take you? Who do you think is coming?" She sucked in a tight breath. "It's the Black Skulls, isn't it?"

He tilted his head. "They're closer than they sound. They're using a sound wall to keep their noise in, the better to sneak up on people."

"Cast the *don't look* on both of us," she ordered.

"I want to meet them, Mara." He risked the honesty. He didn't want to play this any other way with her. "Daegan said the High Councilor stabbed their leader with the needle, too. He might know something about living like this."

"Gregor, no. The Skulls are dangerous. You won't learn anything from them about being wayward. I'll teach you whatever you want to know. We have to hide."

He grabbed her arms. "You are hiding. Go. Now."

"I'm not leaving you! Remember? I already left you twice. I don't get to do it again."

And then it was too late. A dark line spread out on the horizon, focusing into dozens of vehicles.

The West was sending its welcoming committee.

13

Mara could hardly catch her breath as the motorbikes closed in. Everyone in the Wild West knew the Black Skulls took what they wanted and left the rest to rot, including people. Their rallies were infamous for blowing through western settlements and scooping up every working-age man, drafting them on the spot.

"Do you know how they initiate people?" she asked, her voice shaking with fear. He shook his head and she continued, raising her voice over the growing noise. "However they do it, it's quick, effective, and no one gets out."

It reminded her of Power United.

"We'll get out." He clipped off each word.

The line of black motorbikes closed in on them, their roars ferocious and ugly. She'd seen them in action once, a couple of years ago, when her train stopped in a small town on the way to the city of Kansas. She'd watched from the train windows, along with the other passengers, as the outlaws gathered the men and boys of the town in the middle of the road. A minute later, they rode off with them, new gang members riding shotgun on the backs of the motorbikes. Not a single man protested, though a few women had chased after them to no avail. The train didn't stop there anymore. Nothing was left of that town but ghosts and memories.

But the Black Skulls weren't known to inhabit this part of the Wild West on a regular basis. Perhaps the threat of the Republic kept them away, or the city had some sort of agreement with them. She shivered at the thought of what kind of deal it would take to keep the outlaws away.

The motorbikes roared, their engines so loud it had to be partly for effect. Chills rose over her skin as if the noise was created to draw out goosebumps and shivers.

The riders circled them. The men stared, sizing them up, dooming them to trouble. Goggles squatted on their heads or hung around their necks by black leather straps. Tattoos lined every arm and were scattered over the chests of those who were shirtless. Others wore black vests. Muscles bulged from their arms as if they'd all used *beefcake* potion. Not the safest choice, but safety probably wasn't an outlaw's priority.

The motorbikes varied in size and style—some with two wheels, some with three or four. Some had sidecars with passengers.

Both bikes and riders emanated a mass of tough, violent vibes.

She spun around, watching all of them. Her pack bumped Gregor as she went.

He wrapped his arm around her waist. "Easy, firefly. We'll bluff our way through this."

"And if that doesn't work?" she whispered, though there was no way a normal person could hear her over the growling engines. Some of the riders revved their bikes. She jumped, panting at the sight of the cruel smiles on the drivers' faces.

He shrugged, staring at the outlaw who was slightly in the lead. "I'll fight our way out. And I swear to you I'm not leaving you behind."

She believed him. "Do you think this is going to hurt my chances at making it to the city on time?" She managed to form the question with a hint of humor.

"That's my girl," he whispered.

How were they going to get out of this? She had one ability—one—that could act as a weapon, not including her long spindle. She'd used it once, but she'd been a different person then.

He surveyed the land. "We'll be in the city today. Before sundown."

She flung a hand over her eyes to search for signs of his insanity, squinting against the bright day. Before she could ask questions, the engines silenced at the signal of the leader's hand. The motors clicked and chimed in the sudden quiet as they cooled.

Gregor stepped forward. "Morning, gentlemen." It was a calm, clear greeting.

The pony-tailed leader gave them a leering grin, and Mara's heart took it as permission to race away. "You're on private property, folks."

Gregor tilted his head. "I didn't realize the West had gone private."

She might have reached for his hand but moving would draw attention to her and she was as scared as a sheep quivering under the hot breath of a wolf.

"Lots of changes coming to the Wild West." The leader got off his motorcycle. Strands of hair, a darker blond than Gregor's, had come loose from his ponytail and framed his face. Goggles hung around his neck and his black leather jacket was opened to reveal a plain white T-shirt. Fingerless gloves covered his hands. His face was freshly shaven and showed off the tattoo of the black skull on the side of his neck.

He strode over and surveyed them. "What are you two? A mixed couple fleeing the Republic for their messed-up lives?"

A mixed couple. He thought she was a Non-mage because of her spectacles. Mixes were illegal in the Republic.

"Been awhile since I caught a new one coming through." He turned to his men. "What we got here is a Romeo mage and his four-eyed Juliet." He looked at Gregor. "She's a pretty one. You oughta fix her eyes though. They can do that over here. Maybe we'll even help you with that. The Black Skulls are benevolent."

His men chuckled, obnoxious and loud.

"I like my girl the way she is." Gregor pulled her closer. "I'm afraid you've pegged us wrong. We're both mages. Just letting you know. Wouldn't want to give you the wrong impression or anything."

"She's a mage?" The biker to Mara's right sneered. "What's wrong with her then?" He spat on the ground. "She's a freak, ain't she?"

"Paulie, shut the fuck up." The leader yelled but never took his gaze off Gregor. "You'll have to excuse him. He's new to us. Fresh from the Republic and we haven't quite cured him of its taint." He flexed his fingers in his leather gloves. "Not a day goes by that I don't thank the damn stars I was born here instead of there." He turned to his gang. "Paulie seems to have forgotten who we work for."

"I ain't forgot nothing."

"Shut up, Paulie," another Skull said.

Some of the men shook their heads. None of them made eye contact with the newbie.

"You wouldn't know where we can get some transportation to the city, would you?" Gregor asked.

The leader laughed. "Well, the train was headed in that direction. But we'll see what we can do for you." He pointed eastward. "Come with us, and we'll get you fixed up right nice."

"You're heading east. We need to go west."

"There's only one direction around here, and that's the one we tell you to go in." He put the fingertips of both hands together in a pyramid and rubbed.

Mara recognized the habitual move. It was common in

sensate mages to ready their vibes. They had to touch the source of their power as well as touch the object of their spell. Perfect for finding flaws in most anything. She had one on staff to inspect her fabric and clothing.

Paulie shifted on his seat and swung his leg over his four-wheeler, his stare grinding into her. He spat again, his vibes pulsing out. His spit hit the flattened weeds with a smack and then flew up in a dirty mass—a *mud* spell—heading straight toward her, but it splattered in mid-air and sank like a flat, drippy pancake. It never touched her.

She gasped, her fingers tingling from the sudden rush of fear.

The men jumped off their bikes, hands to guns. Tension shot to the moon.

She didn't need her mage sense open to know that Gregor had cast a *shield* spell, protecting her from the muddy mess. When was he going to figure out that he wasn't broken?

"You going to control your man?" Gregor asked, a sharp curiosity in his tone, one that implied that if the leader didn't control him, then Gregor would. It was the same way he'd dealt with the bounty hunter on the train.

Paulie laughed. "I couldn't resist, man. She's such a freak with those things on."

The leader rubbed his fingers. Mara could imagine the energy crackling beneath the sensate's skin, ready to shoot out. Her heart pounded.

"What's your name?" The leader stared at her.

The first thought that jumped into her head was to give him a fake name as if concealing her identity might save her from nefariousness, but it had already found her. She took a breath. "Mara." She imitated Gregor's calm tone with moderate success.

"Paulie, apologize to Mara."

"What?" the spitter snapped back, disbelief in his squinted eyes.

The sensate grabbed the leather whip at his side and tossed it out with a spell. It flashed through the air, lengthening, and smacked the man in the face with precision. The black strip recoiled as quickly as it had arrived, spinning back into its coil and returning to its master. A thick, bloody line streaked Paulie's cheek.

She shuddered. This was how the Black Skulls lived.

"Sorry," Paulie croaked.

The other men shook their heads. Their frowns conveyed disapproval, but she didn't put much stock in their code of honor.

"Miss Mara, your man has a speedy touch with his spells." The leader fastened his whip at his belt without looking. "Is he that fast on the draw everywhere?" He winked. "Bet you inspire him." He ogled her form. This was veering into dangerous territory.

"She inspires me on many levels, Mr...." Gregor's last word faded into a question as he stepped slightly in front of her.

"Seth Kenner." He nodded at Mara. "You'll ride with me, little lady. And you," he squinted at Gregor. "You'll be riding in Rickie's sidecar. He'll drive in front of me. Try anything and my whip will break your neck, right, Rickie?"

The man to his left, spiked hair spread over his skull, pulled his gun, spun it around his finger, and pointed it at Gregor. Then he holstered it with a grin. "You got it, boss."

"Seth, do you know you've got visitors coming in behind you?" Gregor nodded toward the west. "They friends of yours?"

"As a matter of fact, they are." He looked over his shoulder as a half-dozen machines came into view, each with four legs, a swishing tail, and a bobbing neck. Five of the six were headless. The mechanical horses were in two lines, and they vibed with power as they pulled a wide wagon. Its load towered high and was covered with a tarp.

The driver, seated on the bench at the front of the wagon, held up his hand. He had dark, curly hair and suntanned skin and the requisite goggles on his head.

"Hold!" he shouted. Power ricocheted through the word.

The engines of the motorized horses softened. The man jumped down from his seat. He patted each mechanical horse, working up the line to the one in front, the only one with a head. He offered it extra attention, touching his forehead to the beast.

Its wings were tucked tightly against its body, the mechanized muscles protruding in subtle ridges along its sides.

Mara met Gregor's eyes. Unless the Wild West had become home to a herd of flying horses, this was the Pegasus they'd spotted out the broken window of the Rarefied Library. They just hadn't realized it was a machine running on mage power and not an animal.

The horse master glared at Seth. "Thanks for the protection, dumbass!" He thrust a thumb over his shoulder toward the wagon. "This shit is weighing down my horses. I'm straining them till they're sick. You're fucking with my engines with all these racing shenanigans. I can't believe you left us."

"Us?" Seth laughed. "You and your headless horses, Ichabod?"

"You left me stranded with no guns, no blaster mages, no nothing!" He noticed her and Gregor for the first time and jumped back. "Who the hell are these people?" He shoved on his goggles, looked left and right, jerking his head around to see out of the corners of his eyes since the goggles' glass had a black circle in the middle. They covered the spot where a wearer's direct line of sight was. He couldn't see through it.

"Houston, you gotta relax." Seth crossed his arms over his chest. "Your fucking head is going to start pouring out steam like one of your precious prototypes, and we don't have another engine mage around to address it. You owe it to Prophet and to your horses to vibe out and cool down." He reached out to pull the man's goggles off.

Houston slapped him away.

Seth rolled his eyes. "You gotta trust somebody, Hous. Sometime. Someplace." He gestured toward the two of them. "Meet Mara...and her man." He pointed at Gregor. "He just cast a *shield* spell that was so fast even Prophet couldn't top it. We're gonna *have* to acquire this guy. No question about it."

Acquire. The word sent a sick lurch through her.

Houston shoved Seth's shoulder. "I don't give a flying vibe what your new little friends can do. Leave 'em and let's roll." He spun back to his vehicle.

"Nope. They're coming." He pointed at them. "Move it, new little friends."

She could get them out of this. She had to. No matter what Gregor might think of her afterwards. Her panic must have shown on her face because he squeezed her hand.

"I've got this, firefly." He cast the words to her ear. "Trust me."

The only person she'd ever trusted to ensure her freedom was herself. Anyone who did otherwise had never had their freedom taken away.

Seth reached for her. Mara jumped back as he pulled her spindle from its sheath. "Can't let you keep this, sweetheart." He pointed its end toward her.

That decided it. He thought to disarm her, but her mage power wasn't helpless. *She* wasn't helpless. She didn't need her spindle to fight. Gregor might have a plan for later, but she had one now.

"Come on, Juliet. Climb on behind me." He nodded toward his motorcycle.

She reached for her power twirled up on her inner spindle. She could do it. There was no other choice. She just had to relax.

Suddenly, the wind blew hard, her curls stretching across her face.

"Vibing shite!" Houston hollered as the tarp blew off the wagon's load from the force of the hot wind, revealing its contents. Spinning wheels.

Mara gasped.

Over a hundred of them were piled high, precariously balanced. One wrong move and they'd tumble over. They must have been spelled to stay in place. Toward the back of the load, one large wheel circled around and around on its shaft in the breeze. It was a Standish Walking Wheel. Mara had one too.

Evil's clutch. The prophecy jumped through her mind. The outlaws surely qualified as evil. Power United might have the monopoly on that in the East. But there was another player in the West.

She looked around the mowed fields to the bales of green hay beyond.

The Black Skulls had wheels and they had hay, which meant somewhere they had sorceresses spinning copper.

14

GREGOR READ THE DUSTY, rotting sign as Rickie bounced the motorcycle over the railroad tracks into a ghost town.

Fort Prower. Est 1902.

Every school kid learned about the late Douglas Prower, the third son of the then-senator. Prower, a charisma mage, had led a group of disgruntled citizens into the Wild West, dissatisfied with the government policies of the times. The truth was that the thrice-removed heir to the senate seat had wanted his own territory.

Apparently, Prower and his followers had been more successful than history reported, establishing a town. In the Republic's version, the story had ended quickly and tragically. The entire group—men, women, and children—had been taken under by fairies. Judging by the size of the town before Gregor, the fairies would have needed an army to defeat the mages who'd lived here.

There hadn't been a fairy army in the history of the Republic.

Rickie guided his bike into the crumbling town, leading the parade of outlaws. As they passed the only building on the street that still had glass in its windows, Major Stanford Madding stomped out the door. Now known as the Mad Prophet, he was a former Republic army officer, founder and leader of the Black Skulls and, apparently, the first victim of the fairy needle.

Gregor eyed the man as the sidecar sped past, his driver circling around and then coming to a stop.

The Mad Prophet watched the parade move in, hands on hips, legs spread, fat cigar clenched between his teeth.

Keeping the man in his peripheral vision, Gregor scanned the street, top to bottom in one sweeping glance.

Approximately fifty men stood on the street or lounged against the buildings. More men hustled out doors and windows along the dilapidated row of businesses that bracketed both sides of the street, at least doubling the crowd. Three leaned out the upper windows on the north side. They were armed with mage rifles. An additional three snipers hid on the roof of the western-most building, each with a mage-automatic twelve and one-half in his hands.

The s-shaped grip was a giveaway even from this distance. It could hold twelve and one-half different types of *bullet* spells, the half being the most dangerous since it held a mix of poisons that immobilized but couldn't kill, no matter how much its victim longed for death.

He calculated the odds and came up with a tiny number.

Rickie vibed off his engine, and Gregor hopped out of the sidecar.

"Where ya going?" Rickie called.

Gregor pointed at Mara in the midst of all the other vehicles and kept moving. He shouldn't have listened to her refusal of his *don't look*. He should have cast it, stashed her away, and retrieved her when he had his answers.

Seth stepped in front of him just before he got to Mara. He poked a finger into Gregor's chest. "One wrong move, and it's my bullet and everyone else's."

Gregor held out his hands, peaceful but confident. The idiot hadn't even searched him for weapons. Stupid. If he were the Mad Prophet, he'd hang the man out to dry. "No worries. Just looking to stand next to my girl."

Mara swung her leg off the bike. Her lips were flat as she looked around, taking on everyone's stare with narrowed eyes and a courage that made him wonder if she had her own twelve and one-half tucked away. He took her hand.

At least there weren't any fairies.

The Mad Prophet strode over to Seth through the dust the vehicles had stirred up. A crowd closed in behind him.

The former army man still had the build of a soldier—posture straight, eyes focused, vibes alert. He towered over Seth even though the other man was above-average height.

His shoulders had lost little of the muscle he was once known for. His leather vest exposed the tattoos on both arms—black skulls. Another one marked his chest. His buzzed hair had gone gray, and he sported a scar on his cheek that hadn't been in his army *image* spells.

Gregor did another calculation. The Mad Prophet must have survived the needle's prick for twenty or thirty years. That was the good news. The bad news? The *mad* part of his title hadn't been there before he'd been pricked.

"Well?" the Mad Prophet demanded around the cigar between his teeth.

The town went quiet. Everyone listened.

"Some success, Prophet," Seth reported. "Houston's on his way with the wheels. We turned three shipyards onto our side and most of the holdouts along the river and the western blocks. They all support the take-over."

He took the cigar from his mouth. "Including the whore?"

Seth took a deep breath, his lips tight. "She isn't hearing the message at the moment. She's all about being in charge of her own destiny and isn't interested in being tied to anyone. Most especially...you." He dropped the last word softly, like trying to lower a *grenade* potion to the ground without it exploding.

Prophet tossed his cigar away. It bounced twice in the dust. He exhaled between clenched teeth, a steam engine on the verge of exploding. "What the fuck?" His shout echoed against the empty buildings, his body jerking with every word. "Above all else, get the whore to sign. Those were your orders." He stepped up nose to nose with Seth. "That woman is everything! Sign her and everyone else falls in line. The city loves her. She is the linchpin to our success." He held his hands wide. "How can I fulfill my destiny if we can't woo one measly woman to our side? We rule the West! *She* does not!" His volume grew louder. "We rule the West!"

"We rule the West!" The crowd echoed the cheer.

Gregor raised an eyebrow at the insanity. If this is what the needle had done to the man, his own future looked grim. How the hell did Prophet think he would bring the entire place under his command? The Wild West was a sparsely populated, wide expanse of land with few paved roads.

Prophet tipped his head back. "And conquer the East!" he howled.

What?

Was the Mad Prophet so off his vibes that he thought to invade the Republic? That didn't add up. The Black Skulls would be nothing more than a speck of dust to the Republic's army.

Next to him, Mara went as still as a little rabbit. He squeezed her hand.

The High Councilor's eyeballs were going to pop right through her stitches at this. Equally baffling was that the Republic was in the dark about the former Major Madding's anticipated destiny.

The crowd repeated the mind-boggling words with enthusiasm over and over.

Gregor dragged Mara closer to him while the outlaws pumped their fists to the mindfucked rhythm pulsing through them.

Madding raised his hand for silence and the chant faded away.

"We're roasting the whore out as we speak," Seth explained. "She won't be able to stay in business without electricity. 'Specially not when her competitors are blowing nice, cool air conditioning."

From the other side of Seth's bike, Paulie snickered. "That ain't all they're blowing."

The Mad Prophet gave him a hard look, the kind that Gregor had learned early in his army career that he didn't want from his commanding officer.

"We're subsidizing the merchandise of the ones who've signed on," Seth continued. "They might as well be giving it away for free with the dancing girls they got left. Your madame won't have any choice, sir. We'll get a percentage of her girls too and start them spinning copper. We'll have this land strung in no time, electricity flowing, and the people will owe it all to you."

"I don't want a percentage. I'm taking all her girls!"

Next to him, Mara took a sharp breath. She'd been right. The hay fields were for copper. The Black Skulls had become farmers and future utility providers, all in one. This had to be the biggest scheme the Wild West had ever seen. He glanced down at Mara and caught her gulping surprise. Her dark brown eyes were wide. He squeezed her shoulder.

"Rule the Wild West!" a man hollered across the street. Another cheer erupted.

The Mad Prophet held up his hand for silence and then gestured toward him and Mara. "And them? She from one of the houses? Why didn't they fix her eyes?"

"She's no whore," Seth said. "Yet."

And she damn well never would be. Gregor silently vowed that whether or not Mara would have approved.

"They're citizens," Seth continued. "Found 'em twenty miles back. I'm guessing they got kicked off the train for not having a ticket."

Sure. They'd go with that.

"Fucking shit, Seth. I didn't ask for the Republic's stowaways!" He craned his neck and hollered back, "Summon my assimilators, Goddess damn it!"

Assimilators? That sounded like all kinds of new fun. Mara must have agreed because her rapid, fearful breathing pushed against him.

"Goggles on!" Seth yelled, loud and long. "Fairies coming in! Goggles on!"

Ah, fuck. He should have known. He couldn't seem to escape the creatures. His lungs picked up their pace, matching Mara's and then surpassing it. Cold sweat dripped down his back.

All around them, the Black Skulls donned the goggles that hung around their necks or rested on their heads.

The black circles in the middle of the goggles suddenly made sense. They blocked out their direct vision. It was protection from the silvery hypnotic gaze of fairies. Not exactly perfect. It almost blinded the wearer.

"Glister. That's how they initiate people," Mara whispered.

"It's all right," he offered. But it wasn't. He was quaking in his combat boots.

Seth laughed. "You sound scared."

"Fuck you."

A group of men, tall and lean, strode down the middle of the road. Ten fairies...no, eleven...eyed him and Mara like they were supper on a stick. The man in the middle was the one exception. Gregor caught glimpses of him as they moved forward. He was bald. His only clothes were a tattered pair of shorts. His feet were bare and his bones stuck out beneath his skin.

Seth pulled his gun. Goggles on, he pointed it at Gregor, blind except for his side vision. It almost didn't matter to Gregor. He'd face down a gun over a fairy any day of the week.

"Don't resist. Keep your eyes open or I'll blow off your head," Seth ordered.

"With those goggles, how can you see whether my eyes are open or not?" Gregor's words tripped over each other. Fear permeated the tip of his tongue and every other inch of his body.

Seth pressed the gun against Gregor's temple. "How's this, friend?"

"Not feeling that's much more accurate."

The mass of fairies stopped just before them. Their expressions varied from indifferent to disgusted to smug. Three months ago, whoever had pricked him with needle had probably looked just like them. But at least then there'd only been one. He'd never seen so many fairies at one time.

A cyclone of fright swayed right and left inside him, scooping up every vibe of his energy. He couldn't catch a breath.

Shit. Not here. Not now.

Panic was all-consuming. He knew this from experience. It had happened three times since the incident for nowhere near as good a reason as this was. Once it got a good grip, stopping it was impossible.

Mara stepped in front of him.

Goddess, he could not cower behind her. But he had a gun to his temple and his feet were iron blocks. The distance to her side was one step but it might have been a hundred miles.

"Does Daegan know you're here?" Mara didn't sound a bit intimidated.

He was her guard. He had to protect her. He yanked on that dark sea that the needle's power had churned up, the one that Daegan had dared him to swim in. He wasn't even sure what the fuck was in there, but anger, fury, even grief was better than panic's grip.

"Who's Daegan?" Prophet demanded, turning his head to see her through the corner of his goggles.

None of the fairies reacted to her comment.

"A glister friend." Mara's chin was high, her voice steady. Gregor took a breath and a hint of her courage slipped into him.

"Glister?" Prophet laughed. "The glister are no one's friend. Get to work, boys."

The group parted to let the bald guy forward. His gaunt face was pale. His head hung down. If he weren't a fairy, Gregor would have deemed him no threat.

One of the fairies shoved the pathetic creature from behind. "Do it!"

The beleaguered fairy lifted his head. One long blink and his eyes swirled with silver, his obedience as instant as the stark terror that flooded through Gregor. The fairy leaned toward Mara with his hypnotic gaze. "You belong to the wild, lost man who rules the tribe here. You follow his edicts. His wish is your command. Yes?"

"Yes. Sure." Mara's soft, steady reply was carefree. Gregor hardly believed it, and yet it offered an anchor against his fear, a tiny hum of hope. But he wasn't sure Prophet believed it either. The man looked askance at Mara from his goggles' edges.

The fairy shifted his alien gaze to Gregor, moving like the gears in his neck were insufficient to move his fucked-up head.

Goddess protect him, he thought. It was his turn. He gritted his teeth, his temple moving against Seth's gun barrel. But he was weak, and the fairy's silver swirl sucked him in. A sense of nothingness washed through him, eclipsing the terror, smothering his panic. Empty, wandering, desolate...waiting to be filled.

"And you, consort of the lost man's girl—"

Gregor wanted to shake his head at the words. What the hell did that mean? There wasn't enough of his mind left to understand.

"Wait!" The Mad Prophet shouted. "What the still-hells is on your neck?"

The words were far away, muffled and stilted.

Prophet yanked off his goggles, strode forward, and squatted until he was eye-level with Gregor's neck. "You have the needle's scars. You are glister-marked!" He belted out a laugh, bending over, hands to knees. It reminded Gregor of Daegan.

"Glister-marked and you came to me! This is a sign." The Mad Prophet addressed the crowd, his fists to the sky. "Praise the Goddess and her forgiven consort for they have sent a sign," he shouted. He turned to the fairy. "Leave. Now. I want him untouched. Remember. You'll get yours when I have mine," he added.

The gaunt fairy's eyes went blank, emptying of the silver swirl, leaving a hollow, pale blue. All the pieces of Gregor's mind and soul that had scattered away slammed back. He stumbled under the onslaught while the fairy marched off with the rest of his kind as if he hadn't just momentarily erased another's essence.

Mara caught his hand, studying him as if he looked as strange to her as he felt inside.

Prophet moved Seth's gun away from Gregor's face with a flick of his finger. "Who the hell are you?" Like Mara, Prophet inspected him with a searching stare.

Gregor was as wrung out as an old *dishrag* spell. He willed his strength to flood back, but it was a no go. He was going to have to get through this on the fumes of his vibes because that was all he had left. A trickle of sweat danced down his cheek.

Seth yanked off his goggles. "He cast a *shield* spell faster than any mage I've ever seen."

Prophet spun around to him. "And you thought it was a good idea to bring him into our camp? Never trust a citizen mage!" he shouted.

Poor Seth was having a bad day.

"I thought that was *never trust a fairy*," Gregor said. His voice was faint and rough. He cleared his throat. He needed to get this situation under control and find out what he came for...answers... before the fairies came back. "Gregor Whitman, Major Madding. I've heard a lot about you."

"Call me Prophet. What brings you here, boy?"

"He's here because of his girl," Seth interjected. "She's an incomparable."

Gregor tilted his head at that. "An incomparable?" He squeezed Mara's hand.

"Wayward." Prophet spat on the ground at the word and then he scowled at his lieutenant. "You, fool! He's here because *he's* an incomparable." He held out his hand, palm up. A young lackey scrambled over with a cigar. The kid held up a flame, balanced on his finger, a fire mage.

Prophet lit his cigar with it and then puffed, smoke drifting out. "The needle has given me a beautiful life." His eyes brightened, glowing a pale yellow as his power brushed them. "I didn't think so at first. But look what I've got now. Prophecies spill from me. Men flock to me—mages, Normals, fairies. I'm about to have a land twice the size of the Republic under my control." The excitement in his voice grew with each pronouncement. "And then I will take the Republic too. The old bitch will wither next to me. I will pluck her out and take what should have been mine."

"Wagon coming in!" The shout came from one of the snipers on the roof.

The six mechanized horses and their over-packed wagon bumbled into view. It careened back and forth as it traveled over the tracks. Houston stopped his beasts in front of Prophet, jumped down, and strode around to the front, checking on his creations, the Pegasus in the lead.

"Sir, we loaded as many as she would hold. There's a few

dozen more waiting in a cargo hold at the station in the city. We left seven guards on it."

"Unload quick. Then go back and get 'em," Prophet barked. "This time, I'm sending in my suit. He'll get the whore for sure. We'll put the sorceresses to work on the copper, and we'll show the High Councilor what happens when I rule the place."

15

MARA LEANED against the side of a building. Its naked wood was cracked and rough against her shirt, but a sliver of shade graced the spot. In the middle of the street, the outlaws unloaded the spinning wheels. Prophet had ordered Gregor to help.

The gang's leader wanted him; speculation lit the man's eyes every time he'd looked at Gregor. He would not let them go. She was certain of that. She watched Gregor lift and carry. If she could see him, she felt safer though it was nothing but an illusion.

Standing here, she'd formed an escape plan, but if she enacted it, Gregor would want nothing to do with her. He'd take his charming smile and kind heart as far away from her as he could. She should have kissed him when she'd had the chance, after he'd saved her from the train.

Too late now.

Regret rustled through her.

It took almost an hour for the Skulls to line up the spinning wheels under Prophet's exacting eye. The long row stretched across the dusty road just shy of her shade.

A few elderly men, black vests showcasing tattooed skulls on their skinny biceps, sauntered up and shared the protection from the sun. Ignoring her, their chatter rehashed the challenges of harvesting the sprawling hay fields and the fate of the botanist mages who had, in their opinions, gotten what they'd deserved.

Mara listened but couldn't determine the details of that fate. Something bad, no doubt.

Suddenly, Prophet screamed. Mara jumped, straightening from her slouch. She refocused on the man she never should have looked away from. He was close, his body tense. She followed his wide-eyed gaze, but she didn't see whatever he saw in the distance. The outlaws froze, silent, but their eyes gleamed, excitement sparking.

"Goddess damn. It's another fit," one of the old men said, glee in his voice.

"Scribe! Scribe!" Prophet staggered, stopping six feet away from her. His head twitched to the side, a hard jerk that must have rattled his brain. His mouth worked, forming words that never sounded. White flecks of spit scattered over his lips. His eyes glowed softly, a wayward's power coming to the fore.

Every member of the Black Skulls rushed forth as if Prophet were about to scatter gold coins everywhere. The curse of the evil, wayward eye was not an issue for these men.

In the milieu, Gregor sidestepped over to Mara and she instantly reached for his hand. "Can you drive a motorcycle?" she whispered. "We need our packs. They're in that sidecar." She pointed at the motorcycles parked in the middle of the road.

"I've got a plan," they both said at the same time.

"Great. We'll enact yours if mine fails." He didn't stop for a breath. "We don't have time to debate, and your life is more important than your pack."

"Wrong. My pack *is* my life. If your plan doesn't include grabbing it, then I'm going with my plan," she whispered at a furious pace. All she needed was to be in sight of every outlaw here. Considering the location of the sun, she needed to get across the street; otherwise, she'd be nothing but a shadow to half of them.

"We'll go with my plan and I'll get your pack." Gregor's tone was matter-of-fact. "Just stay put. Trust me?"

She did. Which took her by surprise. She never thought he'd be one of the few mages she trusted.

"Scribe!" Prophet twitched again.

A man rushed across the street with the shiniest black boots she'd ever seen. "Scribe, coming through!" He waved a scroll high in the air as if it contained the cure to Prophet's fit, his brilliant boots reflecting sunshine all the while.

Prophet pulled at his hair as foam dripped from his mouth, his cigar clenched in his fingers. *"Glister mistress, twined delight."*

Her breath quickened. She knew those words.

Prophet's glowing eyes brightened. He was an oracle mage like the High Councilor. Power pulsed as inky black strands spread around him. Those nearby leaned in as if they might inhale the prophecy.

The wind blew, carrying the prophecy's power toward her. A tingle of rightness passed through her, nothing like the High Councilor's prophecies. This was light and easy. No wonder his men wanted to be close. Prophet's vibes were velvet against her skin. Gregor stepped forward, but she caught his hand, stopping him from joining in. He blinked at her and shook his head as if to clear it. A worried whisper blossomed inside her. What if it wasn't just the fairies' power that made all these men loyal to Prophet?

The scribe's pen recorded Prophet's words, powered by a *scribble* spell.

Prophet twitched. *"Wields the relics, a royal right. Spin without line of blooded descent, a deadly choice."*

Mara whispered the next words along with the elderly outlaws. *"Spin and lament."*

Gregor turned to her, questions in his eyes, but now wasn't the time for answers.

Prophet came out of his trance with a shiver, and the townsmen gave a collective sigh.

"Well?" He glared at his scribe.

The scribe re-rolled his scroll and held out a handkerchief. "Repeat, sir. About the glister mistress wielding the relics."

Prophet smeared the handkerchief across his mouth. "The relics." He spoke the words as if they were a mix of curse and blessing. "We need that damn wheel."

Shock wrapped around her with a sharp, tight thread. He needed the wheel?

"When it arrives, I won't be the one lamenting," Prophet spat. "That will be her high and mighty bitch majesty."

This relic had been haunting her for far too long. Fate was herding her toward a destiny she'd refused to see on the horizon and now it was too late to flee. The white wheel. Why her? She had to open her mouth to catch a breath against the fear squeezing at her chest.

Prophet pointed at Gregor with his slightly crushed cigar. "Glister-marked." It was as if the man had forgotten about Gregor and suddenly remembered. Mad was an accurate nickname.

He marched three long paces toward them. His eyes held a wild gleam and specks of spit still dotted his chin.

Adrenaline renewed its rush and quivers flowed down her spine. How much terror could a body hold before it lost its potency? Surely, she should have reached maximum by now.

Gregor pushed her back, shielding her from the crazed man. Prophet grabbed him by the chin and peered at his scars. Gregor didn't move under the examination.

"Two pricks, eh?" Prophet thumped his fist against his chest. "She stabbed my heart. Now all I hear are the prophecies of the glister. Couldn't stand the creatures for the longest time, but they ain't so bad as long as you control them." He smiled with vicious satisfaction. "And they're not a bad lay."

The outlaws whooped. Some thrust their hips, mimicking things she didn't want to see.

Prophet pointed his cigar at Gregor as if he were about to impart some wisdom. "Always fuck a fairy from behind. You don't have to worry about getting caught by her lying eyes." He took another drag off the cigar. "You ever done one?"

"Never have. Never will."

"I recommend 'em, actually." With a growl, Prophet twitched his head to the left. "Scribe!" The word blasted through his clenched teeth. Spit flew in Gregor's face.

"Still here," the man called from behind him.

The previous scene repeated itself. The scribe's *scribble* spell wrote furiously on the scroll as Prophet recited, inky strands of smoke drifting out.

> *"The needle sings for the stitcher's dance,*
> *But claims the songs of warrior chants.*
> *Guard the quest of the one who spins.*
> *Seek her truth and healing begins."*

Her truth?

That's not what the High Councilor had said. Mara would never have noticed that one little word except that it referred to her. Her sense of equilibrium with the world tumbled. Had the High Councilor spoken incorrectly or had she lied? She met Gregor's eyes as he looked back at her. She shook her head at the hope kindled in his face. She had no truth that would heal him.

Did she?

"Well?" Prophet demanded of his scribe.

The man read the prophecy from his scroll. "A new one, but it poured forth with no hesitation. No stutters. No pauses." He slumped. "I'm sorry, sir."

"Hell! The old bitch beat me to it. I wonder how long ago she spoke it. That was about you, eh, Whitman? A cadence mage, are you?" At Gregor's stiff nod, Prophet continued. "A singing man! Worthy entertainment at last. Sing us something."

"I cannot." Gregor's words held such grief that even the wind responded, swirling around him in sympathy. If she had a truth that would heal him, she would have handed it over right then.

"Your prophecy speaks the truth. The needle stole my songs from me. I cannot hear them; therefore, I cannot sing them."

"Well, that fucking sucks." Prophet turned to the crowd, switching on his dark charisma. "Who's ever heard of a cadence mage with no songs?" They roared with laughter and boos on cue.

Mara stepped forward and took a sharp inhale, ready to defend, but Gregor squeezed her hand. "Don't."

"Did she share that prophecy with you?" Prophet puffed his cigar.

He nodded in slow motion. "Something like it, yes."

"So you know her. Did she send you to me?"

"No." Gregor's word must have rung with truth.

"I didn't think so. She'd never want two glister-marked together," Prophet said. "But there's no healing for you. Just as there wasn't for me. Your precious power is damaged beyond repair. And there isn't a woman alive—not your uppity bitch on her throne or the one you're dragging across the West—who has the power to fix it." He held out his arms. "You're ruined. Welcome to the club."

The cigar's sweet smoke drifted around them. Mara's stomach ached and she wasn't sure if it was from the smoke or from what the High Councilor had done to Gregor.

"Did she make it seem like you were going to be greater than ever? Immune to fairies? Gain amazing power? Lies. All of it. She uses people, molds them in her palms and shapes them into exactly what she wants. And woe to those who are scooped up."

He held out the cigar. "But you're here now. You're with us and out of her reach." Prophet tilted his head. "How did she speak the words of the prophecy? Easy and flowing? Or did she choke on every word?"

Gregor shrugged. "Easy, I suppose."

"She already knew it then. She probably choked up the words ages ago and then searched her ranks of warriors for one who chants. A little poke with the needle and bam! Prophecy in motion. Wily bitch."

He pointed at Mara. "Is she the one who spins?" His eyes lit up. "Another sorceress. They are falling from the sky. My mission is truly blessed!" He spun on his heels and held out his hands. "Bring the women!"

Across the pockmarked pavement, a man opened the door of an old shop in the middle of the row of buildings. The windows on either side of the door were lined with bars, and the glass in each was shattered in a web of damage. The man reached into the shadows beyond the doorway and pulled out a woman, shoving her in their direction. He impatiently summoned with his hand and women filed out, marching toward Prophet with barely disguised annoyance.

Mara covered her mouth with her hand. This was Power United all over again. Memories twirled through her mind like thread on a bobbin, conjuring sights she didn't want to remember. Drained sorceresses forced to spin, bleeding fingers, lifeless eyes that had long since forgotten what hope looked like.

The women paraded out. Their clothes were skimpy, corsets, sheer skirts or shorts so tiny their bottoms hung out, strapless tube dresses that wouldn't stay up on top or down on the bottom. There was more skin than cloth.

The women came in all shapes and sizes, but every curve, big or small, was flaunted to its maximum potential. A mix of defiance, caution, and fear sprinkled across their faces.

"Line up," Prophet commanded

The first obeyed with a roll of her striking green eyes. The others followed, at least fifty of them.

Green Eyes lifted her chin. "You got three more busy with your colleague. He's a slow draw." She cackled and some of the women joined in.

It had never occurred to Mara that some entity other than Power United could be in the business of gobbling up sorceresses.

"Meet my women, monk mage." Prophet pointed at Mara. "She spins? Then *this* is her quest. The end of it. She's here to join my sorceresses. And you have found your truth with me. You were made wayward by the order of the High Councilor for the good of the Republic. Congratulations, soldier. Your mission is over, and a new one has begun. For you and your woman."

No. She'd die first. Fight flooded into her as a river of never forgotten rage and regrets poured forth. "They don't know why they're here, do they?" she asked. "Because if they did, they'd be fleeing for their lives."

Prophet laughed. "They'll do what they're told. As will you."

No, she wouldn't.

Two of the women put their heads together, looked at her, and laughed, probably at her specs. Bully for them. They still had energy for making fun. The dark despair of spinning metal had not yet seeped into these women.

All joy the wheel will steal, she thought. Prophetic for every sorceress forced to spin.

"You must have emptied a dozen bordellos to get them all," she said.

He lifted an eyebrow. "That I did." He pulled on the cigar. "How much experience do you have spinning?"

She stared him down. "I am the finest spinner you'll ever meet."

Beside her, Gregor stiffened, but she didn't look at him.

Prophet laughed. "Confident and bold." He flicked ashes and they landed on the scribe's polished boot. "Have to be, I guess, to wear those spectacles." He gestured to the women. "They've never spun. Not a one of them. I'm afraid you won't find them very ladylike. I've heard that, unlike my Wild West, the Republic has a multitude of spinning sorceresses who do their patriotic duty."

"With fat asses squished wide from so much sitting! And they wouldn't know a cock from a spindle!" the green-eyed woman shouted. She tossed her long blond hair over her shoulder and thrust her chin high. "I told ya it's not for me, and I'm sticking to that."

"That's Flossy," Prophet said.

"I ain't spinning no yarn either!" another cried. Others followed her lead until it was a chorus of protests.

Prophet took another puff on his cigar, studying them. Then he leaned close to Gregor as if he might embrace him. Instead, he pulled the gun hidden at his side beneath the hem of his shirt. Prophet pointed it at the sorceresses.

"Wait," Mara cried. "They can spin yarn. I can teach them." Her voice cracked.

Prophet moved his finger on the trigger three times. Flossy jerked on her feet, yanked right and left by the bullets.

The ferocious noise pummeled Mara's mind, stealing sound and thought, leaving her frozen.

Flossy fell to the ground.

Prophet pivoted, pointing the gun at Mara. Before she could flinch, before she could hold up her hands in surrender, silence surrounded her. Vibes encased her—Gregor's.

Prophet pulled the trigger again.

She was going to die.

It was the only thought she had time for. There was no chance to worry for her sorceresses or regret the past. At least not until she saw where the bullet landed. It gleamed in the dust, two feet away from her. A tiny moan slipped from her lips as she stared at it, her gaze as paralyzed as the rest of her.

Gregor's vibes had stopped a bullet. He was that fast, that powerful. He'd guarded her like the prophecy had said. She managed to shift her gaze to look at him through the faint shimmer of his vibes.

His lips were flat, his stare hard on Prophet. He didn't glance over to check on her, as if he knew he'd solved her most pressing problem and she could handle the remainder of her issues. She supposed she should appreciate his confidence in her, but the truth was her face was going numb. Icy cold crept down her neck and into her arms and legs.

Shock, perhaps?

Prophet pointed the gun in the air and held up his other arm as if he'd performed a trick. The Skulls applauded, a silent celebration to her ears. All she could hear was her panting gasps.

Get it under control, she thought. She couldn't get the hell out of this place if she passed out.

Prophet pointed the gun at Seth. Clouds of dust burst from the ground, burying Seth's boots. The man's eyes were wide as he danced backward with every bullet.

The spell around her disintegrated. The noise of the world rushed in. She gulped down a breath of hot, dusty air. Gregor glanced at her, his forehead tight with worry at her gasps.

"—forgot to check him for a Goddess damn gun, you fuckhead," Prophet shouted at Seth. He shot the gun again. More dust exploded. Another pull of his finger and the dull click of the trigger sounded. The gun was empty. "What kind of lieutenant are you? Always pat the fuckers down. Next time you bring a guest into our town and he still has a gun on him, you're dead. This time, dig me a fucking hole for the whore!"

Prophet stomped over to his sorceresses who were bunched together, seeking comfort for their horror and grief, but they'd turned themselves into one big fat target if he'd had any bullets left. He kicked Flossy's body, his boot thudding against her corpse. The women screamed and sobbed, their vibes leaking out into the air. High emotions could do that to mages, but in the Republic, all citizens learned at a young age to control it. It wasn't optional. Unlike the West, the Republic ensured all mages were properly schooled.

Mara had been so schooled that she had the opposite problem. Fright or anger scared her vibes into hiding. Right now, she wasn't sure they'd ever see the light of day again.

But they had to.

Prophet leaned toward the women, arms wide. "Anyone else refuse to spin?"

The sorceresses cried louder.

He pivoted to Mara. "Pick out your wheel," he ordered. "And spin me some copper."

Those words poured through her like molten steel and hardened in a flash. She would never spin copper again and sure as hell not for a man who killed a sorceress before her eyes. She lifted her chin and tried to loosen the tight tension on her vibes.

Free. Go free.

"Gold is worth more." She spoke slowly, softly, buying time. Prophet leaned closer to hear her over the wailing women. "Why not gold instead?" she asked.

Come on. Let go.

But her vibes clung to her inner spindle.

"It's not worth more to me. Copper wire to string across the land. That's what I want." A wild light flickered in Prophet's eyes. "The entire span of the continent will be mine. He who controls the power controls the world." He raised his voice to be heard over the women. A few of the outlaws had their fingers in their ears, shutting out the grief.

"Enough!" Prophet roared. The women's sobs ceased as if they had an *off* switch on their tears. Their vibes didn't.

"You're aiming for world domination?" Gregor asked.

Prophet tossed Gregor's empty gun to him. He caught it with a snap and re-holstered it.

"Only my world, Whitman. This town is the beginning of my empire." Prophet flicked more ashes from his cigar. Once again, the scribe's boots were its victim.

The wrinkled scribe tried to kick them off with little success. He grabbed another handkerchief from his pocket...no, two of them. Setting the scroll to the ground, he polished them, a handkerchief in each hand.

"The beginning of an empire?" Gregor asked. His power brushed against her for a moment. He was casting a spell. She might not have noticed if she hadn't been standing next to him... not with the sorceresses leaking their grief through their vibes.

"Yeah," Prophet replied.

The word resounded in her ear with an echo of mage vibes. She tried not to frown, to keep her expression free of whatever deceit Gregor was brewing.

"Tell him to let the women go," he cast to her ear.

"You should let the women go." She spoke without giving it thought. Her trust in him still caught her by surprise. "They have no experience with spinning. Even Power United prefers sorceresses who have experience at spinning. Otherwise, they train them for a year before they're put to work at hay."

"I don't have a Goddess damn year, girl!"

She swallowed hard, fighting the urge to flinch.

"Tell him again," Gregor cast. "Keep going."

If anyone might have noticed his lips moving, Seth provided an inadvertent distraction, dragging away Flossy's body feet first. Her arms stretched along the ground. A stain darkened the dirt beneath her.

"You'll kill them if you force them to spin metal. You have to let them go."

"Let them go?" Prophet bellowed. His face turned red from chin to hairline. His vibes streamed out with his fury. His time in the West must have erased the Republic's training.

Gregor's energy shot past and pulled Prophet's words back as if he'd caught them in a net. She glanced around, but no one else noticed, too distracted by Prophet's building fury.

"Let them go?" He raged on.

Gregor's energy shot forth again, casting out the net of vibes and yanking it back.

Prophet's mouth moved, but, this time, no words sounded. His vocal cords refused to cooperate. He squinted and leaned forward, hands to knees, his lips working. But his roar was silenced.

"Boss." Seth put his hand on Prophet's back. "What's wrong? You having another fit?"

Prophet shoved the man away. Seth went flying, kicking the scribe's scroll that rested on the ground. It landed near the motorcycles. Seth landed on his back.

Prophet turned to them. The rage in his eyes was nearly enough to send Mara flying too. He pointed at them. "Let them go!" His command didn't match the movements of his mouth. His lips shifted with a hundred words but none of them made it past his throat. "Let them go! Let them go!"

Somehow, Gregor had captured Prophet's words and was replaying them. She'd never heard of a spell like that in her life.

The Black Skulls looked at Seth, seeking guidance, though he was clearly in the doghouse with Prophet. "Sure, boss," Seth said, still on the ground. "Let them go!"

"How 'bout a bike so we get out of your hair completely?" Gregor asked.

"Yeah." Prophet's single word snapped through the air, annoyed, but his mouth moved with a thousand other things.

"Definitely another fit," the scribe muttered. "And it's a doozy. Where's my scroll?"

Prophet shook his head furiously at the man, but the same words erupted from his out-of-control mouth. "Let them go!" Same tone. Same rhythm. He was on repeat.

Gregor took her hand and pulled her toward the bikes. "We'll take your bike, Seth. You don't mind, right?"

"Yeah," Prophet snapped while his lips carried on another silent conversation.

Mara stumbled, conveniently, at the right spot, her hand steady as she scooped up the scroll and stuck it inside her pocket. Knowledge was power and she needed every bit she could get.

They grabbed their packs from a bike's sidecar, along with her spindle.

Mara looked back one last time. Prophet clutched at his throat and then covered his mouth with his hands. "Let them go!" The words burst through.

"Goddess help us," an outlaw said. "He's lost it for sure this time."

16

GREGOR PUSHED the motorcycle's engine hard. The image of Prophet pointing his own gun at Mara played in a loop in his mind.

He'd almost lost her. This time, it would have been forever. Any future that might have played out between them would have been erased. He hadn't thought she was his to lose. Not like that. He hadn't realized how much he was counting on the chance to win her over.

He used to be better at introspection than this. Before the needle, he knew himself, from his first vibe to his last, from his evil thoughts—and everyone had them, acknowledged or not—to his greatest hopes. Mara had become the latter...probably from the minute he'd opened her file. He just hadn't realized the extent of it until the barrel of his gun had targeted her.

What the hell had happened to him that he needed a bullet to shatter the fog encasing his mind?

Maybe death did that for everyone. It cleared things up in a jiffy. Wanting to die, on the other hand, did the opposite. It blinded you to everything.

From her seat on the bike behind him, Mara leaned against

him, her cheek against his back. It felt right having her there, leaning on him.

His spell had protected her, repelling the bullet that would have ripped into her chest. Mara was right. The needle hadn't diminished his strength, but Goddess above, he'd never dreamed of testing it like that.

He put his hand on hers where she held him around the waist. She'd tied herself there with a knot of her power just before she'd fallen asleep. He'd added his own spell, anchoring his power around her back.

At least she hadn't run away from him this time. He hadn't needed to pull out the tracker to find her.

Progress.

He pushed the bike faster. It came close to flying as it sped across the Wild West. Houston was a hell of an engine mage if he was responsible for the capabilities of this machine.

He glanced at the side mirror, still nothing but empty terrain behind them and before them, the cityscape. For safety's sake, he sent out another pulse of vibes to the east, seeking any blip that might indicate they were being followed.

The spell he'd used to steal Prophet's sounds should have lasted about four hours. The *rumble* spell he'd attached to the man's hands, a parting gift just before they'd fled, had a similar life. Any movement with his fingers would rumble the air. The booming noise should have deterred Prophet from writing down a command to pursue them. But they were two hours past that window.

Mara's dark curls tossed in the wind and brushed against the back of his neck, a seductive touch independent of their mistress. Goddess, after everything they'd been through, if he could have his power back right now, the first thing he'd do was sing her a song. How many women had he sang to in his past? Too many to remember if he was honest. But the spark it ignited in their eyes, the gentle smiles tinged with lust...those parts he remembered.

Now, when it counted, when it mattered, he couldn't hum a single note. But he had to wonder if even at his best his song would have been enough to entice Mara into a thief's arms.

He guided the bike into the bustling city. The streets were clogged with everything from trucks and cars to riders on horseback, bicyclists, and pedestrians. The buildings were a mix of brick and wood, tightly side by side, and rose only four or five stories. Most dated back to the beginning of the century, though there were a few modern ones, plain and stark compared to their older companions.

He navigated over the brick-paved street slowly. Their borrowed bike got suspicious looks.

Mara shifted against his back, the feel of her soft breasts prompting an instant response in his blood.

"I've been thinking," she said.

Probably not what he was suddenly thinking about.

"I thought you were asleep." If sound hadn't been his specialty, he never would have heard her over the engine.

She shrugged against him, loosening her knotted power around her hands. He slowly freed his spell.

"We need to talk," she said.

"I booked us in a hotel. We're almost there."

"No. Not a hotel." Her words were adamant.

A caution flag waved in his mind. For now, he didn't argue.

He'd find them a secluded spot first. He continued in the direction of the river, passing Fifth Street and then Fourth. He turned down a small alley and cut through an old parking lot behind a factory to an abandoned dock on the river.

These old docks were everywhere. This one was empty and isolated, surrounded by a patch of overgrown trees and bushes. Perfect. He almost had to duck under them as he drove out on it, casting a *concealment* spell as he went. The risk of Nons being close enough to sense his mage vibes was minimal.

The motorcycle's wheels bumped over the boards. He shut off

the engine and activated the *kickstand* spell near his feet. Mara swung her leg over the bike and got off. He instantly missed the feel of her against him, her warmth, her softness.

She walked to where the dock met the concrete and looked out beyond the trees. If she hadn't dropped her pack—her strange sword stuck out its top—he would have worried she was leaving despite the fact she requested this talk.

She turned to him and pointed over her shoulder toward the old factory about two hundred yards from the dock. "That's the mill I use to weave the denim."

"I know. Part of your file. I studied a map of the area." He continued at her raised eyebrow. "I did a thorough job back when I was gainfully employed."

Reaching out, she brushed her hand through his *concealment* spell and her touch resonated against him—a warm whisper dashing along his skin. "I can't believe he killed that woman." A visible shiver ran along her shoulders. She edged in closer to his spell as if it was a source of comfort. His arms could have comforted her better, but he didn't move.

"I can't stop thinking about it. Do you think the High Councilor foresaw Flossy's death?"

He shook his head. "I don't think she knows anything about the Black Skulls' involvement in this. Surely, she would have taken a different tactic if she knew. She could have sent professionals instead of risking you."

"Prophet said *seek her truth*—my truth—to heal."

"I'd choose the High Councilor over him any day." Prophet was vibing crazy. His prophecy had stirred Gregor's hope, but only for a moment.

"But what if he's right?" She put a finger to her lush lips. "I can only think of one truth I have that no one else would see or consider. What if the gray repose spider silk could help you?"

"No." He choked on the word. He would never touch a fairy creature's cast-offs like that.

A dozen rejections clogged his throat, none of which were polite. He swallowed them down. She was only trying to help, but she didn't understand the needle's horror if she was suggesting that.

No one did.

"That's not the answer. That will never be the answer. I want nothing to do with the fairies. Their power is malicious." His volume grew. He exhaled hard seeking control. He didn't want to shout. Not at her. "Nothing should have the power to steal a mage's free will."

She stepped toward him, stopping within arm's reach. "But the spiders don't take anything. They rebalance systems. They restore them."

He looked away. "Please, Mara. Stop."

And for a moment she did. But then she finished her plea in a small voice. "Isn't it worth a try if they could help you hear your songs again?"

He closed his eyes, trying to find the memories of the tunes and songs and chants he'd spent a lifetime listening to, but they were gone. Erased. He couldn't even replay them. Simply trying seemed to open a drain somewhere deep inside him and the songs faded further away. "Do you know how a cadence mage recognizes his mate?" The words scraped against his throat.

She shook her head, her lips tugging into a solemn frown. Sadness drooped along the corners of her eyes. He didn't want her sympathy, but he had to make her understand.

"He hears the sound of her vibes. It can be a melody or a simple tone. Either way, it resonates in perfect harmony with his. I never found mine." He struggled to get the words past his tightening throat. "And I never will. Fairies and their relics took that from me. There is nothing good about them. Some residue from one of their creatures isn't going to fix it. If I could, I'd make you promise me that you'd never use them again."

She straightened. "I'd never promise you that."

"I know." It created a distance between them, one that he wondered if they could bridge.

"I want to help. But that's all I have to offer you."

"You've helped me believe in my power again. That's something I never thought would happen." He stroked his fingers over her cheek and he felt the flutter in her breath. "Though I would rather it not have involved a crazy man shooting a gun at you."

"Me too. Especially one who wants the white wheel. He talked like he knew where it was. That's what this bait seasoned with evil has found for the High Councilor so far."

Thinking about it set prickles through his teeth.

"Maybe we should go back," she said, "and spy on his little town."

Fear rumbled through him. He put his hands on her shoulders and dropped his chin until his gaze matched hers. "No. Not you. Don't get any ideas."

"Well, I'm certainly not going without you." Her words were easy, matter-of-fact and he felt like he could breathe again for the first time in a long while. A weight he hadn't know he carried dissipated.

They were in this together.

MARA SAT on the edge of the dock, her feet hanging over the edge. Gregor rummaged through his pack and pulled out food. When he'd insisted they eat, she'd expected a *meal* potion shaken in a bottle of water. Instead, he'd brought a loaf of bread, a hunk of cheese, grapes, olives, and meat kabobs.

"I can't believe you packed all that."

He smiled. "When was the last time you went on a picnic?" Without the smile, he was handsome; with it, she almost missed the question. She had to focus.

Having tea with her sorceresses at the back of her mill was as close as she'd ever come to having a picnic, but she wasn't sure she wanted to share that. She didn't want him to feel sorry for her. "It feels a little frivolous considering the circumstances."

He gave a small laugh. "I'm in the company of a beautiful sorceress. She's smart. She's courageous. We're next to a river that's"—he eyed it—"scenic in its own way. I'd say that's the perfect circumstance for a picnic." He pulled out a blanket and spread it out. He patted the edge of it and she sat next to him.

His moves were efficient as he made sure she could reach the food. Evidently, plates hadn't made the trip, but she wasn't complaining. "Is this what life is always like with you?" she asked. "Jumping off trains, bad guys with guns, and charming picnics afterwards, Captain?"

He took a drink of his water and handed it over to her. "I'm not a captain anymore. And I think this is life with you. The excitement never stops."

She laughed. "It's only exciting when you're around. Otherwise it's just stressful and worrisome."

"Then it's a good thing I'm here."

"Yes." And once again she pondered that kiss that hadn't happened.

For a long moment, they were silent, focused on the food. She hadn't eaten since her drive through the Republic. It felt like days. She was almost done with a steak kabob—its spices flooded her mouth—and he was on his third when he spoke. "You know what I wonder?" Mischief played through his voice.

"Is this going to be something charming? Should I brace myself?"

"What if we'd met for the first time in a bar or in the library? What if we were just regular mages?"

"You and I, Gregor Whitman, will never be regular mages." She took a bite of bread and cheese, a sense of satiety settling in.

He tucked his lips to the side in a half-smile. "Then what if it was just us. No ties to prophecies, no commands from on high.

Just us. Would we be on our second kiss by now? Would you have said yes to that dinner?"

"A second kiss." Her heart skipped. "What happened to the first?" The one she'd been wondering about.

"That happened when we met for the first time in the library. You were so overcome by my charm that you lifted up on your toes and kissed me."

She almost lifted a hand to her lips as if their kiss already lingered there. Her blood tingled through her as if the thought of kissing him was effervescent. She tilted her head. "What were we doing in the library if there were no commands from on high to bring us together?"

"I was researching ancient chants and you were...."

"Looking up old spinning methods."

He pointed at her like she had it exactly right. His smile spread. She was moonstruck beneath its power, like some kind of spell.

"Oddly enough, those topics are shelved right beside each other," he said. "So there we are. In the library. Completely smitten. We go out to dinner that very night. I'm fascinated by everything about you as we sit across from each other at a secluded table. It's in some tiny bistro that one of us knew about. Probably you."

"Me?" She never went out anywhere for pleasure. But she played along. "Only because I stumbled across it the day before."

"It's quite a find because the food's delicious." As they sat on the dock, he held up a small grape. "I give you a taste of mine." He placed the grape near her lips.

She smiled, struck by the charm of his game but feeding her was too far. A nervous blush burned her cheeks. She couldn't bring herself to take the grape with her lips. She reached out, took it with her fingers and put it in her mouth. Their gazes met. His flickered with satisfaction even though she'd not taken it as he'd intended. It held a promise of things to come.

"You tell me of your work"—he continued with the fantasy —"and I'm amazed at your genius and your kind heart and stunned at your soft beauty. I can't believe how lucky I am to find such a treasure in the library. And you're overcome by my charm and handsomeness."

"It's your smile. It's a highly effective weapon."

"In which case, I plan to use it."

She dropped her gaze. Maybe she shouldn't have said that. He didn't need any extra ammo to win her over. She could afford a kiss, perhaps, but not much more than that. She knew better than to assume her heart would be cautious.

"After dinner I walk you home through the park. Somewhere along the trail, there's a mage playing a slow tune on his trumpet. And beneath the light of the moon, I take you in my arms and we dance."

She held up her hand, stopping him. "No dancing." But her heart bounced with an enthusiastic *yes*. Dancing did things to her power, things she never let anyone see. No matter how much she loved it.

He narrowed his gaze, clearly suspicious at her protest. "I assure you I'm a very capable dancer." He raised an eyebrow. "Did you know that cadence mages go to a special school?"

She swallowed a sip of water from his canteen. "Is it a dancing school?"

"Every Saturday night was dancing. The school was in the middle of an enormous clearing that was surrounded by woods. It was a boarding school."

She frowned. "It sounds like SWWM."

"Hell, no. The Cadence School was a good way to grow up, though I did miss my family a lot. The school was all boys."

"Did you import girls on the weekends for dancing?" She could imagine him as a boy because his smile held a vibrant energy as if he believed the world would always offer him a good time no matter where he was...like among the anarchy of the Wild West while on the run from outlaws.

"No girls. But they did import a dance instructor." He grinned again. "She was something. Every boy in the class had a crush on her. Her power flowed everywhere. We all soaked it in. I think she must have been a sorceress."

"Probably."

"We did line dances mostly. Stomping and kicking. Manly dancing."

She laughed. "Manly dancing. Would you demonstrate?"

"If I'm dancing, then you're dancing, too."

"No." But oh, the temptation pulled at her body to move with him, to be next to him.

"When your power depends on chants and songs, dancing is a proper fit, an easy one. I would have liked to hold you in my arms while we danced to my song." His voice drooped with such sadness that she had to reach out to him. She put her hand on his and he threaded their fingers together. "How about you sing?" He stood and pulled her up, not giving her a chance to resist.

"I don't sing." She stepped back, shaking free of his grip, and crossed her arms over her chest. "And I'm not dancing."

He pulled her close, wrapping his arms around her waist, her crossed arms between them. "It doesn't matter if you're out of tune. I won't be able to hear you." He swayed with her. "And we're dancing, Mara Rand. Just us." He tugged one of her hands free and held it in his. She moved her other hand to his shoulder as if on automatic.

"This is a bad idea," she whispered.

His possessive touch against her lower back promised more, and heat traveled through her body. He pulled her closer yet and rested his cheek against the side of her hair.

A spark ignited deep inside her as he guided them slowly through the easy steps of their silent dance. Her mage power loosened, but she wasn't on the verge of losing control. If this was the extent of his dancing, she could relax.

She let herself pretend, just for the moment, that this abandoned dock hidden away from everyone was their own kingdom. She imagined turning her head and laying it against his chest.

He pulled away slightly and looked down at her. "Someday when we can be just us, I'm going to figure out a proper substitute for my song. Meanwhile, we're still dancing in the park to some mysterious trumpet player's tune."

"We are?" The words were breathy.

"Yes. And you let me kiss you." His gaze fell to her lips.

"Is this our third kiss?" she whispered. "I think I lost count."

He smiled and pressed his lips against hers, soft and gentle. Heat cascaded through her, traveling to her core, a miracle of a kiss for all that it lasted the barest moment. It ended and then another began, just as brief, before she could take a breath.

"Yes," he whispered. "We're on our third kiss." This time he sealed his lips to hers and teased her lips open with gentle caresses. His tongue darted in and she pressed closer. He took her mouth, claiming it. The cascade of heat turned to a flood, sizzling through the corners of her body.

The moment was plucked from her imagination as exactly what a kiss should be. Or maybe it was more...she'd never thought to imagine a kiss could feel like this. It was doused in heat and ignited need, but an undercurrent of happiness drifted within it. Kissing him let her taste the easygoing man he must have been when he was off-duty, when his life was normal, and his power perfect.

She wrapped her hands around his arms, his muscles hard beneath her. She breathed him in, inundating her senses with his strength, letting herself fall under his spell. Easy and free.

He pulled back but kept his arms wrapped around her. "I could lose myself in you, firefly. If it were just us, I'd spend all day kissing you." He stroked a gentle finger over her bottom lip and then her cheek and her neck.

But they weren't *just us.* And their lives weren't normal. The Black Skulls were probably looking for them. The white wheel lurked somewhere unknown. And she had jeans to assemble.

He looked at her like he couldn't look away. "I booked two rooms at—"

"I'm not staying with you." She didn't want to tell him. She kept her voice soft as she broke the news. Regret twined through her as she stepped out of his arms. "I have another place I have to stay. That had to be in my file, too."

"No, actually. Where are you staying?" His eyes hardened. The sun's ray touched the edge of the trees enclosing the beginning of the dock and the light dimmed. With it, his blue eyes darkened and while there wasn't quite thunder in them, she could sense the storm forming between them.

"I have to stay with my friend," she explained. "She's my go-between for the mill."

"I'll stay with you." A bold statement. She couldn't imagine saying the same to him if the situation were reversed. But then he was probably more comfortable with the opposite sex than she was, confident that he had something worth offering.

"That won't work."

"I'm your guard. I can't guard you if I'm not with you." His logic held a tight snap. Gone was the dancing man swaying to imaginary trumpets. She wanted him back.

"I promise you I'll be safe. And we can meet tomorrow night. My guesting duties will be satisfied by then."

He frowned, disapproval waving off him. "And you're a guest where?"

GREGOR KILLED the motorcycle's engine across the street from house number 32. Around them, houses stood grand and bold, mixed with businesses, a few stables and one parking lot.

He studied the house. Tall, wide columns framed the old mansion's carved double door. The house gleamed in emerald paint, shiny and clean, despite being surrounded by dust. A plaque above the front door read *The Green House*. A woman in a negligee lounged on the front porch swing. She wiggled her fingers at them. He didn't wave back, but Mara did. He caught the move from the corner of his eye.

She got off the back of the motorcycle. He grabbed her hand. "This is the wrong address," he said. He'd known a few soldiers over the years who'd visited these types of women. Most of them never matured into men he'd introduce his mother to.

Mara squeezed his hand like she was consoling him and then shook free. "This is it. I know it's unconventional."

"Unconventional?" Shock lifted his tone. "That woman you just waved to is a prostitute." Mara did not belong with them. And right or wrong, he didn't want her around them.

She poked her finger into his chest. "The madame and her women are friends of mine." Her voice was gentle.

He pulled in a long breath. Of course they were her friends... beleaguered sorceresses who, instead of spinning for a living, sold their bodies. He'd seen the depths of Mara's loyalty. The odds of prying her away from a friend were nil.

"Without Fancy, my mill wouldn't be nearly as successful," she said. "She helped me find all kinds of contacts in this city. I started out selling my clothes and fabric in this town. I'll be fine here. Now, what are you going to do with the motorcycle?"

"I'm going to drive back to the dock and drown it in the river." He would not be distracted from the issue at hand. He got off the bike, towering over her. "Mara, a bordello is no place for a lady." He fumed as he spoke, but he tried to keep it out of his voice.

She grabbed her heavy pack, balancing it on the edge of her seat.

He put his hand on one of the straps. "Prophet is raiding them."

She pulled the strap away. "Trust me, none of the Black Skulls will get in here. Fancy has power like I've never seen. Not to mention her bouncer. No one gets in without Valeska's consent."

He got off the bike. "If you're going in there, I'm coming with you."

"No." Instead of poking him, this time she put a hand on his chest. He pressed his over it, holding her to him.

"Tell them I'm your boyfriend." He liked the sound of that anyway. "Surely they wouldn't expect you to leave me stranded while you stay in a whorehouse."

"They wouldn't expect me to have a boyfriend. They'd never believe that."

"Why not?"

"Gregor, look at me." She wiggled the frames of her specs at him.

His chest hurt that she thought so little of herself. "I see you, Mara. I look at you every chance I get, and I marvel at how beautiful you are. Your lips, your eyes. Yes, your eyes. This way or glowing with power. And all I want to do is touch every inch of you." He caught her tiny inhale, but he didn't stop. "If those women think you aren't worthy of a man because of your specs, they are no friends of yours. I'm not leaving your side." He lowered his voice, leaning into her. "The High Councilor is dangling you as her bait. Prophet nearly emptied my gun into a sorceress from one of these places."

"I know. But I have to do this." Her tone wasn't as hard as the day he'd stolen her wheels, but the underlying firmness was the exact match.

Goddess, he was going to lose this argument. He stuck his hands in his pants' pocket. His lucky charm was in there. Once again, it wasn't working.

She looked up at him. "Thompson Mill wants nothing to do

with mages. The owner is a Non, but he has a soft spot for Fancy. This is how I get my denim. I've worked for years to earn a reputation that shows I can handle myself inside that house and in this city. Fancy's a tough businesswoman. She respects other tough women. I can't bring a man in there with me."

"I thought she was your friend. Surely a friend would value your safety."

"I won't even make it through the door if Valeska thinks I can't hold my own. Weak freaks are problems waiting to burst from their bottles like genies. Or so she's told me more than once."

"That's not what friends do. That's not what they say."

She eyed him and bit her lip. "Tomorrow night. I'll meet you on the porch and we can go be just us again. It will be like a date." She rifled through her pack and pulled out a folded-up blanket. "Take this. There's an epidemic of sense sickness here, especially in the east end where all the better hotels are. Sleep with it around you. It's got a *shield* spell woven into it and if that fails, there's another spell in there that absorbs trash vibes. It's my invention, and my patent hasn't come through yet. So don't go giving it away." She pushed it against his chest.

He tossed it on the bike and put a tight hand on her wrist. "Visit here if you have to, but you don't need to spend the night. Stay with me." He drifted his hand up her arm and shoulder and into her soft hair. His instincts demanded he keep her close at all costs. It was a battle to keep them at bay.

"I'll be safe here."

He frowned hard. "I'm going to have to camp out here to keep an eye on you."

She poked her finger into his chest. "If you camp out here, then it's a warning to Valeska that I'm nothing but trouble. If you don't leave, I might not get my thread woven into fabric."

"Fine." One hundred percent lie. He'd camp out. They'd never see him. "But I hope you know this isn't friendship between you and this woman. It's manipulation." He wanted nothing more than to sweep her back onto the bike and slip her between the sheets of his hotel bed. Then he could bar the doors and windows with every security spell he knew. "Do you have my calling card?" He ground out the words...frustrated, worried, pissed.

She patted her pocket.

He reached out and lifted the nosepiece of her specs and stuck them on top of her head. He pulled her to him, fast and hard, one arm low at the top of her ass and the other around her shoulders. He leaned into her, and she arched into his arms.

Need flared to life inside him. And from the way she sucked in a sudden breath, that need washed through her too. He claimed her mouth and her body sank into his hold, melting under their flame. Their tongues danced. A slow, hot burn flamed to life between them.

He savored the taste of her lips and she moaned softly. Kissing Mara made him feel like he was the king of everything. But he forced himself to pull back. He looked down at her. Her lips were swollen, her eyes half open, and her cheeks were flushed. He slipped her specs back on her nose. "Tomorrow night." He issued the words like they were an order. She damn well better play it safe until then. "And it's not like a date. It *is* a date."

17

"ROASTING HOT IN THERE, Mara, darling. Power's off. You oughta stay out here and keep me company." Rosemary sat on The Green House's porch swing. The silky strap of her negligee nearly fell off as she patted the seat. "We could have a little fun. I'll do you for free right here."

"Here?" Mara took it in stride, familiar with the lack of boundaries in this house.

"Bet your guy would stick around if he caught a glimpse of the action. That was a helluva kiss, girl. He's cute, and he's got shoulders like a horse. You could hold on tight to those while you go for a ride." She blew Gregor a kiss. "He new to the Black Skulls? Don't tell Fancy. She's not keen on them."

Mara could still taste him on her lips, warm silk with a tang of smoky sweetness. She pressed them together, holding on to the feel of his kiss. She wanted to remember that one. "He's not a Black Skull. He's just borrowing the bike."

"Borrowing a bike from the Skulls?" another woman asked.

Mara turned as Sage stepped out the door and shut it behind her. Her long dark hair was twisted into a high knot on her head. Her cowboy boots were scuffed and her denim shorts ragged. Her black tank top exposed her tattoo, a long trail of thin vines and tiny red flowers cascading down her right arm. Though she was just as pretty as any other woman who lived here, she wasn't a prostitute. Sage was the bartender. "No one borrows anything from the outlaws."

Mara tipped her head. "He's pretty persuasive."

And when he couldn't persuade, he just took a mage's voice and silenced his objections. She'd never imagined such a thing was possible. He was a valuable ally. And a damn good kisser.

"He can persuade me, that's for sure." Rosemary patted the porch swing again. "Sit. Trust me. You don't want to go in there if you don't have to."

She had to. Gregor wouldn't leave until she was inside.

Two men walked by on the street. Rosemary shimmied. The negligee sagged down until only her nipple caught the fabric. She winked, and they tripped over each other as they stared.

Mara headed for the door, getting out of the way of any business that might come Rosemary's way. "I need to talk to Fancy."

Rosie gave the men a come-hither stare as she replied to Mara. "Fancy's on a tear. A damn sweaty one at that. It smells in there. She's sprayed a half-dozen bottles of perfume to mask the odor of the few customers we have." She fanned herself, looking over at Mara as the men moved on. "Hard to catch a breath. She should cast a *cooling* spell. I told her we should go mages only tonight, but she threw a fit. Maybe you can convince her." She gave her a teasing smile. "Fancy got your room all freshened up for you. I hope you're staying for a while this time. Madame is in a better mood when you're here."

Valeska, guard and bouncer extraordinaire, opened the door. "You." It was her standard greeting. The single word exposed her accent, which came from far overseas and lent a stiff slur to her speech.

Her hard voice matched her appearance. She wore a black sleeveless T-shirt with a long cut down the center as if the strength of her cleavage had ripped the shirt right down the middle. Her bared arms bulged with muscles. She had long straight hair with bangs cut in a sharp line. She looked like an ancient Egyptian princess who'd won her throne through fistfights.

No one messed with Valeska. "Bag check," she snapped.

Mara slipped off her pack and opened it. She shrugged off her vest as Valeska rifled through it.

While the woman worked, two more girls slipped out the door.

"Mara!" Lavender kissed her on the cheek.

Marigold walked right past, not even looking her way. "Don't go in there, spinner girl."

Both of them plopped down next to Rosemary on the swing. "I've tried to explain, but she's on a mission."

They had no idea how true Rosemary's words were. Mara shrugged away the advice and pulled at the back of her sweaty shirt. She'd cast a gentle *keep cool* spell through the weave of the shirt, weak enough that it wouldn't bother the Nons even if they'd sat beside her on the train. Not that she'd actually gotten to sit down. But the weak spell hadn't been enough to fight off sweaty nerves from an encounter with the Black Skulls. The shirt was damp and sticky.

"Yarn." Valeska spat the word like a curse as she looked up from the contents of the pack. "Again. You are predictable, Miss Rand." Something about her accent made that sound like a bigger insult than it might have been. She nodded at Gregor still leaning against his bike, legs extended, arms crossed as he stared at her. The line of his mouth conveyed his disapproval.

"The wild men of Prophet like a woman who keeps them guessing," Valeska continued. "You'll never keep him if you always lead him on a straight path. He is glister-marked."

"You can see that?"

She shrugged and tapped her temple next to her eye. "New

potion is better than ever." Valeska dosed her eyes with *see-all* potion on a daily basis, a fact that everyone in the bordello knew. The dangerous, costly potion made her an all-seeing threat to rule breakers inside. She nodded at Gregor. "If you can't find a natural one of your own kind, make one."

Mara squinted. "Does being glister-marked make every mage a wayward?"

Valeska slapped her on the shoulder. "You are a stupid woman." Her voice sounded matter-of-fact as if the answer to her question—whatever it was—was common sense. The West knew more about glister than the east.

"This is not a good time for visiting." The bouncer shook her head as if she wanted to add *stupid woman* to the end of that sentence as well. "But Fancy is at the bar."

Mara shouldered her pack and then turned to Gregor, still watching across the street. She waved. He lifted his hand in a two-fingered salute. Passersby on the street gave him and his Black Skull bike a wide berth.

She could have stayed all day in his arms...enjoying him touching every inch of her. Those words of his replayed through her head and she had to take a deep breath. But falling for him was a heartbreak in the making.

Gregor came with ties and not just the satin ones that threatened her heart. His connections reached to the High Councilor, the army, and Power United, connections that could strangle her. They were easy to forget when he smiled much less kissed her.

She turned and entered the dark house. The crystal chandelier was off. She couldn't remember it ever being completely off, though Valeska always kept the entryway dim. It made the customers stepping in from the sunshine partially blinded, giving her the advantage.

Although she'd been warned about the heat, it still caught her by surprise. It was hotter inside than out. Mara strode past the parlor and the grand staircase and paused at the small table in the hallway that held a landline. She looked around. The only light was from the windows, but from what she could see, Valeska had moved on, and no one else was around. It wasn't that she'd be prohibited from using it, but all the better if she could complete this task with no one the wiser...or curious.

She picked up the receiver.

"Operator," the woman on the other end said.

"Collect call." Mara rattled off the landline number and waited for Nils to pick up and accept the charge. He had his number forwarded wherever he went in case the underground needed him, though he told everyone it was in case of work emergencies.

"Mara, what's the matter?" The words were sharp with urgency.

She'd called him before, and he never appreciated it, but this was too important not to call. "The Black Skulls are kidnapping sorceresses in the Wild West. How many have we sent here? Did you know—"

"Yes, I already know." His voice was full of impatience. "Why do you think I risked the trip to the West? Do you think it was a coincidence that I was on the train? I'm in the city. I'm not leaving until I've contacted all the transportees and warned them. I know where they are...or at least where I sent them."

"How are you managing that with Cecilia and the bounty hunters right there with you?" Her whisper vibrated against the receiver.

"I can handle them. I do it all the time."

"Have you talked to Fancy? She might know where our sorceresses are." She'd put Nils and Fancy in touch a few years ago when the underground had contemplated sending the liberated sorceresses to the West.

"I'll take care of it. Trust me to handle this. You're too high profile to get wrapped up in it. You attract attention like a flower to a bee. You always have. It's why you stepped back from the Trail of Strings in the first place."

The gentle reminders irritated, mostly because he was right.

Nils continued, "Let me play my role. I have to go." He disconnected with a click.

She hung up. She always felt like a fool next to Nils. He was suave and polished, and she was an outcast. But she'd had to make that call. She couldn't let their sorceress refugees fall victim to Prophet's plan.

She strode into the courtroom. Fancy called it that because it was where she judged the size of every man's purse, where customers courted her girls and vice versa, and where everyone present was guilty of something. The courtroom consisted of the old mansion's former dining room and ballroom, the walls removed between the two. It was almost as dim as the foyer, lit by candles and lanterns, two of which sat on the edge of the stage.

The bar lined the majority of the wall to Mara's right. Tables and chairs lined the floor in front of her, and booths and couches lined the remaining walls. A violinist sat in the corner of the room playing a slow, sultry tune while a woman lounged on a divan at the front of the stage. The lanterns provided just enough light to see by. Her long legs, topped with high heeled, laced-up boots, were slung over the back of the couch, and partly covered in old-fashioned bloomers. Her corset was open, her breasts bare. She circled a finger around one nipple. Not much of a dance, but it captured her audience of two.

A sudden smack against the wooden bar yanked Mara's attention.

"Mara!" Fancy stood up, her arms wide and hugged her. "Oh, this backpack! Threads and yarn. You never stop. All work and no play, darling!" She kissed both of her cheeks. "The train came in hours ago. Where have you been?" She patted her cheek. "I had a feeling you'd be late."

"How did you know that? You have your own oracle mage locked up in a cage out back?" Mara teased.

"What do you think?" Fancy winked. "Bartender!" Her holler echoed through the room.

"Here, madame," Sage's sarcasm came from behind the bar.

"Bare Witches Whiskey for my favorite citizen and another for me." Fancy's shiny red hair was piled on her head in a loose knot. Her black corset pushed her breasts high and left her arms bare. Four-inch heels gleamed sharply beneath the wide legs of her black trousers. She returned to her barstool.

Mara took the next one over.

"Business must be good if you're back already," Fancy said. "I saw your image spell in the paper. *Sorceress dares new fabric with spider silk.*" She held up her hands as she recited the headline. "Bravo for you." Fancy touched her hand to her chest. "You make a mama proud, spinner girl."

Mara definitely hadn't done that. Her mother had left her as soon as she was old enough to be shipped to SWWM. Her father was unknown.

Fancy had taken her under her wing after Mara's cheap, rundown motel had caught fire, displacing all the guests, on Mara's first trip to the Wild West. The two had stood in the street gawking at the towering flames. An instant kinship had ignited. That had been years ago. Ever since, Fancy had done everything she could to help Mara sell her wares, including finding weavers for her fabric. Mara owed Fancy a lot.

Sage set two whiskeys in front of them. The ball of ice in Mara's glass sparkled beneath the candlelight like it had been slipped off one of the chandeliers. Fancy lifted her drink, and Mara tapped hers against it.

"To the wild place," Fancy said. It was the first half of the traditional Wild West toast.

"And freedom's grace," Mara finished. She lifted the drink to her lips. The spicy scent burst against her nose. She swallowed and washed away the dust of the road, the insanity of Prophet's plan, and a kiss that melted her bones.

"You find a supplier for your spider silk yet?" Fancy asked. "If you haven't, I can help."

The day after they'd first met, Fancy had suggested she spin with the webs that had coated the burned remains of her motel. The madame had even collected them for her. It had taken Mara years to dare to attempt it, though the webs had been waiting, packed between sheets of waxed paper. Once she'd tried it, she'd wished she hadn't waited so long.

"I don't need a supplier anymore. I've been banned from spinning it."

"What?" Fancy snapped.

Sage took her polishing rag and headed for the other end of the bar as if avoiding the madame's temper.

"That made the newspaper, too," Mara said. "I'm sure that issue is on its way to the land of Kansas as we speak. I'm willing to push society's boundaries, but I can't disobey the High Councilor."

"That bitch!" Fancy set her glass down with a bang against the dark wooden bar. "How dare she?"

"She dares what she wants. It's her country."

"That's why I live here. You should, too." She finished her drink and slammed it down again, snapping her fingers for another. Sage obliged.

"Luck's balls, Mara! You can't stop. A grand breakthrough is your destiny. You've told me what enormous potential it has. I've been excited for you." Fancy had listened to her drone on about the gray repose fabric during her last few visits.

Mara shrugged. "Politics and prejudice. The two pillars of life in the Republic. There's not much I can do to get around them."

Fancy stabbed her finger at her. "That's vibe shite. You've got to make it happen. This is your moment to shine."

She glanced at her reflection in the mirror behind the bar. "I don't want to shine. It would do no good to my employees or my customers."

On the stage, the reclining woman rolled off her sofa and stood. Mara recognized her now. Ginger. All of Fancy's girls were named after herbs, spices, and flowers, appropriate for The Green House.

Ginger leaped off the stage and strutted over to a customer's table. She laid back on it, arching up, her fingers traveling over her nipples. The man picked up his drink and wiped it across his forehead.

Fancy turned away from the show. "Don't tell me this is because you're wayward." She slipped her hand under Mara's chin. "You deserve to shine as bright as anyone else in that fucked up country of yours. I don't care how crippled or lame you think your power is. I'm telling you that you're perfectly normal. You should move here."

Sometimes Fancy really was as proud as a mama and as blind as one, too.

Mara smiled. "Life isn't so different on this side of the Mississippi. Freedom doesn't really grace everyone here. People live in fear of the outlaws and anyone else who's strong enough to take them over. If you're powerful and capable, then you can fight for your freedom. If you're weak or lame, you either go with the flow or hide. It's the same in the Republic." She didn't want to shine... here or there. She couldn't afford anyone looking into her background or examining her power closely. She didn't want to imagine what they'd find.

"You're just scared."

Yes. Exactly. "Speaking of scared, did you know that the Mad Prophet has it out for bordellos and their girls? And I think he might have it in for you in particular."

Fancy tsked. "Of course he does. This town is mine. The man's tried, failed, and knows what will happen to him if he attempts to force me. He thinks he can intimidate everyone into bowing down before him. I'm not giving in."

"What does he want you to do?"

"Hook up to his new power supply lines." She rolled her eyes. "Like I'm going to unhook from what I already have, even if it is shit and sparks rain down all the time."

"It doesn't seem to be working at the moment," Mara said.

"I'll get it back on. Don't you worry. Prophet doesn't have a tenth of the wire he needs to string around this city." She shrugged. "Don't know where he's going to get it. He's sure as hell not taking my sorceresses to do it. But Janie and Kate have already signed up."

Janie and Kate ran the bordellos down the street. Mara had never met either woman.

"They've given him ten sorceresses each," Fancy continued. "They have a fucking quota of women to provide for him. And we're not talking about a quota of little fucky-fucks."

"What do those girls know about spinning wire? Even if they are sorceresses?" Fancy rolled her eyes. "I fear for the West if he's gonna use wire spun by whores to light us up.

"The girls who are left at Janie and Kate's are about to riot. The only way those two bitches keep them around is with *lock* spells on the doors. Both of 'em have confiscated their girls' clothes. They're forcing them to work if they want them back, along with food, water, and liquor. Can you believe it? Janie and Kate have turned downright evil on their girls. Never thought I'd see the day."

Sage gave her boss a hard look from the other end of the bar and pointed at Mara. "She shouldn't be here. It's too damn dangerous."

"I've heard that one too many times today." Mara glanced between the two of them.

"How'd you hear about Prophet?" Fancy asked.

"I was at the Black Skulls' hideout or whatever they're calling it."

Fancy's eyes went wide. "Luck be with us all!" Luck was a much more popular god in the West than he was in the East thanks to the glister population. "What the still-hells were you doing there?" she shouted, grabbing the attention of the two customers at the tables.

Mara explained her capture.

"I cannot believe you." Again, the madame smacked her hand against the bar.

"It's not like I did it on purpose," Mara protested.

Anger rolled over Fancy's face as if she was personally offended that Mara had associated with the crazy man. "Prophet's path is not yours."

Mara had never been able to determine what kind of mage Fancy was. She talked about destiny as if she were an oracle mage, but Mara had seen her dance and had been certain she had sorceress power. A charisma mage also seemed a possibility since she could charm anyone into doing what she wanted.

"He has glister on his side," Mara continued. "Prophet made one hypnotize us...or try to."

Fancy stared at her, eyes hard, the look she turned on her girls when they disobeyed. "Those fuckers. Traitors to their own kind." She stabbed her finger toward her. "I know you, Mara Kathryn Rand. Don't think for a minute that you're gonna go rescue that bunch of sorceresses. They're worthless. I know every house he took them from, and there's not a quality mage among them."

Rosemary sauntered in. She stuck her face between Fancy and Mara. Her grin stretched to mischievous proportions. "She got a ride into the city from a man on a Black Skull bike." The woman stirred up trouble between the girls on a regular basis, but this was the first time she'd ever done it to Mara.

Mara hastened to explain. "Because taking one of their vehicles was the only viable option to escape. Gregor is not a Black Skull."

Fancy's eyes darkened. "You leave my sight for three weeks and look what kind of trouble you get into. You're lucky you made it out!"

"Well, I'm here now," Mara reasoned gently.

Rosemary plopped her fist on her curvy hip. "I told Mara you had her room free."

"Free?" Fancy's voice went high. "I've got nothing free for someone stupid enough to get caught by the Mad Prophet."

Mara raised an eyebrow. She was thankful Gregor wasn't here for this. Fancy had a temper that got the better of her occasionally, but it didn't disqualify her as a friend. "It's rather unfair to lay the blame on me." She'd always been able to calm Fancy.

"You could have died! Or worse. Death and misery do not deal in fairness. And neither do I. You can have a room, but I expect you to work your way back into my good graces. Otherwise, don't plan on me helping with Thompson Mill. Not if coming west is going to cost you your freedom or your life."

"Work? You want me to...."

"No! I don't want you selling your girl parts. I want you to dance."

Dance. The word struck fear in her...along with something else she didn't want to identify. Mara flattened her hand on the bar. "No." This was not negotiable. "I'll give you the finest cloth on the continent. It will flow and drape and soothe your skin like nothing else. But I'm not dancing. I don't dance for audiences." She lowered her voice into a furious whisper. "You know what my dancing does to people!" She'd told Fancy her story the last time she was here. Clearly, that had been a mistake.

"I don't want cloth." A stubborn note saturated Fancy's tone. "I want you to dance with everything you've got. If my customers aren't falling at your feet in awe and lust, you're out on your ass.

Dance with every joule of your power and you'll have a bed...all alone if that's what you want...for the duration of your trip."

Mara looked away. "You don't know what you're asking."

"All or nothing."

"I can't dance, Fancy. I'm sorry."

"Then that drink is ten golds. Only working girls get one on the house."

"Ten golds? That's ridiculous."

But Fancy wasn't done. "And you can kiss your appointment with Thompson goodbye." The hard look turned colder.

"What the hell, Fancy?" If it weren't for her appointment, she'd leave.

Rosemary tsked. "Told you she was in a bad mood."

Valeska slid close. "Want me to take it out of her skin, boss?" She pulled a joule stealer from the holster at her side. They were illegal in the Republic.

Fancy leaned toward Mara. "I've watched you tiptoe around your power for years. You want to use it. I can see it in your eyes. How would it feel to let your power flow and not cut it off at the balls just before it gets to the good part? How long has it been since you've done it?"

"I should never have told you."

"Too late. I want to see it for myself."

Mara shook her head. "You'll regret it." Part of her wanted to say yes just to show her friend exactly what she was asking for. She'd get what she deserved for making such a request.

"I regret letting you walk through life with your potential clamped down tighter than a virgin's ass. Don't tell me the thought of spinning out all your power doesn't sound enticing. One night to let it all flow, to let your energy brim forth and take what it desires."

Mara closed her eyes and sucked in a hard breath. Tomorrow was her date with Gregor. She tamped down the anger crackling against her vibes. But worse than the anger was the excitement.

Goddess above and Luck below, she had no business being excited. She blamed the wild vibes of the West.

Fancy laughed, tossing her head back. "You want to do it. Don't bother denying it. Dance. Tomorrow night."

"Mages only!" Rosemary piped in. "Finally! Let's get the *cooling* spells blowing, woman!"

Fancy turned and swatted the woman's ass. "Watch yourself. And no spells until tomorrow."

The sharp crack drew the attention of two customers. As if it were the catalyst he needed, the man at the nearest table stood and led the dancer to the far door, his arm around her waist.

"One dance," Fancy said. "No one touches you. No one approaches the stage. You have your room for as long as you need it."

Mara stared at her. "One dance."

The bouncer tucked her shooter away.

The madame stood. "Get a good night's sleep. I want you fully rested for tomorrow's show." She kissed Mara's cheek. "This is for your own good. I can't wait to applaud your power."

18

"Sexiest sorceress in the West! Dancing tonight!" The teenaged boy's voice cracked on the last word. He stood in front of The Green House, a pile of handbills resting in his arm. He tossed them to every man walking by. The black papers littered the road. Gregor picked one up.

One night only! Hottest dance in the West! No Nons Permitted. The words surrounded the silhouette of a woman reclining sideways on a chair.

The same words graced a banner draped across the entrance to the house. He was getting Mara out of here. Tonight was guaranteed to get rowdy.

He took the stairs two at a time. A wooden sign hung on the door.

No weapons of any kind.

He had his weapon stuck inside his invisible pocket, along with the rest of his pack, and he sure as hell wasn't giving them up. Lincoln had assured him the *invisible pocket* spell was undetectable. Gregor had stuffed his entire pack in it every time he'd ventured out of his hotel. He needed to ask Lincoln to teach him how to cast it.

He strode inside, past the gaggle of whores greeting newcomers and a bouncer who looked qualified to guard the gates of hell.

"Ooo. Motorcycle man is here." A young woman, scantily clad in a barely-there dress, slipped her arm through his. She'd been lounging on the porch when he'd dropped Mara off yesterday.

He stepped back. She stepped with him. "I'm here for—"

"Oh, I know." She gave him a coquettish smile. "You're here for Mara. She can't come out though...not until 9:30. She said she called and told you."

Gregor hadn't believed her story about taking care of some business first. She'd acted like it had to do with her yarn, but he'd gotten the same feeling as when she'd said she'd wait for him after they were sprung from the dungeon. If she was about to pull another disappearing act, he wasn't about to wait around and let it happen.

"She figured you'd show up early. She asked me to meet you at the door and not let you in. But seeing as you're already in...." She sang the words as she rubbed up against him. "I'm certainly not going to turn away the most handsome man here tonight. I'm Rosemary, by the way, but you can call me whatever you like."

"Rosemary, I'd like to see Mara." Gregor had spent last night outside their back fence, patrolling the grounds every hour. Plus he'd knocked on the door yesterday evening but had been told Mara was asleep. The bouncer hadn't let him through. He'd checked the tracking device Cecilia had given him to verify her location. He'd spent hours looking at it ever since.

His escort pulled him deeper into the house. Her breast brushed his arm.

"Patience, big guy. Let's get you a drink." She led him into a dark room big enough to house a couple hundred customers. A stage lined the front, its curtain drawn. Another banner hung over it in the air, fastened with a hover spell.

Sorceress. Sensual. Sexy. No Nons Permitted.

He gritted his teeth. He should have tied Mara to the motor-cycle with a spell and locked her in his hotel room. That would have gone over really well.

He eyed the room with one glance. Mara was nowhere to be seen. There was one exit behind him, two on either side of the stage. A short staircase rose along the stage's right side. The room roared with the sounds of drunken men. If the proprietor was smart, she'd start watering down the drinks.

Most of the tables were occupied with two men or more. A few singles and a few empties were scattered around the room. The booths at the back and along the sides were full. Nearly-naked girls lounged against the men.

"Now, don't worry. Mara's off-limits. Fancy has strict orders about that. Everyone knows." She trailed a finger over his chest as she guided him to the bar. "Buy me a drink?"

He frowned.

She giggled. "I didn't think so." She escorted him to the last empty bar stool and snapped her fingers at the bartender. "Sage, this man needs a drink." Leaning in, Rosemary kissed his cheek. "Enjoy the show, Mr. Motorcycle Man." She sashayed away.

As the kiss, almost chaste, settled into his skin, he studied the mage power that vibrated through the room. No electrical lights shined, just a plethora of bobbing mage lights strategically placed. A *cooling* spell pulsed throughout, but underneath was something else.

It wasn't until he sat down that he recognized it. A *heat* spell mingled beneath all the cool air, a line that drifted just at his lap. A keen but devious business practice for a whorehouse, the spell was almost unnoticeable. It slipped through the fabric of his cargos. He hummed his power into his throat and sent a wall of vibes around his lap, pushing the spell away.

"What do you want?" the bartender asked.

He recognized her. She'd joined Mara and Rosemary on the porch yesterday.

She poured a shot for another customer with one hand and readied more glasses with the other. Farther down, the bouncer stood at the edge of the bar and glared at him. Her dark jacket reminded him of the dress uniforms of the Old World military organizations. A gold braid looped around one shoulder. Gold buttons lined the front to hold together the thick, dark fabric. They were buttoned halfway, exposing a deep slice of ample cleavage. Her straight, dark hair added to her harshness and her arms were ready at her sides.

She sneered. "You are a bad man." She had a strong accent that sharpened the words. Her comment drew the attention of the men at the bar. They looked at him but not for long. They had better things to anticipate than action from the bouncer.

"Valeska, git." The bartender shooed her away, but the battleship didn't budge. "You're scaring my customers, and I get an extra half-percent tonight from our generous endower. Now move it."

To his surprise, the battleship exited the harbor with an indifferent shrug. "Whatever you wish, Sage," she said over her shoulder.

"Bourbon. Neat. If you please," he ordered.

"I don't please." She plopped down drinks in front of other customers and then returned. She pulled out two shot glasses and poured a long stream of clear liquid from a green bottle into each, full to the brim. Not a drop splashed over.

Putting the bottle back under the bar, she stuck her finger into one drink and sucked it dry. Her gaze stayed glued to his. She lifted her glass and waited from him to do the same. "To you, Mara's chauffeur. May you live long enough to take another drive."

He lifted his shot glass and, keeping pace with her, tipped the liquid back. The kick nearly chopped his gut in half. He sucked in the little air he could manage. "What is this?"

"Native's Piss."

He nodded. "Sounds about right." He gazed around the room waiting for the burn to die down. "Where is Mara?"

"Busy."

"With what? Helping a wayward mage? Teaching someone to spin yarn?" He didn't like the shrug he got as an answer. "Is she in trouble? Because I wouldn't like it if she was and someone kept it from me."

She narrowed her eyes. "This place is trouble. I really doubt anyone kept that from you. You let her waltz right in. You have the muscles to stop her. I bet you have handcuffs too. Not sure why you didn't use them." She shrugged again. "But she's safe enough right now. She likes you." She looked to her right and then dropped her gaze, nervously fingering her empty glass.

"I like her too, but I don't think she'd appreciate handcuffs." Gregor turned to see what had caused the nervous expression.

Just beyond the bar, a woman sat at a plush velvet booth, the nicest in the room. She met his eyes over the glow of a flame that she played with, dancing it from finger to finger. Her face was perfection, smooth cheeks, and eyes heavy with the experience of a rich life and ready for more, lips full and plump. Her red hair was piled high on her head tempting a man to free it down her back. Lust rolled off her in waves like it was a type of power.

His vibes shuddered. It wasn't entirely comfortable. He couldn't quite figure out what she was—not that he could identify mage type easily. Few mages could.

Despite the flame, he was certain she was no fire mage. Her vibes seemed to send out conflicting messages on purpose.

He leaned toward the bartender, nodding at the woman. "How does she manage that?"

"The flame? Or do you mean how does the madame look like she's waiting for the fuck of her life?"

Neither, he thought. But there was no denying the madame projected that image.

The bartender tucked away her empty glass. "She's a professional."

"And I am a professional torturer." Valeska's words popped in his ear. She cast her voice from her position in the doorway. "I will fuck you up if you cause trouble. Unlike the sorceress, I don't like you." Her *sound* spell traveled with ease across the room. "You left Mara at a whorehouse with no money. Only thread. Spools and spools of thread." She sneered again, the expression clear despite the distance and the dim light. "How do you think a penniless girl survives in the Wild West? There is a reason she ended up here."

A red sheen descended over his vision though he knew the woman was goading him. Mara would never sell herself. Power vibed in his throat.

"Oh my. That scarred throat can growl." She strode away.

He reached into his pocket and yanked out the palm-sized tracker, keeping it below the bar and out of sight.

Mara was thirty feet away and off to his left, which put her on the other side of the wall. He put the device away. He should have cast a *tracker* spell on her, but they were hard to stick to clothes. Skin or hair was better, but he'd miss his chance, too distracted by that kiss.

The bartender leaned her arms on the bar and opened her mouth, but whatever she'd planned to say was wiped away by the crackle and zap of a serious electrical charge. Sparks rained out and showered over his head. The mirror above the bar reflected their image. He ducked, casting a shield over him and the bartender. The crowd rumbled, uneasy, and one man dumped his beer on his sleeve to put out the spark that had caught there.

"Stupid power lines," she muttered. She glanced up at him. "You're a quick caster."

The electrical lights over the bar flickered to life and then off again. Behind him, glass shattered.

He spun around on his barstool. Above, a small chandelier

with one broken bulb swayed as if a hard wind had blown past. It attracted little attention from the patrons except for one.

Nils Lusman looked up at the crystal structure with a frown and stepped away from it as if worried it would fall. "The power lines around here are shit," he muttered, scooting onto the newly vacated stool next to him. He blinked in surprise at Gregor and then held out his hand. "Captain? How are you?"

Gregor tried to recover his shock at seeing the man. He shook his hand. Static electricity popped between them, but neither complained. "Former captain," Gregor said.

"Once a warrior, always a warrior."

Gregor tipped his head at that truth, still stumbling through utter surprise. "Never thought to meet you here," he finally said.

Nils laughed. "I was about to say the same." He took the drink the bartender poured him without asking—water with a hefty shake of what looked like salt in it—and downed it in one gulp. He shrugged. "I get so damned dehydrated out here."

He arched an eyebrow in surprise. "I guess you're a regular?"

Nils laughed again. "When in the West, one should always make time to appreciate its charms." He eyed the woman at the nearest table. Her breasts sat above her corset. Her nipples were pierced. "And The Green House has charm galore."

Rosemary walked up to Nils. It was his turn to have her breasts pressed against him. Gregor turned away while the two talked. If they were transacting business, he didn't want to know.

A moment later, Nils tapped him. "Listen, about that job offer...." He was missing his tie and the top buttons of his shirt were undone. A lipstick print of a kiss marred his cheek.

Gregor swiped at his own cheek hoping he didn't sport such evidence.

"I really need someone with your skills and your reputation," Nils said. "If one of the Republic's finest army officers headed up our security, it might polish away these unfortunate rumors of poorly treated sorceresses. Mara Rand means well, but what she claims is simply not true. If you were on board, it would free up my time to focus on more pressing needs. Power United is a good company and it's vital to the future of our country. I know we talked about it once, but I thought you might reconsider. Hell, you should talk to Mara about it. Her answer might surprise you."

Gregor shook his head. "Not interested." He could guess what Mara would say, and he wouldn't strain the little trust between them for Power United. Plus, he hadn't liked what he'd seen of their workers.

"I'm not taking no for an answer, at least not tonight." Nils slapped him on the back. "The pay is superb. The hours suck. Think about it." He nodded to someone across the room. "Pardon me for leaving you, but I see my friend." He patted his jacket pocket and pulled out a piece of paper. "I've been carrying this around, though I sure as hell didn't think I'd give it to you here. Your paycheck. Power United is appreciative of your services leading our team of men, and we look forward to a long, productive relationship." He handed it over and walked away.

"WHAT TOOK YOU SO LONG?" The madame's whine was a whisper that no one else but Nils was meant to hear. Gregor pulled her voice to him with a hum of power. He didn't make a habit of this, but Mara was here. He wasn't going to risk missing something that might affect her.

She stood and leaned in to give Nils a lingering kiss on the lips. "I've missed you, my darling. Come sit and keep me company."

Nils stared at her cleavage, missing the shrewdness in her eyes. Her gaze landed on Gregor before she slid back in her seat, facing the bar. Nils took the booth's other side, his back to the bar.

"I'll tell you all about those nasty outlaws who were here two days ago and then most of this morning." She placed her fingertips to the top of her breasts. "Nils, the men barely left me alive. I needed a big, strong man like you around to protect me."

Outlaws. She had to mean the Black Skulls. And they'd been here this morning.

Shit. He'd been watching the place all day. How the hell had he missed that?

Gregor squeezed his hands to fists.

"Problem, cowboy? You look a little sick." The bartender switched her gaze between him and the drink she was mixing.

He cast his words to her ear. "Have the Black Skulls been by since Mara's been here?"

She rolled her eyes. "I told you this place was trouble. But don't worry about your girl in that regard. Fancy would never let anyone take Mara from her. She loves that girl in her weird way."

He studied the vibes of her words. "Truth, but you didn't answer my question."

She shrugged and returned to her more favored patrons. He went back to eavesdropping, pulling sound with his vibes.

"Fancy, I seriously doubt you needed protection," Nils said. "If you had men here who weren't welcome, your patrons would be tripping over dead bodies tonight."

"That's not true. I'm no killer."

Gregor could find no fault or lie in the madame's words, but he still didn't believe them. Something about her was off. Something more than her manipulating Mara into staying here. His vibes hadn't settled down since he'd noticed her.

"They wanted me to hook up to their power lines and hand over half my girls to them," Fancy said. "Half! I'd go broke. Besides, none of my girls has ever spun a damn thread. They spin their nipple tassels and their asses on my stage. But to spin yarn or wire? Forget it."

Gregor looked around the room as he listened in. One of the working girls stopped a few feet from him and looked him up and down. She winked and walked away as if she knew he was off limits. Her high heels clacked softly against the floor. He looked down at the sound, unusual in the east among properly schooled mages, and caught sight of burn marks on the floor. Must have been a popular spot to drop a cigar. The madame probably didn't appreciate that.

"Your girls could always learn to spin," Nils said to Fancy. "However, I can take care of your electricity. I believe I've mentioned that before. Let me do this for you."

The madame's laugh trickled out over the crowd's noise. "Oh, Nils, you always say the sweetest things. I thought Power United only did work in mageland. They're such a patriotic organization. Do they know what a victory they scored when they hired you? You are a wonderfully proper citizen, with the best interests of the Republic at heart...unlike some."

Nils laughed sharply. "Unlike some I work with."

"Oh dear." Sarcasm tainted her tone. "Do they seek glory for themselves instead of the righteous Republic?"

"Cut it out, Fancy. I know you don't like the Republic. You're playing me."

"No, darling. Tell me about it. I respect you and your beliefs. I know you're all for Goddess and country."

"I do my duty for her great land. Always. Even when some cannot see what it's meant to be. The Republic is under serious threat thanks to a few small-minded people."

"Mmm. Let me ease your worries." She leaned in, her hand under the table.

Gregor registered Nils's hard inhale. Hell, some things he didn't need to hear. He tuned out for a few minutes. By the time he listened in again, they'd jumped topics.

"If that's the case, then the Mad Prophet is a fool," Nils said. "He's going to use up his sorceresses for nothing. If I had those women, I'd be twenty-five percent ahead of where I am now."

Fancy waved his comment away like it was nonsense. "Those women are not sappy, silly citizens of the Republic. If you had those whores, you'd be lounging around your office fully sucked dry but with no more copper wire than you have now. Even a proper citizen like you wouldn't be able to resist their true talents." She lifted her drink and finished it off. "I don't know what he was like before he was all fucked up by the glister relic, but Prophet's only out for himself now. He wants to rule the West on a grand throne custom built for his tight ass and then take over the Republic."

"He's a fool. Only Power United has the resources to string the entire land, east to west." He shook his head. "Cecilia would shit herself if we powered the entire stretch of the continent."

Fancy cracked a laugh. "I hear that excitement in your voice. You're a manifester! Nils, you are keeping secrets from me." Surprise laced her tone with an unexpected delight. "I had no idea. If your Republic stretched from Atlantic to Pacific for the pleasure of the Lady's blessed people, what would happen to the rest of us?"

"Think of the good the Republic could bring to this wild land."

"You'll find that a number of people disagree with that. The fairies, the natives, the Normals. Seriously, darling. If uniting the two halves of the continent were as simple as a geo mage flicking a spell at a measly river dividing the land, someone would have done it already. There are good reasons why citizen mages are east and the rest of us are west. It's a necessary balance of power. Lucky for us all that Prophet doesn't have the tools he needs to do it." She leaned in close.

"Goddess, Fancy," Nils gasped.

"So big, so hard for me already. I think you have a tool that could unite two lands," she giggled. It was an odd sound coming from the experienced woman. "I hear you've been confiscating spinning wheels."

"For the good of the Republic." Nils sucked in a hard breath.

The mage lights in the room dimmed and the audience quieted.

"Oh, it's showtime," Fancy whispered.

Nils groaned.

Gregor cut off his spell, relieved he didn't need to hear any more of that. He tapped his fingers against the bar, impatient for Mara.

Somewhere behind the stage's curtain came the beat of a drum. It had a soft, steady touch. His fingers automatically matched its rhythm, his body recognizing the magnetism of the sound before his mind did. Despite the beat's lightness, strength permeated it, as if it might carry across forever without needing to raise its volume. The drum called to him, somehow waving *come hither* with its simple beat. He wanted to cross over to it, like stepping over a threshold he'd never noticed before.

He caught Fancy's stare as he looked across the room. She closed her eyes as if in that moment the power swept her away.

The curtain lifted.

Mara stood in the center of the stage, lit by a hundred tiny mage lights hovering in the air.

His mouth went dry. A primal urge forced him to his feet, demanding he wrap her up and hide her away. Another part of him couldn't move any farther, too amazed, stunned. Awed.

He could sense now that it wasn't the drum that had such unexplained power. It was Mara. Energy pulsed from her, an invisible rope whipping over her audience in time with the drum. He'd never encountered anything like it.

Her body was draped in a complicated pattern of strings that sparkled with gold against her pale bronze skin. The thin ropes graced her arms, crisscrossing around her biceps in a wide, open mesh. Her belly and hips were draped in loops of the fine string. Her breasts were bare—Goddess, her breasts—the golden rope encircling their fullness. Low on her hips, a skirt of airy layers floated on the currents of her power.

She was motion and stillness at the same time.

A black blindfold wrapped around her eyes. If anyone had been cognitive enough to think and reason, they might have compared her to Justice. Only instead of judging and weighing guilt, Mara invited their guilt, beckoned their imperfect hearts, and filled their souls with the call of her energy.

Her power surrounded him with its luscious touch. The energy that had engulfed their dungeon cell was nothing compared to this. This was indescribable.

He wouldn't have been surprised if Luck suddenly appeared, standing next to her, for this power was no gift from the Goddess. No, this was the Goddess's competition.

The drum stopped suddenly, only to start again exactly in time with the lift of her hips, up and down, side to side. The hard, rhythmic move flowed into tight, graceful circles of her hips and he wanted to rein them in and hold her tight. He could feel the softness of her skin under his touch already.

She lifted her hands, circling them as she reached in a graceful stretch. Her power had an edge to it, sharp and tight, and he savored the sting of its cut as her dance lured him in. Desire pulsed, an offering to her audience....

An offering to him.

Gregor wanted to steal her away. What kind of man let the woman he wanted in his bed dance half-naked in front of other men? But to take her from this would be a sacrilege. He guessed that everyone in the audience felt the same. It was the only explanation for why they stayed in their seats. To interrupt her, to touch her, would violate the purity of her power.

She stepped side-to-side, shimmying and quivering, her simple skirt parting as if it was spelled to offer glimpses of her innermost secrets.

This dance was about temptation. It was about the primordial power that somehow lived within her, and it offered to alter his reality, to close a rift he hadn't known existed. With every circle of her hips, she rode the energy and invited his to join in.

He leaned forward, bumping his empty shot glass. It rolled down the bar. A moment passed before he thought to grab it. The bartender beat him to it.

She leaned in. "This is who Mara is. This is her power unleashed. Can you handle it, motorcycle man? If not, leave. And don't come back."

19

MARA'S ROOM measured fourteen steps from the wall to the dresser, and ten steps from the door to the edge of the poster bed. As she paced, her mage power puffed around her in a dense, tangled mess, exposed and vibrating with a need that left her feeling like a tigress in a cage.

She turned and paced toward the bed with its red satin sheets. It took a moment for her vibes to flow with her. Like a train of silk, her power spread out behind her.

She took a breath. Deep and full. Eyes closed. She was wound up...or rather wound out. Every joule floated around her, refusing to be tamed. The soft glow of her eyes refused to quit as well. She kept her face turned away from the mirror. She didn't want the reminder.

As Fancy had commanded, she'd given her audience every-thing inside her. She'd given in to the wicked temptation to let her power spin wild and free. Her body had warmed with every mage her power brushed against, ensnaring their energy just as surely as they were ensnared within hers.

The Wild West had never seen anything like her.

She took another breath and drifted her hands over the silk of her robe. It had been waiting for her, draped over the bed. Her nipples hardened, and her belly twitched as she dropped her touch lower.

Her power wanted an outlet, a companion...a victim, someone to wrap in its tangles and hold on to. By the stars, she had to wind this back in. She had to meet Gregor out front in fifteen minutes.

A knock sounded at the door.

"Wrong room!" No customers. That was part of the deal. "Go away!"

"Mara."

She halted her pacing with a hard inhale. Gregor.

His hard body. His broad shoulders.

The trim cut of his belly beneath her hands. The strength of his vibes, the security they promised.

Need quivered through her.

"I was supposed to meet you outside," she called. Her voice faltered as the implications of his presence washed over her. Dread followed in a hot wave.

Rosemary had promised she wouldn't let him in. She put her fingers to her lips. "Tell me you didn't see me," she whispered to herself.

"I can't tell you that, firefly."

She dropped her head to her hands. What had she done? "Go away, Gregor. You have to go away." She clutched her robe tight. He'd seen her naked...or as good as naked. "I've spellbound you. That's what my dance does. For your own sake, leave."

His scoff carried through the door. "There's no such thing as spellbound." He paused for a moment. "I've never seen anything as sexy and utterly lovely as you were on that stage. I wanted to toss my shirt over you and hustle you away, but another part of me was captivated." He sighed, and her vibes scattered like they could feel his breath. They were light and soft against her skin, the total opposite of shame's weight that sat against her.

"Right. That's because you were spellbound." She shook her head even though he couldn't see it. "Didn't you see what my power did to those men? It coated them in desire. Like some kind of mind trick or contamination. That's why you're here. My dance pulled you in and now it won't let you go." That's what her wayward power did fully unleashed. The knowledge of what she'd done to him slammed down. "Go away."

The door rattled as if he leaned against it. "If I were spell-bound, I'd obey your order and leave. I'm still here. We need to talk about your misperceptions regarding your power. But first, why is the key to your room on top of your door frame?"

She squinted.

Surely not....

The scrape of a key in a lock clicked through the door. The knob twisted. The door opened and his broad frame took up the doorway. "That's not very safe," he said. The look in his eyes nearly brought her to her knees—need, wanton desire. It pulsed from him.

She swallowed hard. She had to clear her throat before she could speak. "I'm sure the key was an oversight."

He slipped the key from the lock, stepped inside, and closed the door. A soft, low hum emanated from his lips and his vibes spread out over the door.

"You can't cast that *lock* spell. Fancy doesn't allow spells on this side of the house."

He narrowed his eyes. "Someone left a key up there so they could get in. The *lock* spell stays. No one's going to notice my vibes unless they try to open the door. Besides, it's all mages, all night. No Nons permitted because you put on a show that could have knocked every man in the city to his knees." He stepped forward and stroked a finger along her jawline.

His touch was a flame. Heat spread through her. But if her dance had pulled him here, what would her touch do to him?

She backed away, her legs bumping against the bed, her hand

trailing over the silk sheets. Their cool touch would delight her hot skin. A little voice whispered in her head that he would feel even better.

He stepped closer, trapping her between his body and the bed, a soft cage she could break free from.

If she wanted to.

Stars above, she shouldn't do this to him.

"Where did you get such mixed-up ideas about your power?" He tucked her hair behind her left ear. It was so familiar, so comforting. So loving.

She froze, the hot flames of need still burning, suddenly afraid that if she picked up a foot she'd step closer, not farther away. "It's not mixed-up. It's true."

Instead, he was the one who backed off. The moment his touch left, her nerves flickered against her skin as if reaching for him.

He leaned his arm high against the column of the poster bed. "All right then, who told you this truth?"

Those memories were a dark shadow woven through her soul with threads that cut if she pulled too hard. But it calmed her body's cravings enough for her to slide away, to put her beyond arm's reach.

He tilted his head and pressed his lips in a tight smile. Not a happy one, a worried one.

She averted her gaze, staring at the open vee of his buttoned-down shirt. It was nicely pressed, his jeans too, as if he were a cowboy who'd come a'courting in his finest. "Did you wear that for me?"

"I did. I'm looking to impress."

She gazed at his neck, the line of his jaw, wanting to trace her fingers over the same path. Everything her body called out for was right here waiting.

"Who, Mara? Who told you that you capture people's minds

with your vibes?" He didn't seem as distracted as she was. "Some wayward-hater?"

"Why does it matter?"

"I want to know you." The words were gruff, demanding.

She swayed on her feet, battling desire and the past. It was too hard to fight them both. "The headmaster at the school I went to." She'd never talked about it with anyone. "He told me more than once. I danced there on my first day of school." She swallowed hard. "It wasn't anything like this dance, of course," she rushed to tell him. "I was very young. It was just a silly little girl's dance. It was both the autumnal equinox and the headmaster's mageday. There was a celebration, and I joined in. After, I was forced to vow never to do that again because it was detrimental to the goodness of those around me. I tainted them."

He didn't even need to say anything. The upset at her breaking a vow trickled down his face.

"Vows are just words to me, Gregor. I didn't believe then, and I don't believe now. That's who I am."

He frowned. "I don't care about the vow." He leaned forward, wrapped his hand around her wrist and pulled. Gently. She didn't need much encouragement.

The heat of his body wafted through her robe. She imagined undoing his buttons one by one.

"Your headmaster lied to you. I am not spellbound. No one was. You had a captive audience tonight but only because they chose not to look away. Nothing more than that. But if you thought that, why did you dance tonight?"

She dropped her gaze, but even the dread at telling him couldn't cool her ardor. She fought to keep her hips still, to keep from pressing against him. She squeezed her core, trying to burn off the need. "Fancy insisted. I had to dance if I wanted a room. I didn't know that would be the deal when I left you."

She continued, talking over his angry objections, "And I wanted to do it." She hardened her tone. "I wanted to let my vibes

free. All of them. I didn't care what would happen to those men."
She lifted her chin, letting him see her defiance. "You should let
me go. You're tempting me and my morals aren't as strong as my
desire."

He put his hands low around her hips and pulled her to him.
She sucked in a tight breath at the sensations—the buttons on his
jeans, the toughness of the denim, the hard press of him beneath.

"Does Fancy know you didn't live up to your end of the deal?"

"What?" Her mind struggled to grasp the question.

"You might have been nearly naked up there with every joule
of your power on display, but you're still shielding yourself. The
next time you dance, firefly, I want it to be just for me. And I want
to see your eyes."

The truth was she danced only for herself. It was like an
offering to her own body and soul. The thought of him—only
him—witnessing it, struck a profound sense of intimacy in her.
And she wanted it. She wanted it now, as if his words had set
loose some beast in her she hadn't known existed. She wanted to
dig her claws into the sensation and hold onto it forever, to
connect herself to someone...to him...to not be so alone in
this power.

She reached out and dragged a finger down the open section
of his shirt. "Maybe I'm the one who's spellbound," she whispered. "You're a dangerous man, Gregor."

"I'm no danger to you."

She shifted her hips against him, wrapping one leg around
his, anchoring him. His hardness pressed against her core in just
the right spot. Pulling him down to her by the collar of his shirt,
she pressed her lips against his mouth. He tasted of spice and
strength and heat.

"I'm a bad influence," she whispered against his lips. She'd
skated too close to her edge and she'd fallen over it, landing in
the middle of a temptation she couldn't resist. She trailed her
fingertips against the stubble that shadowed his face.

"I love your influence." His lips tickled hers. "And your body and your vibes. They sing with such perfection that even a deaf man can hear it."

She stroked her tongue along the line of his lips. He opened his mouth beneath her gentle assault and then took control for himself. He pulled her tight, sealing his lips against hers, his tongue sliding in.

A moan escaped from her. She didn't mean to. It sounded of desperation, of absolute need. She didn't want to be this needy.

As if in response to such a traitorous thought, the pool of heat at the juncture of her legs heightened, demanding its cure.

She pulled the tie of the silky robe free. It sank down to her feet with a silent slither.

He broke their kiss and stepped back, eyeing her as if he couldn't help himself.

He growled. "I think you're sense drunk on your own vibes, firefly. If I were a gentleman, I'd leave and stand guard outside your door." His words vibrated with desire, with his power, their roughness sounding like the fabled voices of the Wild West's wolfmen.

"Your sense of honor, while admirable, is misplaced." Under his gaze, her vibes flowed faster, harder. She wondered if he could sense it.

He reached out and she jumped when he lightly set his hand against that spot between the curve of her waist and the start of her lower ribs. She felt cherished, wanted, but it was a teasing touch. Only his fingertips rested against her, and it was not enough. She guided his hand to cup her heavy breast and closed her eyes in pleasure.

"Is that what you want?" he asked, his voice low and soft. He brushed his thumbs over the hard pebbles of her nipples. Heat spiraled through the sensitive buds, almost too much to bear. She grabbed his wrists, trying to stay afloat through the pleasure. Had she ever felt so much need? It was like swimming through a newly discovered sea, its warm current pulling her along.

She'd needed to be touched for so long.

"So soft, Mara. And the prettiest sight I've ever seen."

The kindness of his words soaked into her as he stroked higher, over her shoulders. Her breasts still ached for his touch, but he traveled his hands over her neck and into her hair. He held her chin high and gazed into her eyes. Those blue eyes were dark and hot and the connection that clicked between them went to the bottom of her soul, places no one had ever seen.

An unexpected fear tangled through her that he'd see her and find her lacking, that her doubts, her past, her power were too much.

"You give me hope," he whispered. "You make me believe in me."

GREGOR PRESSED his lips against hers, a whisper of a kiss, a promise of what was to come. He'd caught the fear in her eyes, that fright that might lead to escape. More than anything, he needed her to let him cherish her, to let him keep her safe, to let him make her his. For tonight. And the next night. And the one after that.

How could he make a kiss say all that?

He opened his mouth, teasing hers to open too. He delved his tongue into her, tasting her. His need heightened as she clenched at his waist, pulling his shirt from its tuck. She ran her hands under the fabric.

He stepped back, not quite releasing her from his kiss, to wrench off his shirt. He needed to feel her skin against his. Needed inside her. He bent slightly, wrapping one arm low under her lush ass and the other at the nape of her neck. He lifted her. "Wrap your legs around me."

She obeyed. Her breasts pillowed against his chest. Her wetness smeared against his belly and his cock jumped. Goddess, that was what his fucking pants were blocking him from.

He sent a stream of vibes with a hard, fast hum toward the bedspread. The blankets and top sheet flew off as if they'd grown wings. He cast a quick glance at the remaining sheet and threw down another spell, plastering the bed with a solid layer of his vibes. Goddess only knew how clean the sheets were in a place like this.

He laid her down on the bed, her legs falling open. He swallowed hard at the sight and dropped to his knees. He pressed a kiss onto her inner thigh. Her chest rose with a deep breath, a smile playing across her lips.

He unfastened his jeans. They were tight and getting more so by the minute as her feminine scent brushed against his nose. He held back the urge to slide inside her. He wanted this to last.

More, he wanted it to be good for her. Hell, he didn't want to mess this up.

He lowered his head again and pressed a soft kiss to her clit.

She cried out and he kissed her there again, drifting a gentle finger between her lush pink lips. He circled her opening. Her heat surrounded him. "How do you like it, darling?"

"Soft. So soft. Just like that," she whispered. Her eyes were closed, feet on the bed and her knees bent, soaking up his touch and letting him worship her. He circled his finger again.

Her energy waved over him, like tiny strands in an ocean of desire. He watched her with his mage sense. Short tendrils of power danced on her skin, silky and fine. Her vibes had changed, relaxing even as her body wound tighter and hotter.

He slipped his finger into her passage and she sucked in a breath, her breasts shivering with the move. His cock hardened impossibly at his front row seat to her pleasure.

She arched up into his steady rhythm. Her sparkly, bright eyes opened under his assault. "I want you with me." Her words were so earnest he almost froze. They echoed his own heart so perfectly, words that he wanted to reflect right back at her but hadn't any hope she'd feel the same...at least not yet. Still, he wasn't sure if her words had the same meaning for her as they did for him. He was determined to win more than her body. He'd never known anyone so strong and brave, but the truth was he never would have recognized her for who she was if it hadn't been for the needle. He would have let her slip right by him. A fierceness roared through him, driving his need for her higher yet.

She scooted farther back onto the bed, moving away from his touch and propping herself on her elbows. "Take off your jeans."

He complied, stepping out of his pants and she held out her hand, beckoning him onto the bed beside her. He slid over the sheets until he was even with her. Lying back, he threaded his fingers through hers, and helped her over him.

He was so hard his cock stood up off his belly, gripped with a need so tight it hurt. He caught her hips as she lowered herself down on him, slowing with a gasp as they joined together. He fought the urge to close his eyes as her heat surrounded him. He didn't want to miss any of this.

Forcing himself to stay with her, he stared up at her. Her breasts dangled in front of him and he lifted his head to take her nipple into his mouth. She cried out, lifting her hips, stretching the connection between them until only the tip of his cock was left in her. He held her there tight, his hands clutching the back of her hips, the edge of her lush ass, and guided her down again. "My sweet firefly."

～

MARA DANCED her hips against his with an ancient rhythm as Gregor held her like he'd never let go. The madness of desire spun through her core, tighter and hotter than anything she'd ever felt.

She clutched at his arms. "I don't want this to end." The words rang with a hint of fear she didn't want him to hear.

"This is just the beginning, baby." He rolled her onto her back, taking the lead on their dance and slowing their pace, forcing her desire to hover a single spin away from the pinnacle.

He pulled back even as he dropped his forehead to hers. "My sweet Mara." He loomed over her, his cock at her opening and she strained toward it, his heat burning through her until she thought she might ignite.

The sound of her name on his lips held an intimacy, connecting her heart to him, and opening her to a vulnerability she didn't want, but once stirred up, it wouldn't be denied. She knew she was his.

He gently thrust his hips, stretching her until they were again fully connected. She wrapped her arms low around his ass and pulled him into her, lifting her hips again and setting a slow rhythm.

"That's it," he whispered. "You guide me. Just like that."

She held onto him, her fingers clenching against the muscles of his backside, moving their bodies to the tempo of her desire.

Need wrapped around her and heightened until her passion saturated her skin. Her core burst in pleasure. She cried out, her toes curling.

His shout followed as he spilled into her. Lowering one arm at a time, he lay on her chest, his cock still throbbing against her passage as aftershocks vibrated through her. He pressed a kiss against the bare skin of her shoulder.

When he gently pulled out of her, her core twitched and vibrated all over again. He put a hand on her hip, tugging her into the curve of his body.

She settled, boneless, into his embrace. Her heart swelled

with too many emotions to hold...freed by the perfection of his touch and by the connection between them.

She closed her eyes as he dragged her blanket over them, tucking it against her with its protective shields and holding her close all night long.

20

WHEN MORNING CAME, they had time for a kiss and nothing more. Gregor had woken early but he'd let her sleep, holding her. His arms had never felt stronger than they did when she was in them.

She'd left for her meeting, on her own, two minutes ago. Last night hadn't changed anything in that regard. She was still adamant about showing the world she was independent and strong. And alone. He wasn't sure he understood. Though he'd agreed to wait five minutes before he left, he left now, his pace fast and urgent.

Ten seconds earlier, the *tracker* spell that he'd put on her with her permission had gone dead. What the hell had happened? Valeska had damn well better be with her, as Mara had claimed she would.

He raced down the back stairs of the bordello—Goddess, he was in a bordello. His invisible pocket, which contained his pack, was attached to his vibes and floating within reach. As he strode past the stage, he wondered if Lincoln's spell had an expiration date. He headed toward the bar. It was deserted this early, but the air smelled like last night's booze and smoke.

The bartender sat alone at a table. A tobacco stick rested between her fingers. Its smoke drifted in streams.

"Have you seen Mara?" he demanded. Thanks to Cecilia's tracker—he still hadn't confessed that part—he knew where she was, but where the hell had his spell gone?

The bartender narrowed her eyes. "Have *you* seen Mara?" Her glare held so much power that he had to rein in his instinct to free his vibes, ready to defend himself. "Have you truly seen her, warrior mage whose songs have been claimed?"

"How did you know that?" he snapped.

She put a finger to her lips. "Shh. Secrets are best spoken in soft voices." She leaned forward. "And I know all the secrets." She took a hard inhale from the tobacco stick as if it offered a necessary strength to bear those secrets. "Mara comes to the West to be used by higher powers like everyone else. Like you, like me, even Valeska. And there's nothing you can do about it...nothing you can do to stop it. You can't hide from fate. Believe me. I keep trying. I keep failing."

"What the hell does that mean?"

"Well, good morning, you handsome stud." The madame strode in wearing a white corset, white dress slacks, and matching high heels. She spared a suspicious look for the bartender and then pivoted back to him. "I must meet the man who's caught my Mara's attention." She stopped too close to him.

He held his ground. "And you are the woman who forced Mara to dance in exchange for shelter."

"Oh my, I can feel all those vibes you've got simmering under there. Maybe Mara was the privileged one last night instead of the other way around." She tilted her head. "I like the marks on your neck. Naturally, the girl would find herself a glister-marked man. I'm not sure you left your lover satisfied though. She left earlier than I expected. She's not coming back."

He knew that. They had plans to meet outside the mill.

She smiled. "But if you're in need of attention...." She slid her hand over his groin.

He grabbed her wrist, pushing her away as a blast of her power hit him. He nearly staggered under its force before it disappeared. What the hell was that? Some kind of test to see if he could handle it? "Madame, you overstep." His words crackled with his power.

"Habit." She shrugged. "I always have business on my mind." She took her bartender's tobacco stick and sucked on it hard. Smoke curled to the ceiling. "You should know that I value Mara above all others. Truly," she added as he raised his eyebrow. "She's at the mill. You should chase after her. Do you know where it is? Four blocks west."

No, it wasn't. He fought not to react. He knew damn well the mill was east of here. The madame's vibes didn't waver with her lie. She had to be a sorceress.

And for whatever reason, she didn't want him to find Mara. He bet she was the one who'd erased his *tracker* spell. He had no idea how she'd managed it. Nor did he have time for an interrogation.

She smiled. "I wish you Luck, monk mage. He's on your side." Laughing at her own joke, she stroked her finger down the side of his neck.

He didn't knock her away. He didn't blast her with a spell. He didn't break her fingers...though all three occurred to him. Refusing to give her the pleasure of his reaction, he didn't even ask how the hell she knew his mage type.

With a curt nod to the bartender, he strode out of the house. The madame's power still lingered around him. He wanted to shower. Maybe he could find a *cleansing* potion at the train station.

He pulled out the tracker. The device was designed and manufactured by a Non-mage mobster who ran his men like a small army in the slums of Rallis Territory's capital city. The man doled out his technology for exorbitant sums to the army, police, and apparently Power United.

Mara's dot was due east. Gregor paced down the street to her location.

Thompson Mill claimed almost an entire city block, a four-story brick building. Two guards stood outside the front door. Was that normal or because of Mara? Valeska was nowhere to be seen. But the tracker indicated Mara was right where she was supposed to be, inside the mill.

Gregor strode down an alley and found a secluded spot to dart behind the building. It wasn't hard. The mill's fence was already slashed and pulled open toward the back of the lot. He ducked in. The place was empty. No cars, bikes, or horses lined the back lot, no employees on break, no shipments of fabric coming in and out. No boats on the river beyond the lot. It was as if someone had swept the place clean for him, except for the fishy scent sharp against his nose.

He opened his mage sense. Again, no whisper of power lurked. He edged along the back of the building. Large windows lined the wall, most likely the offices where Mara was. Farther down the wall, the windows were high up and wide—the factory floor, he guessed.

Overgrown bushes lined the back wall of the factory. He crouched behind them, beneath the first set of windows. His invisible pocket journeyed beside him. He double-checked the weapons lining his belt. Three knives, two *stop-'em-dead* potions, and his gun. He stretched his mage sense wider. Bits of sound waved through his vibes—the river's slap against the bank, the harsh hum of the weaving machines, the shouts of the workers.

"You should consider sending a normal the next time, Miss Rand." The man spoke from inside the building.

The pair was in the office above him.

"I thought we'd passed the formal part of this relationship. I used to be Mara."

"It's not safe for sorceresses here anymore. Even a normal like me has heard that rumor. Although if I weren't in the weaving business, I might not have paid attention. Hire a courier next time."

"That wasn't an option," Mara's voice was calm and smooth, every inch the confident businesswoman.

"The last sorceress I hosted in my office was removed by uninvited Black Skull members." The man's words carried a hard bite. "I wove your threads today as a courtesy to Fancy, one that I will not extend again."

Gregor could hear Mara suck in a hard breath. "I certainly do not want to bring any danger to you or your employees—"

"You do that simply by being here." His whisper was sharp like he was trying to conceal their conversation. "Hence my messenger asking for your yarn last night."

"How did you know where I was?"

"Really, Miss Rand. It wasn't difficult." Scorn lined his voice. "Sexiest sorceress in the West? One night only?"

Gregor could imagine her blush.

"You figured it out yet?" Daegan's voice bounced against his ears and blurred out Mara's response.

Gregor jerked around, readied his vibes, seeking the man's location.

"Over here, you idiot." Daegan's boat drifted into view on the river, far away, though his voice sounded as if he were right next to him.

Ice formed in Gregor's veins. His teeth chattered in the sudden winter of his fear.

Daegan shook his head. "You've got to stop being scared of us."

"I'm not fucking scared of you!" He sent the words in a wicked *sound* spell that smacked against the fairy's chest as he stood on the deck of his shitty boat.

Daegan stumbled back. "I'm trying to help." The fairy held out his hands.

"By giving away my hiding place?" The nausea that rose in his gut was not helpful. Nor was it necessary. The damn fairy was a long sprint away. There was no way Daegan could catch him if Gregor didn't let him. "Go the fuck away."

"I'm not giving anything away. You're the only one who can see me. Now, the weapon. The unsung song. Have you conquered a glister's power? Have you listened to your heart and heard the song?"

"Listened to my heart?" He floundered for a moment, unsure what to even say to that. "What kind of man actually asks that? I can't hear songs, asshole. Why don't you go sing it if it's so damn important?"

"I can't." Daegan's tone might have held regret. "I don't know what it sounds like. But I know it exists. And I know you have all the qualifications to hear it."

The fairy was full of shit.

"I also know you will never be able to protect her until you do it." Daegan shook his head. "Your mage power is not enough to save her. It will never be enough."

"Mage power is all I have." By the Goddess, he hated fairies.

Daegan's raft pulled away. "Try, mage. Don't let us all fall because of your stubborn fear. By the way, you've got trouble coming around the corner. Don't know how you're going to get her out of this one." He drifted down the river without a glance back.

"What kind of trouble?" He wrapped the furious question in a spell and tossed it like a mageball at the man's head. Daegan ignored it.

A knock on the door from somewhere inside the building yanked his attention back to Mara.

"Sir, there's a mage here," a woman said. The secretary, probably.

"Send him away." The derision in the words was thick.

"It's a woman. And she's not here for you. She's here for the sorceress."

Fast footsteps tapped against the floor.

"Sage?" Mara asked. "What's wrong?"

"They're coming for you."

Gregor recognized the bartender's voice.

He focused his mage sense—listening, sensing, ready to defend. He wished his mage power had come with vision enhancement like ghostsight mages who could see through walls.

Energy vibed into his sense. A half-dozen mages, each with his own frequency pinging against him, were marching down the side of the building, exactly where he'd ducked through the fence. Sure enough, six...no, seven men strode into the lot. Their black leather clothes and dangerous vibes were instantly familiar though they'd left behind their signature goggles. Gregor didn't recognize any of them.

They strode closer, no rush, just confidence. They ignored their surroundings, their false sense of superiority blinding them to threats as if no one would dare oppose them.

They were wrong.

From inside the building, Sage explained. "The Black Skulls." Panic wracked her words. "They came back to talk to Fancy. They know you're here. They're coming around the back." The words were rushed, tripping over each other.

"Did you see Gregor out front?" Mara's voice was as focused as he was. "He needs to know."

He wanted to puff up his chest with pride at her calm readiness. His heart thumped at her concern for him.

"And what about Valeska?" she continued.

"Valeska?" Sage cried. "I have no idea where she is. And your man wasn't out there either."

Behind the building, the Skulls moved into place, covering the back entrance like they were expecting a small army.

"Get your cloth and get out," Thompson demanded from inside the building.

Gregor shuffled quietly to the edge of the shrubbery, casting a gentle *don't look* as he went. The spell pushed away from him, crawling through the air as he made his way to the corner. His cast would tug the men's vibes away from him, drawing their attention to the far side of the building, but it wasn't foolproof. It was too weak for guarantees. He couldn't risk a stronger spell. Any strong cast would attract the attention of experienced mage fighters even if it were designed to do the exact opposite.

He broke out of the bushes and turned the corner. Out of sight, he sprinted to the front. It was a risk. If this had been his mission, he would have spotters around the entire perimeter of the building. But he'd plow through them to get to Mara.

The street was crowded, more so than a few minutes ago. The train station sat at the end of the road, and a train had come in recently, spewing its passengers everywhere—the same train he and Mara were scheduled to leave on shortly.

City-goers heaved luggage and travel bags up and down the street. Guns sat at most hips, a part of the Wild West uniform. Considering the number of Nons present, he didn't dare cast another spell. He'd face a shower of bullets. He couldn't defend against so many guns. This held every possibility of disaster.

He would have to fight his way out with as few vibes as possible, or the Nons on this street would morph into an army of enemies.

He made for the mill's front door dodging one pedestrian after the other, caught in a stream of travelers heading toward the train. He fought the urge to blast them out of the way.

One of Prophet's men rounded the other side of the building and sprinted up the steps of the mill.

Mara opened the door right into his arms.

21

A WIDE, evil grin greeted her. Mara stumbled to a stop along with every nerve in her body, but it was too late. Her speed thrust her straight into the man's arms...and into his cruel anticipation and sinister joy. It wrapped around her as tightly as his muscled arms.

"Gotcha, girl." He laughed as if it were all so simple.

A misplaced sense of bitterness rose in her. Just like that, she could be caught? He wasn't even supposed to be here. Hadn't Sage said they'd be out back? Mara's confusion weakened her reaction, and the man moved to throw her over his shoulder. It was pure luck that she yanked in the opposite direction at the right time, throwing them both off balance. Her heavy backpack, strapped to both shoulders and full of cloth, helped her cause.

Past her kidnapper's shoulder, she could see the crowd on the street move in a noisy, blurry wave away from the building. None of them would help her, but where was Gregor?

She struggled, her arms pinned to her sides. This time, the man pulled her hard into his chest and dragged her toward the street. Her spindle banged uselessly at her side.

As she dug in the toes of her hiking boots, she punched the

edge of her fist into his thigh, but she couldn't reach the target she really wanted. He didn't even grunt at her efforts.

"Take your hands off her!" Gregor. He stood at the corner of the building, gun raised.

Shouts of fright erupted from the crowded street. Her assailant spun her around to face Gregor's gun, but she made an awkward shield with her pack.

He let go of her right arm, going for his own gun. She pulled the top of her spindle high enough in its sheath to freely move it. With all her might, she jammed it into the man's shin.

She instantly hit boot, but the force was enough to hurt. He screamed.

Gregor was at her side before he shut up. Her would-be kidnapper fell back. His chin whipped high with Gregor's swift punch and then he crumpled over with a knee to the groin. Two more blows and he fell to the side and didn't get up.

She was still staring at his prone form as Gregor yanked her away from the mill. Her lungs seemed to have shrunk in the scuffle and she panted for air.

"We're getting out of this, firefly, but we have to move." He hustled her down the street. The buildings passed in a blur. "We get to the train and get the hell out of here."

On cue, the train whistle blew.

They dashed down the street, pressing into the crowd. There were so many faces and bodies her mind couldn't process them all. Each was a threat. Panic clung to her skin.

As Gregor shoved through, people hollered at their rudeness, leaving a clear signal for their pursuers. Her pack jostled on her shoulders. Sweat didn't get a chance to drip before the pack smashed against the forming droplets, soaking them against her shirt. Their boots pounded against the brick road. The uneven surface grabbed at her footing every chance it got.

Gregor dashed in front of her with a single step and turned to face the buildings on her left, almost running sideways. Outlaws rounded the corner, guns in hand. Gregor's shots rang out before they could aim.

She bit back a scream.

He tugged on her hand. "Keep moving. All we have to do is get to that station."

One job. She could focus on that. She stared at the station as if it might move if she looked away, but then another line of thugs came at them from the right.

She reached with a shaky hand and pulled her spindle free. The potion on the end was good for three uses or so the potion-ness had claimed. She'd already used it once. And there were five outlaws...no, six...heading her way. She sucked in as much of a breath as their sprint and her panic would let her.

Gregor switched sides again, protecting her with his body. "Run, Mara. Cast a *don't look* and sprint to the train."

"Can't! Not my type of spell! Too many Nons around to risk it anyway." The Nons in this town would not stand for mage battles in their streets.

But he didn't heed her warning. He hummed low in his throat. The essence of him surrounded her as his *don't look* spell locked onto her. "Go!" he ordered.

Another hum of his vibes, louder and more forceful, and he formed a shield. He was revealing his mage power and it was going to cost him in a city dominated by Nons. She'd seen mages gunned down for less and left to rot in the streets.

"Get to the train, Mara." His voice spoke in her ear, the words dashing at her, as he turned to face their attackers, tossing spells at them.

"Come with me!" she cried.

"Soon. Now go. I'll find you." He shoved his vibes at her, forcing her down the street.

A sob choked her, lodging in her throat, as she left him behind.

Gunshots cracked out, their noise muffled and echoing at the same time.

She looked back. Gregor was surrounded. Light flashed with a spell. It glinted off the knife in his hand. One mage fell to the ground and then another.

He backed down the street, drawing the men off her trail. She almost called out as he vanished around the corner.

She swallowed a cry and ran on, promptly bumping into someone. The man squinted, unable to see her thanks to the *don't look*. He fled, running in the opposite direction, and she made for the train station as fast as her pack would let her. The sound of her breath mixed with the sloshing of the pack and the pounding of her footsteps. Someone was going to hear her, but she didn't have time to be quiet.

Three more blocks. Every building seemed to stretch longer. She dodged right, missing another unsuspecting pedestrian by a thread.

A horse with two riders ambled straight for her. Another dodge. The animal's musky scent blew into her nose as she took a smack to her face with its tail.

The train station awaited, now a block and a half away. Five columns held up the front of the stone building like a row of teeth ready to consume the coming passengers.

All of a sudden, Sage appeared from between the last of the two buildings on the block. "Mara."

"You can see me?" Mara skidded to a stop. It was either that or run her over.

"Don't trust him." She looked right and left, her eyes wide and desperate. "Your motorcycle guy...I saw him take a check from the Power United man."

"What Power United man?" Mara's voice snapped with fright...and impatience. They had more urgent matters. "There's a mage battle heading this way. Black Skulls. Get out of here!"

"Listen to me. You can't trust your lover."

"I do trust him." The words were automatic. "Gregor used to work for Power United. But he doesn't anymore."

"Then explain the check," Sage demanded.

A group of leather-clad outlaws raced at them. Mara froze. By the lost girls, she was caught. Her feet were ice. "Run, Sage!" She could barely talk through her frozen lips.

The other woman disappeared between two buildings. Mara braced herself for their hit. If the bartender could see her, then they could too. Instead, they looked right through her and sprinted on. The wind from their speed blew her hair. Gregor's spell still held.

She'd been given a second chance. She couldn't waste it.

She forced her feet to move, tiptoeing at first, as if a full stride was too bold a move and would attract the gaze of fate. But gentleness wouldn't save her. She took a breath and ran.

One block remained before the station. It was an abandoned lot, and she steered clear of its edge. The lot, heavily wooded with thin, tall trees, was haunted by a lost tribe of river maidens and the ghosts of the mages who'd tried to trap them two centuries ago. The legend was common knowledge in the city.

Posts stood at each corner sporting *No Trespassing* signs.

As she readied to cross the busy street to the station, a flicker of white waved along the side of the small, forbidden woods.

She turned.

Lacy silk gleamed in the sunshine. Its picot-point ends fluttered in a non-existent breeze. She blinked. She'd made that scarf two days ago. Had it only been two days? She stepped over and caught it, the cool silk slipping through her hands. What was this doing here?

Footsteps shuffled behind her. Dropping the scarf, she spun around. Her pack bumped against the thin trees.

An outlaw stood six feet away, blocking her path to the station. A Black Skull tattoo was drawn in stark lines on his neck, the same spot where Gregor bore the needle's scars.

Closing his eyes, he sniffed and held out his hands, scenting her out. A howl rumbled from his throat as he lifted his head.

A wolfman.

Her legs went weak.

The legends about them were almost as bad as the woods that stood at her back. In all her trips west, she'd never encountered one. Suddenly, she longed for the safety of the Republic. But truly, there was no safety there either. Not for her.

She was lost. Lost to the train and its path to freedom. Lost to Gregor and his promise to find her.

Soon, he'd said.

Not anymore. She felt their chance at a future slip away from her like silk threads blowing on the wind.

The wolfman paced forward. His nostrils flared. He snapped his teeth in her direction. "Found you, bitch." The words were a growl.

She did the only thing she could.

Pinned between a wolfman and the forbidden land, she turned and stepped into the woods.

A THOUSAND SLIM, green trees stretched out wide and long as if space expanded inside the block's borders. It held a different world. The sun's light danced among the sparse canopies, lending a bright yellow to the hue surrounding her. The color gave the impression of saplings in spring. It was all false. They'd been standing for over two hundred years.

Mara pivoted to face the street. The outlaw stood on the other side of the trees. Only a few layers of thin, pale green trunks separated them. "I see you," he taunted.

Gregor's *don't look* had worn off.

Baring his teeth, almost a smile, he howled again. Victory echoed in the sound. "I got her!"

"Then grab her already!" Another man approached. He had curly red hair and a beard and mustache to match. He slowed his sprint at her imminent capture.

The outlaw reached in with a dirty hand. She scrambled back, a desperate moan gurgling in her throat as she moved deeper into the deadly territory. The stories about this place rarely included people coming out alive.

He followed her inside the tree line, the leer on his face encircled by long stringy hair that hadn't seen enough *shampoo* potion. His teeth were yellow and sharpened to points. The wolfmen in the High Councilor's tapestry looked much more well-kept.

"Hey, Stephens! You find her in there?" the red-haired man called from the street, squinting like he couldn't see them.

As if the world whispered some signal to the forest, the leaves and branches shivered and rustled. The sound was like a thousand ghosts hushing the mournful and forlorn. Goosebumps prickled along her spine as the trees seemed to creep closer, stepping forth on legs and reaching with hands. A solid mass of green stood all around her. Like the red-haired man on the other side of the trees, she could see nothing else. She was surrounded.

A low muffle of protest and a shout of pain sounded in front of her and then silence. With another shiver, the mass of green disappeared. The trees once again stood in their proper places. The street was just beyond, the train station on its other side. She might have imagined it all.

But her pursuer was gone.

Outside the trees, another red-headed man had joined the first. Brothers, she thought. Their sharp, beaked noses matched, too. "Where'd Stephens go?"

Brother One squinted into the trees. Judging by his side-to-side movements, he couldn't see her anymore.

This land was full of power, and now it blocked her from them.

"Gone," he said. "Can't believe he went in. Stupid man. You know the stories about this place."

"Of course he went in. That's his job." Brother Two looked around and then nodded toward the street. "Lordan! Get over here!" Another outlaw jogged over. Brother Two grabbed the white scarf from the branch. "I'm knotting this around your belt loop. You go in as far as you can. See what you can see. I'll pull you out."

"Yes, sir." Lordan was a fool.

This time the forest let her see. The scene played before Mara like a story come to life—otherworldly and horrific.

The man came through the trees. He looked around, his eyes widening and mouth gaping, as if everything he saw terrified him. But Mara saw only green trees and the city beyond.

Lordan's gaze passed over her as if she were invisible. Shadowed clouds coalesced between them, gathered from nothing, until he almost disappeared in the fog. His scream echoed as the cloud molded into a mass of women, translucent and wispy—the ghosts of the river maidens. Their naked shapes got lost each time they moved into the sunlight.

Another long scream and a shuffle of clothes, a hard crack—was that bone?—and then the cloud disappeared.

Like before, the outlaw was gone.

"What do you see?" the first brother called, his tone impatient.

Mara cried out, a quiet, quick noise that held her own terror. She tripped over her feet as she backed up. But her stumble was abruptly halted as she bumped into the sturdy softness of a person, cold and wet. She spun, her scream dying before it could form.

The river maiden queen stood in the forest. Around her, the trees had parted as if they walked on their roots, clearing the area around her, framing her naked body. A path behind her stretched deeper into the woods.

The light trickling through the trees played beneath the queen's skin. Translucent rainbows flashed in muted colors. Her irises glowed blue and silver, the colors moving in a current, waving in and out. They were so large there was little white left in her eyes. Her pale skin dripped with water as if she'd just stepped out of her bath or a pool...or the river.

"A safe course lies this way, mistress." Her voice was in multiple pitches and played through the air as if more than one person spoke.

Mara stepped back, a fresh shot of fright coursing through her. She tried to control it, to act normal so she didn't spook the river maiden queen. One boat trip across the river hardly qualified them as friends and the creature wasn't known for leaving her findings alive.

Mara pointed behind her. Her hand shook. "There was another man just there. Two men, actually. Do you know where they are?" Her voice was too high, too fast.

"Your course lies this way," the queen repeated, pointing in the other direction from Mara.

She shook her head. "I need to go this way to get to the train. I'm meeting someone there, the mage who crossed over with Daegan. I need to get out of here." She looked toward the street, but there were only trees now. Surely that was the right direction. Where had the road gone?

"It's not in my power to leave, mistress."

"Is it in my power? Can I leave?" The words dashed out, claustrophobia dancing on their heels. Mara spun toward the street. She stomped through the trees, determined to march to freedom. She *would* get out of here.

Step after step led only to more green saplings that reached so high they should have drooped over. The road that had been just a short distance away remained hidden.

The river maiden queen walked beside her in silence. Her pace was calm and sedate. Mara's was frantic. Water dripped from the queen's skin and sweat dripped from Mara's. As they progressed, trees moved out of their way, but Mara did not reach the forest's edge. By now she should be past the train station and walking on the tracks out of the city.

She was trapped. There was no way out.

The river queen looked over when Mara stopped as if waiting for her to lead.

Where exactly was she to go? Mara slipped off her spectacles, pocketed them, and let her mage power flood around her.

The river queen inhaled sharply, the gills along her neck snapped closed. Her shoulders sank down as if relieved though her expression was unchanging.

With her mage sight in place, the thin tree saplings disappeared. Enormous white glister oaks stood in place of the whip-thin green trees, giants born from a cocoon of premature saplings. Mara gasped. Wonder and impossibility settled around her. Like the wolfman, she'd seen this before too...the grand forests were depicted in one of the High Councilor's tapestries. But the glister oaks were supposed to be extinct.

She looked up. The tops of the trees stretched higher than she'd ever imagined. She blinked at the motionless clouds above that erased the bright blue of the sunny day. Another blink and she saw the truth. Those weren't clouds. The trees' canopies blossomed across the entire sky in a span of pure white too stalwart to blow in the breeze.

Mara looked beyond the ancient woods toward the train station and found she was only feet from the edge of the forest. Out there, Gregor jogged up the station's steps and disappeared inside. Then Cecilia, of all people, strode up to the building. The two bounty hunters from the train walked on either side of her. They didn't have their AWOL sorceress. They were going home empty-handed.

Thank the lost girls for that.

Directly outside the trees, the red-headed brothers still waited though Mara felt like she'd been in here forever, walking miles. The forest's power played with her perceptions.

The brother on the right held the scarf. Its pointy hem was gone, a ragged curve left in its place as if someone had taken a bite out of it. Blood soaked it.

Mara clamped her hands over her mouth. She backed away, one small step at a time.

Brother Two eyed the scarf as if it might devour him. "What the fuck! Is he dead? Does that mean she's dead? Damn it all!"

"That could explain why the tracker isn't working." Brother One held up a rectangular box, smaller than his hand.

Brother Two scowled. "What the hell is that?"

"Tracker tech. I've seen this stuff once before. The other guy must've put it on her. The receiver fell outta his pocket when he was on the run."

"The other guy? Her boyfriend?"

"Some boyfriend, huh? I picked it up. But it stopped working when she went in here." Brother One turned the device over. An emblem marked its back. Mara could see it through the trees. It was a picture of a wire wrapped around a bolt of lightning. Its gold paint shined against the black of the device.

Power United.

Gregor had been tracking her with Power United equipment.

Betrayal stabbed her with its sharp spikes.

"Shit." Brother Two grabbed the tracker and tossed it into the trees.

22

THE POWER of the ancient glister forest played around Mara, picking up tendrils of her energy and fluttering in circles like streamers on a Maypole. Time and space frolicked here too, shaking off their ridged confines and basking in the magic. They danced around her, flying out of reach.

Mara sat against the thick trunk of a white glister oak tree. She should get up, she thought. But she felt anchored here. An odd sense of fragile safety had settled around her. She'd been seeking safety at one point. When had that been? Before her heart broke or after? She'd been here for so long now, hadn't she? Accuracy was beyond her grip. Just like her mage power. It hovered, free and easy, as if it had never been tucked away, as if it would never know captivity again.

Somewhere at the edge of her consciousness, the train whistle blew.

Two blasts.

Was the train only now moving out? Was that possible? Or had days passed and a half-dozen trains come and gone?

Did it matter?

No one could get to her here. Not Power United's bounty

hunters or the Black Skulls. Not Cecilia with her vindictive campaign against her.

Not Gregor...who'd lost his tracker.

How had her life spun so out of control?

"The forest...it will keep you, mistress, if you wish it." The river maiden's queen bowed her head. "Housed and fed with its power."

As she spoke, pale pink berries grew up from the soil on a thin vine.

"If I eat it...." Mara's voice faded.

"It will nourish you."

She picked one and put it in her mouth. The sweetest taste flooded her senses.

"I should go home," she whispered. But there, she had to hide and keep her mage energy wound up tight. Here, her power had unraveled. Uninhibited. Free.

Strong.

"Why do I feel like this here?" she asked though she wasn't certain her companion would know the answer.

The river maiden lifted her gaze, moving with the grace of an underwater dancer. "Glister land calls forth true self."

"I feel drunk." But it was more than that. Her power floated, barely tethered to her. One snip of a thin thread and she'd never tame it again. She was unrestrained and unchecked. "Is that the true me?"

"Your power is potent." The river maiden queen held out her arms and tipped her head back as if she pulled it into her and savored it. "The finest blood."

"Are you going to eat me?" Somewhere in the back of her mind, she cared about the answer.

"Never." She tilted her head at Mara, her brow pinched and puzzled. "The forest blossoms for the brave and honorable. For others"—she shrugged—"it does not do this." Her harmonic voice flowed as if she stood beneath her river and not in the air. "Not many dare to walk it now."

"What about those men?"

"They were not brave."

Mara wasn't brave either though she was grateful the glister land had a different opinion. Regardless, she did have to go back home. Her sorceresses waited. She stood.

The river maiden queen gestured deeper into the woods, away from the city. "The current flows this way."

With no more than a few steps, Mara found herself in front of a small, white sailboat bobbing in a minuscule pool of water. Its sail was delicate white lace. The tiny craft was carved with intricate swirls and ripples as if it mirrored the river. It had a regal allure. Neither the boat nor the pool had been there a moment before.

The river queen touched her wet hair with her webbed fingers, and the scarf suddenly appeared draped over her head. No blood marred the fabric. It was perfectly repaired as if it had stepped back in time. A neat trick.

"I will take you to the brother." The queen turned and paced toward her boat. She walked into the small body of water and sank down as if it were a bottomless pool.

The small craft bobbed back and forth, beckoning Mara to climb aboard.

"Who's the brother?"

But the river maiden had descended beneath the water.

She looked back in the direction of the train station. She was alone. No allies. No city beyond the trees.

If she ever let herself cry, this might have been the time for tears. But the futility of tears had been hammered home early. She'd given them up long ago.

Tossing her pack into the front of the boat, she took the single seat.

The small craft shoved forward and picked up speed. The

wind pressed her back. The trees passed her by and gave way to an ethereal cloud, glistening like stars, stretched and swirling. In seconds, the scenery changed into a wide river, the land around it vast, rolling with hills and dotted with stands of woods. The air was hot and the sun high, burning the blue sky to white. The boat slowed without a lurch, bobbing along leisurely.

In the distance ahead, a train raced along tracks, its rumble a persistent whisper. It barreled on, traveling into a sparse wood. Far away, birds took flight from their resting places on leafy branches as the train's noise disturbed their peace. The train was a flicker, darting between hills and trees.

Was that the train she was supposed to be on? Was Gregor on board? Did he know she wasn't? Where was the other part of the tracking device? The part attached to her? She had no idea what it was called. She brushed her arms and legs and ran her fingers over her scalp but found nothing. How could he have done that to her?

The cloudy veil of stars descended again bringing silence with it as if someone had cast a *mute* spell. The boat surged forward.

No one in the Republic would ever admit that the glister might have fantastical abilities. They believed the glister had nothing worth coveting. But no mage in existence could do this. Skipping through the land was dazzling...and highly convenient, assuming the destination was correct.

Once again, the cloud dissipated. The scenery re-formed, and a sigh of relief tumbled from her chest.

Daegan stood waiting for her on his ferry on the Mississippi's west bank, the same place where the river queen had let her off to catch the train. Was that still only two days ago?

Mara's small craft came to a graceful halt next to the ferry and held still like the maiden had paused the current.

He sucked in a breath. "You've been in the forest. It's left its mark on you."

The maiden lifted her head from the water, and she and Daegan shared a stare, some silent communication passing between them.

The queen turned to Mara, bowed her head, and disappeared beneath the water.

Mara scrambled up, heaving her pack to Daegan, before the maiden decided she wanted her boat back. The boat tossed side to side with her clumsy efforts, but Daegan pulled her out with a strong hand.

Standing on his ferry, Mara eyed the Republic across the river. How would she find the strength to stand up to everything that land held? Maybe she should have stayed in the forest. "Are you the river maiden's brother?" Her words were flat and tired.

"She spoke to you." He studied her, his face tight. "And no, I'm not her brother. Where's the mage?" His eyes swirled with silver, but they lacked the usual threat, their twirl slow and casual.

"On the train, I presume." Her voice felt fragile. If she said too much, it might break. *She* might break.

Daegan frowned and looked up at the grassy bank as if he might see the train and the mage in question. "Why is he not with you?"

She leaned against the boat's railing, her body heavy. Betrayal ought to weigh down its perpetrator, not its victim. "How well do you know him?"

"I know his heart."

She was so shocked she almost laughed. "And what do glister know of hearts?" Perhaps if she'd been more levelheaded, she wouldn't have said it so coldly.

"What do you know of hearts, Mara Rand, who's never bothered to love?" His retort kicked at her chest.

"I loved once." Her shrill words stirred a small rabbit in the bank's tall grass. Frightened, it fled, sprinting. Smart creature. She could never move, much less sprint, when fear crept forth, much like now. The memories threatened to freeze her. "And it nearly killed me."

"Because you were a stupid girl."

"Well, maybe I'm still that stupid girl. Maybe I'd still fall for a guy who only wants to sell me to the highest bidder." Her fear came tumbling out of her mouth and she wanted to eat the words right back up and never let them see the light of day much less the inside of her head. She didn't even want to think them. Her throat ached, seizing up, and she gasped for a breath that sounded too much like a sob.

"I think you can spot a bounty hunter at a hundred paces now, even with your power wrapped up tight and those fucking spectacles. If you were wearing them right now, I think I'd rip them off."

She hardly registered his comment. "What if he's one of them and I can't see it?" She thrust out her hands. "He has connections to Power United and they keep cropping up. He works for them. He was tracking me!"

Daegan lifted a disapproving eyebrow. "Perhaps because you run away from him?"

She flinched. Whose side was he on?

"A glister-marked would never be a bounty hunter," he said. "And if one dared, we would take care of that. We would not stand for one of the marked to hurt sorceresses."

Sorceresses were the mothers of the original glister if one believed the stories. But every sorceress avoided that connection.

Mara avoided most connections in life.

What do you know of hearts? Daegan's question reverberated around her. Did she know her own heart? Her focus was on surviving. It was hard to look inward when the outside world stampeded forward with derision and judgment, censure and rules. She had constructed a well-weathered shield and embodied it inside and out.

She patted the pocket that housed her spectacles.

Gregor was right. She hadn't given Fancy what she'd bargained for. She'd danced and her power had swelled through the space, delighting herself and her audience. But she'd covered her eyes, hiding behind a curtain of her own making.

She'd shut herself away. Somewhere she'd lost hope that she'd live any freer than she'd started out in life, though perhaps she'd never had such hope to begin with. Yet she'd spent years trying to push beyond the wall that mage culture had built around the wayward, the weak, and the imperfect. She'd wanted to knock it down a few stones and climb over. But who was she to wave hope around, a scarf of silky promise, to hold it high and show the people in the discard bin that there was possibility and potential? She certainly didn't live up to her own.

Along the bank, a bird with a wingspan as wide as she was tall took off and flew over the river. Its gray wings tilted, turning its sleek body to glide over the steel-colored water. Its fast flight took it far down the river, but it stayed crystal-clear to her eyes, and she watched it soar.

"You don't have to go back," Daegan said.

She nodded slowly, cognizant of her vibes fluffing around her. In a way, he was right. She couldn't go back to the way things were. Not anymore. Not ever again.

She studied the brilliant blue of the sky that swept wide and everlasting, above and beyond her sight, gracing both east and west. The sun lifted high, reaching its peak, casting the vast depths of the universe behind it invisible...but not forgotten. "The Rose Moon is coming. Since you know the prophecies, I assume you're aware that's the supposed deadline for all this." She felt the moon's pull behind the spotlight of the sun. She felt its threat. "Considering everything that's happened to me lately, my luck is not going to hold out forever."

Daegan raised an eyebrow at her. "You can rest easy in that." His voice was full and certain. "Luck will always hold out for you."

She dropped her gaze to the water. He was talking about his god. She was talking about chance.

She took one.

She pulled her spectacles out of her pocket, reached back, and tossed them as far as she could into the Mississippi. Her shield fell away without a splash.

23

THE STAINED GLASS windows of her house were dark and dim. No light shined behind them. Mara eyed the place as she drove past, blinking wearily. She was exhausted despite staying in a hotel last night. She'd hoped to be well-rested for the drive across the Republic. That had been a waste of money.

To her tired eyes, her house looked intact. She wouldn't have put it past the women of the High Councilor's receiving chamber to have cast *rock* or *graffiti* spells against it because of their fear of her spider silk cloth. Then again, those high-society types probably would have hired underlings for such activities, unwilling to enter her low-class neighborhood. It was close to the Drainpipe, where the dark mages lived.

A push of vibes tingled against her ear. It was the tenth time... maybe the eleventh. Somehow Gregor had found her calling card connection, and he'd been ringing her since she'd crossed back into the Republic.

"Mara." Gregor's voice was close. Too close. He'd cast that word directly to her ear, not through a calling card. Could he see her?

A slow burn of anger built as she pictured him inside her

house staring through the stained glass windows. That was as high-handed as putting Power United tracker tech on her.

She sped up, her car squealing through the last two turns to get to her carriage house. Gravel crunched as she pulled into the alley that bisected the block. She parked her car in its spot, grabbed her pack, got out, and kicked the door shut. Four paces later, she turned back to get her purse.

She'd left the thing sitting on the passenger seat.

Again.

With a swirl of her finger, she caught a thread of power, simple and easy, and spun out vibes to close the large carriage door and open the smaller one—person-sized, not vehicle-sized —that led into her gated backyard. She'd never used her power for those simple actions, and it felt brave and bold. And she needed brave and bold to face Gregor.

He stood on her back porch—not inside her house. He must have spied her over the fence as she drove past the front. She faced him with her glowing eyes and swallowed down her heart that had lodged in her throat. She let anger bubble up in its place. That was much easier to handle.

"I've been so worried." Lines traced his temples. His jaw was shadowed with golden whiskers. His shirt was rumpled. "You weren't on the train. I couldn't find you."

She stopped on the stone path that led up to the porch steps, needing to maintain distance between them. "I imagine it's tough to find a person when you drop your tracker," she snapped. "You should be more careful with your Non-mage tech. I don't think your employer will appreciate you losing it."

He sucked in a slow breath. Remorse ran down his face. "It was a back-up. A necessary one considering what we'd already encountered. The madame destroyed the *tracking* spell I put on you before you left for the mill."

She squinted. Her face felt tight. "Why would Fancy do that?"

"I would guess she wanted me off your trail so the Skulls could take you."

Fancy's betrayal was yet another layer in all this, but she couldn't get her mind around it, too distracted by the hurt of Gregor and his tracker.

He held out his hands. "The tracker tech was all I had left."

"Thanks to Power United! How could you do that to me? After everything I told you. Do you work for them?" She was shouting. She never shouted.

He pulled his fingers through his hair. "I should have told you. I'm sorry. But I knew you'd say no." He looked at her from the porch, his lips parted, his face tight. He didn't come down the steps. Maybe he needed distance too. "The tracker helped keep you safe. If I hadn't used it, you would have faced that bounty hunter on the train alone."

So much had happened between now and then that it took her a moment to remember that awful encounter.

"He would have had you in his cuffs and carted you off. Without that tracker, I never would have been able to find you fast enough."

She shivered as the memory crept up her spine.

He combed his fingers through his hair again, leaving it spiky and scattered. "I can't even think about what would have happened then, but you can be damn sure I would have tracked you down."

She knew exactly what would have happened. She'd lived it once. Though Nils had been right there, he wouldn't have been able to save her. Not without blowing his cover. He'd never risk that.

"You can call it deceptive or high-handed," he said. "And you'd be right. But nothing I've done to keep you safe has worked. You've got enemies coming from every direction. I haven't stopped one of them from getting their hands on you. Bounty hunters on a train, Black Skulls in the middle of the Wild West and then again outside the mill, and"—a fast shield of vibes formed around them blocking out the neighborhood's sounds —"threats from our own government, too."

His spell disintegrated as quickly as it formed. "Of all the people in the world, it's you that I want to keep safe. And I'm failing. Mara"—his voice softened—"you gave me my hope back. I'm damn well going to do everything possible to protect you. Hence, the tracker. Like it or not." His eyes held worry, his face haggard, but she didn't offer him any solace. She didn't want protection. Though even as she thought it, she knew it wasn't quite right. She didn't want to *need* protection.

"You never answered my question about your employment."

His gaze sharpened. "I can explain. But I need more time than we have right now. I just need you to trust me on this."

That was answer enough.

She stomped up the steps ready to tell him exactly where he could put his plea for trust. But then she saw the pillow on the porch floor. Beside it was the blanket she'd given him, wadded up. He'd slept on her porch last night while she'd stayed in a hotel after crossing the Mississippi. Was he that desperate to find her? He would have been better off searching the roads. Surely he knew that, but she didn't bother asking.

She unlocked her door with the key. This was the last time she'd use it. She'd cast a *lock* spell from now on. If the neighbors didn't like seeing her eyes glow, then they shouldn't look.

As she'd driven home, she'd gotten horrified looks from every bounder mage at the territory checkpoints between the Wild West and here. Two had tried to stop her, but they were powerless against her citizenship card.

"Wait, Mara. Can we just talk for a minute longer?" His shoulders went crooked again.

Some part of her begged to say yes. But she could still see the Power United emblem glistening on the back of that device. "Did Nils give you the tracker?"

He looked away and sighed hard and short as if the question made him mad. But she knew him well enough to realize it was the answer that angered him. "Cecilia did."

Of course. She gave a bitter laugh at the new betrayal. Her chest hurt from its sharp stab. Gregor knew the woman was no friend of hers. How could he have accepted Cecilia's offering? She was full of greed and vengeance and nothing more. "How long had she been tracking me? Is she still?"

"I don't know. On either count." A desperate regret pulled at his face.

She knew that feeling, wanting to beg for forgiveness and knowing it would never come. Carrying that burden was a never-ending punishment. She was quite familiar with it. Whether it was weak or not, she didn't really want to do that to him, but she couldn't puzzle it out now.

"I have to get the cloth to the mill. I really don't have time for this." She pressed her lips tight as she turned her back on him and stepped inside. She paused for a moment, her heart fluttering like a tiny bird in its last throes, and then she closed the door, forcing herself to keep moving.

Dropping her keys into the bowl on the counter, she slung her purse over the back of a kitchen chair and left the pack on the floor. The air smelled like dust though she'd only been gone for two days. Bits of it danced over the kitchen sink where the window hosted a beam of sunshine. She looked out the window. He was still there. Was his chest hurting as much as hers or was it all a lie? Maybe there was some spell she could learn that would judge his trueness.

"Not exactly a practical option," she whispered aloud. Not for her. And not when the countdown clock on the jeans was ticking away.

She should have driven straight to the mill, but she needed fresh clothes; it was partly vanity, partly a simple need for cleanliness. The mild version of her *keep clean* spells woven through this outfit could only do so much. Because of the Nons in the Wild West, she kept the spells subtle in her traveling garments. Her Republic clothes contained much stronger spells. She could wear them for two weeks, day and night, and they'd still look fresh.

She headed for her bedroom, striding through the kitchen and then the dining room with its high ceilings and ornate molding. Stillness drenched the atmosphere.

She'd bought the house years ago on a lucky fluke. The owner had wanted out fast, the neighborhood going to trash, he'd said, improper mage powers moving in all around.

Her kind of place.

It was more than big enough for two. But she'd never had a person in her life with whom she might have been *two*. The man she'd just left on her porch was the only one.

Just us.

Damn that tracker.

A wave of pressure smashed against her as she stepped into the front parlor. She stumbled back. What the hell was that?

A crackle ripped through the room. The windows shook in their frames, and the illusion of emptiness vanished.

Her living room was crowded with men. And one woman.

Mara forgot to breathe.

Two older distinguished-looking men sat on her couch in front of the windows. The one on the left was Senator Rallis, and on the right, Senator Warren. Three others stood along the wall with her winged back chairs and fireplace—Senators Standish, Prower, and Howland. Senator Alden, Harry's grandfather, sat in one of the chairs. All were dressed in the finest wool suits and silk ties, and all wore Medallions around their necks, indicating they each ruled a territory.

Most citizen mages would have recognized them, though few would expect them to appear out of thin air in their living rooms.

Scariest of all, the High Councilor stood at Senator Rallis's left. She strode forward, weaving smoke trails between her fingers. "My monk boy says you have the Mad Prophet's scroll."

Mara froze. He'd told on her. She couldn't trust him. But then she couldn't trust anyone when it came to the High Councilor's power.

"He had to tell me," the High Councilor replied as if she'd read her mind and then peered around Mara as if her eyes worked. "Did you leave him behind? I know he hasn't left." She clicked her tongue. "Better go get him."

Retreat. The word rang through her mind.

Mara pivoted on her heel and retraced her steps with a flurry. Outside, she shut the door behind her, putting a barrier between her and her unexpected guests.

Gregor paced the porch. His eyes flickered with the same useless anger burning in her gut. "She wouldn't let me tell you they were in there."

She tried to ignore the know-it-all voice in her head that chirped the facts at her, that if she'd answered his calls, if she'd given him the chance to explain, none of this would have caught her by surprise.

He offered no defense. He offered nothing. He stayed silent and pacing as if that's all he could do.

"Are you coming in?" she asked. "I can't go back in there without you." Not just because that was her order, but because she needed his strength. She looked away, not wanting him to see the truth.

He paced on.

She squinted at him, impatient, and finally saw it. "What is that?" Her body went tight at the view before her.

Ropes of energy tethered him to the far column of the porch. It must have had some stretch to it, long enough to let him pace a few feet beyond the door. She crouched by the knot, the twists and turns of the thin energy visible to her mage sense. "She tied you up like a dog." Sharp pricks of outrage tingled through her like coarse wool against her skin.

"Mara," he whispered with a furious force. His vibes popped around her, eating away at her words. "Be. Careful."

She stood with a jerk. "I'm tired of being careful. I'm tired of tiptoeing around these people who won't leave me alone." But he was right. She closed her eyes and dropped her shoulders. His vibes caressed the aura around her. "Don't," she whispered, but she wasn't sure she meant it because when he obeyed, she missed them.

She crouched back down and studied the knot, sending the thinnest stream of her vibes into the powerful strands that spelled him in place. Letting her vibes merge into the strands, she loosened them, pulling the tight knot apart and making it hers.

"What are you doing?" Panic saturated his voice. "Stop." He pulled her up hard by the shoulders.

"I almost had it," she cried.

"I know." His *silence* spell descended. He leaned down, face to face with her. "Mara, you can't do that. That should be impossible. That's the High Councilor's spell—"

His bubble of silence popped with a sharp shot of vibes. The High Councilor, standing in the dining room, had a clear view through the kitchen window. "I can hear you!" she sang.

Mara closed her eyes. The consequences of what she'd almost done played in her mind. Gregor had stopped her from breaking the crone's *leash* spell just in time. The leader of the Republic would never stand for someone breaking her spells.

He'd saved her life.

She dropped her head to her hands. "I'm out of my league. I can't do this."

He wrapped his hands around her arms, his touch gentle. "You can. You are brave and smart."

"I'm not. I chose a Power United man. Again. That's not smart." She was so close to him that his warm scent teased at her nose. He'd soaked in the sunshine. She shrugged free of his hold, twisting away and moving back. Was she really going to let her history repeat itself? "Now, how am I supposed to retrieve you if I can't unravel the spell?"

"I'm not allowed to tell you that either."

Frustration and dismay rolled over her. She was sick of these games. She doubted she was smart enough to survive them for much longer. She stepped closer for a better look at the *leash* spell. It weakened as she watched, and not because of what she'd done to the knot. That had faded the moment she'd let go. She sidled toward him again. The spell's vibes weakened further. "It's being near you, isn't it?"

She looked up at him...so close she could lean in and be in his arms. "By the lost girls, it's a kiss, isn't it?" she whispered. She didn't hesitate, needing to get it over with. Threading her fingers through his short hair, she pulled him down to her lips and pressed gently, reacquainting herself with his touch, and then tilting her head to press deeper still. Their tongues danced, their connection sealed. His sunshine scent warmed her from the inside out. He wrapped his arms around her...they were strong and safe.

Just like that, she wanted to forget about the tracker. Was she that weak? The answer was apparent as a sense of rightness settled over her, of comfort, of heat. A hungry flame flickered to life in her core, devouring the fuel his kiss provided and demanding more.

Somewhere, a foreign energy snapped and released. The *leash* was gone. She shoved back, her lips tingling, her chest pushing and pulling for air. She held out her hands between them, holding him back while she waited for that flame to taper off. It took its sweet time.

He bent down to her. "Listen to me." His whispered words were rushed. "I think you were right all along about Power United having the white wheel."

She squinted at him, her mind hesitating at leaping away from the kiss and toward such an unpleasant subject. "But Prophet talked like he knew where it was."

"I've been thinking about this while I waited for you. There's no way the Black Skulls have the capability to string the West with electricity. They're either working with P.U. or Prophet is planning to hijack their company somehow when the border falls. And we know Power United's people were in the West at the same time we were." He wrapped his hands around her arms. "I'm going to find the white wheel. I'm going to search Power United high and low. That's why I accepted the job. I won't stop until it's found and you're safe."

A TSUNAMI of vibes hit Gregor so hard he lost track of space, time, and his own mind. He let them go instead of fighting to hold on to them. Like his last experience with this, the spell retreated as quickly as it arrived. He and Mara stood in her front parlor instead of her back porch.

The High Councilor had moved them.

Mara looked green but kept her composure, unlike his first time. The acrid scent of sulfur burned through the air, the same as yesterday when she'd swooped him up from the east bank of the Mississippi and dropped him on Mara's porch.

He eyed the highbrow crowd around them. He and Mara hadn't left danger behind when they'd left the West. His firefly, already a supposed threat to the purity of good mages everywhere, had come home daring to show her true colors. While he saw the beauty in her bright eyes, he also saw the fear in the men before him. He wanted to stand in front of her and shield her from this group who would not let such a thing pass without consequence.

These men were powerful enough to smite them a thousand times over.

Senator Rallis, seated on the couch, tilted his head, and the front windows slid up in their tracks as if they were brilliantly oiled and brand new. "I don't know what that spell is, Madame Glender, but it stinks."

"Oh, Burr, stop it. You're gonna make a girl blush." The High Councilor waved away his comment.

"She's got the evil eye!" Senator Prower pointed at Mara. He stood in front of the fireplace, practically baring his teeth, and vibrating with power.

Of all the senators present, Gregor knew Prower would be the one to cause trouble. He was an ass. Gregor had encountered all of the Republic's senators on various missions.

"Prower, watch where you point that," the High Councilor snapped. "Behave. Or I'll cast my *misplace* spell and send you home. Ask my monk mage how much fun that is."

It fucking sucked. He'd lost his lunch...all of them through at least last Tuesday.

Senator Prower was a long way from home—his territory covered most of the southern peninsula of the Republic. A spell powerful enough to transport him that far away in a blink might kill him.

"Not kill him," the High Councilor said. "But it would cost him more than a few lunches."

Gregor took a fortifying breath. He needed to censor his thoughts.

"The Rand woman is a freak." Prower didn't know when to stop. "No mistaking that. I make a motion to cease with this charade and go straight to the plan proposed earlier."

"I've already told you, senator." The old crone's voice cracked like ice on a thawing lake. "Your camping proposal is not on the agenda this afternoon." She lifted her hands toward Mara and felt the air around her. "All this sweet, delicious power. Makes me want to take a bite out of you. Now fetch the scroll, Candy Girl, before I chomp down. Does it have any clues about what evil I'm up against?"

Gregor could give her a clue. She'd sent them to the Wild West to find evil's clutch, but the only ones with the resources to destroy the Republic's borders were those who lived within it.

Mara retrieved the scroll and his brave girl held it out with steady hands.

The High Councilor tapped it against her cheek, a pensive move. She studied Mara and then pointed the scroll at Gregor. "I *misplaced* him as soon as he crossed the Mississippi. Bzzzzt. Right onto your porch. I thought you'd be with him. Where were you?"

"I missed the train. And you tied him up with a *leash* spell!"

Gregor put one foot in front of her, shielding her with his body. If the crone was going to take her down, she'd have to take him too.

"I gave him your calling card." Logic dripped through the comment. "I have every citizen's calling card in my spell-o-dex," she offered. "I thought you'd race home as soon as you heard I'd caught him. I figured you'd rescue him. I should have known better. You didn't answer him." She laughed. "There's a reason I admire your style, sorceress. A man should sleep in the doghouse now and then. It's good for him. Makes him appreciate what he's got." She shoved the scroll back to Mara. "Read to me. I don't feel like seeing."

24

Mara took the scroll as the crone's words spun through her mind.

I figured you'd rescue him.

How many times had he rescued her? How many times had he tried to call her and she'd refused to answer? Guilt nibbled on her insides before she mentally reached out and grabbed it by the muzzle. Gregor was the one who'd put Power United between them, and it was a daunting task to reach around it to get to him.

She unwound the top of the scroll. *"Glister, fairy, gray, tomorrow or today—"*

"I spoke that one already. Next!" the High Councilor snapped.

"The king's forbidden land alight—"

"Next!"

Mara skipped on, and to her surprise, made it through a complete stanza. The crone didn't stop her.

> *"In the hand of royal's heir,*
> *Three relics claim the regal chair.*
> *It sits in east and rules in west,*
> *Destiny shall manifest."*

Mara eyed Gregor as she spoke. They both knew where it had come from...the stolen scrolls from the Rarified Library.

The crone stroked her chin. "Oh now, that is new. Destiny shall manifest." She clapped her hands and then bent over laughing. "Very funny." She sucked in a big gulp of air, trying, only partially successful, to catch her breath and regain composure. She waved her hand in the air. "Keep going, sorceress."

"The needle sings for the stitcher's dance—"

"What?" Offense flashed through the High Councilor's tone.

"I said—"

"I know what you said! Read!"

Mara jerked her attention to her task.

> *"But claims the songs of warrior chants.*
> *Guard the quest of the one who spins.*
> *Seek her truth and healing begins."*

"Stanford said this? Well, crap on a trash tower. I thought I'd made up the thing." The old woman shook her head. "Wait a minute! Her truth? That's not what I said! I said *the* truth." She tapped her temple. "*Mind like a steel trap.* It's my favorite spell. Do you know it? I cast it every morning before my feet touch the floor. I remember everything."

"You made up a prophecy?" Mara gasped. Her sentiment was echoed in the open mouths and protests of the men in the room.

"Lady, surely that is not the case!" Standish said.

Senator Rallis was the only one who looked unperturbed and not a single vibe surprised.

The High Councilor pointed at Gregor. "I had to motivate him somehow! Otherwise, he was all doom and gloom and *I'm going to abandon my country because they don't like me anymore and they were mean to me,*" she whined. She glared at Gregor. "So what's her truth, monkey?"

He didn't miss a beat. "Exactly what you see, Lady. Her truth is written in the air around her. It resonates with strength and courage and virtue."

"Pfft. You make her sound like Justice. That's who I'm supposed to be." She tossed up her hands and let them fall.

Inky smoke drifted around her, morphing from nothing. "Where's my scribe?" Her voice changed, dipping deeper. She looked around as if a scribe might be standing in the room somewhere unnoticed. "Oh, I don't have one. Major Stanford Madding has a scribe and I don't! That's wrong. Just wrong." She played her hand through the black strands of smoke building around her, lifting a cloudy strand and playing with it on her palm. She spoke.

"Glow Eyes spins webs as Luck commands.
Abandoned to the dance in the western lands.
The relics await her touch. Their fate?"

The words reverberated through the room and then faded away. The High Councilor stomped her foot. "Their fate?" she screamed, but no more words came.

Mara backed away. Her head felt heavy and she swayed on her feet, but it wasn't surprise or shock. It was more like utter doom. The relics awaited her touch. And yet to use them without royal glister blood was death.

Gregor wrapped his arms around her. "Breathe, firefly. Just breathe."

The High Councilor's frustrated screams flooded the room. Mara wanted to flee, a primal instinct at the shriek.

The inky blackness paused in the air as if winter tiptoed in and held it frozen. The oracle reached out and gripped the smoke in her fists, smashing the dark wisps. The rest of the smoke dropped as if it suddenly lost its power and landed on the floor like a deflated storm.

"What the vibing hell is their fate?" the old crone shouted.

"Raise your hands, gentlemen. Who knows their fate?" Anger vibrated around the room, squeezing as if it might shake the answers out of the house.

She turned her blind eyes to Mara. "Glow Eyes! The relics await your touch! What have you done?"

"Nothing! I've done nothing!" Her protests of innocence sounded weak even to her own ears, like a peasant begging for mercy. If she'd learned anything from her times with the High Councilor, it was never to show weakness. She pushed away Gregor's arms and stood straight, chin lifted. "I have spun with the webs, but you don't need a prophecy to tell you that. And I help the disabled mages you would discard with a swoop of your wand. That is all I have done."

"I beg your pardon! I haven't swooped a wand since way before your unwed mother was born. And I don't discard mages! I exist only to protect them."

Mara kept her chin high. "If you say so."

At least one of the senators gasped at her scorn, but the High Councilor ignored him. She held out her arms, her long, full sleeves flowing out beneath. "Those relics will kill you, girl." Her voice softened with a hopelessness that Mara had already accepted.

"I haven't used the relics."

"Yet. It's a slippery path, my dear. Don't you feel it? First the webs, then the relics," the High Councilor whispered. And then her voice turned sharp. "Besides, you know the prophecies." Vibes released with a taut snap and dozens of cards came into view on the coffee table. The crone had been shielding them with an *illusion* spell, one Mara was quite skilled at, too. She used it to hide the mess in her office every time she hosted meetings there.

She stared down at the crisp white cards, free of their envelopes. She'd known this day was coming. She'd imagined it a thousand times. People like her weren't permitted to know prophecies. Perhaps she should have destroyed the cards as they'd arrived, but if she'd ever decided to solve the mystery, she needed them.

There was no dodging this. She eyed the old woman. "I've known the prophecies for years." She picked up one of the thick squares of paper neatly arranged on her table. "I received the first when I was still at SWWM, the day I turned seventeen. Usually I would get one or two a year. Lately it's been much more frequent. Most are prophecies—it took me a while to figure out that's what they were. Some are old nursery tales." She tapped the corner of the card against another square of paper on the table and read aloud.

"A white glister oak wheel
And a silver spindle's prick,
Twelve moonbeam spokes whirl
And endless threads twirl."

"Endless threads would be quite a boon to my business." Mara shrugged. "But I've never been interested in the wheel. It defies logic that it's even real. Someone's been trying to warn me, but they've done a poor job conveying the specifics. I thought I knew who, but he denied it."

The High Councilor took the card from her. "They're from an oracle, a sage who is trying to influence the way all this turns out. The fool."

"A sage." Mara took a slow breath. Sage had been hiding in plain sight, tending bar and pouring drinks. She probably smoked tobacco sticks to cover up her inky prophecy smoke. Stupid not to have figured it out. She glanced at Gregor. "Why, I wonder?"

"Perhaps someone cares what happens to you," he said. The words dripped with meaning. He cared.

Senator Rallis picked up a card from the coffee table. "You've quite a collection here, sorceress. He read aloud.

"When evil's clutch shares the relic's touch,
All joy the wheel will steal.
Then West devours the mages' powers.
The Lady's cry, her land to die."

The High Councilor stepped forward. "Which brings us to the point of this meeting. I now call to order session 59A-3 of the Republic year 314, a hearing regarding the possible evil inherent in Blue Light Mill's owner Mara Rand, resident of the family seat of Rallis Territory," she proclaimed.

Mara gasped, but the oracle continued, "If I had a scribe, I'd look so much more official." Exasperation lined her face as she heaved a sigh.

"You're accusing me of evil." Mara laughed though no humor graced the noise.

The High Councilor shrugged. "What else are we supposed to do?" She ticked off the facts on her fingers. "You know about the prophecies. You're mentioned in them. You have a personal collection of them. You know about the wheel. You spin with so much power you could be a senator. Don't think I don't know that. And worst of all, you spin with silk that carries glister power. This does not look good for you, girl! I even banned you from spinning the silk, but you did it anyway." She looked pointedly at Gregor. "Uh huh. That's right. He's a snitch."

She turned to Gregor.

He held her gaze for a moment and then looked away with a long sigh. "I'm sorry."

He was a danger to her, and she'd made him so, letting him get close, showing him her secrets. She had complicated her life when she'd let him in her bed. She pulled in a slow breath. Let him? No, she'd enticed him with such force that he could never have refused. Since then, the complications had multiplied.

"Let's be honest, freak," the crone began. "Considering the facts, how could I proclaim you innocent?"

Mara held out her hands. "Because I'm not the evil that's trying to destroy the country's borders."

"Her waywardness meets the very definition of evil." Prower spoke as if he'd been waiting for that cue. "Cursed to evilness by the fallen consort! Those were the exact words in the descriptions of the waywards. The evidence of evil is clear. She touches the webs of the fairies' creatures—"

"Glister," the oracle corrected, speaking over him.

"Making a fabric that taints this Republic with the gray. We cannot stand for that. She is a threat to the sanctity of this land. She has already corrupted a lady of Casteel." He lifted his hands. "May the Goddess be merciful and grant a cleansing of the syphon's soul."

Senator Rallis laughed. "I'll have to tell Bronte you said that. Vinny too."

Prower might have paled at that, but he didn't get a chance to backtrack. The High Councilor spoke, "The fabric balances the power of the over-burdened, those born with too much mage energy for their bodies to carry easily."

Mara hadn't expected such a defense.

"Power a burden? Then that mage is weak," Prower retorted.

"Oh, stuff that," the crone said, her tone scathing. "Having too many vibes is like having big boobs. Your back hurts and they weigh so much you might fall over and smash them to pieces."

The room fell silent for a moment.

Prower cleared his throat. "The Rand woman needs to die before she does irreparable damage and the Republic falls. All those in favor of death?"

Standish raised his hand, as did Senator Alden, Harry's grandfather, and Senator Howland.

"Death?" Mara cried. She looked at the High Councilor.

The old crone's hand was high in the air too. She shrugged at Mara's gasp. "Just keeping it interesting." A gavel's knock resonated through the room. "By vote of committee, Mara

Rand is deemed evil. Such mages are sentenced to death by dragon fire until nothing is left but a pile of ashes." She pointed a finger, bobbing it around and encompassing everyone in its swoop. "We will execute her as soon as a dragon can be found." She studied the tips of her fingernails as if she could see them. "Might be awhile. In the meantime, Whitman, guard the dead mage walking as she finishes my jeans. Keep her alive."

Gregor bowed slightly. "I apologize, Lady, but I am unavailable. While I was on the back porch, I accepted an official job offer from Power United. I start today."

Though she already knew, Mara couldn't breathe at the words. Fate was playing a game with her. How many hits could she take and stay standing?

"Alrighty, then," the old crone said lightly. "I'll assign another man to guard my mage-to-be-smote." The oracle turned to face the members of the Senate. "Let me be clear, boys. The execution is delayed. We need her. For now. The relics await her touch. Relics. Plural. We only have one of them. If we're going to find the relics, we need her. They will come to her by the Rose Moon. Poor wayward girl."

The oracle shook her head. "I'll keep you alive for as long as I can, but you're like Sleeping Beauty. Every spinning wheel has been confiscated, but you're still doomed to prick your finger and die."

～

HER HOUSE HAD EMPTIED of all but one guest. The High Councilor puttered around her kitchen, but Mara paid no attention. She sat at the kitchen table waiting for the icy cold hole in her chest to fill in again.

The High Councilor slid a cup and saucer down the table. Sloshing with tea, it stopped in front of her. "Drink up."

Spicy fumes drifted out and Mara flinched back, surprised. "You spiked it."

"How could I resist? Fifty-year-old Bare Witches Whiskey?"

Her mouth fell open. "You opened it?"

"That's what it's for, sister! Seize the moment now or regret it as wasted forever...if you believe in regret, that is. I don't. I believe in drinking."

A knock on the back door sounded, and the High Councilor spelled it open. "We're in the kitchen."

"Yes, thank you, Lady, I see." Lincoln Sinclair stepped into the kitchen.

"Commander, I hereby command you to vow to protect sorceress Mara Rand with your life."

"My life?" Lincoln raised his eyebrows.

"Do it." She stuck a pointy finger in his gut.

He took the poke valiantly. "I vow to protect Mara Rand with my life."

The High Councilor disappeared in a flash of white smoke. Mara waved the air away and eyed Lincoln.

For all that he was her majesty's personal guard, he looked more like a tough bouncer in a bar. His eyes were hooded and hard. His chest was thick and broad, and his legs were in perfect proportion to it. Before he'd become one of her clients, he'd had a hard time finding shirts and pants that fit properly.

He had a sculpted beard, and the sides and back of his hair were trimmed very short. The top was long, and he pulled it into a ponytail at the back of his crown.

Evidently the High Councilor didn't mind an unpolished look in her House.

"Captain Whitman filled me in on the situation," he said.

"And what is the situation, Lincoln?" The whiskey was already going to her head, loosening her thoughts and letting Gregor nest in their nooks and crannies.

She'd thought they'd be in this together. Or at least that's what she assumed before she'd found the tracker, which she could admit had saved her once. Maybe twice. She wasn't sure how she was going to let the deception go, but now she sat here alone and her hands were shaking and her throat was tight.

She didn't want to be without him.

Power United didn't bother playing games with its enemies. If Gregor was right and they had the wheel and if they found out what he was up to, she'd never see him again.

Plus, Cecilia would be all over him.

A tightness coiled inside her. Power United couldn't keep its hands out of her life. They couldn't stop grabbing at everything she had. Now they had Gregor. And she had to trust that he wouldn't become one of them.

"Call me Linc," he said. "And the situation is—"

She held up her hand. "I know actually. I don't need a recap." The heat of the Bare Witches Whiskey churning in her stomach did nothing to melt the icy fear or quell the sour bitterness that she would always have a *situation*, that she would never have average or regular or normal. That was how life would be for a Glow Eyes. But she'd settle for simply having Gregor back at her side.

Just us.

"He's going to get himself in trouble if he's not careful," she said.

"Nah. He's smart and capable." He studied her. "And he cares for you a lot. I've had an earful about how bold and brave you are. That I'm not to give you a chance to sneak off by yourself. And that I'm to keep my hands off your vibes." He squinted. "That particular command came with a harsh expletive."

THEY LEFT THE HOUSE, and Linc drove her to her mill. She gave him directions. He put up with her guidance.

Outside the mill's fence, a dozen protestors lined the road.

Their signs bobbed up and down above their heads, spelled into place with vibes.

No fairy power.

Spiders are evil.

Republic for Mages Only.

This was the result of that newspaper article.

Linc's vibes shot out. "Sergeant, get 'em out of here." He cast the message away, and two guards stationed at the front doors jogged out.

Linc pulled his vehicle around the back where her sorceresses had gathered for a break.

They occupied the large picnic tables, their lunches spread out. Faded umbrellas shaded the space.

Esther stood as Mara approached. "Hey, lady boss, you travel safe?" She brushed her hands free of crumbs. Her hair was shorter now, almost buzzed, and it stuck up in spikes all over her scalp. It was a striking blend of silver and gold. A swirl of a new tuning circle tattoo played on her right bicep.

"I survived in one piece, and so did the denim, which is the important part." She handed it over to the forewoman. Thank the stars above she'd gotten it this far.

"I like your shine there." Esther tapped a finger next to her eye.

Mara took a breath. There was going to be a lot more of that, and not everyone would be accepting.

"Did you find yourself a new gentleman?" Esther nodded at Linc.

"This is Lincoln Sinclair. He and his men are overseeing security here now."

"Security. Huh. Don't know if it's good that we have protection or bad that we need it." She eyed his government uniform. "That is, if it's actually protection he's providing. I hope you don't mind me saying so, lady boss, but he's dressed like he's ready to arrest you or confiscate some more of our stuff."

Mara silently agreed with that. She eyed her workers. Considering the events around here, if they'd had other job opportunities available, they'd probably all quit. "Time will tell."

Esther shrugged off the unpredictability. "I'm ready to go." She nodded at her lunch. "We took one last food break. I scoured the sewing room vibe-free myself. And we got a new order while you were gone. A nice big one."

"Interesting." Mara kept her tone flat and crossed her arms over her chest. She'd known her sorceresses wouldn't let their confiscated wheels stop them while she was away. "How are you spinning it? On drop spindles?" She felt like the mother of naughty children. She knew what was coming.

Esther shook her finger. "Yeah, about that, there's something you should know." She pointed at the building. "We got some wheels spinning in there. They ain't all that hard to fashion out of a little bit of this and that."

A fact Mara knew well. She'd made a few of her own.

"We went to the Drainpipe," Esther said.

Mara raised her eyebrows. "You went to the junkyard?" It was called the Drainpipe because the trash vibes from the city drained into the trash towers there. It was also a repository for metal junk. And guarded by tough guys with dark mage powers.

"They've got a nice supply of old bicycle wheels, and after the first few, we got pretty good at constructing spinning wheel frames out of pipe." Her forewoman lifted her chin. "Spinning production is at sixty percent and has been for the past two days. Not good but not bad considering. The powers-that-be can't possibly want to steal these. Hell, they probably wouldn't even recognize what they are. They sure don't look like anything Sleeping Beauty would use."

"Perfect."

25

"WHAT THE HELL are you doing here?"

Gregor spun around in the dank hallway, deep beneath the main offices of Power United, to find Daegan standing behind him.

"Goddess, I fucking hate fairies...glister...whatever." His heart pounded. He hadn't sensed him at all. "I work here." He tightened his grip on his scroll as if he might use it as a weapon. Officially, he was inspecting security functions. He'd been working on it for a day and a half. The scroll listed the current processes and procedures in place. It was short. "What the hell are you doing here?"

The fairy stood in a shallow puddle. Not even a puddle really, more of a smear on the concrete floor. This glister had an affinity with water.

Gregor lifted a quick eyebrow at the realization that his mind was calm enough in a glister's presence to think. Panic hadn't appeared. Maybe the third time was the charm. Or maybe Mara's tough-as-shit attitude toward the man had rubbed off.

He kept his eyes on the fairy's chin as Daegan frowned at their surroundings.

This level of the building was three stories below ground, and it smelled every inch of a damp basement. They were too close to the river to have so many basements, and there was an additional one lower yet that he still had to inspect.

Power United had offices all over town, but not one of them sported a white spinning wheel. In the guise of security inspections, Gregor had done an initial overview of the facilities that produced wire. He'd seen sorceresses spinning at their wheels, guards pacing among them. The women's small piles of copper wire had grown slowly as the straw disappeared from their hands and morphed into metal with their vibes.

As a group, the sorceresses looked tired, but they still had hair, teeth, and enough energy to move back and forth to the cafeteria and then to their dormitories at the day's end. But he'd seen the copper quotas posted in the hallways, and these women weren't producing near enough copper to meet them.

"You're supposed to be Mara's guard. And unless she's here, you're falling down on the job. You fall. She falls," Daegan said.

"Mara has at least six guards now. Better than I could offer. Someone needs to focus on finding the wheel." He contained his words with a spell, but he kept his voice to a whisper anyway.

"No, asshole." Daegan's voice blasted right past his spell and echoed around the halls. "The wheel will find her. You should be practicing the weapon. Can you do it yet?"

He'd hoped the fairy would give up on this. Gregor had no problem with the idea that a song could be a weapon. He knew plenty of songs and chants that qualified and was skilled enough to use them even if he couldn't hear them anymore. But he had no idea what Daegan meant by the unsung song—and probably never would.

"Fuck. You haven't done anything on it. What the hell is wrong with you?" The fairy's eyes flashed.

"Watch it." Panic drenched his mind.

Daegan threw his hands up. "Luck's balls! Relax. Look, I

thought cadence mages were supposed to meditate and look deep into themselves. If you don't look, we're all doomed."

"So I'm going to look into my soul—"

"Heart," Daegan corrected.

"And find a song that I've never noticed before."

"Right."

"Don't you think that if a love song is all it takes to stop a fairy's power, someone would have figured it out?" He couldn't even believe he was saying such vibe shite. Thank the Goddess no one was around to hear him.

"Who? Who's going to open their heart to a fairy in order to kill one?"

Gregor shifted his stance. "That's a fair point."

"Monk mages are the only ones who have the ability to do it, and how many of them are in battle? How many of them fight to defend their people?"

His decision to go into the army had baffled every teacher and apprentice chanter mage he'd known. Only one other was in the army.

"How many of them have been pricked by the needle?" Daegan asked.

"Fuck you." Gregor glared. The fairy knew the answer to that question.

"Come on. I'm going to show you something." Daegan put his hand on Gregor's shoulder, and the basement zapped away, replaced by sunshine and the heat of summer.

"Goddess damn it! How the hell did you do that? The High Councilor did that shit to me yesterday."

Daegan frowned. "No mage has a spell like that. It's glister power."

"Then she borrowed it from one of your people. A friend of Mara's. That's what the old crone said. You're Mara's glister friend."

Daegan squared off to him. "Let's get something straight,

witch. I hate that crone. She has nothing of mine and she never will. Now, do you know where we are?"

He looked around. They were behind Mara's mill. A food truck was parked nearby and the sorceresses had gathered outside. He would have scanned the crowd for Mara, but he knew she wasn't there. Her energy was absent. He could recognize it in a flash.

"This happens every week. She'll come out eventually," Daegan explained. "They can't see us."

"You spy on her. You dirty shit." But he didn't step away.

"That normal boy over there...he's Mara's gardener."

An older teen stood at the distant corner of the fence pulling weeds. The required N, the designation for Non-mage, was pinned to the right side of his shirt. He ignored the sorceresses and the food truck.

"I pay him twenty bucks a week to keep this puddle here. Open to him. Focus your heart on him. Harness the unsung song within him."

Gregor laughed, incredulous. "Do you have any idea how idiotic that sounds?"

"If you don't figure this out, it's over. Everything the West stands for and everything the East is will be gone." His eyes flashed between silver and brown like he was struggling to control his power. "I don't know what the song sounds like, so I can't describe it. But I know it exists. And I know that you, wayward monk, have what is necessary to hear it. You can't save her without it.

"Harness the song and you can stop a glister, a mage, a Normal. Anyone. And anything. It's that simple. Now, grab that boy with the song of hearts. Grab his power."

Gregor stared at the fairy for the length of a long, slow breath. Daegan was sincere in this. That much was clear, so Gregor tried to offer the same, keeping the disbelief from his face and his eyes from rolling. "That's a Non-mage. They don't have power. There's nothing to grab."

Daegan looked up at the sky. "I can't believe it's come to this. The king is gone. And our only hope is a monk mage who drained not only his chants and songs down the eye of the needle, but also his gumption and his courage."

Gregor squinted. "What king?" He was secure enough in his gumption and courage that he didn't bother to argue about that part.

"The glister king. We have a leader, you know." Daegan's voice picked up an accent that had been missing before. Something old and far away.

"I thought the fairies—the glister—were into anarchy."

"Don't confuse the Wild West with the glister."

In the distance, Linc exited the mill and held the door for Mara. Gregor stared at her, soaking her in as she strode across the lot. Goddess, he missed her, and it had only been a day since he'd left her standing shocked in her living room, no time to explain, leaving her safety in another man's hands. He'd been searching for the wheel almost every hour since.

She gave a closed-lip smile to a pair of her workers who lingered near the door, but there wasn't real happiness in her expression. He needed to find the damn wheel so this could all end.

"She can't see us. And I can't afford to stay long, so listen up," Daegan said. "That normal kid has energy. It exists. That's the first thing you have to change—your fucked up little mind." He spoke fast. "Every living being has power. Mages and the glister have harnessed it. The normals dwell in oblivion by stubborn choice. Don't be as stubborn as they are.

"Listen to your heart and listen to his. Merge with his power and take control. Be one."

One with all. Gregor had grown up with that slogan. It was

the motto of the monastery. They hadn't really meant it. Not when it came to the glister or the Nons. Or waywards.

He quit looking at Mara and shifted to the kid. He opened his mage power and prodded at him. A shiver ran along the boy's shoulders.

"Not your mage power, fool. Your heart."

He tried again, but to the same effect. The kid looked around with wide eyes, his forehead tight, his mouth in a circle. He was scared to death. Gregor gave up before the kid had a heart attack.

Daegan crossed his arms and glared. "Do you enjoy being helpless against glister? I have to ask because you haven't made a shit's worth of progress. Sought any truth recently? Has healing begun in your needle-pricked soul? Hurry up. Try harder."

He disappeared in a blink.

What the hell?

The glister had left him here, miles from work on a Wednesday afternoon. Nothing ever went as planned with Daegan around.

Gregor knew he should cast a *don't look,* jump the fence, and cast a spell for a taxi. He should get back to work and find the damn wheel before someone else did. Mara had a death threat over her head and those fucked up senators were going to demand her execution the moment the wheel fell into govern-ment control. Instead, he watched her, opening his mage sense, seeking her essence.

He would have given anything to know what Mara's power sounded like. Instead, he had to settle for his other senses. It tasted sweet. It flowed with a lyrical softness that had no end and could soar to the heavens, and it sparkled and swirled like a nebula of stars. He was pretty sure she surpassed him in strength. He was certain she was his better in courage and kindness.

He'd had to be broken before he could recognize her. He'd been listening for the one ever since he knew how. He didn't care what his friends said. Every man he knew was looking for the right woman whether he admitted it or not. Without the needle's effects, he never would have looked at Mara, and that would have been the biggest tragedy of his life.

She stood in line at the tea truck. Her eyes sparkled softly, a dark bronze, more glitter than shine. Her mage power puffed around her in a soft, full cloud. It was relaxed, vibing with just enough energy for her eyes to focus without her specs, he supposed. Her hair was tucked behind one ear. She wore a black, sleeveless dress that covered her from her neck to above her knees, gently gracing her long curves.

Screw the damn taxi.

He paced toward her.

"It's him! He's back." The shout came from the bald girl with the scarf.

A dismayed clamor rumbled through the tea party. The sorceresses stood, a few pulling out their drop spindles. Lady Harry smiled, quickly hiding her expression behind her hand. Mara strode right for him.

Linc jogged past her. "How the hell did you get in here?" His tone was hard and unfriendly. "I've got the whole place locked down."

"Did you find it?" Mara asked.

He held up his hands, palms in, before anyone could decide to cast a spell he could only grunt and bear. "I haven't found it yet." He turned to Linc. "And it's an odd story as to how I got here."

"A glister escorted him in," Mara offered. She studied him, her lush lips parted, her eyes focused. He couldn't read forgiveness in her expression. He couldn't read anything.

"You saw that?" Gregor asked. Daegan wasn't as sneaky as he thought...or he was underestimating Mara. Everyone underestimated the wayward.

"No. But I've seen Daegan do it before."

"A fairy," Linc ground out and turned to Gregor. "Hell. There's nothing I can spell against one of them. I tried to shoot one once. It didn't work. I can't keep them out of the Council House either."

"Glister invade the Council House?" Mara asked, her tone easy with the other man. Gregor wanted to step between them.

"Not so much invade. Visit. And it's always unexpected to me."

Gregor didn't want to talk about anything that Linc was an expert in. Jealousy was a new feeling. He nodded toward the party. "What's the occasion?"

"The Tea Time truck comes every Wednesday at two o'clock. It keeps up morale." She folded her hands in front of her, entwining her fingers. Nervous, maybe. "Are you thirsty?"

He'd had no hope of being invited. His chest lightened.

She gave him a small smile. "Though perhaps the real question is are you brave enough to face them?"

It was the second time today that his courage had been questioned.

As if sensing their cue, a few of the women stepped forward. "You took our wheels," the forewoman hollered. Esther, that was her name. At least her spindle was no longer pointed in his direction.

"I did. And I'm sorry."

The bald one walked up beside Esther and studied him. "I like his eyes."

Gregor glanced at Mara. Was he supposed to say thank you to that?

"They look kind. Troubled, but kind." She looked up at Esther. "I think he's going to help us get our wheels back."

"You a soothsayer now, Stella Woodson?" The forewoman put her hands to her hips in false outrage.

"I might be. I foresee your cup of tea getting cold." She gave the forewoman a cute grin and strolled back to the tables with a spirited step. Esther shook her head and stomped after her.

The sorceresses relaxed and most sat back down to their teacups.

"Let's talk in my office." Mara headed toward the building and he followed.

"If you've got her, I'll take a break." Linc turned his gaze, much softened, to Lady Harry. The man had only been here for a day and a half. Maybe he didn't know a woman like that was a shot in a million for a guy like him. But Gregor wasn't going to bring the man down.

Mara's employees were agog as he passed. One of them fumbled with her porcelain teacup, dropping it at his approach. A quick hum of his power and it halted in mid-air. He palmed the delicate cup and handed it over. The woman gave a blushing thanks.

Mara led him inside. Two flights of stairs weren't long enough to ogle her ass. He didn't even try to avert his gaze, remembering the way it looked on stage, the feel of it cupped in his hands.

They walked down a hallway and into a large office. Mara closed the door behind them.

The room was white and airy. Her long, simple desk, made of pale wood, was straight ahead. A wall of windows was on the left and looked down onto the factory floor. At the other end of the room was a couch with an old-fashioned curve to it. A bunch of yarn sat on a low table in front of it.

He nodded in the direction of the spinning wheel he'd concealed. "Did you find it?"

"I haven't dared yet. Linc is about at his breaking point with all the unconventional activities that go on around here. I didn't want to push it. But it's a comfort to know it's there." She sat on the couch. "How's Power United?" The bitter curl to her lips hurt his heart. "Have you found the spinning floors?"

"There are three." He sat beside her, slowly, as if he moved too fast she might scamper away. "The sorceresses work hard, but there's no obvious abuse going on. They're not anywhere close to reaching their posted quota though."

"Those women don't sleep or eat until the quota is met. The floors you've found must be for show. We worked in one long, cavernous room. That's what you need to look for. If they have the white wheel and they're using it, it would have to be close to the sorceresses."

"That's the type of room I've found. But the women look healthy." He was about to reassure her that he believed her accounts of what happened there, but she kept going like she was unable to stop now that she'd started. "Row upon row of women tied up to spinning wheels. The guards are zapper mages and they have wands or whips. If you look up from your work or you don't spin fast enough, you get punished."

She paused for a moment, and then her next words tumbled out. "What if they corrupt you? What if they turn you against me too?" She looked away. "That's what plays through my mind when I think about you there."

He tucked a curl behind her ear. "Firefly, nothing could ever do that. I know you. There's nothing that could make me turn from you."

She looked at him, her eyes bleak and dull. "Oh, there might be something. You don't know everything about me...."

"I can't imagine what that something would be."

She stared at him. "When I escaped Power United, I left all the sorceresses that I was imprisoned with behind. I never went back for them. They all watched me break the bonds that tied me to my spinning wheel. That part of my escape was simple brute vibes...no finesse, just sheer power. They were spells none of them had the strength to do. And then I danced like I did on Fancy's stage. I know you don't believe in my power to spellbind, but it's true. I can." She held out her fingers and looked down at them. "I bound them all. Guards, sorceresses, bosses, secretaries."

She slumped back on the couch. "I abandoned those sorceresses. Just as that asshole bounty hunter abandoned me. And I never went back. P.U. has forty-eight spinning facilities in the Republic and each one is allotted one hundred new sorceresses a year. You'd think that would be plenty, but the company is always clamoring for more because over half of them die. It's very hard for them to spin copper. They can't produce much. But it's still far cheaper than mining. The rest of the world uses aluminum for their overhead wires. It's lighter, easier to hang, but here we just cast a simple spell to hang copper high and then cast a *don't look* on it so it doesn't mar the landscape. Out of sight, out of mind. Just like P.U.'s sorceresses."

He sat back.

She leaned her head on his shoulder. "They don't care if they die, and I didn't care if I left them behind, spellbound."

That was a lie. Her anguish was clear.

"Mara, you couldn't have taken hundreds of women with you."

She shook her head against him. "At the time, there were thirty-four of us still alive. Two were pregnant by guards. The rest were dead."

Goddess above.

"It's why Cecilia hates me so much. She was there, a Power United sorceress. Somehow, she managed to climb the ranks. She's done well for herself, but she isn't doing anything for the sorceresses. Though who am I to throw stones?

"I did try to get help, after I escaped, to let people know. I contacted a few reporters, but the story never saw the light of day. Once, I went to the receiving hours where Senator Rallis listens to the commoners, but no sentry would let me in. My glowing eyes, my rags for clothes. That's when I left for the West."

He put his arm around her and she leaned into him, holding him with a desperation that broke his heart. "You did the best you could."

"It wasn't enough."

"Sometimes it isn't." He shifted her closer. "Sometimes you can't fix it and you just have to live with it." Like his wayward power. He pressed a kiss to the top of her head and held her. He let himself hope that he still had her, that he hadn't ruined everything with the damn tracker.

A wave of vibes brushed against his sense. Not now, he thought, but he didn't get his wish. A knock sounded against the door.

26

As she strode across her office, Mara cast out her vibes to open the office door. It wasn't something she'd done in the past. With her vibes free now, it was a new practice.

Lady Harry stood on the other side, her lips pursed, her eyes looking off into a corner of the hallway as if she was averting her gaze from any sordid scene that might be playing out in her office.

Mara had hired Lady Harry five years ago. The woman was levelheaded. Mara was too. It's why they got along. Harry could have worked anywhere she wanted though she didn't need to work at all. Her Mayflower family had buckets of money.

"I have bad news and a letter," Harry said.

Clearly it was no common letter or it would have been in the mail pile on her secretary's desk. Some new gremlin was sneaking around the corners of their lives with more trouble. She braced herself and held out her hand for it, but Harry passed it to Gregor.

He glanced at the business-sized envelope with his name scrawled on the front. "It's from my mother." He ripped it open.

Mara squinted at him. "How did she know you'd be here?"

"My mother has always been able to find me. Don't ask me how."

"Mrs. Whitman is a reporter with the *New Ashton Times*." Harry offered.

"How did you know that?" Gregor asked.

She eyed Mara. "After you were shuffled off to the dungeon with him, I looked him up. I needed to make sure you weren't locked up with some dangerous freak."

Mara frowned. "That was a waste of time. There would have been nothing you could do if he'd proven to be dangerous. You would have just worried."

"I knew you would say that, but if the tables were turned, you would have done the same thing, lady boss. And don't tell me you don't want to know what else I found out." She didn't wait for an answer. "His colleagues think highly of him. Bronte Casteel sings his praises so high she might as well compose a song about him, and his ex-girlfriends, of which there aren't as many as I'd assumed, smile fondly at his name. Two asked for his calling card."

Ex-girlfriends. A sharp tingle plucked against her skin. She wanted to rub the sensation away. She didn't want to be in that category, not that one night qualified her. But what if *just us* became *just once*? She bit her lip at that and tried to breathe around the ball of wool suddenly lodged in her chest.

"Ex-girlfriends?" Mara asked. "Is that your bad news?"

"No. This is the bad news." Gregor scanned the letter. "Apparently there's a bill in the Senate, one that's been lounging around for a long time, that would require all waywards to be rounded up and put in an internment camp. The bill got a hard nudge two days ago."

For a moment, Mara couldn't speak. "An internment camp? They can't do that to us. We're citizens of this Republic."

"My mother says the bill comes up for a vote the day after

tomorrow. It's expected to pass and go into effect immediately. The land for the camp has been donated by Senator Prower."

"But why would he do that? He's not known for hating waywards," Harry said.

"Oh, he hates waywards. Or at least he hates me," Mara said.

Harry shook her head. Her knowledge of the founding families and their secrets had helped Blue Light Mills grow. The families were all about power and appearances. Many of them paid a lot of money for Mara's special clothes that addressed their shortcomings. "Standish hates them. So does Noble. But not Prower. He's known to be...tolerant. Rumor has it that some of his servants are glister."

"Glister?" Gregor's word held disdain.

"I've never been able to confirm that. I do know that he's on Power United's board."

"He's not my biggest fan," Mara said. "Maybe I should have kept my glow to myself when he invaded my house."

Harry frowned. "No offense, lady boss, but you're overstating your importance if you think he donated land to house all the waywards because of you. How many waywards do you think there are? A few thousand? All because he doesn't like one of them? But that wasn't the bad news to which I referred."

Of course, it wasn't.

"The delivery date on the jeans has been moved. It's tomorrow. Not Saturday. The message came from the High Councilor's assistant's assistant."

Mara pinched her lips. "Makes sense. If I'm going to be locked up in an internment camp on Saturday then the High Councilor needs her jeans before then." Images of guards and razor-sharp fences played through her mind...cold cells, hard cots, and thin streams of sunshine timidly passing through high windows. She turned to Gregor and took his hand. "Now's probably the time to go find your mountain."

His handsome face was hard and determined. "You're coming

with me, firefly. Do you trust me to keep you safe?" His eyes tightened at the question as if he were bracing himself for the answer.

She nodded as her heart swelled in her chest. "I just have to
get the jeans done first."

27

GREGOR HAD LEFT Mara with a kiss on her cheek. She'd stood in her office looking lost and afraid. It was the first time he'd seen that expression on her face. He'd given her instructions to pack lightly, knowing that no matter how scared she was, she'd keep moving. It's what she did.

Meanwhile, he'd returned to Power United. He had less than twenty-four hours to find the white wheel before the internment bill kicked in.

The negative vibes that lingered in sub-level four hit Gregor with his first step off the elevator. He flipped on his flashlight, forgoing casting mage lights. He wouldn't broadcast his presence any more than necessary, although if Power United had a decent tracker mage on staff, they could figure out he'd been here whether or not he cast mage lights.

He strode down the dark halls, made a left, and then another, forming a mental map of the interior hallways and rooms. He checked each one, finding nothing but storage areas behind locked doors which he opened by jimmying the cheap locks with vibe packs, small containers of vibes that would power a spell anonymously. Donating vibes for the packs was dangerous. For the desperate, it provided a meager but draining income.

The fifth room he came to held scroll cabinets, floor to ceiling, rows of them, leaving just enough space for one person to walk between them. His flashlight played among the rows, sharpening the shadows to a sinister edge.

The wheel clearly wasn't in this room, but he took a minute to examine the files, alphabetized by name...all women. He'd bet they were sorceresses. He pulled out two at random and stuffed them in his invisible pocket. It was still functioning, an unseen valet.

He scanned for *Rand, Mara.* Sure enough. He took it and looked on for his little champion—Stella Woodson. But hers wasn't there.

He paced on, skimming fast, to the lowest drawer in the last cabinet, which should have held the last of the alphabetized names. Instead, it held a small selection of names from A-Z. The drawer's handle had a decided lack of dust, unlike the others, and inside, it contained around a hundred scrolls. He scanned them, stopping on the name he'd missed before—*Woodson, Stella.*

He pulled it out as vibes burst against his senses. He went still, readying his power. Shoving the scroll into his invisible pocket, he crept out of the room, racing silently toward the vibes, and casting a *don't look* as he went. So much for anonymity.

He turned a corner and had to brace himself. A wave of vibes, distraught and fearful, lashed at him.

By the Goddess, what had happened here?

He took a breath and strode into it. A small door stood at the heart of the rotten energy. He opened it to find a closet.

Nils Lusman stood inside. The man jumped at the open door, fierceness in his flaring nose and his pulled back lips.

Gregor dropped his *don't look* and revealed himself.

Nils panted. "Goddess above, man. What the fuck are you doing down here?" Sweat dripped down his face.

Gregor scowled. "My job. Inspecting for security leaks. What the fuck are you doing in a closet?"

Nils closed his eyes. "Long story."

Gregor sank into the power of his vibes, a mage's fighting stance of sorts, as a hint of distrust trickled through him. "Uh huh. Does it have anything to do with why this place feels like shit?"

"Look, man." His voice was rough. He took a swallow from the bottle in his left hand. "There's a reason for that. I can't afford for you to be here or to tell anyone about this. And you know who else can't afford for you to be here?" His lengthy pause made it clear he wouldn't continue without an answer.

Gregor obliged. "Who?"

"Mara."

GREGOR SAT in the hard chair across from Nils's luxurious desk, biting back his demands to know what the hell this had to do with Mara. He waited while the man downed another bottle of some blue drink and reached for a third from the refrigerator behind him. Empty bottles of the same kind piled high in his trashcan.

Gregor raised an eyebrow. "Thirsty?"

Nils puffed out his lips and sighed. "This job dries out your soul. Some days I walk around here feeling like a fucking raisin. I hate raisins." He cracked open the bottle and started coughing. "See. It's literally drying me out. Goddess, I hope I'm not getting sick. Here. Have one." He tossed a bottle through the air. "They've got lots of healthy supplements in them."

Gregor caught it. He took a cautious sip. Sweet but drinkable.

The other man downed a quarter of his bottle. "We can talk freely in here. I've spelled the room with everything I've got."

Gregor had sensed the *silence* spell when he'd passed through the doorway. "Let me help you with that." Sending out a stream of vibes, he prodded for *hearing* spells. No ears lurked. With another push of vibes, he recoated the office in his own *silence* spell, stronger than the previous spell.

Nils nodded. "Impressive."

"A little extra protection. That's all. You had it locked down pretty well, but it's my specialty. Now tell me why Mara can't afford for me to be on sub-level four."

"There's no way I'd tell you if I weren't certain of your loyalty to Mara.... Yeah, I know about that. You shielded her at the expense of yourself on the train. I saw that. I'm damn glad you were there. That's love, man."

Gregor straightened at the word, and a sense of possessiveness crashed through him.

Nils fiddled with his bottle, rolling it around on his desk. "She's a pretty girl. And on that stage at The Green House ... Goddess almighty. She was something. I've never seen anything like that. You're a damn lucky man to have that rolling around on you."

Possessiveness erupted to rage like a flame to dry kindling. It whooshed to the top of his head, painting his vision. "Nils, you don't want to talk about that." He spoke behind clenched teeth.

"Right, right." He sat back in his chair. "I guess she probably told you she was one of ours about fifteen years ago." He shook his head. "Not ours. Theirs. I want nothing to do with it. That closet you found...there's a door at the back of it and a tunnel that leads"—he shrugged with one shoulder—"out. I help them out when I can."

"You help them? As in, help them escape?" Gregor continued as Nils nodded. "Where are the sorceresses around here?"

The other man frowned. "Haven't you seen the spinning rooms? I assumed you'd given yourself a thorough tour."

"I did, and I've found three floors."

"Well, there you go. You have seen them."

Gregor tested the man's vibes. Steady. Normal flow. Truth. "There are no others?"

"Some big cavernous one with girls shackled to their wheels?" Nils asked. "Cecilia shut it down as soon as she became a VP. It was well after Mara left here."

He nodded. Mara had said the other woman had moved through P.U.'s ranks. "Were you here then?"

"Nah. I was still in secondary school."

Gregor wanted to ask about the scroll room, but he kept his snooping to himself. "So you disapprove of the way the sorceresses are handled?"

"Poor girls...low-powered things that are little more than Nons." His voice vibed with scorn. "Glad it's not me, but if I can help them get to a better place, then that's what I do. I want to make this world better. Mara helps too, when she can. That's what I was doing on the train."

Gregor kept his expression steady at the gut-churning news that Mara helped government-conscripted sorceresses escape. Goddess, his girl was brave and sneaky and risking her precious life. "Why not put a stop to it instead? Better the lives of the sorceresses?"

He cracked a laugh. "Have you seen the men who are on our board? A senator, two heirs, and three of the richest men in the Republic. All of them own a considerable amount of stock in this company and wield clout that I can't hold a single vibe to. They don't want to spend their beloved profit on those weaklings. And I can't afford to stir up controversy. I have to keep a low profile. Cecilia knows I'm up to something. I need her off my back. That's part of the reason I hired you, army man, with your reputation beyond reproach." He cocked his finger at him. "You make me look like an upstanding citizen to the higher-ups."

Nils ran his hand down his face. "I believe in helping these sorceresses live life to their true potential. But the best I can do is work within Power United's rules. Mara and I go way back doing just that." He smiled softly. "I had no idea she could dance like that. I'm glad she hid her eyes away though." He winked at Gregor. "That girl needs me. I'm her inside guy."

28

MARA FUMBLED with the lock on her front door. The key refused to turn. Though she'd locked her back door with a spell, she rarely used her front door and hadn't bothered changing from deadbolt to vibes.

Gregor waited at her side. She wasn't sure if she was imagining the impatience waving off him. She'd guessed...hoped... that he'd show up tonight, but she hadn't expected to find him waiting on her front porch. Linc had driven her home and then left after the two men had exchanged nods.

"Linc said he has someplace to hide from the internment camp." Mara continued jiggling the stuck lock. She'd offered Linc the chance to come with them, but he'd declined. "He didn't say where."

"I'd expect no less from him."

"Right. Because that's how you soldier people are?" Finally the key turned and she opened the door.

Gregor picked up the paper bags sitting on the porch and led the way into her quiet house. With a hum of his power, he cast his own *lock* spell on the door.

"Am I going to be able to undo that?" she asked.

He took her hand and laced his fingers through hers. "Sing this tone with me." He hummed a note.

"I don't sing in front of people." It was a hard and fast rule of hers.

"I can't hear it. Come on. Match the tone." He hummed again. She sighed with displeasure and then hummed his note. His vibes sang out and the spell formed. "Now all you need to do is touch the door and hum. Any note. Doesn't have to be that one. The spell will recognize you. No more pesky keys." An edge lined his tone.

"Bad day at the office, dear?" she asked, one eyebrow raised as he strode into the dining room and began to unpack the food at a brisk speed.

"Something like that."

She lagged behind him. "This is a new mood. I haven't encountered this one in our...fling." Uncertainty tugged at her. She had no experience with this. Maybe this wasn't a fling.

Angry lines stretched across his forehead. "This is not a fling."

That answered that. But what were they? She took a breath, studying his frown. Now wasn't the time for that conversation. "What's the matter? I mean, other than the entries filling up our calendar of doom?"

"I hate Nils Lusman. That's what's the matter."

There were times when she wasn't happy with Nils either... impatient, guilt-ridden days when she wished he'd hurry up and find a way to free another sorceress. "Sometimes he can be a little hard to take." She glanced down at the white takeout boxes. Despite the tension, her mouth watered at their spicy, rich scent. She opened a box. A huge piece of chocolate cake sat inside.

He rubbed his hand across his forehead. "Ah, hell, Mara. I messed up."

She waited in that bad news stillness to hear which way the scale would tip—to the *easily fixable* side or the *someone was dead* side.

"He saw you dance."

For a few seconds, the words refused to make sense. It was a blissful moment, one her mind clung to for as long as it could, denying the meaning of such a simple sentence. It wasn't nearly long enough. A cascade of hot and cold poured over her. She clutched her hands to her cheeks. No one was dead, but by the stars, she almost wished she was. "Nils was at Fancy's?"

"I should have cast a *fog* spell over his eyes...over everyone's eyes."

"That's...embarrassing." But she could still feel the vibes of her dance playing on her skin.

When the curtain rose, she'd known in her heart that she needed to wring every moment of pleasure from that experience for herself. It hadn't been about the audience or Fancy but about her power, her connection to it, and her acceptance of it. It's why she'd covered her eyes. It wasn't about letting other people see them...or so she'd told herself at the time. Now she realized she'd been fooling herself, still partly in hiding.

She dropped her hands from her cheeks. "No, you couldn't have hidden me away. Fancy would have booted you to the Pacific if you'd ruined the show. And, besides, I don't want to hide anymore." She offered him a small smile. "Although if I still wore my specs, Prower might not have pushed for interning the wayward." She bit her lip.

He closed the distance between them and cupped her cheek. "This is not your fault. You can't think that."

But she did. She looked away from him.

"Nils told me how you help sorceresses escape Power United. That's dangerous work, Mara."

"It's worth the risk," she said, as solemn as he was. She hadn't thought to tell him that secret. And now that he knew, all she could wonder was whether or not he'd help them get sorceresses out. Some part of her mind noted the depth of her trust and pondered at it.

He nodded. "How does he know Fancy?"

"I think she helps him move the sorceresses in the West. I hope she doesn't put them in brothels." She shrugged like she was helpless, but she wasn't. She needed to question more. "I don't know. Nils doesn't like it when I ask."

She walked into the kitchen and pulled out two wine glasses and a bottle of red. Setting them on the dining room table, she sent a sharp stream of vibes along the foil of the wine bottle. With a needle-thin thread of power, she pushed her vibes into the cork, secured it with a knot at its bottom, and pulled. Her very own *corkscrew* spell.

He nodded at the bottle. "Impressive spell, sorceress. With a stream of vibes that thin, you could slit a man's throat."

"At the rate I'm going, that might come in handy." For an unwitting moment, she tried to picture it and couldn't. Not that she wanted to. But experience had taught her she was capable of things that were unpleasant to think about.

"Goddess, I hope it doesn't come in handy."

They sat down together. Over their dinner, she told him about her second encounter with the river maiden's queen and how she made it out of the City of Kansas...more unpleasantness. He didn't smile once during their dinner. Of course, her story wasn't humorous, but there was something more there.

Something heavy.

She tried not to make it about her...about them. She didn't want to be that insecure, but she'd never done this not-a-fling thing before.

"Thank you for this." She nodded at the empty boxes. The wine bottle had nary a drop left. "When are you going to tell me whatever still has your eyes tight? It's not just Nils."

He rubbed at the telltale wrinkles. "I was trying to hide it until we were done."

"Well, we're done." The words were tighter than she wanted.

He took a breath. "I found a file with your name on it at Power United. Yours and Stella's."

HE SHOULD HAVE GIVEN her some warning instead of dropping the topic on her. Gregor watched her as she stared at the empty bottle of wine, her eyes bronze and glowing...and far away. He wanted to protect her from this, not lay it out before her. But he didn't have a choice.

She was silent for a long time.

"What do you think happened to the AWOL sorceress on the train?" she finally asked.

He knew she wasn't changing the subject. She was working her way up to it, preparing herself. He reached out, offering his hand to her, and when she took it, he helped her up and then led her deeper into her house without an offer from his hostess. He pulled her next to him on her soft couch in her den.

"Do you think she jumped?" Mara asked. "If she did, then she probably didn't make it. She was so skinny and frail. I wouldn't have made it without you." She shivered.

He pulled the blanket that was draped along the back corner of the couch over her and then pulled the four scrolls out of his invisible pocket.

"Where did those come from?" she asked. To her eyes, it had to look as if he'd pulled them from thin air. He explained about the invisible pocket.

"Could you teach me how to cast that spell?" she asked.

He instantly frowned. "It's not mine. It's Lincoln's." He nearly growled the man's name.

"Oh. Would you mind if I asked him?"

"No." But he gritted his teeth.

Mara laughed. "Gregor, are you jealous of Linc?"

"No." He couldn't disguise the lie in such a blunt question.

She leaned over and kissed his cheek and then his lips.

The gentle touch almost made him smile.

"You have no reason to be. I would never kiss him." She put her hand on his arm and studied him, but her gaze held a vulnerability that he wanted to cherish as much as soothe.

"You like me better than him?"

"I do."

"I like you better than him too." He appreciated the oddly honest moment, but knew his tone still held a grudge.

"Have you ever had a conversation like this before?"

"No." But then he'd never needed to. He'd never been with a woman whose answers to those questions would have mattered.

She gave him a small smile and after a moment, nodded at the scrolls. "Did you steal those?"

"I'm not sure I like this reputation I have with you as a thief, but, yes, I did."

"Looks like you stole a few extra." She picked up the first. "Veronica Guyson. Know her?" She glanced over at him, and he shook his head. "Me either." She unrolled it. He read over her shoulder.

Guyson, Veronica
FJ: 3.01
Lottery year: 233
Ticket: 19
Born: 215/12/01
Training: Intro – 233/6/1
SWW: 1597 days
Total: 0.34 tons
Released: 237/10/15
Deceased: 237/11/21
Cause: Suicide

Most of it didn't make sense to him. But he understood the

second line. FJ stood for Frederick-Johnson, the last names of the two mages who had created a scale to measure mage strength. Every mage was tested and officially categorized as a light or dark mage and their specific power named at sixteen years old.

"Poor Veronica should have missed Power United's cutoff based on her FJ score. A sorceress has to be 3.0 or lower to be put in the lottery," Mara explained.

"That's one thing I don't understand. How did they get away with taking you? You must have a nearly perfect FJ score."

"They don't test waywards. They just assume we're all weak."

"That's not right."

She shrugged. "It's the way it is."

He didn't believe her easy acceptance, but they had enough problems to conquer right now. "What's SWW?" He pointed at the initials on the scroll.

"Standish Walking Wheel. It's a type of spinning wheel. They're one of the largest wheels. It's an old method of spinning. The spinner walks back and forth next to the wheel as her thread or yarn or wire grows longer and then she stops the wheel, winds the thread on the bobbin, and starts the process over again. This particular wheel is made in Standish Territory."

She tapped against the bottom line. "Veronica spun less than half a ton of copper over four years on it."

He calculated the days that were listed. "Longer than four years. 137 days past to be exact. She killed herself a little over a month after she was released."

"That's not unusual," Mara rolled up the scroll and reached for her own. Her hands shook. She almost dropped it.

He took it from her and unrolled it.

Mara Rand—RELEASED
FJ – unknown.
Wayward.
SWW – 27 days.

Some parts were blacked out with a spell. He cast an *erase* spell toward it, humming deep in his throat, but the black ink didn't budge.

"Short and sweet." Her words were clipped. "It was a long time before I could bring myself to spin on a walking wheel again." She tossed it across the room.

He wanted to tug her close, but she unrolled Stella's scroll. He leaned closer to see.

Stella Greer

FJ: 74.3

Lottery: 239

Ticket #1

Born: 223/5/6

Orphan

SVW – 701 days

LSIIW – 27 days

LLW – 13 hours, 42 min.

Deceased. 241/5/6

"By the stars, I knew they'd gotten her when she was sixteen, which is illegal, but Stella was far too powerful to be conscripted. 74.3. That puts her...what...in the top five percent of mages? She's not up there anymore."

Top two percent, he thought. But he didn't share. "It lists her as deceased."

"Yes." Her voice was quiet. "Stella's rescue was different from the others. Power United believed she was dead. They took her body to the morgue. P.U. has their own." She delivered the facts gently. "Their morgue attendant realized she was still alive. My guess is that the attendant has seen enough sorceress bodies that she joined Nils's organization. But she came directly to me. I don't know why. I could hardly ask her as she dropped Stella in my arms. I have no idea what happened to the poor girl there. She doesn't remember much of her time at P.U. at all."

She refocused on the scroll, pointing to the abbreviations. "SVW is Standish Victorian Wheel. LSIIW is Lashford Sorceress II Wheel. The Standish Spinning Wheel Company and the Lashford Company are the two big manufacturers. The LLW is the Lashford Lourne Wheel. It's the one you saw in my window upstairs, remember?

"Julia Lourne was the most well-known craftswoman in the business...an enormously powerful mechanic mage. Her wheels channel incredible power. If a sorceress isn't skilled enough, a Lourne wheel could drain her dry. If she was spinning copper on it"—she shrugged—"perhaps it could kill her.

"Julia collaborated with Lashford on one wheel. But they only made a few. I didn't know P.U. had one. She wouldn't have liked that."

"Would she know where the white wheel is?"

"She's dead." Rolling up the scroll, she stared down at it. "From how sick Stella was, I knew she had more power than a 3.0, but 74.3? That's a lot of vibes to drain." Her anger and dismay pulsed through her energy, pushing against him. "I need more gray repose silk. It would give her back her vibes. But I used up my supply of webs on a Rallis...like they aren't privileged enough. And then I gave that scarf to the river maiden queen."

She shook her head as if she couldn't believe it and then leaned against his shoulder. A protective urge rushed forth. He took the scroll and laid it on the table, bringing her into his arms.

The energy between them changed with the simple movement, sparking something unexpected. She looked up at him and stroked the side of his whiskered cheek. That was all the encouragement he needed.

"Come on, firefly." Bending to put an arm around her legs, he scooped her up and strode through her living room and upstairs, following her residual vibes to her bedroom. He lay down with her on her bed, face to face. Her eyes glowed with everything he wanted—heart, home, and a heady sense of lust powerful enough to make him dizzy.

She leaned over and took his mouth with hers, nibbling softly and he tasted her sweetness. A primal need to reassure himself that she was his washed over him, as demanding as it was uncertain. He palmed the back of her head and pressed their kiss deeper. Anyone who thought they had a claim on her would have to come through him first...man or woman, renegade or ruler.

She reached for the buttons on his shirt and twisted her vibes around them all, undoing them with a spell. She straddled him as her vibes clouded around his chest, gentle touches everywhere.

He sucked in a breath as her hand caressed his chest, her fingers drifting over his nipples and the hair that traveled in a line to his belly and below. He'd wanted her back in his arms since the instant she'd left them.

She tugged open his pants with her spell. With a soft hum, he added his own power to hers, tickling her skin.

She shivered and giggled. He'd never heard her make that sound and a heaviness within his chest lightened. "Take off your shirt with that spell," he ordered with a whisper.

She obliged, shucking the garment to the floor. He unfastened her bra with a quick flick of the fabric. He lifted her heavy breasts, loving their weight, their softness. Brushing his thumbs over her nipples, he toyed with the hard buds. He watched as she tipped her head back, pressing into his touch, her eyelids heavy with desire.

He craved this closeness, this naked need that bonded them.

Beneath the press of her core against his, his cock stood ready. He wanted her skin against his.

"Off," she said, as if she sensed his need. She tugged at the fastening of his pants and then stood, wiggled her pants off, and waited for him to do the same.

Sitting against her headboard, he helped her back on his lap, spreading her wide over his legs. He pulled her forward and her wetness slipped over him. Goddess, she was pure fire and heat. With a gentle thrust, he found her opening. She shuddered as he stretched her tightness.

Intoxicating pleasure washed over him and with it was an awareness that at this moment everything in his world was exactly right. "Ah, Mara, what you do to me...."

Eye to eye, her power shined through, connecting with his, open and unguarded. He leaned into it and so did she. Holding her ass with a soft touch, he guided her movements, her narrow passage grasping at his cock. Time fled, leaving only devastating need.

They moved as one, her hips meeting his, the core of her womanhood brushing against him.

Her body went taut above him. She cried out as her climax hit, her pulsing rhythm driving him over right behind her, sending his seed deep inside her.

As she relaxed forward, he pulled her onto his chest. Cradling his hand against her head, he held her and prayed to whatever deity was listening for the strength to keep her safe.

THE SUN WAS up long before either of them, but Mara knew from the line of the light in her room that she still had time to get to work at a decent hour. She stayed still, savoring the feel of his warmth and strength behind her, holding her. His breath tickled the back of her neck and then his nose nudged her.

"I know you're awake," he whispered. "I like your room." His voice was scratchy with sleep. "It looks like it should be in the middle of a forest."

"A dark forest." She turned over in his arms, burying into his chest.

"I grew up wandering around a dark forest. It suits me."

The wallpaper, with its large tapestry-like forest scenes, was printed in shades of gray and showcased a grand, wise owl in every repeat of the wide, tall pattern. The wallpaper met the dark molding that took up the lower half of the wall at the chair railing. Her bed stood proud and regal in the center of the room, black carved wood topped with a dark gray duvet.

Dark. It was all dark.

When she'd finished decorating the room, she'd stepped back and observed the final effect. She'd nearly slammed the door on it. It was glamorous, sophisticated...and bleak. Not a hint of color marred the landscape. She'd created a fancy dungeon for herself, one with an artist's rendition of a forest and birds that might have surrounded a crumbling castle, home to a dark queen who brought catastrophe upon the world.

White sheets and a hint of white background in the charcoal wallpaper softened the effect. But it wasn't enough.

This morning, however, her dark dungeon of a bedroom held a prince of a man for the first time ever.

She smiled at him and pressed a kiss against his chest that turned into a round of gentle lovemaking. The rest of their morning was oddly domestic considering what was coming.

After a breakfast of toast and coffee, she started to cast a *stay good* spell on her milk.

"Stop," he ordered.

"Should I just drain it then? If we're leaving—"

"We don't want anyone to think it was planned. Just leave everything. Dirty dishes in the sink, too."

He kissed her goodbye when he closed her into Linc's car. He would meet her at the mill at half till evening-tide and accompany her to the Council House.

By the time she arrived at work, Harry was waiting in her office, a plan to hide her at the ready.

"Thank you, my friend, but no." She wouldn't let Harry get wrapped up in hiding them. Mara sat down at her desk.

Harry took a chair across from it. "You can't just let them take you."

She couldn't afford to tell anyone the plan. Harry was safer not knowing.

"If I don't come back, make sure everyone gets their paycheck on time. Esther knows enough to keep the floor running and to handle the orders, but she won't know how to coordinate anything else. Feel free to give yourself a raise." She handed over a thick envelope. "This contains a list of clients you'll have to handle personally. It also contains my will. If anything happens to me, the mill is yours. Not that it's much of a prize, but I don't have anyone else to leave it to." Her voice faded with the last part. It was embarrassing to admit. "You can sell it, of course. But...."

"I'll keep it going. I vow it, Mara."

She nodded. Refusing to let the silence build to sadness, she switched subjects. "How was the Black Cat last night?"

Harry was a creature of habit, and her Thursday nights were always spent at the sleazy bar looking for a hookup.

"Boring. Nothing looked good." She gave her half a smile. "Nothing that would bring a glowing flush to my cheeks that still remained the next day."

Mara smiled back. "That would be a lucky find, indeed."

After a quick knock at the door, Esther walked in without waiting for a welcome. Two dozen pairs of jeans weighed down her arms.

29

"HURRY UP! I'm naked under these robes!" The High Councilor's words echoed around the massive atrium.

Mara climbed the stairs that crisscrossed the middle of the three-story space, turning to the next set of steps at a landing that was wide enough for a living room. Gregor was at her side. They both carried two bags of jeans.

To get to the Council House, they'd entered the portal that stood in the middle of Columbus, taken a few steps, and walked out hundreds of miles away in the middle of the Republic's capital city. The average mage citizen believed portals were impossible, and she'd been warned to keep it that way.

Linc had accompanied them. He waited for them outside the Council House.

Mara nodded to the guard at the top of the stairs as she rounded the corner and crossed the hall to the doors straight ahead. Linc usually stood there when the crone was inside.

The guard shoved something into her hand as she passed. "For my shirts," he muttered. "And I need three more."

"Contact the mill," she whispered, frowning. What was he thinking paying her here? If he weren't more discreet, his secret—

that his power flowed too strongly to handle comfortably—wouldn't stay hidden for long.

Gregor raised an eyebrow but kept quiet.

Ahead, two large wooden doors opened with a spell. She and Gregor stopped in the doorway. The High Councilor stood in the center of the room, perfectly framed. Ornate moldings graced the top, middle, and bottom of the walls, which were a pale gray. White silk curtains hung open around the windows that dominated the wall behind her. A couch and chairs sat off to Mara's right. On the left, a screen stood, sectioning off the corner of the room. She wasn't sure what this room was used for other than the fittings that she did for the High Councilor.

"I'm going to spell wheels to take the place of your feet the next time. You're entirely slower than turtles!" the High Councilor said.

Mara bowed. "I'm not sure we could manage your stairs, Lady, if we did not have feet."

"Oh, shut it, my little wayward citizen, and hand over the goods. I'm late for my date." The old woman grabbed one bag and swirled away, robes fluttering behind her, as she disappeared behind the dressing screen. An instant later, the white robes flew over the top of the screen and the shuffling of clothes whispered out.

"I thought your date was Saturday," Mara said.

"It got moved up. My date's impatient."

That was a convenient excuse for changing the delivery day. Mara buried the thought before the crone could read her mind.

A moment later, a young woman with big brown eyes, long, dark hair, and a gleaming red smile stepped out. She wore Mara's white jeans. Her blouse, also white, had straps at her shoulders but her sleeves started at mid-bicep. It was cropped short. If she lifted her arms, she'd reveal her belly. Her feet were bare, toes painted yellow. She was stunning and about twenty years old. She winked at Gregor. "Wanna give me a kiss, handsome?" she asked in the old crone's voice.

Gregor's jaw dropped.

"No kiss?" She turned to Mara. "How about you, lovely?" This time her voice matched her body, youthful and seductive. She puckered up, waited for a moment and then shrugged. "Your loss." She spun away toward the side of the grand room. "Chop, chop. You want to be paid for your work? Follow me." She sashayed away and disappeared out a door at the side of the room.

"Was that...." Mara squinted around the room. She tried again, "Who was...." But still the words would not come. She peeked behind the dressing screen. Vacant. She gestured toward the exit. "My check just walked out the door." She dropped the other shopping bag and rushed after the young woman.

The next room featured clusters of fancy couches and chairs among ornate paintings but no beauty queen or old crone. Mara rushed through the long space, the carpet deep and as plush as a cloud. The next open door led to an office.

The desk and chair were delicately feminine, carved, painted, and created before the New World was truly conquered. She couldn't imagine the High Councilor sitting there. She passed it and rushed toward the next door, closed but straight ahead.

This place was laid out like a never-ending row of rooms, impossible based on the outside dimensions. There were spells afoot, and they were getting thicker.

Gregor pulled her to a stop. "I'm going first." His eyes were hard, his lips flat.

"Why?"

"The door is another portal. The power around it is sparking out like fireworks. Can you not sense it?"

She should have recognized it for what it was. The portal to the capital city felt the same.

"The question is, where will this one take us?" He opened the door and power flooded out, tingling against her like a fizzy drink. Gregor stepped in. "There's a *silence* spell here. No one can hear us." He reached for her hand and ushered her in.

They walked down a long, narrow corridor, a wall on their left and enormous tapestries that hung from the ceiling on their right. They passed the first tapestry and the second. Mara gawked, drinking them in. Even from the back where the threads were thick and tied, the scenes were clearly erotic. Naked women cavorted in the first, and the second pictured multiple couples in the midst of a variety of acts.

"Where are we?" she whispered.

"No idea. There's a place like this in the receiving room, behind the tapestries, but this is different. Yeah," he added at her sharp look. "I was there when you were with those ladies-in-waiting."

She'd ended up on her knees in that room with all that power and all those prophecies. And then she'd landed in a dungeon. She hoped for a better outcome today.

When they got to the third tapestry, it turned transparent.

In front of them stood the beautiful woman who wore the High Councilor's jeans. She faced them, but her eyes were focused elsewhere.

"She can't see us," Gregor said.

The room was lined with cushions and backless couches. Toward the far end, a grand bed dominated, draped with hundreds of yards of silk fabric. It was a room fit for a royal harem. The air felt thick and dirty. Dust stuck in Mara's nose.

A chandelier hung in the middle of the room. Crystals dangled from it. It was a near match to the one in the courtroom in Fancy's bordello.

"By the lost girls," Mara breathed. "We're in the Wild West."

On the other side of the spelled tapestry, the young woman spun around and gave them her back.

Fancy strutted in.

30

THE HIGH COUNCILOR had a portal that led to a bedroom in The Green House. It was the finest bedroom Mara had ever seen. But she knew it wasn't Fancy's room. The madame would never let someone into such a personal space.

Mara's mind felt seared with shock. Fancy was acquainted with the High Councilor...or at least some version of her, one that held no resemblance to the crone. Did Fancy know who she was dealing with?

"It's about time you got here. I thought you were going to stand me up." Fancy's black corset lifted her breasts high. Her leather pants shined in the candlelight, and her heels granted her an extra five inches. The contrast from one woman to the next stretched from sexy youth to experienced seductress.

"Why are you so late? A bad hair day again, High Councilor?"

Okay, Fancy knew who she was dealing with.

If Mara had needed it, the madame had given her confirmation that the High Councilor had a youthful alter ego buried beneath her wrinkles and white hair.

"I've heard Mara has an excellent hair mage on staff. Perhaps you should ask her for a referral." Fancy sauntered forward. The High Councilor turned so that she stood in profile to the tapestry. Fancy did the same, facing the young beauty. "I do like your ass in those jeans though. Did you wear them for me, gorgeous?"

"Baby, I'm all for you. If you're woman enough to take it, that is, and let's be honest, that has yet to be determined." The former crone, now sexy vixen, smiled, her red lips shining with the best *lipstick* spell Mara had ever seen.

Fancy laughed. "Oh, please, woman. I've already had you. I can handle whatever you want to dish out." She tapped a sharp, red fingernail against her chin. "Can the same be said for you?" Her eyes swirled silver, the metallic gleam catching the candle-light that sparkled dimly in the colorful chandelier.

Silver.

Shocked once again flashed a bright streak through Mara's mind.

"Goddess above, she's a fucking glister." Gregor's whisper whipped with fury. She put her hand on his arm, giving comfort as much as she was seeking it.

All these years, Fancy had been masquerading as a mage, and Mara had fallen for it. Everyone had fallen for it. Stars above, how could she not have known?

Gregor yanked her around, hiding her face against his chest. His heart sprinted beneath her ear. "Don't look," he growled. "She'll catch your mind."

"Gregor, it's all right." She pushed him away. "She can't catch me. No glister can. But how could she let me believe she was a mage?" If she could reach the woman right now, she might grip her by her corset strings and shake her.

On the other side of the tapestry, the young High Councilor stroked a finger over her bare shoulders. "No silver eyes, glister girl. That's not playing fair," she whimpered with a sexy hitch. She dropped her gaze, so innocent, so dangerous.

Fancy ran a finger along the young woman's lips. "Since this is both love and war, all's fair goes doubly true. And by the way, when are you going to return my spell? Haven't you had enough fun with it yet? I know you've been misplacing people...west to east and north to south."

The young crone shrugged and hummed her lips together in a song of *I don't know.*

"Shall I take it out on your hide?" Fancy rubbed the High Councilor's ass.

"Try it," the vixen crone whispered. "And see what happens." It was offered softly, but a threat lay beneath.

Fancy laughed and strutted away, her derriere perfect in her shiny pants. She opened a low chest at the foot of the bed and came back with a pair of white scissors in hand, pointed at the High Councilor's youthful body.

On the other side of the tapestry, the High Councilor scrambled back. "Goddess of the great country! Don't point those things at me! Are you trying to kill me?"

Though she'd never seen them before, Mara realized what they were: scissors that endowed the power of dance into anything they snipped...one of the fairy relics.

Gregor grabbed her hand, his face pale. She angled in front of him as if she might protect him.

"It's a gift, my sweet," Fancy said. "Are you brave enough to take it? Spin, snip or stitch, it all ends badly for a mage with a relic." Her voice was low and sexy as if a mage reaching a bad end was a sensual delight. "You ruined a very handsome mage with the needle. Two of them actually. The Prophet. And the young, proud Captain Whitman. Now he's as good as one of us, you know."

Gregor glared at the High Councilor, such loathing in his eyes, such fear, that Mara wanted to push past the invisible wall separating her from the woman, brave those scissors, and snip the crafty, cold-hearted woman out of their lives.

The vixen crone shrugged. "He had a job to do. He's loyal to his country, and so he did it. Besides, he got to screw the girl, didn't he?"

Fancy smiled, and the High Councilor smiled back. It reminded Mara of an *image* spell she once saw of two sharks circling each other.

Fancy held out the scissors again. "They were a gift to the Goddess, you know. And they are in your hands now."

"A gift from a philandering sicko wanna-be-god." She pinched one of the handles with the tips of her fingers, touching them as little as possible.

Fancy dusted off her hands and gave a relieved sigh. "The Republic now has the needle and the scissors. That only leaves the wheel. If you're not smart enough to find that one on your own and keep your borders standing, then that's on you."

"What would your brother say about that?" She stuck the scissors in her pocket. The white handles poked out, an uncomfortable accessory for the outfit.

"My brother has been missing for thirty years. I can't remember anything he said."

"I miss him. He was a worthy opponent."

Fancy shrugged. "Perhaps he still is. Who can say? Considering the prophecies, he'd want the relics in the Republic. No glister wants citizen mages in their land."

"Apparently there's one citizen mage you like having in your land. About her, that sorceress, did you know she gets notes with prophecies written on them?"

Mara stiffened. Why did the High Councilor want them to see this?

"Notes? Like in the mail?" Fancy asked with a whisper of uncertainty.

"Exactly so." The High Councilor tilted her head. "Someone's scribbling bad poems and shooting them through her mail slot." The young woman stepped closer, something threatening about her posture. "You wouldn't happen to know an oracle mage spouting prophecies about the end of the world?"

Fancy stepped back.

"I thought you were going to keep her quiet. I've foreseen what happens if there are two high-powered oracles in the Republic during my rule and it ain't pretty."

Fancy rolled her eyes. "She's not in the Republic."

The High Councilor reached out and trailed her fingertips over Fancy's high, deep cleavage. "I can't believe I had to let her live."

"Had to?" Fancy gave a bitter laugh. "You don't do anything you don't want to."

"Then you know nothing of ruling," the young High Councilor snapped softly. "How did you meet my wayward sorceress?"

"Yours? Oh, she's not yours. Never mistake her for yours." Fancy strode over to a large, wooden armoire and opened the doors. Crops and whips lined the interior. She pulled one out and tested it in her hand. "I met Mara during the seventh dark moon of the 274th year of the king's reign."

"Pfft. Gray time." She paced over to Fancy, slipped the crop from her hand, and snapped it in two. Tossing it to the floor, she skipped over to the huge bed and jumped on it, bouncing high and then landing, seated, against the fluffy pillows.

"Glister," Fancy corrected, her tone full of warning. "Years ago, Mara's hotel in the city of Kansas caught fire. She was standing in the middle of the street in a crowd, staring up at the inferno. I met her by chance, of course. It was the middle of the night." She shrugged. "She needed a bed. I had one."

"Your bed." The words were flat.

"By Luck's ass, no. You're the only mage girl I've ever fucked." She lifted a bottle of champagne out of an ice bucket standing next to the couch. She filled the two glasses sitting on the low coffee table and strutted over to the bed. The High Councilor took it and sniffed, cautious.

Fancy dipped her finger in hers and sucked it dry. "Besides, Glow Eyes is in bed with the deaf monk now. Isn't it all going the way you planned?"

The High Councilor laughed, high and pretty. "I wish." She gestured with her glass. "How does it go again? Glow Eyes spins webs as Luck commands, abandoned to the dance...blah, blah blah. The relics await her touch. Their fate...." She was fishing for information as if the other woman might spill out the rest of the prophecy.

The vixen crone cocked her head, her eyes high, a picture of innocence so ripe it was spoiled. "Hmm. No matter. She's not spinning webs at the moment, you know. She's run into a bit of a supply issue with the raw material. Banned." She shrugged like these things happened.

"What a shame," Fancy retorted, drawing out the words. The madame leaned over the bed and stroked her hand over the High Councilor's thigh. "White is such a pretty color on you. So pure. So sweet. And these jeans...perfection encasing perfection. You sent Mara across the continent like a Manifester on a pilgrimage to make them so you could look pretty for me."

The High Councilor leaned in. She sniffed. "You smell like smoke."

"I'm aflame for you." Fancy sealed her lips to the other woman's. It was a gentle kiss.

"What have you done?" the High Councilor demanded softly when Fancy pulled away.

"I've given my favorite sorceress what her heart most desires. That's what I've done. Now, you, on the other hand...you're allowing your Senate to break the rules. Your land shall pay a steep price if this internment is enacted."

The High Councilor frowned. "The Senate is full of fools."

"They think to put roadblocks on Mara's destiny. I shall burn them away."

The young High Councilor gave her a slow blink and got up

on her knees, tugging at the ties that held together Fancy's leather corset. "You started a fire."

"It's what I do." Fancy's tone was heavy and sensual.

The young woman tilted her head, studying her lover. "This time your fire might burn your favorite sorceress to a crisp." She loosened the corset's laces.

Mara looked away before Fancy's breasts spilled out, but it was a close thing. From the corner of her eye, she saw the tapestry lose its *transparency* spell. Fibers and threads dangled in front of their noses instead of the bedroom scene. Thank the stars for modesty. She had no desire to see anything more.

"Show's over." Gregor tugged her out and they retraced their steps, through the corridors, the exquisite rooms, and down the stairs.

She still hadn't gotten paid.

MARA STOOD at the entrance of the capital city's portal waiting to cross back into Rallis Territory. They were fleeing westward the moment they returned. They'd reach Daegan's ferry before nightfall. Or at least, that had been the plan. She was about to change it.

Linc gestured for her to enter the portal.

Like the one that stood in Rallis Territory, the portal in the Republic's capital was in the base of a tall bronze statue. In her home city, it was a statue of Christopher Columbus. Here it was a statue of the first High Councilor, his lips in a firm line, hiding his wooden teeth, his proud nose arching gracefully above it. Mara had always thought he had an arresting face.

She stepped in, Gregor behind her. The stone walls were rough and cave-like, glowing with a soft light. The door to Rallis Territory awaited a dozen strides ahead. Some trick of the portal made the inside of the statue longer than the outside.

A shatter of power flickered around her. She paused. That had never happened before.

The light faded, darkness falling like a smothering cloth. Her heart pounded. "Gregor?" she tested. She couldn't see a thing. A hard push at her back sent her crashing into the wall. She cried out.

"Don't hurt her," someone hissed, a man, behind her. An impossibility since the wall was right there...and then it wasn't. She nearly fell into the newly empty space. She spun away, too hard, and fell to the floor. Power flooded around her. It was another portal.

"Mara!" Gregor shouted.

"Get 'er guards!" the man ordered.

"She wasn't supposed to have fucking guards!" Another mumble of words sounded, but she couldn't make them out.

Someone grabbed underneath her arms and yanked her back. Her head jerked, straining her neck. She dug her heels into the ground. "Gregor!" she screamed. The sound bounced. A punch, a thud against the wall...she couldn't see anything.

She reached high behind her, the only way left to her with the strong man's arms under hers. She yanked at his hair, threw an elbow into his ear.

It all happened so fast. There was no time to make sense of it. No time to do anything but flail with everything she had.

His hand struck her in the face and she cried out, gripping his hair harder.

"Shit! Outta here! Retreat!" The man yanked away, her hand tearing something from his head.

The door at the other end of the portal opened. Light flooded in. Gregor scooped her up and sprinted. The jostle addled what was left of her mind.

And then they were in the middle of the sidewalk in Columbus. Linc slammed the portal door shut.

As sunshine flooded around them, she stared at the black goggles in her hand.

31

Clutching Mara, Gregor paced as fast as he could without running across the wide expanse of concrete that spread out before the statue. Running would have drawn too much attention, even considering the powerful *don't look* spell that surrounded the portal. Linc was just in front of him, navigating their way through the downtown streets and sidewalks. They were crowded. The sounds of a festival near the river filled the air.

"Put me down," Mara whispered.

"No. Don't." Linc's voice was clipped. "You'll slow us down." The car was a block away.

She wiggled. "I want to walk. This is ridiculous."

Gregor let her go, even knowing Linc was right. She'd been tossed around in the damn portal and her mage energy was clamped down tight. She wouldn't be able to see. He kept his hand around her elbow.

She held up the goggles.

Goddess above, they'd nearly had her. His fingers itched to clutch her to his chest and never let go.

"It was the Black Skulls," she whispered, squinting up at him. Her glow was gone, and her pace was too slow by far.

He nodded. "One outlaw. Two glister." He pulled her down the sidewalk.

She shook her head. "All sent for me? That's a lot of work for one spinner. Guess that's what I get for bragging to him that I'm the finest. Remind me to be humble." Her words were breathy.

He scanned their surroundings with his vibes but refocused on Mara when she stumbled over a crack in the sidewalk. "Do you have your specs?" he whispered.

"They're in the Mississippi."

He nodded, taking that in stride. "You need to unwind your power so you can see."

Their speed slowed to a crawl as she sought her vibes. Linc alternated between glaring at the portal, alert for the enemy to emerge, and rolling his eyes at Gregor appeasing Mara. It took her over a minute to unwind her vibes, as if she struggled to find them. Finally, her vibes puffed around her. Her eyes glowed.

"Nicely done," he said. Someday they'd work on her mage sense's reaction time. He was certain she could improve despite SWWM's teachings. After all, Linc had managed to overcome their strict instruction to tuck away his power. The man wouldn't be chief of the High Councilor's security if he hadn't.

He pulled her faster toward her car, Linc taking point again as they made their way through the meandering crowd here for the simple pleasure of having fun. How many of them were wayward? How many would be locked up when the decree came down?

"Gregor," she whispered, "when my hotel burned down in the city of Kansas, the night that I met Fancy, do you think...is it too farfetched that she started it?"

"I wouldn't put anything past her."

"That's quite an undertaking for a mere introduction." Her voice wobbled. "She told the High Councilor she set a fire. I think

I know where she set it. The forbidden forest. The gray repose spiders build their webs on glister land. Nowhere else."

Gregor frowned. "The forest belongs to the Republic." They stepped off the curb and crossed the street to her car.

"No. Daegan told me once. The forbidden forests are glister land. I need to go there. Now. If there are webs, I want them."

"We don't have time for that. We're leaving here, remember? Internment?" Linc said, opening the car's back door for Mara. Gregor slid in beside her.

"I need them to heal Stella. I'm not going to miss another opportunity to help her. She's lost so much."

Linc got behind the wheel. Mara leaned forward on the seat toward him. "Linc, you've seen her for yourself. I will not turn my back on this."

"This is a bad idea," he muttered.

Gregor agreed, but he was too smart to argue. He laid his hand flat on the middle seat and she put hers in his. Simply touching her eased him.

"How did the Black Skulls know I would be in the portal? It couldn't have been Fancy. If she set the forbidden forest on fire, then she wants me to go there."

Linc glanced in the mirror at her as he guided the car into the street. "Every woman in the receiving room knew you were delivering the jeans on...."

"On Saturday," Mara finished for him. "It's Friday. The delivery was moved up because of the impending internment."

"Sponsored by Prower," Gregor added. He replayed the scene in his mind, flipping through the words that had been spoken by all of the ladies-in-waiting. "His wife was the one who talked about her trips to the Wild West. Maybe Lady Prower knows Prophet."

"That should be the most baffling sentence any mage has ever spoken," Linc drawled.

Gregor remembered the motorcycle ride into the Black Skulls' hideout. "Prophet is holed up in old Fort Prower."

"From a hundred years ago?" Linc asked. "Isn't that a coincidence. Shit. How badly do you need those webs, Mara? I say we just go straight into hiding. Now. Prower is a damn powerful bastard."

"I have a chance to help Stella and I'm taking it." Her voice was firm. There'd be no talking her out of this.

He might not have lost his vibes, but he'd lost his songs. And he would do anything to change that.

She looked up at him. "You understand," she said softly. "I'm not turning my back on this. I'm getting those webs."

MARA SENT a spin of vibes at her high heels, spreading a spell along their soles so they wouldn't sink in the dirt or get caught in the brush. With her vibes waving around her, she walked into the forest, Gregor a pace ahead of her.

She'd never been in here before. Thick silence swirled around her and the ancient beauty took her breath, her mage power seeing the forest for what it really was...a land of white glister oak.

"By the Goddess," Gregor gasped. "The trees look different. They're white. How did they change? They never looked like this before."

"You can see it, too?" she asked. "This is what the forest looked like in the City of Kansas." She'd told him about it over their take-out dinner. "Is it a wayward thing then?"

"They're not white. They're green," Linc corrected, his voice hard, his eyes squinted in confusion.

"Look with your mage sense," Gregor said.

The other man gasped. "How did that happen?"

She looked up at the white canopies, so regal and untouchable...untainted.

"Waywards resonate with a glister's power," Gregor said.

"What? How do you know that?" She sure as starry vibes hadn't, and she'd been wayward all her life, not mere weeks or months.

"I just figured it out." He bit off the words and reached for her hand. "Let's get what we came for and get out of here." He guided her deeper into the forest, the land swallowing them up and claiming them as its own, tempting her to forget what waited outside. And then he stopped.

"Shit," Linc hissed. He scrambled back a step.

"They know we're here." Gregor's voice was tight and low.

"Six of them. Two are off the charts. The others...."

"Sentries," Gregor finished.

She looked around the white trees and saw no one. "Where?" Her hand shook inside Gregor's.

"By order of Lord Rallis, come forward and show yourselves!" The order popped around them with an ear-blasting roar.

"Great," Linc muttered.

Mara let the remorse wash over her and then packed it away for later. She should have insisted she walk in here alone. She'd just gotten them all in trouble. She straightened her shoulders as Gregor guided her around a maze of trees. Lincoln stayed at her back. Both men's vibes circled around her.

Fancy had indeed set a fire. The damage spread out before them. It had consumed a small section of trees—about the size of her front parlor—down to the ground.

Smoke still lingered in the air like steam from a cauldron bubbling with a potent brew. From the odor, the forest ought to have been black and craggily with burned tree trunks. Instead, it was covered with spider silk so thick it might have been long strands of snow instead of strings of webs.

Lord Edmund Rallis, heir to the territory, and his wife, Lady

Aurora, were across the wide pool of white. Her face was pale, her eyes watery. He looked as hard as stone. They sat on tree trunks cut to the size of stools. Four Rallis sentries stood around them wearing gray uniforms with scarlet sashes.

"Four sentries. And one fairy." Linc's whisper was just loud enough for Mara to hear.

Daegan sat alone at the top end of the pool of white webs. He stared at her. "Lord Rallis has no authority here. You didn't have to show yourselves, but I am glad you joined us."

She glanced around again, uncertain what to make of this. It looked like they were interrupting a meeting.

"You were expecting us," Gregor said, his hand on her elbow as he drew her closer. Two more logs, at seat height, stood empty directly in front of them.

Daegan shrugged. "It was inevitable."

That summed up her life at the moment. Inevitable and uncontrollable.

"Mara Rand." Lord Edmund Rallis cocked his head at her. "It was my understanding that you could no longer make any more of your repose fabric because you had run out of spider silk. At the time, I was disappointed to hear that because my family has a use for such cloth, but when the land that is so close to my home catches fire to provide you with webs, I find myself feeling unkindly toward both you and your products."

"I did not start this fire," she replied, speaking with the same tone she used on the High Councilor—firm and tough. Their kind of people never wanted to listen to her kind.

She eyed the webs, wishing she could just grab them and run. They glistened in the soft light of the forest, waving gently. That last part gave her pause, but she chose to believe it was the non-existent wind moving the webs and not a thousand spiders beneath it. That was too creepy even for her.

Small shoots of green poked up through the silk. The loss of the majestic trees that had been here before struck her.

"Lord Rallis, we know who set the fire," Gregor said. "We have no evidence. But if the culprit were here, she'd probably tell you herself that she started it."

Lord Rallis eyed him. "Then set us straight, and tell us who did it, Captain."

"I've never met a mage who can be straight about anything," Daegan said.

The sentries stirred. Their vibes sprang out.

"Don't think to pull your weapons on me. This is glister land, and no one invited you." Daegan's sneer matched his disdainful tone.

"Glister land? You mean the gray?" Lord Rallis asked. "We're in the middle of the Republic. The gray do not rule here."

"Wrong, young Lord Rallis." Daegan's eyes shimmered with heat but not with power.

"I don't understand. Glister?" Lady Rallis asked.

"An ancient name for the gray, Lady Aurora," Gregor explained.

Mara couldn't stop her frown. This was Gregor's former life raising its head, and for a moment she was jealous...that she hadn't known him then, that they knew him as she didn't. It was silly. She had a past without him too.

As if he sensed her feeling of displacement, he took her hand and stepped closer.

Daegan glared at Lord Rallis. "The people of the great Goddess choose to have short memories about us, to forget the past that joins us together. It is a shame. Has your grandfather passed down the knowledge? Or has he forgotten too?" He didn't wait for an answer. "Mara, lady boss of Blue Light Mills, and her guard"—he nodded regally—"please, do us the honor of sitting at our table."

He held out his hand. A rumble sounded from beneath the ground. Twigs and branches burst from the soil around the two empty stools. Twisting and braiding, they formed into backs and armrests for the stools.

Mara swallowed hard. She was the lowest rank here and this was the grandest seat, but Daegan waited, and so she sat, Gregor beside her. She looked back at Linc. He had no place.

"I'm used to standing." He didn't smile.

The glister eyed them all. "Once when the great white sails danced across the ocean, glister and mage were twined, two strands united and each of great power. One was bold, resolute, and unbending. The other was free and brave. Together they conquered a land to make a new home, but the freedom seekers dashed on through the new forests while the bold stayed to gather the power of their slice of land and tie it to them.

"The two peoples agreed to keep peace between them despite the unraveling of their unity. The glister promised portals that led to their kings so their mage allies could call on them in times of need. In return, the mages promised forestland to the glister so they might roam wherever their hearts called them.

"Years passed, and the mages cleaned their lands of all except for themselves and their servants. The glister lands in the territories came to be called forbidden and the heart of the treaty was lost from the common minds of magekind."

Daegan frowned. "The forbidden forests are our paths, meant to be traveled by any glister who so chooses. The old crone remembers, but even she has been careless with the treaty, allowing others to occupy the lands."

"No one occupies them here. Not now," Lady Aurora said.

Daegan nodded slowly. "The little girl no longer hides here. No more Lily." He almost sounded bereft.

"She doesn't need to hide anymore. But we...."

"We enjoy the forest as our own," Lord Edmund finished.

"It is not yours." Daegan's voice snapped. "It is ours to burn, to cull, to abandon, whatever the king sees fit."

"The king has been missing for thirty years," Lord Rallis said. "Are you saying he has returned and ordered the forest burned?"

"With our king gone, our hearts grow bitter and weaken under the strain of temptation...though perhaps this was meant to be." He looked at Mara. "The silk is yours. If the mages will not allow you to spin and create with it, you may do so here. This land is yours to roam freely wherever your heart may call you."

"Why?"

Daegan stared at her for a long moment, his eyes began to go silver at the edges, but they did not flood with his power. "Because you are brave."

She didn't feel brave. She felt in over her head and scared. "If I am brave, it is only because others cannot be and they need someone to stand up for them." She trailed a finger over the webs and came away with a sticky strand.

"Maybe that's the best reason to be brave."

She didn't get a chance to respond. A loud crack sounded through the air. Her whole world turned to fire. Pain vibrated through every cell of her body.

"Mara!" Gregor's shout was so far away.

Lightning flashed behind her eyes.

And then darkness.

32

SHE WAS GONE in a blaze of light as if the hand of destiny had grabbed her. Formless. Undetectable. Gregor had sensed nothing coming though his power had been, and still was, open and ready.

He wanted to run after her, to scream her name, but there was nothing to chase, no one to shout at. She was simply gone. She'd been sitting right next to him. What the hell had happened? Who had the power to do this?

Across the webs the Rallis sentries grabbed their targets, yanking them from the chairs. "Out! Move!" one of them ordered.

If he'd had a chance to grab Mara he'd be doing the same. But there'd been no warning. Where the hell was she? Mages didn't disappear in thin air. A few could use their power to turn invisible but they were still present. He reached out though he knew she wasn't there. Her vibes were completely absent.

He was hollow as if she'd taken some piece of him with her.

Linc acted, unlike Gregor's silence, casting orders through *comm* spells that connected to his men at Mara's mill. "Tanner, bring three men to the forbidden forest, west quadrant. The sorceress is missing. We need a search party now."

"She's not here," he whispered. There was no point to searching here. He could feel it in his heart, his soul, and his energy. He managed to harness the edge of his focus, but only because of years of training and the sliver of his mind that refused to believe what he'd seen...mages didn't disappear.

His surroundings crystallized. The scent of smoke blended with a sharp, acrid burn. Black scorch marks marred the earth where she had stood. The webs vibrated with a staticky crackle.

He remembered Mara's story about the man who disappeared from the forest and left behind a bloody, ripped scarf. He shoved a finger in Daegan's direction. "Did the forest take her?"

The fairy sat in total stillness with his eyes closed. "No." The word sounded hard and hopeless. "The forest would never do that to her...could never do that to her."

Linc crouched in front of her makeshift chair and ran his fingers through the scorch marks on the ground. He took a sniff of the residue and coughed hard. "Nothing but trash vibes. Not a glister spell, then." Only mages left residual vibes. He wiped his finger on the dirt around him trying to get it off. "What the hell kind of spell does that?"

"You know who set the fire, fairy." Gregor's accusation shot out.

"My sister," Daegan said.

"Your sister? Fancy is your fucking sister?" Gregor dropped his head back.

"Fancy is focused on Mara living up to the prophecies. I disagree but ordering the king's sister to do something is no easy task."

"The king's sister," Linc repeated. "That makes you...."

"The king's brother," Gregor answered. Goddess, what next? He reined in the anger. He needed to keep thinking, needed to climb past the towering wall of rage and despair that had formed in the same blink in which she'd disappeared. "You didn't want Mara to go west. You wanted her to stay in the east."

"Because I wanted to keep her away from the Black Skulls... and Fancy. But that did not work." His words were flat, emotionless. "Mara is with the wheel now. And you did not find it, monk mage."

Gregor's mind roared with thunder, its raging boom so loud he nearly missed the glister's next words.

Daegan looked at him with dead eyes. "When the time comes, remember that I tried to keep this from happening."

Gregor charged at him, fueled by loss and anger, but Linc was in front of him in a flash. The man snapped his fingers in Gregor's face. "Focus on the problem. Getting her back. Glister, is there a way to track the relics?"

Daegan shook his head. "Not even the king could sense it. But I am certain it is in the East. The other relics are already here. It must be close."

"All right then. The only people who have wheels in the East are Power United. The High Councilor has made certain of that," Linc said. "We start there."

Gregor clenched his jaw. "I've searched everywhere at their offices in this city. It's not here."

Linc gave him a hard look. "Maybe you missed something. You're rather new at using wayward power."

"Fuck you."

"There must be someone we can shake down over there. The High Councilor's guard has an entire team of torturers on staff. I'm still their commander. Who's first?"

"Nils." Gregor closed his burning eyes, remembering. "He knows Fancy very well."

"We'll start with him."

～

HER NEW WORLD was cold and hard as if she'd been transported to the top of the earth and abandoned in a desert of ice. The air cut like knives against her, flaking away at her skin until only crumbling specks existed. She was a wasteland of a tundra, inside and out.

She fought for control of what used to be muscles, squeezing and tensing and contracting. It took hours for her body to respond, or so it felt. After a long while, she managed to shift her head.

Her fingers lay beside her, tangled in a lock of hair, numb, too far away to move.

Breath stirred in her lungs like dust under a ray of white moonlight, floating idle and aimless. Pain burst with it.

Darkness fell.

33

THE POWER UNITED emblem was painted in gold on the grand doors of Nils's office. Gregor marched toward them, Linc beside him. No one looked up from their work as they passed row after row of cubicles.

Gregor's rage and grief were walled up tight, but they battled for freedom. No matter what, he couldn't let them loose.

Nils's office door was locked. He'd expected that. He sent his vibes rumbling into it, but the bolt didn't budge, a quality lock. He readied to break down the door, but Linc held out a packet of *melter* potion—it paid to have friends with security clearance. Gregor pressed the packet against the latch and the metal dissolved. The knob fell to pieces.

From within the office, a blast of mage power erupted. The lights surged, visible through the seam of the doors.

On automatic, Gregor hummed a *shield* spell in front of him, and as Linc cast his own, he shoved the doors open.

Nils stood toward the far corner of his spacious office. His eyes were red, his face pale, his suit rumpled. His tie was thrown over his shoulder as if he'd encountered a strong wind, but nothing in the office was disturbed. Everything was in its place.

The stylish black glass desk was neat except for a few empty drink bottles. Papers, pens, and chairs were arranged just so. Thick cologne scented the air as well as a hint of smoke.

"Did you knock? I guess I didn't hear you over my sneeze," Nils said, locking eyes with Gregor. "Having a little problem with my vibes. Embarrassing," he muttered. "Goddess, I hope this isn't a vibe virus."

Vibe viruses were contagious, unpleasant, and had permanent side effects if left untreated. But that blast was no vibing sneeze.

Nils leaned his head against the wall as if he were exhausted. Static electricity popped faintly as he touched the wall. "What can I do for you, Captain?" He gestured at Linc. "And friend."

"Where's Mara?" Gregor demanded. He clenched his fists to keep from grabbing him.

He straightened. "I have no idea. Don't tell me she's missing. Shit." He grabbed a bottle of his blue drink from the pile by the wall and took a swig of it.

Linc stood at Gregor's shoulder. "What are you drinking?"

"A little juice," Nils said, his voice hoarse. He held it up for the man to see.

"Reballa Potion," Linc read. He tipped his head. "Looks addictive."

"Nothing like that. A simple hydration formula. I worked out and I need to rehydrate." Nils brushed away Linc's comment and stared at Gregor. "Where was she taken?"

"Taken? That information is not available," Linc replied.

Nils straightened and finally focused on Linc. "You sound official, Mr...."

"Lincoln Sinclair, commander of the High Councilor's personal guard, on assignment to guard Mara Rand. And I don't think you work out."

He shrugged. "I've been a little dry lately. This stuff helps soothe my throat." It all rang true. His vibes were smooth as ice.

Linc scrunched up his nose. "And you puff on *cologne* spells instead of taking a shower."

He shrugged again like he was too exhausted for a retort.

Gregor almost missed the piece of fabric looped around Nils's neck. It was stuck inside his collar, poking out at the side. "What's this?" He pointed to his own neck with a lifted chin.

Nils eyes went wide and his Adam's apple bobbed with a hard swallow. "Uh..."

Linc walked over to him and ripped it off.

He blanched at the invasion. "Captain Whitman, you have rude friends."

Linc held it up. A blindfold. "Kinky. Exactly what kind of working out did you do?" He didn't wait for an answer. "When was the last time you saw Mara Rand?"

"I sense that I'm a suspect. That's a shame." Nils slapped his palm against the wall in time with his last words as if he was smacking out his anger at being under suspicion.

Gregor narrowed his eyes at the odd move. Before he could register what was going on, the wall disappeared where Nils had slapped it. A black hole gaped in its place. Power sparked. A tall, slender man appeared from the darkness.

It happened so fast.

Gun. Draw your gun.

But the glister's eyes swirled silver, and Gregor thought nothing more. He'd had no time to cast a spell, no time to open his heart or sing a fucking love song. No moment to look away, to shout for help.

He failed.

Linc failed.

His body slipped away from him, ripped from his control. Rage enveloped him as the glister smiled.

"This is bigger than you, Captain Whitman, but I would have liked a man like you at my side." Nils stepped into the hole. The glister followed. The portal closed up the moment both were inside as if it had never been.

Their powers flooded back to them and they stumbled. Gregor reached for the desk for balance. Bottles bumped over the surface, bouncing to the ground. Linc fell to his knees.

Nils had Mara. Gregor was certain of it. Somehow, the bastard had taken her. A vast anger bellowed from the depths of his soul. Losing part of his hearing was horrific; losing Mara was indescribable. He shoved it all down with a ruthless punch.

Linc glared at the wall. "We've got to fucking figure out how to stop those portals." He stood. "Your boy Nils is working with fairies who are working with the Black Skulls who live on Prower land."

That summed it up.

Linc stepped toward the door, but his gaze caught on the floor. "What's this?"

Scorch marks lined the carpet, a dozen short streaks, maybe more. The streaks were just below an electrical outlet. Linc swiped a finger through it. "Trash vibes."

"Like the forest," Gregor said.

Linc gave a curt nod. "This isn't because Power United's headquarters has poor electrical wiring. What the hell is going on?"

They needed reinforcements. Gregor picked up Nils's landline and dialed Vin. He filled him in on the Black Skull and his glister friends hopping the Republic's border and trying to kidnap a citizen from inside the capital's portal, as well as Nils's disappearing act and their suspicions about Prower. His voice cracked when he told him of Mara's disappearance.

In ten minutes, Power United was crawling with analysts, trackers, and reader mages scrounging through the office scrolls, the residual vibes, and the words of the employees. It took hours to figure out that no one in this office knew anything of Nils' activities. Judging by that, he might have been a one-man show, yet half of the board of executives couldn't be located.

Cecilia started talking without prompting the moment Gregor walked into her office. She'd already suffered through a couple of rounds with the interrogators. "I don't know where Nils went. Look, I knew he was corrupt when it came to the sorceresses. I suspected a few others were too."

Gregor knew she'd given the interrogators some names.

She shrugged like she didn't care. "But they were far above me. Nothing I could do about them. Sorceresses kept disappearing. I'd try tracking them down, but more often than not, I failed." Her voice was flat. "I had no idea what he was doing with them, but I knew it wasn't anything good."

"Did you tell anyone? Your boss? His boss?"

"I tried a couple of times. But no one cares about those sorceresses. Just me. They're too weak, too poor to matter. I work every day to get them more food, shorter hours. I try to change the rules around here."

Gregor squinted at her. "Mara cares about the sorceresses."

"Mara breaks the law," she snapped. "Taking in runaways doesn't result in permanent change for the better. It just makes things worse. And I would never ask that bitch for help."

He picked up a crop that lay across her desk. One of the interrogators had found it in her briefcase along with a few other items. "Nils into this kind of stuff, too?"

She shuddered. "I never wanted anything to do with that man."

"He enjoys wearing a blindfold. Maybe you two...you know... have fun together?"

She jutted her chin forward, her eyes tight. "Obviously he wears a blindfold, dumbass. I figured that out a long time ago. He wears it so he can speak the truth when he's asked where the sorceresses are who go missing." Her voice snapped louder. "He can honestly say he hasn't seen them."

He set down the crop with a snap. Fuck. He'd let Nils slip through his fingers—the man who professed to be Mara's ally but was her enemy. It was right in front of him and he'd missed it. "Does Nils have the white wheel?" His lips felt numb.

"If he does, then he can keep it. I don't want it. Why would I? To steal the joy of my sorceresses? Kill them by having them spin on it?" She shook her head. "I'm willing to do my patriotic duty and help the High Councilor find it. But that's it." Truth. All of it. "My top priority has always been the mages who work here, from the time I worked my way up from a conscripted sorceress until now. Unlike your wayward freak. Wherever Mara is, I hope that betrayer is getting every damn thing she has coming to her."

34

MARA SAT in the corner of her stone prison. Her mouth was dry, her skin tight and itchy. A hollowness pushed out from the inside of her body.

She wanted to sink into a cool pool of water and gulp it all down. It hurt to open her eyes. It hurt to close them. She could hardly see. She didn't have enough vibes to power her vision, leaving the world a blur.

She was used up. Every joule, every bit of energy.

Her clothes were in tatters. Her pants were missing one leg and most of the other. Her sleeves were gone and her back felt a breeze where her shirt should have protected her.

But unlike her clothes and her soul and her body, the white glister oak wheel created for Luck's lady stood in the center of the room, gleaming like new as if it had never felt the rub and pull of fiber.

It had found her.

The prophecies echoed through her aching head. Her destiny was manifest here and now. A shriek of denial churned in her gut. It rushed into her throat, but all that came out was a wounded moan. Her mind pulled away from her, panic flooding in.

She closed her eyes and breathed deeply. She had to stop this panic. Now. If she gave it rein, it would sprint away and take her with it. She forced herself to focus. She squinted at the wheel, lit by mage lights hovering at the ceiling as if it were perpetual noon in this place. It throbbed with potential energy.

Diagonal from the white wheel was a mess of green. Hay. She knew its shape. With a quick breath, she caught its scent.

Copper. That's what they wanted, though there was hardly enough to make a few coils of wire.

And where was she exactly? With the Black Skulls or with Power United?

She looked around for answers, but the stone room held nothing else that she could see. Even the door was hidden to her blurry sight. Maybe there wasn't one. Maybe she'd been portaled in.

That thought was all it took. The walls closed around her, claustrophobia's long fingers squeezing her chest. She panted, digging her hands into her palms, fighting. She'd find a way out. She would. She'd escaped once from hell. She could do it again.

"Wake up!" The man's voice sounded all around her. "Wake up!"

The noise pummeled at her ears, thrusting her out of her thoughts. "I'm awake," she croaked, but all that came out was the last syllable.

"Drink both bottles. Or I'll come in there and force you and you won't like that."

She looked around. Two bottles of pink liquid sat to her left, opened and ready. By the lost girls, she hadn't even noticed.

The air in the room tightened. A crackle of energy zapped through her. Her body arched back. Her head bounced against the stone wall. Her fingers curled from the force of it. And then it was gone, leaving her panting from the utter ache.

"I'll give you another crack if you don't drink them. Don't spill. You won't like that either."

Pressure built in the air. Her ears popped. Another crack was coming.

Please, wait. She moved her lips, but no sound came out. She reached out, forcing the little strength she had to the fore, and clasped the bottle. It wobbled as she brought it to her lips, the pressure in the room still ripe for a crackle of electricity. She let it flow into her mouth.

She was so thirsty. It tasted perfect.

"Are you drinking?" The voice popped into existence from nowhere.

Mara jumped. Pink sloshed over the bottle's edge. "Yes."

Wherever he was...however his spell worked...he couldn't see her. That was odd. Surely there was some type of *spy* spell or *image* spell with a distance extender that would have allowed her captors to see in...or the *transparency* spell the High Councilor seemed so fond of. Mara didn't know how to cast such things, but her spells knowledge was limited.

"You've got twenty minutes to drink all that," the man said. "Then start spinning. You've got work to do."

She had no idea how long twenty minutes was. There was no clock, no windows, only the bright light from above. She counted. One sip every ten seconds. She had to change it to twenty when her stomach started to protest, but she wouldn't stop. She needed her strength to get the hell out of here.

When the bottles were empty, she stood, shaky but strong enough to work, coherent enough to keep escape in her mind. Another piece of her pants fell to the ground, leaving her bare at mid-thigh on her right side. The last layer of her shock fell with it, leaving steely resolve in its wake.

If she would flee for her life with clothes dripping off her, then so be it. They'd fallen to tatters in such a way that she was wearing shorts on one leg and tap pants on the other.

At least she wasn't naked. At least she wasn't wearing the horrid gowns that Power United gave their sorceresses. She still had her own clothes.

She walked over to the wheel, circling it. Something about it called to her and before she could think about it, she stroked it. The white glister oak was cool and soft. Its power hummed like velvet beneath her fingertips.

This was a wheel to covet.

She sucked in a breath, catching the dangerous thought before it could lure her further. This was the wheel that would steal all joy, that would bring only lament.

How could it feel so inviting?

She touched a spoke on the wheel and gave it a spin.

A whisper breathed through the air. She almost caught a voice, but it stopped. She held still and listened, but silence filled her prison. Had it been the man again, whispering instructions? If so, he needed to speak up.

She leaned closer to bring the relic into focus. Symbols and figurines decorated the surface. The spokes were carved with flowers and vines. A carved pair of lovers were entwined on the tilted bench that supported the wheel.

Luck's Lady's wheel was stunning.

She straightened. LLW. That's what had been in the files. How long had Power United had it? How many sorceresses had they forced to use it?

How fast would it kill her? Probably not as quickly as the man and his lightning zaps.

She unraveled her power from her inner spindle. Whatever was in that drink worked. Her vibes were replenished. She let her energy puff around her. Her vision cleared.

Holding out her hand, she guided a stream of green hay to flow, one stalk after the other, into her palm. She knew how to do this. It was almost comforting. She eyed the wheel, and somewhere in her mind, she wanted to whisper a challenge to it.

Pulling on a spoke of the wheel, she set it spinning.

Her power and the wheel spun together with the simplest of ease, and the partnership between spinner and walking wheel began. Vibes pushing with a whispered caress, the hay flowed toward the spindle, twisting as it went, circling with her power, and revolving into shiny wire. As the new metal stretched out from the spindle, Mara paced back with it resting in her hand, letting the wire lengthen.

Spinning was about rhythm. It was a dance among the spinner, the fiber, and the string. As the wire lengthened, Mara stepped forward to wind her wire creation around the bobbin. She repeated the process, pacing away to give the hay space and power to evolve, then walking forward to wind the new wire.

"Lost girl." The scratchy words whispered through the air.

Her rhythm vanished. Hay fluttered to the ground. She grabbed a spoke on the wheel and stopped its spin.

Silence fell in her cell. She looked around at the emptiness, the solitude. "Who's there?" she whispered back.

No answer.

Lifting a shaky hand, she tucked a lock of hair behind her ear and started again, tiptoeing through the room as she spun.

"Despair not...girl, for I shall...a story." The whisper scratched through the air, its words cracking and fading.

Mara sucked in a tight breath, but this time she didn't stop her spinning walk.

By the stars, it was the wheel.

"Once upon a time," it whispered.

No. She stopped. She couldn't do this. Her heart thudded in her ears. Fright flowed through her veins with a hundred prickly needles. The wheel's power made its spinner crazy.

On cue, the man's voice boomed out. "Are you spinning?" The air tightened and crackled as if a bolt of lightning readied to flash out.

She whispered a *yes* and made it the truth, starting the rhythm again.

"Once upon a time...." The voice was soft and hoarse. "A king wandered the...western lands." A long noise rasped out from the wheel, piercing her ears. She wasn't meant to hear this. She almost stopped again, but a squeak sounded from the wall. A piece of it slid open. The door was right where she'd been lying when she'd awoken.

Two men strode in, a lightning bolt on their breast pockets. That answered one question. This was Power United. Old fears she'd long since left behind burst from hiding places in her mind. She froze. The wheel spun on from the momentum she'd given it.

"Shit! Look what she's done. The hay's nearly all gone," the first man said.

"Keep going, girl! Don't stop." The other man smacked a short, thin stick against his hand.

She tried to swallow, her mouth dry, her throat burning. Lost girls, she remembered that whip.

"Nah, we need to get her out of here. Much longer and it'll kill 'er. She's been in here long enough for it to trance her. She'll spin like crazy now. We'll put her on a wheel out on the floor, and she'll spin until her teeth fall out."

"We don't have an open wheel on the floor right now, dumb-ass. Bring in more hay. We'll keep her in here since she's doing so fine."

The first man shook his head. "Number forty-seven's about to keel over. There'll be an opening soon enough." But the other man glared. "Fine. You're the boss." He turned and obeyed, piling ten bales inside with a *screw you* glare. Dissension in the ranks, she thought.

"Get it done!" The man with the whip poked her hard in the side. In her mind, she could hear the smack of it against a sorceress's skin, the pained cry in response.

She turned to the wheel. For the first time, she noticed the spindle didn't fit right. It was rusted, cheaply made and newer than the rest of the wheel. It was also too small.

Another hard poke. "Spin!" the man ordered.

And like his underling, she, too, obeyed.

"His power was...and strong," the wheel stuttered. "The king united...."

She nearly stumbled to a halt. She knew exactly which spindle was supposed to go with this enormous wheel. It was long and sharp and silver...and she used it as a weapon in the Wild West. Fancy had given it to her years ago.

"I hate that wheel. Listen to it. A bitch of a lullaby. All whiny and out of tune," one man said as they left, the stone door closing behind them.

Mara listened to the wheel that wasn't music at all but a story.

"He held...his land with a gentle but ruthless touch...good. Many years later, he lay with.... By her, he...a daughter with eyes... glowed like gold and a dance in her heart that would captivate. Alas, the king lost her. And then he lost himself."

She spun and listened and learned who she was.

Mara hadn't known she loved him until her heart broke. *Just us* was gone. She spun the wheel and poured her sorrow into it, and not even its stories could cure her sad and lonely heart for Gregor would never want a girl who was born of a fairy.

35

GREGOR WOULD HAVE BEEN RACING toward the Wild West after Nils's portal stunt except for the fact that two of the three relics were here, under government control, and all three needed to be together for the prophecies to come true.

He was leaning on that with his whole heart which was heavy with an unfathomable ache.

Nils and company seemed to be ignoring that detail of the prophecy—foolish—but the bad guys were never as smart as they needed to be.

With an hour to spare until the maging hour and the tick of the clock changing to a new day—the day of internment—he exited Power United through a utility hole in the parking garage, leaving the analysts and interrogators still at their work. Linc was by his side.

A horde of enforcers waited out front to escort them in mage cuffs to the wayward camp, but Gregor and Linc crept through the below-ground tunnels that housed the wires that electrified the city. They emerged four blocks away.

Vin waited in a dark alley between a deli and a shoe store. He pushed off the brick wall where he leaned as Gregor slid the round cover back in place. Two full backpacks sat at the general's feet. "Come to the farm. You'll be safe there. I vow it." His lips were in a grim line, his eyes hard.

"What are you doing here?" Gregor frowned. "I thought you'd send Dane. Not come yourself."

"I didn't know what she was planning to do with the needle. I vow it, Gor."

Gregor shook his head. "No farm. But thanks." If they went to the farm, they'd be stuck there. There'd be no coming and going because if they were caught, the Senate would have Vin's job for defying them. "And...I'm sorry. I know you didn't have anything to do with this." He touched the scars at his throat. "I should have—"

"Don't. This isn't on you. I can only imagine the hell I would have raised if someone had done that to me." Vin nodded at the packs. "Food, ammo, sleeping bags. And every potion I thought you could use. Including two dozen *disguiser* potions."

"You must have emptied the larder."

"Be safe." Vin gave him a man hug, shook Linc's hand, and disappeared into the night.

Linc and Gregor slipped on the packs and headed the other way. An hour later, after walking, jogging, and sprinting through the city and casting *don't looks* to stay unseen, they entered the forbidden forest.

"This is a shitty idea," Linc said. "Every outlaw worth the label has hidden here."

Gregor stepped beside the webs. Their thickness obscured the ground, though the green saplings poking through already stood taller than him. He reached down for the webs.

"What are you doing?" Linc spat the words with disgust.

The webs moved like a sheet of fabric. Gregor lifted them to the new branches above his head and pressed until they stuck. "Making a tent no one would dare to look in." He stepped under the webs he'd raised and lifted another portion to a sapling's branch. The silk was light and sticky. "Hell, they probably wouldn't even come near."

"I'm not going near it. There are spiders in there." Linc's voice pitched higher as his vibes drifted out, pressing against Gregor's sense, and ready to defend against the eight-legged beasts.

Hidden beneath the webs, he hollered out, "I think they're gone, man. They've done their job. They left." He didn't know if it was true or not, but he scanned the ground, testing it with his vibes.

Hell, the thoughts going around in his head were testing everything he'd ever believed, and he needed a sounding board. Linc would work better than most anyone he knew...except for Mara.

He clutched at his chest. Despair and heartache made a lethal venom. He wasn't sure he'd recover. "Mara, wherever she is, is probably scared to death. She's probably hurt." Goddess, let her be alive. "You can handle this tent."

He reached for his invisible pocket, still traveling along with him, and pulled out Mara's blanket. He'd stuck it in there after sleeping on her porch. Spreading it on the ground, he sat down.

Linc slowly ducked under, flinging off the touch of the webs as soon as he was clear. He pointed at the blanket. "Where did that come from?" His tone was laden with suspicion.

"I didn't spin it out of webs, that's for sure. You can sit on it. Tell me something. Why would the glister king's sister tell the High Councilor that imprisoning the waywards is against the rules? What rules?"

"The treaty rules that we've all forgotten? If you believe what that fairy said anyway."

"Why would it be against the rules?"

"Because keeping freaks like us around weakens mage society. The fairies would want that...maybe."

"Waywards don't weaken society." Gregor dismissed that idea with a scowl. "Fancy said I'm one of them. One of the glister now."

Daegan had said it too, but he'd thought it was just more of the man's torture, his usual asshole ways.

Goddess, he wouldn't be able to live with himself if he was one of them. The fairy and his needle had been sheer hell. And his memories, almost two decades old, of the shrill touch of another fairy replayed with such clarity he could still feel it drilling into his mind. He could sense the exact path the creature had taken, leaving a river of silver in his skull.

"Part glister, part mage?" Linc finally sat down next to him. "I thought I was the only one," he confessed softly. "My father was a fairy."

36

GREGOR STOOD in Mara's office, gazing down at the factory floor through the interior window. The vast room below was vacant, but he hardly noticed. He hadn't slept last night, wide awake after Linc's revelation. Then Daegan had shown up. Gregor's mind fogged every time he tried to think it through.

It was a risk coming to the mill. He'd done it anyway. Lady Harry was Mara's closest friend. If anyone knew her truth, it would be Harry. He rubbed his eyes. Hell, he knew the truth.

He'd told Mara that denial was not an effective defense. Evidently, he was a genius at deploying it for himself.

"It's good to see you," Lady Harry said, breaking the mournful silence that had fallen between them after her first words.

Did you find her?

"I've been worried about you. And Linc." She looked around as if the man might appear from nowhere next to him. "Did they...." She leaned forward. "Did they get him? Is he locked up?" She folded her hands and brought them to her chin as if she were ready to beg.

He shook his head. He didn't offer any more information about the half-fairy. Lady Harry was better off without Linc. The thought cracked around him. What the hell had happened to his world that he was thinking such things?

"Oh, thank the Goddess," she whispered. "There have been raids. Lots of them. It's all over the news. Everyone from the old to the newborn. The enforcers have surrounded the school Mara went to."

He pressed his fist against his heart, trying to manage the ache. It was shattered, its pieces as sharp as blades. "Mara's parents...where are they?" His voice was rough.

"Oh." She shook her head. "They won't care that she's missing."

It was a logical assumption as to the reason behind his question, that he'd want to notify them, but she had it wrong. "Who are they?"

Her eyes widen for a moment. His tone was too harsh. But she shrugged, weak and slow. Moving through grief and worry was exhausting. "She never knew her father. And her mother gave her up to SWWM when she was four, two years earlier than SWWM is supposed to take kids. Mara never heard from her again. That's all I know. It's not exactly a happy topic. She never talks much about her past."

He nodded at the empty factory floor below. "Where are all of her sorceresses?"

She lifted her chin. The hint of defiance reminded him of Mara. "I hired the Tea Time food truck to come back. Even though it's Monday and not Wednesday. I thought we could all use some cheering up, some distraction. Would you like to go down together? You look like you could use a drink."

Tea wasn't going to cut it, besides.... "I'm keeping a low profile. The whole wayward internment issue."

Lady Harry tilted her head. "The entire mill knows you're here. You passed right by Stella on your sneaky way in."

"How? I didn't sense a thing." The last thing this place needed was an invasion by the enforcers.

"Stella's mage sense is completely damaged. She has no vibes to sense." She held out a hand. "The tea truck is out back. They have excellent orange blossom tea. It will do our ladies some good to see someone else who cares for Mara." She swallowed so hard he could hear it. "It's certainly done me good." She fought tears as she took his arm and marched him out. She kept her chin up, and he ignored the watery eyes. Any offer of comfort or reassurance and she probably would have lost the little control she did have. He sure as hell would have.

They took the stairs down and headed toward the back hallway, stepping outside to the bright sunshine and blue skies. It ought to have been dim and gray without Mara. He blinked against the light, taking the half-second to steel himself for the crowd of women.

The Tea Time food truck was parked in front of the picnic tables. It was painted dark purple and a garland of flowers floated in an arc above it. Matching bouquets floated above the tables. Pots of tea and plates of cookies and sandwiches rested upon them. Some of the women stood with teacups and saucers in their hands, other sat, and still more were lined up in front of the truck, waiting for their food and drink.

The mood was subdued and quiet and grew heavier the closer he came.

At the far table, Esther stood up. "Any word?"

It pushed against him, their worry, their concern. Their expectations. It was a burden, but it was also a comfort. He wasn't alone in his fear...or his love.

"No word. But we're looking. Everyone is looking. From the army to the enforcers to the Rallis sentries." But he wasn't a part of the team effort. Neither he nor Linc would be welcome. They'd be arrested.

And what would the government do if they found her? Lock her in a camp? At least he'd know where she was.

He'd break her out.

"Why the sentries?" one of the women asked.

"Because when she was taken, the Rallis heir was present, and because Lady Bronte Casteel has a stake in her return, therefore the entire Rallis family does too. She can't wear that dress forever, and it has helped her a great deal."

No one responded for a moment.

"She can wear the dress forever," Esther said.

"Or close enough," another woman piped up.

"It's our highest quality stuff." The forewoman nodded. "Made by the lady boss herself. That's how good she was...is."

Silence wrapped around them at the slip, but it was broken by the least of them.

"You'll find her," Stella said in her high, quiet voice. The purple scarf that covered her bald head almost matched the color of the truck. "You will." She nodded, confident, and then pointed to her eye. "What happened to your face?"

He almost smiled that she had the guts to ask. Lady Harry hadn't, but she was so lost in heartache and trying to keep the mill together that he wasn't sure she'd noticed.

"I ran into a tree." He might have done just that from the shock of Daegan appearing from nowhere inside his tent last night. The tall, lanky man had looked so open and hopeful, but his face had hardened the moment he looked at him, realizing Mara wasn't inside, that she never had been.

"Figured it out yet? Listened to your heart?" the glister had snapped. Defensive, angry, desperate.

Exactly like Gregor.

Daegan had been as ready for Gregor's attack as he had been to spring it on him. Fists flew, elbows jabbed, and Gregor's face ended up in a tree. Daegan looked worse. Linc had wisely stayed out of the whole thing.

"Waywards are half-fairy," Gregor had accused. "That's what I've figured out. Why the fuck didn't you tell me?"

Daegan had spit out a wad of blood, bent over, hands to

knees. "Why should I have told you? Because it would've made you feel all better?"

"Mara's fairy half...what flows through her veins? There's a reason why the prophecies are about her. And it isn't just bad luck." He already knew the reason. There was only one reason a wayward would be so important to Daegan or Fancy. Mara carried their blood. As heartless as they were, it had nothing to do with love. Only blood.

Royal blood.

How could they have left her to suffer in the Republic alone?

Gregor touched the bruise around his eye, aware of the women's stares.

Esther raised her cup. "I bet the tree looks worse. No one gets the better of the lady boss's man."

"Hear, hear." The words echoed through the group.

He shook off their approval. Esther was wrong and everyone knew it. Someone had gotten the better of him, and they'd taken Mara as their prize.

He motioned Lady Harry in front of him to get her tea. The thin veneer of her confidence crumbled and her lower lip trembled as she tried to decide which scone she'd have.

There were two choices.

He put his hand on her shoulder. "How about the cranberry orange scone? It looks nice with those white lines on it. And a pot of that orange blossom tea you mentioned?"

She nodded, her eyes teary. "I'll do that."

The Tea Time woman gave him a grateful nod, wiped her hands on her frilly apron, and got to work.

While they waited, Gregor eyed the truck's shelves of cookies and little cakes along the back wall. A row of teapots sat beneath them, secured with spells. To the left stood a display of bottled juices, all colors. He sucked in a breath at the label. "You sell Reballa Potion."

She set a plate with Lady Harry's scone on the window's

counter. "It's not really a potion. That's a bit of a misnomer. I'm surprised The Tavis Potions Company hasn't filed a complaint against it. It's just a hydration drink. I sell a lot at the parks to all the runners and exercisers. And it's really popular with the zapper mages on Harmon Avenue. I guess it replenishes them after they zap a bunch of stuff."

She gave a huffy laugh and shrugged. "I've never understood what the Power United zappers do exactly. Fix wires or something? Whatever it is, it makes them thirsty. Reballa has a lot of salts and minerals in it." She handed him Harry's teapot. "Careful. It's hot. Hold it by the handle."

He took it. "Zapper mages at Harmon Avenue?" That wasn't anywhere on P.U.'s list of offices.

She nodded. "Harmon and Stimmel Road. I had no idea that was a Power United office. The building's not marked or anything. I pulled up a couple of months ago after driving by and seeing a bunch of lunchers hanging out beside the building. Now I park there around midmorning. They're drinkers, not eaters. A few of them asked me to carry the drink. One guy drinks so much of the blue stuff that I keep an extra box set aside for him. Although, sometimes he buys pink too." She wiggled her eyebrows. "I think he has a girlfriend now."

The world around him went still.

"He's some big executive," the woman continued. "Lucky girl."

No, he did not fucking have a girlfriend. That was his girl. A hard focus pushed him. He activated *comm* spells for Linc, Vin, and Dane and gave them the location.

"What's going on?" Lady Harry asked.

His muscles tense and screaming for action, he strode over to an empty chair and put Lady Harry's teapot on the table. "I've got to go."

"Where?"

He was going to get Mara back.

37

TALL COILS of copper stood throughout her prison cell like a mountain range. Stacked to the ceiling, they left only one crooked path from the concealed door to the wheel.

Mara had left the men an obvious trail, and then she hid, wedging herself between the wall and the far side of the coils that lined the men's path. She had enough room to squeeze past the coil nearest the door and slip free of this place.

She dropped the pieces of the misfit spindle to the floor. It had been simple to destroy. If anything went wrong with her plan, at least she'd sabotaged the wheel as much as she could. She couldn't destroy the wheel itself. Luck had rendered his gifts unmalleable to the hands of mortals. Not that she wanted to destroy it. Not anymore.

She waited for the men, her energy filling the room after spinning for so long with Luck's wheel. Her power was as unwound as if she and Gregor had once again tumbled off the train, encased in his spell, in the Wild West.

The door whooshed open.

"Holy hell. Look what she's done!" The first guard laughed as if he'd discovered an unexpected prize. "The boss is gonna be ex-ci-ted."

The pair stepped forward into the maze of copper.

Mara didn't waste any time. She dashed out the door while they were still in the small jungle of wire, pausing to study the door's controls. Her heart raced.

"No, he's going to be pissed. The transport's scheduled in thirty minutes. We've got to get the wheel out of here now, and there's no Goddess damn room to move. We gotta move all this copper first."

Lost girls, please let this work, she prayed. She pulled the lever on the wall. It didn't move. Damn it. She needed to use her vibes, but after spinning with the white wheel, the mass of her power was puffed out like raw wool. It was in no shape to be focused.

"Hey, freaky girl, you've outdone yourself!" the first man hollered from somewhere in the stacks of copper. "Come 'ere and let me cuff you. You're moving out with the wheel."

She reached for a strand of power but got the full tangle instead.

It was all or nothing. The door slammed closed.

She raced down the stone hallway on her toes. The floor was cold and dirty. Sharp crumbs of rock stabbed into her feet. The hallway ended at a staircase, and she sprinted up.

Behind her, silence dominated. The thick stone walls ate up any protest the guards might have made at their sudden imprisonment, but it wouldn't last long. Whoever was on the other side of that blind *comm* spell would be checking in soon enough when the guards didn't return.

A metal door met her at the top of the stairs. No lever, no doorknob, but no *lock* spell that she could sense. With fear shaking through her, she gathered her chaotic power and sent a clunky push of vibes into it. She'd never trained to do much with her energy beyond spinning and weaving, and she was paying for her shoddy education.

The door opened revealing a cavernous room with a hundred spinners sitting in row after row. They were chained by their ankles to the wheels. Her heart screeched to a halt. This was her nightmare pulled into daytime.

Windows high up along the tall walls let in dim sunshine. Buzzing mage lights, poorly cast, finished the job of lighting the room. The clank and rattle of metal rang out, the soft dings of the production of copper from sorceresses forced to spin. The place stank of desperation.

None of the women noticed her, their eyes glazed over, their mouths open like they were in a trance. As she watched, strands of one woman's hair broke free of her scalp and drifted to the ground. She had to be in terrible pain, yet she just kept spinning. This was worse than Mara remembered.

Across the room, a woman screamed. "No! Please! I'll work harder."

Two men yanked her up by the arms. One raised his hand, a thin stick in his grip. He brought it down across her back.

Another scream.

The jangling of the unstoppable spill of copper seemed to come faster yet.

Mara's back burned at the sound of the slashes. She cupped her hands over her mouth. She didn't want to remember this.

"She needs to go back to the white wheel," the whipper said. "She's come outta her trance."

Mara sucked in a silent breath at the revelation. The wheel must have powers like a glister's silver eyes. It had hypnotized them into working. These women, or most of them, were firmly under the domain of a power stronger than their own, one that pulled on their energy until they had nothing left to give.

This was the wheel in evil's clutch. It had stolen their joy, their freedom. It had devoured their lives.

Mara crawled along the edge of the first row, fear pushing her into a bruising pace. This was exactly what she'd done fifteen years ago. It clung to her mind as if it were yesterday.

She would come back for them. She'd free them all. Her lower lip trembled and her throat tightened. She'd thought the same thing then and she'd failed. She was doing it all over again. But she had no choice.

No, she thought. There was always a choice. And leaving them was hers.

None of the women she passed halted in their spinning rhythm. Unlike the last time, she didn't think they even saw her. The chains of their slavery were so tight they had blinded them.

Or perhaps not....

"Two rights and a left," the sorceress at the front of the row whispered, her lips barely moving with her cryptic phrase. "To freedom."

Mara didn't hesitate. She crawled to the door at the front, stood, and ran out. She sprinted down a wide hallway lined with cubbies on one side and benches and shelves full of tools on the other. The scent of old coffee and sweat saturated the air.

One man sat on a stool by the cubbies, his back to her, stooped over something in his hand.

Her bare feet were soundless against the floor, but her vibes were the problem. They flared out behind her, waving like an oversized flag as she moved.

She saw a doorway on the right and took it, dashing around one bench, only to run into the next one. She winced but stayed silent.

It wasn't enough.

"Hey!"

Just like that, her power recoiled, disappearing inside her with a bolt of fright. The world went fuzzy, her vision blurring, but she didn't let that stop her. She raced forward. Another right and then a left. A wall of windows loomed ahead. She could make out the light of the sun. She ran for them. Maybe there was a door among them. If not, she'd break a window. Hope unfurled her vibes enough to focus her eyes. Yes, she could see a door to the outside among the dirtiest windows she'd ever seen. It was fifty feet ahead, on the other side of a green, faded lobby.

"We got a runner!" the man hollered behind her.

But he needn't have bothered with the alarm. A dozen Black Skulls poured in through the door.

Trapped. She'd been so close. Yet some part of her mind that she almost couldn't recognize refused to give up. She faced down the men.

Their black leather vests, goggles, and tattoos were a menacing sight. They spread out across the lobby, ducking beneath tangles of electrical wires that hung from the ceiling as if someone had removed the lights and dangled fire hazards as decorations.

She had to get past these men. She had to get to that door.

"Oh, look who it is," Seth jeered, pushing his way to the front of the men. "You beat us to the white wheel, sorceress. How was it? And where's your boyfriend? He stole my bike. If he ain't dead yet, he's gonna be." He pulled his gun and spun it on his finger.

She didn't waste time. Some instinct whispered that bare skin was best, more surface area for her power to emanate from. She grabbed what was left of her blouse and yanked. Her bra fell to shreds as if the only thing holding it up was the integrity of her blouse, and now that it was gone, it fell in despair.

"Well, alrighty," an outlaw hollered.

The man behind her cracked a laugh. She looked over her shoulder. He rubbed his hands together in glee. A wide smile split his lips.

By the lost girls, she couldn't believe she was doing this. She shimmied her hips. She grabbed the rhythm of her breathing as her music and moved her body in twists and turns, coaxing her power to the fore. It stuttered forward, her vibes teasing at the men, but not enough. For minutes she held them only with lust as she spun and twirled, her mage energy too tight, too scared.

She looked over her audience. A flash of movement through the window caught her eye.

Gregor. He was racing for the building. Her heart jumped to her throat.

He was coming.

She had to do this. She had to free her vibes because Seth was here and if she lost control of him, he'd kill Gregor.

At the thought, panic stole her breath. Her steps faltered. Her power shriveled tight.

Hands grabbed her from every direction. She lost her audience...if she'd ever had them in the first place. The prickly roughness of rope twisted and squeezed around her ankles and wrists.

Someone pulled a piece of cloth over her head. At first, she thought it was a hood, but a firm yank down freed her head. She lifted her face to see the glister man who'd had the job of hypnotizing her. He was bare-chested, sacrificing his shirt to cover her nakedness though her bound arms couldn't go through the sleeves. The glister tossed her over his shoulder and ran out with the other outlaws. The familiar tingling power of a portal feathered around her and then the bright, hot sun burned against her skin.

She breathed in the dust and cigar smoke of the outlaws' camp.

38

GREGOR STOOD in the doorway of the three-story brick building that had nothing to recommend it from the outside. Five Power United workers stood around the lobby, eyeing the spot where the portal had been.

"What the hell do you want?" one demanded.

"The girl." Gregor's words vibrated with so much power that the dust motes floating in the sunshine shook.

But he was too late. Mara was gone, along with the Skulls and fairies.

He couldn't hold back. His power burst free into a spell of pure sound. Furious thunder poured forth, silent to his ears but knocking the men down and shattering the windows and rumbling the walls. If he'd done that thirty seconds ago, he would have knocked her down too, but at least they wouldn't have taken her.

He'd seen her through the window. The power in her eyes, too dim to start, had faded to nothing as she'd looked at him.

He was the reason she'd stopped dancing.

He yanked the nearest man up by the front of his Power United jumpsuit. "How the hell do you open the portal?"

"I don't know, man! I don't know nothing about a portal. We were supposed to transport the girl in a damn van. The piece of shit's parked out back. But those freaks just disappeared into the wall with her!" His high voice trembled but the words rang true. "They ain't like the zapper chief either. He travels through wires. Not walls."

"Nils Lusman zaps himself through electrical wires?" Gregor asked through clenched teeth. How was that even possible? But it explained how he'd appeared from nowhere in Fancy's bordello. And somehow, the fucker had grabbed Mara from the forest and taken her with him.

"Yeah," the man gasped. "Chief can do that."

Gregor didn't need to hear more. He tossed the man away and left, racing down the street. He needed to get to the Wild West.

Three blocks away, the forbidden forest stood in the road like an invading army, staking fresh territory inch by inch. He fought not to roar at it, to knock it down too, and send it back where it belonged. Nothing was as it was meant to be. Nothing was in its proper place. Not the forest. Not Mara. Not even him. He was supposed to be with her.

The thunder built in his throat again, clamoring for release. *Thunder* spells were dangerous. Just one could drain some cadence mages for days. Even he could only afford a few at a time.

Control.

Outside the forest's edge, a small crowd of people stood, peering into the towering trees. Their conversation reached his ears with ease. Cadence mages were excellent eavesdroppers.

"Have you ever seen a forest so dark?" a woman asked.

"I think the more pertinent question is how did the forest cross into the road like this?" the man next to her replied.

Fairy power.

And his own mix of it rumbled inside him. How much of this had the High Councilor already known? Guard her quest. That was the mission she'd given him. And Mara's? She was to find the white wheel. But not for the reasons the High Councilor had led them to believe. He hadn't questioned any of it, too distracted by the promise of healing if he sought the truth.

As he headed into the forest, the man nearest him held out a hand. "You shouldn't go in there. There's some arbor mage going nuts in there. Better wait for the enforcers. They're coming."

The enforcers would do nothing but arrest him and send him to the internment camp. He sped past, sprinting through the trees. Silence encased the white towering oaks, a stillness that called out to be filled with the power of sound. He ignored it and charged toward the river that ran through the forbidden forest and into the city. It should have been about two miles, but the forest's growth had lengthened that.

Daegan waited there, leaning against the railing of his crumbling ferry. The vessel was docked on the bank. He straightened when he saw Gregor. "Well?" The word was sharp.

"She's gone. The Skulls and their fairy allies took her through a portal." His voice heaved with rage. "Your people helped take her!"

"Yeah? So what? Luck's balls, grow up! Some fairies are dipshits. Just like some mages are."

"Take me to her. Make a portal. She's in the West. Old Fort Prower." He was almost certain.

"I can't. The best I can do is take you to the border." He shook his head. "I guard the river. My power is water. I've been trying to reach her," he whispered, as if he suddenly didn't have the strength to speak any louder. "Wherever she is, there is too little water. Others could do it. My sister, for one." He dropped his head. "Mara doesn't know. She doesn't know she's the king's daughter."

The king's daughter. He hadn't been sure. He'd thought that maybe Daegan was her father or Fancy her mother. "Why didn't you tell her?" Another roar of his power built inside him. "Why isn't the truth about waywards known? They're not broken mages. They just have two types of power running through them."

"So you've finally had a change of heart." Daegan sneered. "What good does it do to make the truth known? With the way you witches look at us now, any child born between glister and mage would have been locked up forever or worse. We have too few children to let that happen. The king dictated that no glister who lay with a mage in the east would reveal his true nature, even if a child came of that union."

Linc's father had not obeyed that.

"His edict stands today though Mara could overturn it if she chose. I suppose you can blame him for all of this," the glister said.

"You're a bunch of cowards, not protecting your own children. Mara grew up in hell."

Daegan shook his head. "The treaty says they must be cared for. Wayward mages are free citizens of the Republic. Or at least they were until the stupid internment camps. But a glister mage? For the past two centuries, they would all have been thrown on the trash towers."

"Your treaty is worthless. No mage knows about it. And you people hide away in holes. You left Mara to fend for herself...to fend for everyone." And he had failed to keep her safe.

Daegan looked away for a moment. "I've been thinking about the glister who took your mind for three days when you were a boy. Did he have markings? A necklace?"

"A necklace?" The memory was as clear as the water of the stream where he'd found it. The tuning circle that was his good luck charm had been on a leather cord.

Gregor pulled it from his pocket and held it out. "I found it at his feet. It was in a shallow creek. That's where he caught me. I picked it up and I held it the entire time he dissected my mind. It cut into my palm. I used it to channel power, to save my sanity."

Daegan sucked in a breath as if he could smell the thing.

"Luck above and below. That is the mark of the glister king." Shock softened his voice. "Tuning circles, as the mages call it, are used for pulling on the gods' power. They originated with the glister. If he was so clumsy with your mind, then he is truly weakened."

"That was seventeen years ago."

But Daegan didn't seem to register his comment. "You, guard to the glister princess, are the last known person to see the king alive. The king must have seen your destiny for what it was. He never would have hurt his daughter's guard. Not on purpose.

"The glister mages were never meant to be cast-off. They were supposed to be treasured, a gift between allies," Daegan said. "Powerful in unique ways."

"Did the needle give me spells that I didn't have before? The *misplace* spell? Portals? Anything?" Something he could use to save her.

"You have the power of the unsung song. But you never bothered to learn it." Daegan heaved a sigh. "I don't know if you can port yourself there, glister mage. Maybe. Perhaps the needle lent you such powers. But she is far away and it might kill you to travel such a distance your first time. At best it will drain you completely."

"I won't let it." His power rose in him like a stubborn beast.

Daegan shrugged. "Very well, then. It is a simple spell. Use that glister eye to see your destination. Let it shine. Let your power flow through the vision and it will pull your body with it. It will hurt like hell."

Before he tried, he reached out to the webs and pinched two small sections and stuffed them in his pocket. He pictured old Fort Prower, the shadows of the building Mara had stood in as he'd unloaded spinning wheels from Houston's cart. He let his power flow into his sight and the world around him disappeared.

39

MARA SAT in a tall-backed wooden chair, her hands fastened behind her, this time with metal cuffs. She'd revealed her skill with rope and knots too soon, and the outlaws had learned from their mistakes. Her legs were bound with chains to the chair. Complete overkill.

The chair's wicker seat pressed sharply against the backs of her legs. The short bloomers one of the sorceresses had offered her were better than being naked, but they offered little protection or modesty.

It was the least of her problems.

Her chair sat in a shadowed corner in the saloon of the Black Skulls' hideout. The saloon's tables and chairs had been pushed against the walls to make way for one large table in the middle of the room. A crisp white tablecloth, fine silver, and porcelain plates lined the surface, elegance among decay. The highest-ranking members of the Black Skulls sat around it, including three fairies and Seth. He'd made her life hell here as much as Prophet allowed it.

Nils and Lord and Lady Prower also sat at the table, as well as six other wealthy Republic citizens, but she didn't recognize them. A few seemed friendly with Nils though, and she guessed they worked for Power United.

"We should wait," Nils said. "Two more days until the Rose Moon. Let's do this right. By the book."

Mara dropped her gaze. She couldn't stand to look at him. His betrayal turned her stomach. He'd used the Trail of Strings organization to send sorceresses to the west to be gathered up by Prophet. She'd tried to think back to the women she'd helped. Had she helped anyone get to the West? Nausea rolled through her at the thought.

"No. The sooner, the better." Seth always disagreed with Nils. "We destroy the Republic's strength now. Let's get started on our destiny."

The conversation went in circles. After three nights of this, she could predict exactly how it would go.

"Oh, boys. So ambitious. Both of you," Lady Prower said. Based on the secret touches and glances that Mara had spied, Lady Prower was sleeping with both of them as well as her husband's glister servant, who stood behind his master.

Someone needed to step up and lead, to quit tiptoeing around and decide. If she ran her mill this way, she'd be bankrupt in a month.

She'd spent the past two days spinning copper for Prophet and helping the other sorceresses reach their ridiculous quota. They'd all been forced to use Luck's Lady's wheel. It sat in the opposite corner from her and was the only reason she was still sane. The wheel provided her a sense of peace and a boost of energy. Who would have thought that would be the case? Mara bit her lip at the realization that Sage had known. She'd sent all those notes through some spell or power.

Still, Mara was no Goddess at the white wheel. Even she had physical limits as to how much she could spin. Her fingertips were sliced with cuts. They were cold and wet, dripping blood, but her hands were tied behind her, and there was nothing she

could do about it. Her corset was so tight she could barely
breathe.

She was tired. If she closed her eyes and fell asleep, she could
go back to dreaming of when Gregor's eyes held wonder and lust
and kindness, back when the thoughtful charm of a man who
packed a picnic on a forced march west was still hers to revel in.
Where was he now?

Safe. Please be safe.

The pressure of a sob in her chest caught her by surprise and
suddenly she couldn't get a breath. By the lost girls, she needed
this corset off.

She closed her eyes, reaching for her power. It quivered deep
inside her like a lost lamb. She coaxed it forward, trying to convince
herself to relax. All she needed was a thread of vibes, but it was
usually an all-or-nothing game for her. Control was not her forte.

Finally, her vibes puffed out like a stuffed toy busting its
seams and exploding with cotton fluff.

She worked quickly. The bow tie of the corset strings was a
simple endeavor and she had it loosened before the glister
servant could whisper a word of warning to his master. He glared
at her. Lady Prower caught the glance. She looked at Mara. "What
are you up to now, sorceress?"

The conversation around the table died as Mara sucked in
lungs full of air, making sure she got her money's worth from that
spell before it was too late.

"Fairy princess," Prophet corrected.

She wasn't sure how he'd figured that out.

"And I have just the thing for her." Lady Prower stood.

Everything inside Mara recoiled, retracted, but she had no
shelter, no hiding place. No way to turn her back on the taunts
and jeers and pain, all of which was promised in the other
woman's eyes.

Lady Prower lifted a wreath of sticks and sauntered forward, placing it on Mara's head. She pressed down. Mara bit back a cry as sharp thorns pierced her skin.

"A crown for our royal guest." She laughed and turned back to the party. "Doesn't it look nice?"

Mara locked eyes with Prophet at the far end of the table. He was chaos on a rampage. His plan, which had seemed so impossible days ago, was on the verge of tipping half a continent into destruction all so he could claim dominion over it.

"The Republic will fight back," she said to Prophet. "The glister will go to war to save their freedom. The Nons of the West will be swept up in the power struggle and their bullets will fly into everyone around them. Don't do this."

Prophet laughed and held out his arms. "Princess, it's as good as done." He looked around the table. "Lady and gentlemen. Enough debate. The Rose Moon is in two nights. The wheel sits in the West." He lifted his glass of champagne in a mock toast to her. "And its mistress with it. The West is about to devour the mage's land and if the Goddess cries, then all the better. Come on, sorceress, you have to admit that last part is satisfying. That bitch in the sky has done nothing for you or me or Willy here." He thrust his thumb over his shoulder to where the beaten glister lay.

Willy was the one who'd pretended to hypnotize her when she and Gregor had arrived here the first time, the one who'd covered her with his shirt when she was naked.

He'd paid a high price.

Prophet raised his glass of champagne again. Its golden liquid sparkled beneath the mage lights floating above. "Here's to healing the gaping slash down this great land and bringing it together at last. To one nation."

His guests drank to the toast. Mara wanted to close her ears against the celebration.

"I've been looking forward to this day for years, gentlemen."

Lady Prower's cold smile pulled at her lips. "I am anxious to start."

Prophet stood and helped the woman scoot back in her chair. "Then we go." He lifted her hand and kissed it. "Destiny shall wait no longer."

40

GREGOR LAY on the ground behind a line of dilapidated buildings in old Fort Prower. The spot was too dry and dusty and hopeless for even the bugs. A small stand of raggedy bushes—their determination to survive was a lesson in stubbornness—hid him from discovery. This was the second time he'd hidden behind bushes to find her. It was becoming an odd habit.

He estimated that he'd been here for one day and part of a night. He should have listened to Daegan's warning. He wasn't even sure what to call the spell he'd cast to come here. Could a mage *misplace* himself?

When he'd first arrived, he hadn't been sure he'd had the strength to take another breath. He didn't remember much of the first day except for dreams of Mara.

Now, he was so thirsty he fought not to choke on his tongue with every dry breath. His mage sense ached like the ringing of an out-of-tune orchestra. His body, too.

He'd lost everything he'd packed...his invisible pocket, his guns, his knives, even his boots. The only things that had stayed with him were his clothes, his supposed good luck charm...the king's necklace that Gregor had refashioned with a leather cord and fastened around his neck...and the webs he'd stuck in his pocket.

He held them in his hands.

Heal me, he thought, too tired for worry or fright. He closed his eyes at the impossibility of being full of hope and completely empty of it at the same time. No cure existed for the needle's damage. But perhaps the webs could restore the energy he'd drained getting here.

He stuffed them in his ears like cotton balls.

In a blink, the world of sound he'd known for so long returned, the energy of the universe hummed, alive and loud in his ears, suddenly resuscitated.

It was like a kiss from the Goddess...a breath from Luck.

Mara had been right. And all he wanted to do was tell her. His hands ached to hold her as the universe sang its eternal song to his listening ear. He would have fallen to his knees if he'd been standing. He didn't fool himself that this was permanent, but he'd gladly take whatever the webs offered him. It was a complete surrender of his fear.

Safely hidden, he soaked in the webs' power until the sun went down again, sleeping without choice. When he woke, he found the strength to stand, his socks already coated with dust and dirt.

The town was empty. Damn it. It hadn't been that way when he'd arrived. He remembered popping into place and seeing the town bustle around. Where the hell had everyone gone?

He reached out with his mage sense, gently probing the buildings. A few mages were down to the right, but their energies were subdued and weak. Whoever they were, they were in no shape to fight. Perhaps there were Nons or fairies around, but he needed to push more power out to search. Not a risk he was willing to take at the moment.

Mara's energy signature was absent. Though her power might have been tucked down tight, he bet his firefly had pulled her escape act again. He'd had plenty of opportunity to hone his instincts when it came to that. He was back to searching for clues for her location.

He prowled though the town, heading for the saloon, the most intact building. He opened the door and peered in. A vacant table, still laden with food and drinks, sat in the middle of the room. Starving and thirsty, he scavenged for bread and water. A spare pair of boots would have been nice too, but apparently everyone had kept their shoes on at this meal.

A moan reached his ears. He followed it to find the fairy who'd tried to hypnotize him. The man was on the floor in a puddle of blood. He opened his eyes when Gregor nudged his leg. His eyes went wide at the king's necklace around his neck.

"Where is she?" Gregor demanded.

"The king," he whispered. "The king returned." His eyes darkened. Power waved out from him, but no silver shined in his eyes. The questing power passed through Gregor, whispering faintly in his ear, a message he couldn't quite catch.

He crouched beside him. The glister wore no shirt and the gaping wound in his belly bled sluggish and dark. There was no healing spell that could fix this.

"River. They took her to the river...with the geo mage. Portal. You just missed them."

"Why?"

"Moving it." He panted for air. "Uniting the lands." The man let go of a breath and the light faded in his eyes.

The first sound of death was silence, a stillness in the liminal moment between realms. The second was a blend of tones, high and low and everything in between. It should have sounded like a crash of noise but there was something undescribably light within it.

Gregor reached out and closed the man's eyes. "Thanks," he whispered though, right or wrong, he felt no grief for this loss.

He didn't have the energy to spell himself to the river. Stealing a motorcycle wouldn't work either. He'd never get there in time to stop the geo mage from destroying the Republic's border. But maybe that didn't matter anymore. He wasn't a soldier. He was the guard of the glister princess. And he would save her regardless of the border or the Rose Moon or the white wheel.

He headed out the door and came face to face with a nightmare. The river maiden queen was naked except for the white lacy scarf on her head. Her body dripped with water and a puddle formed around her. Water spread into the dirt until the puddle became a small pool. Her wide eyes were too big for her face and her lips were nearly colorless.

She pointed at his chest. "He told me the king returned."

"Who told you?" Gregor backed up a step. "Daegan?"

She pointed at the saloon. Maybe the whisper of power from the dead fairy was a *message* spell to the river queen. Was every glister on speaking terms with these creatures?

Her expression didn't change. "You are the guard. I will take you to the battle." The pool around her shimmered with an impossible current.

"Is that where Mara is?"

But she gave no indication she'd heard. A sailboat appeared behind her, bobbing in the growing water. She turned to it and sank into the pool as if it were six feet deep. The boat was no battleship, but he got on, his chest tight. The boat sailed away, the stars and clouds stretching beside him until it suddenly stopped. The Mississippi, wide and deep, slapped against the boat as if they'd blinked into existence right there. Gregor stood in the boat and studied his surroundings.

On the eastern shore, the Republic's soldiers lined the bank. Vin and Dane were over there somewhere, guaranteed. Gregor was much closer to the western shore. It was less than fifty yards away. It held an army of Black Skulls.

The outlaws were armed, some with guns in both hands, all pointing at Gregor and his unexpected company of river maidens. The river was now populated with hundreds of the creatures, all bobbing in the water and eyeing the Skulls.

Prophet stood in the middle of his outlaws at the shore's edge. The Prowers were on one side of him, Nils on the other, along with a handful of other wealthy Republic mages...Gregor identified them by their dress.

Mara stood near Nils. Chains wrapped around her legs all the way to her waist, her hands behind her. Three Skulls pointed guns at her.

The sight sent a wave of fury boiling through him. His vibes shot into his throat.

The river maiden queen treaded water in front of him.

"What can you do to them?" he asked her, his voice a low growl.

"We can eat them."

Goddess above. A pulse of alertness jumped through him. He didn't want to call it fear, but she looked back at him as if she'd sensed it.

"They'll shoot you." He kept it as simple as he could, not sure how much she understood.

"They will kill us."

So they had no fancy tricks like Daegan's ability to repel bullets. They'd all die before they could get close enough to eat anyone. Gregor pondered his options. He couldn't risk a *thunder* spell. It would be too draining. Worse, the force of his vibes might jostle a slippery finger on a gun pointed at Mara.

If he'd understood how to use the unsung song, this would have been the moment to deploy it.

Across the water, Prophet's old scribe stepped up to him and held up his fist, sideways, just below the leader's mouth. Prophet's voice boomed over the distance with the scribe's *voicecaster* spell.

"You ought to thank me for taking her off your hands, General Rallis!" The words reverberated and he waited for them to stop before continuing. "You know who she is?" Prophet paced over to Mara and shook her by the shoulder. He recited the prophecy.

> *"Glow Eyes spins webs as Luck commands,*
> *Abandoned to the dance in the western lands.*
> *The relics await her touch. Their fate?"*

You want to know their fate?" he hollered.

This was as far as the High Councilor had gotten in the prophecy.

Prophet shouted out the rest.

> *"Spin, snip, and stitch for the king's half-witch!*

You hear that? She's a fucking half-breed by the king, no less. The fairy princess is my bitch now!" He rattled Mara like a rag doll.

From the east bank, Vin replied sharply with his own *voice-caster* spell, stating that Mara was a citizen of the Republic with all the protections that entailed.

"She is mine," Gregor whispered to Prophet, pushing the words with a furious stream of vibes straight to the man's ear. "And this will be the last time you ever touch her."

Prophet smiled, the expression full of madness.

Lady Prower lifted her hands. The Mississippi rumbled with a fury, tossing the river maidens. Within seconds, waves built high, sloshing over the boat and dousing the white sail. Gregor stumbled back, his foot catching on the edge of the boat just before he tumbled in. His necklace bumped against his chin. His ears sloshed with water. The world went silent.

Shit. The webs. They'd fallen out as if Prower's spell inspired the water to wrench them away. His songs were gone. He scanned the water. The webs were nowhere in sight.

Waves rose again, and the water foamed. The river maidens screamed a battle cry, but Mara's shout carried above them all.

"Gregor!"

He'd never heard her sound like that. Terror drenched her voice. Her cry hurt his heart like a sharp punch jabbing through him, a blow to his core so strong it left a gaping hole. A new noise resonated free, like her fear had blasted through a wall inside him. A symphony of chaos blared out. The noise was savage and wild. He looked around for its source. But he couldn't pinpoint it. It came from everywhere...and everyone.

From Mara. From Prophet. From the Republic's soldiers on the other side of the river. From the river maidens fighting to swim against the turbulent waves.

This was what Daegan had been trying to get him to hear. But the glister had been wrong. This primal sound was not about love. It wasn't even about hate. It was something else entirely and it took him a moment to figure out how to define it. He knew he hadn't experienced enough of the universe to truly understand it. The closest he could come was to call it something like the power of a vow or an oath. The sound held the promise of a future, but that promise could only be given if it was bound in the turmoil of transformation and change.

This song was the feathered wing of chaos that swept through every second of life. It wasn't soft and pretty. It wasn't happy or sad or any other emotion. It was ferocious and unrelenting, moving all life with a tempestuous force. It saturated every person, every creature, every spark of life around him, constant and changing at the same time.

How could he have missed hearing this his entire life?

Daegan's words came back to him.

I know that you, wayward monk, have what is necessary to hear it.

Wayward...Gregor had needed his other songs silenced before he could hear this one. The needle had given him this.

None of his mage teachers had mentioned this song because they didn't know it existed. Perhaps the unsung song resonated not with the Goddess's vibes, but with the vibes of Luck.

Or maybe that was all a bunch of vibe shite. It didn't matter. All that mattered was that he knew how to access it, to listen for it...and to control it.

He focused on the western shore and gathered their chaos—their futures—to him, yanking it from the depths of their souls, leaving them trapped in the sameness of a single moment, frozen, their energies caught tight. A person couldn't move to the next second, the next minute, the next day without the power of change.

The Black Skulls and their allies, the enemies of the Republic, went motionless on the western bank, an army of statues.

With the geo mage's power now bound by Gregor's, the river stilled. Her spell was erased. The river maidens surged forward to attack, the queen among them. He dove into the water after them. One of the maidens grabbed him, dragging him to shore in the span of a breath. The water was red before he made it to the bank.

He raced to Mara, casting his vibes into the *lock* spell of the cuffs and chains. They tumbled to the ground. Mara's eyes were wide and panicked.

"Close your eyes, firefly." He lifted her into his arms, his world righting, and headed back into the water, swimming for the boat.

Behind him, the battle raged. It wasn't a fair fight. The Skulls couldn't move. All they could do was watch while bloodied teeth came for them. The silence of a conquered enemy lay heavy in the air.

～

THE BOAT BOBBED in the river as Mara rested her head on Gregor's shoulder. They were both dripping wet and she shivered though the evening was still warm. "You swam the Mississippi for me." Her teeth chattered. Gregor's vibes drifted around her with a hum of his power. The *warming* spell soaked into her. She gave a laugh that turned into a sob. "You came for me."

"I will always come for you."

"But don't you know who I am?"

He looked down at her. "I know who you are. You're the woman who knew I wasn't broken, who braved the threat of an internment camp for a chance to collect spider webs to heal her friend, who dances with such power that it captivates a mage's mind."

"Spellbinds," she corrected. Her teeth chattered again, but it had nothing to do with cold and everything to do with fright.

He put his hand under her chin and looked into her eyes. "Hey, now," he crooned. "We're together, Mara. There's nothing to be scared of. Not anymore. I know what your power can do. And I'm thankful you can."

"Why?"

"Almost every mage has a dangerous side to their power, though I swear to you that yours doesn't work on me. But you need a way to protect yourself. If yours is through dancing— though I'd rather you kept your clothes on—then so be it."

"I couldn't do it. I couldn't dance in that place. I was so worried about...." She bit her lip. "I want to go home," she whispered. She was tired inside and out.

"Worried about what?"

"You. My power is like a glister's. You hate them."

His blue eyes gleamed like the water reflecting moonlight. "I was wrong. I was afraid."

"And now you're not?"

The boat rocked in the river as his vibes pushed it east. "The only thing I'm afraid of right now is that you're going to tell me again that you don't need me to be your hero, that you work better alone."

"I'm part glister."

He pulled off the spell that covered his glowing eye. It was only the left, the side of his heart, the side of his scars.

She gave him a small smile. "I like it. It adds a roguish touch to your handsome charm."

"I may not have been born of a glister, but I'm part glister now, too." He pulled off the necklace and held it out. "Daegan said it was your father's." He put it around her neck and fastened it there. "It was your father who...."

She gasped. "Who picked apart your brain when you were sixteen?" Dismay flooded through her, along with a wicked whisper of envy that he'd met the man.

"I probably shouldn't have put it like that."

"You met my father."

"Somehow he knew." He took a breath and cupped her cheek. "He knew that I'm the one for you. Say you'll have me, that you'll dance to my songs and that you'll let me stand by your side."

"Yes," she whispered.

"Let's go home, firefly."

41

THIRTEEN SORCERESSES STOOD in a semi-circle around the concrete picnic table where Mara sat, a scroll open before her. Above, the Rose Moon shined down from a pre-dawn sky. Luck's Lady's wheel stood next to the blue walls of the mill, glowing white beneath the moonlight. Its proper spindle was attached— she still planned to use it as a sword when in the West.

The sorceresses here this morning were formerly of the Wild West, Prophet's victims. They were the only ones who'd accepted Mara's offer to sponsor them in the Republic.

They eyed the wheel warily and stayed far from it. They were still tired and weak from the wheel's effects. It would take them a long time to recover. Mara had already told them they didn't need to be here this morning. They should be resting. They'd only been here for two days.

She started to suggest it once more, but Susette caught her eye. "Uh-uh. Don't even say it. We aren't leaving. You saved us from that wheel and from Prophet. And you got us new jobs." She was one of the girls stolen from the house that was Fancy's main competition. "We're gonna make sure you're saved, too."

They were worried about the coming meeting ever since Lincoln had let something slip about the suspended death sentence.

Gregor smiled at the woman as if he appreciated her sentiment. He sat beside Mara, sharing her bench, reading the details of the treaty with a great deal more focus than she was.

Lady Harry marched around the corner. "They're here."

The chain-link gate squeaked as Harry cast the *unlock* spell. It took a moment before the gate started to move. Gregor cleared his throat and gave Mara a sideways look.

"It's just a little rusty." Mara shook her head at him. "That's all. It works fine."

A line of four limos paraded into the back lot. Their sleek shapes spoke of untold wealth, sophistication, and power.

"Don't offer them a seat. Make them stand," Harry ordered. "This is your territory."

"Oh goody. I haven't missed the party," an old woman said behind her.

Mara recognized the voice immediately. She closed her eyes for a brief second before turning to face the High Councilor. She scooted off the seat to stand. The rough surface tugged at her pants. She should upgrade the seats out here.

"Yes," Harry whispered in her ear, her voice shaky. "This one you can stand for. Equals." The last word squeaked.

"No limo for you?" Mara asked.

The old crone's white robes and hair shined in the moonlight though not as brightly as the wheel. The black thread that held her eyes closed seemed darker than ever. She lifted her staff. "Nothing wrong with a good old-fashioned broom."

Mara didn't bother to point out that it wasn't a broom. If the old crone could turn herself into a young vixen, then morphing a staff to a broom was child's play.

"Child's play, indeed." The crone smiled toothily, satisfaction gleaming through.

By the lost girls, she had to figure out how to cloak her thoughts. Soon.

"I hear you dance. It's almost worth the risk of seeing. Your father danced too though I'm guessing your moves are a little different."

An insight came to Mara in a flash. The High Councilor's closed eyes were an easy defense against a glister's most powerful weapon. And yet her other personae looked at the world with open eyes.

The High Councilor shrugged. "A trade-off. We ultra-powerful women need to have a little fun in our lives. Remember that, girl."

On the other side of the tables, the limos spewed out their passengers.

"Oh look, carpool line!" the High Councilor cackled, and twelve senators eyed her warily.

Senator Rallis stepped forward, buttoning his suit jacket as he moved. "The wheel sits in the east under the Rose Moon. Your doing, Miss Rand?"

She looked at Gregor. "I had help."

"Why are these two not locked up?" Senator Standish marched forward, a sneer on his face.

Harry stepped to the front of the table, blocking Mara from the hateful man. "Her Highness, Mara Rand, daughter of the glister king, princess of the glister, and Gregor Whitman, consort to the princess, are free citizens of the Republic, as are all wayward mages."

They'd argued for quite a while over the words *her highness*. Considering she was the princess, Mara still wasn't sure why she hadn't won that argument.

"And who are they?" Senator Rallis pointed at the sorceresses behind her. "Not your court, I hope, Princess?"

She tried not to blink at the title, to take it all in stride in front of these privileged men. "These women are the former prisoners of the Mad Prophet." Mara watched their faces as she explained his plan to rule the West and the role of Power United.

"A couple of things, Senators. From now on, waywards are known as glister mages, and they're to be treated as equals in all areas of Republic society." She smiled at Standish's gasp of indignation. He looked as if he'd stepped in something questionable. "Accept it with open arms or prepare to cede your land to the glister inch by inch. That is what the founding families and the glister decided at the start of this country as documented in the Treaty of Plymouth Rock."

Gregor held it up, winding the scroll to show the scrawling signatures of the original leaders of the thirteen mage families and the glister king, Mara's ancestor.

"The glister forests will not stop growing until the conditions of the treaty are followed to the letter. The land claimed during the time of abstaining from the treaty will not be returned," Mara explained.

"I've lost four blocks of my capital city because of this foolishness," Senator Rallis barked. "I voted against the internment camp."

"As did I," another man said. "And I've lost far more than that. I've had miles of land overtaken by forest."

"Senator Bradford," Harry whispered to her.

"Perhaps if you'd stood up on behalf of the victims of your senate's bill, you might have had a different outcome," Mara said.

"Prower has lost a few hundred square miles all along the border between his territory and Locke's." The High Councilor stepped forward. "No one can enter or exit Prower Territory without going through glister land."

"And, therefore, my territory is blocked from the rest of the Republic as well!" another senator shouted.

"Howland," Harry offered, but Mara hadn't needed that explanation. She'd guessed who he was since his small territory was on the very tip of the southern peninsula, the rest of which was Prower Territory.

"There are consequences for those ruled by fear," the High Councilor said. "Unlike some of you though, Prower acted out of greed. I'm certain the purpose of his internment camp was to get his hands on one wayward in particular." She wiggled her finger at Mara.

"Where is Prower?" Senator Rallis asked.

"Dead. Gobbled up by river maidens after Lady Prower nearly erased the Mississippi. That's how close you came to losing your Republic. Destiny is manifest," the High Councilor said softly.

The crone moved in front of Luck's Lady's Wheel. She reached out a hand as if she might give it a spin, but she didn't touch it. "The white wheel rests in the east and its glister mistress resides with it." She pivoted toward the senators. "Come on. Perk up. Such a gloomy group. All you have to do is make nice with the fairy princess and her glister mages. If you don't, you'll lose your territory and no one can stop it. Not me. Not you. Not the princess. Forever and ever. So shall it be." She shrugged. "It's not so bad. The fairy princess lives in the Republic with all the rights and privileges of a visiting head of state." She recited the last part with great exaggeration. That was one argument Mara had won against the old crone. "She is as close to a ruler of the West as any will ever get."

"To be clear, you don't rule the West simply because I live here," Mara said.

The High Councilor pressed her lips together and shrugged, a thoughtful expression. "Well, one could look at it that way."

Maybe she hadn't been as victorious as she'd thought. "Only if one didn't know the truth. And the truth is that you have the glister and a glister mage to thank for the fact that your Republic still stands."

"Eh." She shrugged again and changed the subject. "As

requested, the Power United draft for weak-powered sorceress is now erased. Also, SWWM is now under the rule of a board of trustees and you are president of the board." She pulled a box from her pocket and opened it. The scissors and the needle lay inside.

"You carried those in your pocket?" Mara took them. "You certainly cut it close." The full Rose Moon was in about five minutes, peaking in the daylight though it would still look full when nighttime fell. "I'm glad you didn't hit traffic on your way over or the world would have ended."

"Well, I've been busy. I had to expand my dungeons to make room for all my enemies involved in this. Or so I thought. Turns out, all the bad guys got eaten."

Nils hadn't been the only executive involved, but he had been their ambassador—of a sorts—to the West, the one who'd taken all the risks to make it happen.

The High Councilor wagged her finger. "There's a new Senator Prower, by the way. He'd like to meet you and apologize for the actions of his distant uncle." She leaned closer to Mara. "I shifted their ascension plan a wee bit," she whispered, as if the senators weren't aware. "Those Manifesters will think twice about the consequences of their actions now."

"Speaking of consequences...." Mara pulled the receipt from her pocket and handed it to the crone. "$2,975 plus tax. You can send the check to the usual billing address."

"What's this?" Her voice held high-pitched outrage.

"The charge from Redcap and Sons Movers to move my spinning wheels—the ones you stole—back into their proper spots."

Gregor had arranged it the moment they'd arrived home.

"Redcap and Sons." The crone's tone was sharp with disapproval. "They ought to call it Redcap and Daughter-Does-All-the-Moving. Cute little thing. All that hair and that tiny voice make you want to wrap her up and coo at her. Girl's got power like a bull."

She drummed her fingers against her staff. "Now that high blood has Luck's Lady's three and the western border is safe, we can move on to other issues. I have a wee problem. Could you talk to your aunty for me? One of my portals has gone bad and I need a little fixy on it. I thought I was taking the door to my throne room and imagine my surprise when I walked into the locker room of the men's wrestling team at Locke University. If I'd known that was going to happen, I would have worn my jeans." She wiggled her eyebrows. "You know, your aunty could make a portal for us to access each other, too. I have one with her, you know." Her voice turned sly.

Fancy.

Mara had yet to forgive the woman. She'd kept secrets, and she'd used them against her in the worst way. "You'll have to ask her yourself."

Gregor threaded his fingers through hers in comfort.

"Oh, fine. Tootles, princess!" The High Councilor waved her fingers and spun away with appropriate *billowing robes* and *trumpeting* spells. The senators piled back into their cars and drove away with no fanfare.

By the time Mara and Gregor were able to slip away from the business of the mill, the noon sun lit up the sky and her employees were back at their wheels and looms. The women took the new arrivals under their wing.

Mara settled the white wheel in her spinning room in her home, and Gregor paced the perimeter of the yard and then the block, checking in with the team of guards he and Linc had hastily arranged.

She was waiting for him in the kitchen. She leaned against the counter and looked out the window over the sink, fingering the tiny piece of lace she'd made for him from the webs. It was designed to go over the top of his earlobe, but he'd left it behind. She bit her lip, wondering, and then he opened the backyard's gate. His gaze found hers the moment he stepped through. A smile stretched at his lips...the smile he saved for her. Her breath caught in her throat. Everything around her seemed to lighten.

Would it always be like this?

He came inside and took the web from her, putting it in place. She could tell when his songs sounded in his ears again. His eyes sparked with life.

She loved that look. "You didn't take it with you. I was afraid it didn't fit."

"It's perfect. But I haven't figured out how to hear the unsung song over the sound of my mage vibes." He brushed his knuckles against her chin. "I don't want to be without that weapon when it comes to keeping you safe, but I love hearing your sweet power, Mara Rand. You know it resonates in perfect harmony with mine."

Her smile grew. "I was hoping it would."

He cupped her cheek. "I heard your song in my soul before I could hear it with my ears. That day you cast that ritual behind your mill...my heart heard you. With or without the webs, I'll always hear you, firefly."

He put his arms on either side of her and leaned down to kiss her. As their lips met, she felt his vibes stream out toward the back door as he locked it with a spell, closing out the rest of the world.

"Do you remember"—he pressed a kiss against the corner of her lips—"when I told you that if it were just us, I'd spend all day kissing you?"

She tilted her head as he kissed her jaw and then her neck, having a hard time remembering anything beneath the sensual assault. "Did you say that?" She placed her hand against the muscles of his chest, so strong and hard beneath her touch. "All day? We might get hungry." The words were breathless.

"We'll order in food." He nibbled at her skin and a shiver passed through her. "Anything you want, firefly. So long as you'll have me."

"Always. Just us."

Read on for a glimpse of the next *Mayflower Mages* book

PASSION'S POTION

Coming December 2018

CHAPTER 1

THE THIEF who had invaded Thea Redding's potions shop had left behind a footprint in the fairy dust that now coated the shop's floor. The shards of the broken glass bottle that had previously housed the dust pockmarked the mess. Thea pressed a hand to her chest, willing her heart to slow down. She was alone, the shop empty of anyone else's mage vibes. The culprit had fled. Otherwise, he—or she—would have gotten a serious dose of her *repel* potion. She touched the potion's vial, holstered at her waist. She'd grabbed it during her mad dash out her apartment door, summoned here by her *alarm* spell.

She studied the large footprint. Wide and long and prickled with the shoe's traction marks, she guessed it was from a work boot. She also guessed that her would-be-thief had been curious at the unlabeled bottle hidden under her shop's counter. That curiosity had saved Thea from disaster.

Apparently, the fairy dust in the now-broken bottle was impure, cut with the silver pollen of the winger flower, which made many mages sneeze so violently that they might as well have taken flight on invisible wings. The intruder's deep, ear-shattering sneeze had woken her from a sound sleep in her apartment one floor up, and then it had set off her *alarm* spell. Though she'd silenced it the moment she was certain the person had fled, its screech still vibrated through her bones.

At first glance, nothing else was damaged or missing, though she needed to inventory her shop to be certain. A shiver danced across her shoulders as if this invasion crept cold fingers over her skin. It threatened to yank away her confidence and sense of security. Both were too precious to let some faceless mage steal. She straightened her spine. She wouldn't allow that. But she shook her head at the mess, her dismay and regret reserved more for herself than her intruder. She'd purchased the fairy dust last weekend at the neighborhood's farmers market without examining the contents of the bottle.

A newbie mistake. And she was no newbie.

She'd been trying to shop local, wanting to fit in, to show goodwill to her new neighbors and hopefully receive their goodwill in return as well as some local customers of her own.

"You've got to be smarter than this, Redding," she whispered.

She pulled a scarf from her emergency spill kit, attached to the wall at the back of her shop, and tied it over her mouth and nose. Reaching out with her mage vibes, she activated the broom in the back closet. It wobbled forward, ready to attack the mess at her command. Side by side, Thea and the broom approached the dusty spill.

This wasn't her first encounter with criminals, be it thieves or otherwise, and it was unlikely to be her last. Independent potionnesses were often the target of criminals and, almost worse, they were the favored suspects of the enforcers for crimes related to illegal potions. She would not be calling the authorities to report the break-in. In fact, if they found out, they'd probably find a way to turn her into the guilty party.

The quicker she got rid of the evidence, the better. And as soon as she had time, she'd rework her *alarm* spell to only sound inside her apartment and store. If the Goddess were smiling on her, then her neighbors would have slept through the piercing sound.

She cast a dash of mage energy at the broom, and it got to work, swishing back and forth as if invisible hands clutched it, gathering the dust and guiding it toward the door.

It reached the smashed bottle's small cork stopper, but the tiny cylinder rolled away, disappearing beneath her counter. She crouched to retrieve it only to find a dozen slim shards of glass twinkling at her under the counter. Striding down the length of her potion shop's shelves, she selected a bottle of *Shard Searcher*. It was her own invention. With one pull of the spray bottle's trigger, a fine mist showered out. A tiny storm of liquid spheres rolled around the floor, coalescing as they went, gathering the glass and encasing the sharp slivers inside growing bubbles of liquid that merged, one by one, until it formed a single sphere. One squirt had a range of six feet. When the potion had gathered all the shards, Thea tipped the empty trash can to the floor and the shards rolled in.

Glass begone.

She tossed the cork in, too, and then paced to the door, opening it just in time for the broom to shepherd its dirt out onto the old brick sidewalk of the historic neighborhood.

She looked down the street, left and right. The block was quiet, its residents still asleep, nestled safely in their old homes. The houses were well cared for, the wood trim and doors on the all-brick buildings painted with committee-approved colors. The small plots of flowers and bushes that dotted the curb held onto their summer colors thanks to their owners' *preservation* spells, but the trees glowed in their autumn prime, lush with reds and oranges. They wouldn't fall until the powers-that-be deemed it appropriate to release the spells that anchored the leaves artificially, a date that would coincide with the scheduled citywide cleanup. That date was next Tuesday—directly after the Dragon

Harvest Festival that would take place in the park at the end of the block.

Thea paced after her broom as it pushed its cloudy pile off the curb and into the gutter of the brick street, taking a few leaves on the lam with it. With its work complete, she grabbed the broom and scurried back to the open doorway of her shop and waited, yanking the scarf off her face.

The fairy dust particles lingered in a low cloud, swirling in the pale sunshine of the autumn morning. Such a waste of money. Fairy dust made a superb binding agent and also had amplification effects for many potions. She was hoping it would help with her anti-gravity potion that she'd been working on for years. A pipe dream. But, by the stars, what she'd give to fly.

She tapped an impatient finger on top of the broom handle, gazing down the street. She couldn't leave the powder in the gutter and risk the morning's passersby tracking it to their work or homes. There'd be a sneezing epidemic, and with her luck, the enforcers would trace it back to her.

After another minute, the noise of the street sweeper mage rumbled into the quiet neighborhood. Three, maybe four, blocks away.

By order of the neighborhood committee, all cars had been moved off the street either by their owners or by the *tow* spells of the mover mages the committee contracted. Every Wednesday morning, except in the winter, the sweepers came by with their spells roaring like train engines. The committee was full of clean freaks. No other neighborhood in the city swept this often, but it was convenient timing for this spill.

"Come on, now," she spoke aloud, as if she could coax the street sweeper mage to hurry over.

She needed this rotten dust gone before anyone on the street noticed. She'd poured everything she had into her new shop, all of her energy and all of her savings from her contract jobs. The result,

Potions by the Park, was charming and welcoming, and she sold the finest potions anywhere in the city if she said so herself. No one was going to clip this dream and stifle her trajectory. Not a crook, not a foe, not even a suspicious enforcer. If it failed—and it would not fail —she'd have to get a job at the big potion manufacturing plant.

Goddess of the stars, the last thing she ever wanted to do was to step foot into The Tavis Potions Corporation.

The breeze chose that moment to rattle the tree branches. The contaminated dust rose to greet it. From her spot in her doorway, she threw a quick *containment* spell over her cloud of winger pollen and fairy dust, keeping it knee-level. Disaster averted. She let her shoulders drop with a sigh. But it was a premature move, for when the breeze passed on and the leaves stilled, a clattering ring sounded from inside her shop. She looked back.

Surely the keeper's stone hadn't just triggered.

It had been years since she'd heard that sound, though it was as recognizable as the shake of a rattlesnake's tail and just as much of a warning of approaching danger.

Maybe she was hearing things. One catastrophe per morning. That was her limit.

But the short, squat vial on the highest shelf behind her counter wiggled in its spot. It was spelled to stay in place and to look cloudy, though she could see the stone inside with no prob-lem. If the thief had chosen that bottle to inspect, he would have hit a payday.

The bottle jumped. Once, twice, again and again.

Oh no.

Inside the bottle, the stone danced to footsteps or a pulse that she could not hear, a rhythm of disaster stomping forward.

Keeper's stones weren't intended for shopkeepers. They were meant for dragon keepers. They announced the incoming pres-ence of a fellow dragon rider who might try to steal his herd. Dragon riders—an ancient breed of mage that no longer served a useful purpose—never trusted their own kind, even now, though none of them had a herd, much less a single dragon since ancient times.

Likewise, Thea didn't trust any of them either. They were a dangerous temptation, almost always packaged in a handsome, manly wrapping. Their natural instinct was to seek treasure and hide it away in their covert dens. She'd gotten too close to one once and had fallen all over him like raindrops in a storm. He'd tried to stick her in his rider's den and cut her off from friends and family to keep her all to himself. If it hadn't been for her very old grandmother's determined help, she never would have escaped.

She'd learned her lesson and now avoided the mage type at all costs, making good use of the stones that generations of Redding potionnesses had passed down, woman to woman.

The stone rattled again. A rider was definitely coming.

She dashed inside the shop, flipped the lock with a push of vibes and double-checked that the *closed* sign was displayed. Forget guarding her contaminated cloud. That dragon rider mage could just mosey on down the sidewalk. If he stayed out of the gutter and away from her contained dust, he'd be fine. Besides, the street sweeper mage was almost here.

As she turned to her counter, she caught a glimpse of sparkling powder draped across the sidewalk.

Oh no. Oh no. The words replayed in her mind like a broken *recording* spell.

Her broom had missed a spot.

Marcus Tavis leaned against the towering maple tree that had declared the corner of Whittier Street and Mohawk its home long before any of the current neighborhood residents were born. He was alone on the corner. The day was too young for joggers or mothers strolling with babies toward the park at the end of the block, and the street stretched too far from the main thorough-fares for morning rush hour.

Althea Redding was the only other creature stirring. Her black sweater might have kept him from realizing that her black pants were pajamas, but their silky shine gave them away. What-ever vile potion she'd holstered at her waist weighted down her pants and revealed a hint of creamy skin. Her feet were either covered in slippers or some flimsy shoe. Her brown hair was piled in a haphazard knot high on her head, strands falling free as she watched her broom strike against the sidewalk hard enough to loosen a century's worth of dirt and dust.

Hints of the coming sun lightened the sky with a soft orange and pink glow, not enough to see details on this cool autumn morning, but dragon rider mages had keen eyesight, especially when they had eyes on their prey.

Even from across the street he could see her tight brow and the tension in her lips. She was just above average height for a woman, he supposed. But still, he doubted her chin would reach his shoulder. Her form was slight. She'd blow off the back of his motorcycle, which was parked at a discreet distance down the block and on the correct side of the road for the coming street sweeper.

Not that he'd ever give a woman like her a ride.

As intended, she was completely oblivious to his presence. His smoke shrouded his form with a subtle *don't look* spell as he spied. She was connected, somehow, to the poison his sister was addicted to. Independent potionnesses like Althea Redding were every bit the menace to society that their reputations hinted at. Their ethics and morals were as loose as the leash he held when he walked Pilot, his fifteen-year-old retriever.

He clenched his teeth. His sister's sharp, shrewd mind was a wreck, but during her chaotic fits, he'd picked out Thea's name at least a dozen times over the last week. Plus, his sister had strolled past this shop on three occasions in the last four days. He still couldn't believe he'd stooped to secretly following Saxon around, but the Chief Potionness of the world's largest potions manufacturing company, an accomplished and capable woman, was on the brink of destruction.

He had no one to blame but himself. He'd been pulling back from his business duties because he and Saxon had almost freed the company—and the family—from their matriarch's grip. The legal tangles were unwound, and Grandmother Tavis would soon find she had no one's strings to pull. Marcus had relaxed. He'd looked away. And some wicked witch had flown through his lax defenses to poison his sister and play with her mind.

He had to save Saxon before she ran the family business into the ground and cut off the salaries of over two thousand mages in factories around the Republic. His mission this morning was to get the Redding woman to admit to poisoning her with her illegal potions. Then he'd make her pay.

Problem solved.

He'd arrived at his sentry post by the maple tree in time to sense the scratchy vibes of a weak *alarm* spell waving through the air. He might not have noticed if he hadn't been focused on her shop. She hadn't called the enforcers judging by the lack of approaching sirens. He wasn't surprised. As far as he was concerned, it was another strike against her. A potionness who dealt in illegal potions—IPs for short—wouldn't call for help from the authorities.

He shifted against the tree, squinting at her as if his perfect eyesight needed help in bringing her into focus. Her face was populated with delicate features, a perfect disguise for an IP dealer, as was her skill with a broom. He didn't imagine there were many IP dealers who were this tidy.

As she turned back to her shop, he stepped off the curb toward his target. Two seconds after the door shut behind her, a puff of vibes knocked against the door as she locked it with a spell.

No matter. It wouldn't keep him out. He crossed the street as the sweeper mage rounded the corner and began its crawl down Mohawk Street, heading toward him. He slipped off his suit jacket as if he were readying for a confrontation and caught it by the crook of his finger, tossing it over his shoulder. He'd left his tie in the storage compartment of his bike, as was his habit when he rode it to work.

When he was halfway across the intersection, the potionness popped out of her shop again, her broom in hand. She tackled an invisible spot on the brick sidewalk, head down, oblivious to him. He gave a mental shake of his head. IP dealers really should be more aware of their surroundings.

He quickened his pace, ready to capture his target, not worrying about the sound of his footsteps over the roar of the coming street sweeper.

Damn, those machines and their mages were loud.

He stepped on the curb as she smacked at the ground with her broom, her back to him. Her frantic pace suggested she was in a race with the street sweeper. As the giant vehicle closed the distance, a flash of sleek black darted across the street, sprinting in front of the sweeper and right between Marcus's legs.

"Kitty!" the potionness cried, spinning around as Marcus danced about the cat. He tumbled, falling off the uneven curb.

The dirty gray vehicle towered over him as he lost his balance. He shot out a stream of vibes trying to regain his equilibrium, but it wasn't going to be enough. Time slowed, giving him too many seconds to contemplate the disgrace of his demise that would be described in his obituary.

Sucked up by a street sweeper. May he rest in pieces.

He might have slapped his hand to his forehead if the force of the suction hadn't already caught his arms. The buttons on his fine white shirt popped off and disappeared into the looming machine. His suit jacket followed leaving only the burn of the fabric against his fingers as it was sucked away. His skin would be next. He was coming apart.

He couldn't catch a breath. The atmosphere had become a vacuum. It all happened in a moment of time that stretched as thick as the syrup over the pancakes he wished he'd had this morning. That would have made a nice last meal.

A pair of slender arms wrapped around him like soft feathers on a wing. The potionness had stepped in front of him.

Hell, what was she thinking? Before he could toss her aside, her touch was followed by a burst of vibes that showered over him like a gentle rainstorm and anchored them both to the curb.

She squeezed her arms around his torso and buried her head against his chest, now naked and bare, his shirt sucked to its doom. Her muscles quivered against him, her vibes like molten steel hardening in the cool morning.

The motor and vibes of the street sweeper cut off like a pair of scissors had snipped its cord. Silence wrapped around him.

He was still alive.

CHAPTER 2

THEA'S HEAD rose and fell as if it were resting on a bellows that puffed at flames beneath a giant's cauldron. Except for that small movement, she was locked in place. Her chin was tucked. Her cheek pressed against a solid mass. Her eyes were shut hard. Her muscles and mage vibes were as frozen as a rabbit spotted by a hungry dragon flying overhead. Heck, she wasn't even sure her blood was still flowing.

"What the blasted hells are you thinking?" The sweeper mage behind her had a shout that matched the roar of his motor. If the neighbors weren't already awake, they were now. Still, his heated fury wasn't enough to thaw her ill-timed freeze.

Goddess, she sucked in emergencies.

A firm grip around her lower arms pried her off, peeling her away from the one hint of warmth she'd had. A shiver wracked through her, but it rattled her brain into action.

This man was a dragon rider mage.

Right. The stones had sensed him.

She shuffled back. Her foot met the curb and she went flailing, only to be caught by the man again. This time she lifted her head enough to see a sculpted chest so fine that an artist might have carved him.

"I could have sucked your body into my bag," the street sweeper mage shouted. "Then it would be a body bag!"

"My apologies, sir." The rider mage's voice was low and smooth, nothing like her shaking hands or her vibes that were too brittle with icy cold to tuck back into their place. Like an extra appendage or a sixth sense, vibes could reach out on an energetic plane, and like hands, they needed to behave themselves or people took offense. As she scrambled to shove her vibes back, she lifted her head higher and met the dark blue eyes of Marcus Tavis.

A gasp escaped from her mouth, a mix of horror and outrage. What the vibing hell had she'd done to deserve this? A Tavis stood half-naked on the sidewalk outside her shop.

She recognized him from the LifeStyles pages of *The Dispatch*. She'd certainly never met him. Never wanted to. At least not now. Once upon a time, she'd been best friends forever with his sister. She'd shared everything with Saxon. The girl Saxon had been was perceptive, clever, and entertaining, though she wasn't the strongest potionness. She was also oddly protective, too much so.

Since then, Thea had learned enough about herself to know that gravitating toward that last characteristic was her weakness, a dangerous one, but back then that friendship had been her whole life tied up with a pretty bow. She'd been immersed in every aspect of Saxon Tavis's life, though her former friend had never invited her home on their free weekends from Potion School.

"Do you know what happened to me the last time I sucked up somebody?" the sweeper mage hollered.

Thea turned around to see him wrench off the stocking cap that covered his bald head. He shook it at them in a tight fist. "I had to go on unpaid leave for one month! I nearly lost my contract with the city. How am I supposed to feed my kids if bimbo mages like you dash into the street when the signs clearly state to vacate the premises? You are a trash-vibing idiot! You ought to kiss this girl's vibes for saving your worthless life!"

Thea hustled three steps back. "Not necessary." She pointed a finger at Tavis as if she might hold him back with the strength of one digit. But it wouldn't matter if she threw every vibe she had at him. Nothing could hold back a dragon rider mage when he had a goal to acquire.

Retreat!

The word shouted through her mind.

She bent down and picked up her broom.

Leave it!

She should have listened.

When she straightened, Tavis stood in front of her shop door, pushing it open with his vibes.

"Wait! No! You can't go in there. I'm not open. And...you... you...." She shook her finger at him again. "You don't even like independent potionnesses."

He stepped over the shop door's threshold as the street sweeper restarted his roaring engine and chugged away. Tavis looked over his shoulder at her, one eyebrow raised high, his naked back flexing with more muscles than she'd thought possible. The city's two-time bachelor-of-the-year—ever since the Rallis twins found their mates—smoldered on her threshold. She should have stocked *extinguish* potion by the door, hosed him down, and put him out.

Literally.

Instead, he stood inside her shop, holding the door open for her. He gestured her inside with a strong arm.

"I'm not open yet." The words wobbled. She cleared her throat and straightened her shoulders.

He stepped farther in, his arm stretching to keep the door open for her. "I believe it's a violation of the fire code to have your door open inward instead of out."

She scoffed, so aggravated she actually stomped her foot. "So like a Tavis...criticizing, bullying. And by the way, this is a historic building. I was granted an exception."

"An observation, not a criticism." He shuffled inside another step while his vibes propped open the door.

High on her shelf, the stone rattled.

His gaze sharpened like a hawk. Or perhaps like a dragon, but it was impossible to say since the beasts hadn't existed in a few millennia. "What was that noise?"

It wasn't illegal for her to have the keeper stone, but it was beyond unusual and she didn't owe him any explanations. "None of your business."

He looked down at her, moving his head with the slow smoothness of the enormous, dangerous creature his mage type used to tame. "Then let's talk about something that is my business." The words drawled, slipping from between his lips with a honeyed purr. It matched his well-defined pecs and a belly that rippled with cords of muscle. Of course it did. Typical dragon rider. Sultry. Sexy. Dominating. They sucked up a woman's life as if they were cousins with street sweeper mages.

"Mr. Tavis, I assure you there is nothing related to your business that I could possibly discuss with you."

"How's Saxon?" The short words sounded like an accusation.

She might have laughed if she hadn't been consumed by the aftermath of adrenaline. The truth was, she felt a bit sick. "No idea. I haven't seen Saxon since the day she stole my future from me. Surely you heard about that? Or maybe she never confessed to you how she cheated on our graduation exam."

"Thirteen years ago?" He jutted his chin down as if lowering himself a few inches might help him see her better. His vibes glided out and brushed against her, ready to take a hungry chomp out of her energy.

"Twelve." She waved her hand in front of her, swiping at the air as if to freshen it. "And quit that with your vibes. It's bad manners to contaminate a public space like that, though what can one expect with a dragon rider? I'm going to have to air out my shop now."

He sent his vibes against the door, closing it with a quiet click. His eyes were hard and something stark and cold drained through them. "You haven't seen Saxon in twelve years." His words fell flat.

"Oh, I've seen her in newspapers and magazines touting her designer outfits and fancy parties, but that's it. And that's more than I want to see of her."

He frowned hard, his eyebrows—nicely groomed and all around as perfect as his abs—clenched in a vee. "You hate her."

"No. I don't." She paused to ensure that her statement had time to sink into his thick dragon rider skull. "Hate is a waste of energy. I moved on ages ago and doing that was hard work. I have no desire to see her, hear her, or smell her expensive perfumes."

He took two steps backward as if her words had a physical force. "You're telling the truth."

"That's right. Read my vibes. I'm telling the truth."

Most mages could sense the chaotic energy of a lie. It made keeping secrets a challenge.

He straightened, his muscles clenching, his abs tightening like he was bracing to attack before she could. "Have you ever given Saxon an illegal potion or poison?"

"Are you kidding me?" Her mouth dropped. Such accusations were the bane of every independent potionness in existence. "I would say that I'm not going to lower myself to answer that, but it would probably just make you stick around. So here's the truth, again. You'll want to pay attention since truth seems like a novel experience for you. Ready?" She opened her eyes wide, nodding her head. "I do not deal in illegal potions. I do not deal in poisons. I do not make either one of them. I do not sell them. I do not give them away for free. And I have never ever given Saxon, or anyone else, any illegal potions or poisons. There. Have I covered everything?" A bubbling burn stirred through her like a potion boiling over a flame. "Happy now?"

His lips were tight. His glare hard and focused. He turned away from her, giving her his back. He clearly was not happy now, but there was no further reason for him to stay.

Instead of ordering him to leave, she paused at the uncomfortable push in her chest. She tried to tell herself it was simple curiosity. Professional curiosity, she corrected. That was it. "What did she take?"

"You tell me."

She shook her head. Forget it. It was past time to make his marvelous physique and dangerous accusations poof out of her shop.

"And while you're at it, why don't you tell me which rider mage gave you a stone?"

Keeper stones were originally a security system for dragon riders' herds, but Thea would never have a herd to worry about. The stones were her security system for her sanity and her heart and her freedom. She'd never let another rider into her life. Nor would she let Saxon or anything to do with her come close. Too bad she didn't have a warning system for that. She hadn't thought it would be necessary.

"I answered your questions about IPs and Saxon." She opened her shop door with a stream of vibes. Cool, autumn air crept in. "I'm all done with your interrogation."

He pointed at the small bottle that housed her stone on the high shelf. "The key to riders' perpetuity does not belong in the hands of a potionness."

Perpetuity stones.

It was an ancient, archaic name for keeper stones. She

couldn't remember the last time she'd heard someone say it aloud. They certainly didn't use the term in her family.

"I hardly think you can chalk up the survival of dragon rider mages to the existence of those stones," she continued. "If they're key to your type's perpetuity, then they're not doing a very good job." Rider mages weren't a thriving population.

He pivoted, slow and controlled. "We haven't died out."

"No, you're just obsolete." She couldn't help but dig at the annoying man. "Now, if you wouldn't mind"—she nodded at the door—"I have a busy morning."

He didn't move except to cross his arms over his puffed-up chest. Centuries ago that strength was often for hire by aristocratic mages who needed a defender. Nowadays, riders had no true vocation. They were throwback renegades, cowboys without a horse to ride across the land.

She tried again. "I would like you to leave."

"I would like many things, like illegal potions and their dealers wiped from the face of the Republic."

"A noble wish, but impossible....as impossible as dragons returning."

"You don't think dragons will return?"

She could almost hear the charm lurking below his tone, the stuff that lured beauty to his arm. He could keep it buried.

For the love of the Goddess, keep it buried.

She leaned against her opened doorframe and sighed. "I don't think dragons will return. But everyone needs a pipe dream. Don't you have a job to get to? A shirt to find?"

He frowned and strolled deeper into her shop, eyeing her shelves. "I'm doing my job."

"Inspecting the competition? You're a poor secret shopper."

He leaned forward, studying the labels of the bottles on the side wall as a crisp breeze drifted through the door she still held propped open. "*Hellhound* potion?" He looked back at her with a hard frown. One side of his nose might have lifted in a subtle sneer. "What kind of person would give their dog something like this?"

She raised her hand. "I would. I know you find this hard to believe, but there are many people in this world who can't summon a horde of bodyguards with a flick of their fingers or even summon a defensive spell, though they might thrust every vibe they have behind it. The kind of person who would give their dog something like this has no other defenses to employ against nosy bullies who won't leave them alone." She sighed with a flair of drama. "Too bad I don't have a dog."

He tucked his hand into his pants pockets, his arms framing his trimmed torso. It was almost hard to look at, as if it were a mirage that wavered before her. "A woman like you has plenty of defenses."

"Why, thank you," she replied, though he certainly hadn't sounded as if he was paying her a compliment.

She turned her attention away as a blonde woman with copious amounts of shiny curls burst through the open door.

"Oh, good, you're open," she squealed, clapping her hands in applause. "I was afraid you'd still be closed." She pointed at the half-naked Tavis heir. "You do sell *beefcake* potion! Yours works absolutely beautifully! Look at him. A work of art. Those abs... like they'd been sculpted by Michelangelo." She circled her hands in the air. "Those marvelous pecs."

Marcus Tavis's sneer grew, consuming his face.

"I need it so bad." Her tiny waist and rounded hips and breasts screamed *plastic* potion, but she certainly wasn't a *beefcake* user. She was too slender. "Is he your model?" She stuck her hand in her very expensive purse and pulled out a wad of money. "I'll pay whatever you ask."

Thea blinked at the big denominations fluttering past on those bills. That was a loan payment. Maybe two. She heaved a hard sigh. Life always seemed to work this way. She walked a straight and narrow path, but shortcuts and dark alleys jutted along the way in the most unexpected places. Thea had learned a long time ago that if she didn't stay focused on her path, she could fall off it in a single step. Getting back on was tougher than a witch's backside.

She gave an apologetic shrug. "I don't sell *beefcake*. It's a very dangerous potion. It has numerous side effects. And you shouldn't buy it from any potionness who doesn't insist on examining the vibes of the person who will be taking it."

"It's for my husband." She jerked her hands down to her sides. Her breasts jiggled beneath her tight dress. "He's old! Much too old to have to worry about side effects. I wouldn't have married some boy!"

Beefcake could be deadly if taken by those who were still growing.

"Ah, of course. But, again, I don't sell it."

"Then do you know someone who does? I'll pay you for the information." She thrust out the money again.

"I do not. It is a questionable type of potionness who makes such a formula."

The woman gave a rough scream of frustration and rushed out, nearly colliding with Thea's neighbor. Luella Sanders was nearly bent in half. Her light brown hair—a *color* potion that hid the gray—bobbed across her face, hiding her expression. Her beau, Mr. Fielding, held her arm, his eyes wide with alarm.

"Miss Luella!" Thea rushed out and wrapped her arms around the older, ailing woman who normally vibed with good health.

Another emergency. Stars above, have mercy.

Thea's blood pounded in her ears, muffling her hearing. The world went staticky. Panting against her panic, Thea fought for calm as she steered her inside, guiding her to the wingback chairs that sat between the windows on the other wall. She took a deep breath and then another. "I knew this was going to happen," she huffed. "You ran out of your potion, didn't you? Your refill has been sitting on my shelf for a week."

Luella gave a desperate nod.

"I'll be right back." Thea hustled away to grab the tincture in the backroom but paused, tripping over her feet as she halted. She gave Tavis a warning look over her shoulder. "Don't touch anything."

ABOUT THE AUTHOR

Anise Rae is the author of the Mayflower Mages series. She lives in a suburb of Atlanta with her husband—nicest guy ever, two kids who are far smarter than she is, and a Golden Retriever who can never get enough attention. She has degrees in chemistry and library science and spent a few forgettable years in the cubicles of the corporate world. Now she writes romances in an unfinished closet filled with ductwork, wrapping paper, long-forgotten toys, and all those dishes that only get pulled out once a year. It's a very nice place because it has a door that closes, leaving her alone with her characters and her deadlines.

To stay up-to-date on her next releases, sign up for her newsletter at www.aniserae.com

ACKNOWLEDGMENTS

Some books are harder to write than others. In this case, Sorcerer's Spin didn't truly click for me until I spent a weekend learning to spin yarn with an expert spinner. I was the only person who signed up for the session and I will be forever thankful that my teacher, Annie, chose to continue with the class instead of canceling it, making me the lucky recipient of a one-on-one workshop with an amazing woman.

All mistakes regarding the technical aspects of spinning are mine.

Many thanks are also due to my husband, kids, and mom who were encouraging at every turn, and to my writer friends, especially Kimberly, for reading the whole thing when it wasn't quite polished.

Finally, this book is dedicated to the memory of Gunner, without whom the Mayflower Mages might never have found their home.

ISBN 9781732906716 (ebook)

ISBN 9781732906709 (paperback)

This is a work of fiction. Names, characters, places and incidents are either pulled from the author's cavernous imagination or are used in a fictitious manner unrelated to our current reality.

www.ingramcontent.com/pod-product-compliance
Lightning Source LLC
Chambersburg PA
CBHW071734110726
47908CB00006B/1586